Highest Praise

For Duty and Honor

"Leo Maloney has a real winner with *For Duty and Honor*—Gritty and intense, it draws you immediately into the action and doesn't let go."
—**Marc Cameron**

Arch Enemy

"Utterly compelling! This novel will grab you from the beginning and simply not let go. And Dan Morgan is one of the best heroes to come along in ages."
—**Jeffery Deaver**

Twelve Hours

"Fine writing and real insider knowledge make this a must."
—**Lee Child**

Black Skies

"Smart, savvy, and told with the pace and nuance that only a former spook could bring to the page, *Black Skies* is a tour de force novel of twenty-first-century espionage and a great geopolitical thriller. Maloney is the new master of the modern spy game, and this is first-rate storytelling."
—**Mark Sullivan**

"*Black Skies* is rough, tough, and entertaining. Leo J. Maloney has written a ripping story."
—**Meg Gardiner**

Silent Assassin

"Leo Maloney has done it again. Real life often overshadows fiction and *Silent Assassin* is both: a terrifyingly thrilling story of a man on a clandestine mission to save us all from a madman hell bent on murder, written by a man who knows that world all too well."
—**Michele McPhee**

"A deep-ops story presented in an epic style that takes fact mixed with a bit of fiction to create a spy thriller that takes the reader deep into secret spy missions."
—**Cy Hilterman,** *Best Sellers World*

"For fans of spy thrillers seeking a bit of realism mixed into their novels, *Termination Orders* will prove to be an excellent and recommended pick."
—*Midwest Book Reviews*

Books by Leo J. Maloney

The Dan Morgan Thriller Series
TERMINATION ORDERS
SILENT ASSASSIN
BLACK SKIES
TWELVE HOURS*
ARCH ENEMY
FOR DUTY AND HONOR*
ROGUE COMMANDER
DARK TERRITORY*
THREAT LEVEL ALPHA
WAR OF SHADOWS

*e-novellas

WAR OF SHADOWS

A Dan Morgan Thriller

Leo J. Maloney

LYRICAL UNDERGROUND
Kensington Publishing Corp.
www.kensingtonbooks.com

LYRICAL UNDERGROUND BOOKS are published by

Kensington Publishing Corp.
119 West 40th Street
New York, NY 10018

All Kensington titles, imprints, and distributed lines are available at special quantity discounts for bulk purchases for sales promotion, premiums, fundraising, educational, or institutional use.

Special book excerpts or customized printings can also be created to fit specific needs. For details, write or phone the office of the Kensington Sales Manager: Kensington Publishing Corp., 119 West 40th Street, New York, NY 10018. Attn. Sales Department. Phone: 1-800-221-2647.

Lyrical Underground and Lyrical Underground logo Reg. US Pat. & TM Off.

First Electronic Edition: April 2019
eISBN-13: 978-1-5161-0333-1
eISBN-10: 1-5161-0333-5

First Print Edition: April 2019
ISBN-13: 978-1-5161-0334-8
ISBN-10: 1-5161-0334-3

Printed in the United States of America

This book is dedicated to my family, especially my granddaughter Katherine, who inspires me every day. She is smart, kind, gentle, and caring of other people's feelings. She loves books and is an avid reader, reading way above her age level, and coauthored a children's book with me called *The Dolan Sisters' Adventure in India.* Lastly I want to dedicate this book to all my readers who have stuck with me since the beginning, especially Bill Ross and Andy Taylor.

Chapter 1

Dan Morgan's house exploded.

It was so sudden and devastating that Morgan's mind instantly reacted. The husband, father, and classic car dealer part of him went into shock. But the part that was the experienced, knowledgeable, veteran operative of the C.I.A., and now the clandestine organization Zeta Division, went into overdrive.

He had just turned the corner at the end of the Andover, Massachusetts, street where he lived, feeling the comforting purr of the green 1968 Mustang GT his team had presented him with during their last mission. Ironically, he had reluctantly just admitted to himself that he was the happiest he'd ever been….that is, since his wedding day and the day his daughter Alexandra was born.

For once, everything appeared to be going great—both professionally and personally. Together with his team and even his family, he had averted a biological apocalypse. The organization he worked for had never been so respected within the intelligence community, his superiors had come to fully appreciate his abilities, and even the skeletons in his closet had been cleared by his coming clean to his family about his previous double life. And now that the extremely capable young lady who was once his baby girl had moved out, he and his wife Jenny were even talking about having another child. Maybe adopting one from Asia or Africa.

The father and husband in him remembered that he couldn't wait to get home to her, the love of his life, when the unthinkable had happened. But the seasoned secret agent, to his growing rage, recognized the detonation.

It was what the experts called a "toothpick explosion," where fuel and oxygen mix perfectly to render a house into a tearing, shattering, ripping, belching mass of glass, wood, concrete, brick, and metal shards in two blinks of an eye. The husband and father, teetering in shock, stomped on the brake, while the professional military and espionage operative dove to the seat, knowing what came next.

As the walls and windows of his once comfortable happy home erupted in a million swipes of death's scythe, more oxygen rushed in to reignite the explosion's source. Sure enough, less than a second later, a *whomp* that was both sound and pressure filled his ears, light blinded his eyes, and a fireball engulfed, then spewed the house-shaped debris like a horde of maddened wasps.

In the milliseconds that it took, Dan Morgan's eyes snapped back open. The husband and father inside him prayed that it might have been a gas leak accident. The intelligence operative inside him snarled, *bullshit.*

Both personas tromped on the accelerator, sending the Mustang screeching down the street, over the curb, across the lawn, and into the flaming hole where his front door had been.

"Jenny!" he bellowed, certain his voice carried over the detonation's dying roar. He had just been talking to her. With cellphones, she could've been anywhere, but he felt certain she had been talking from home. Even before the car stopped, half on the ruined porch, half in the burning maw where his front door had once been, he was vaulting out of it. "Jenny!"

The heat hit him like an angry monster's slap. He felt his eyebrows singe, but he didn't care. He charged through the conflagration, toward the stairs and the master bedroom. He opened his mouth to call out again, but the heat took that as an invitation and shoved itself down his throat like a hammering fist.

That stopped him. He stood, staring, at the wreckage of what had once been his beloved home. He couldn't recognize it. It looked like someone had shredded his life and sprinkled it onto a sizzling volcano crater.

Dan Morgan had witnessed many an explosion, seen many a dismembered corpse, and smelled many a barbecued victim of fire-bombing. You couldn't live the life he had lived in the military, the C.I.A., and now the Zeta Division without having such memories permanently branded in your brain.

But this wasn't some godforsaken hellhole he was infiltrating. This was his home, and if he stayed here he'd join whoever had been caught there when it happened.

"Jenny," he managed in a combination of a croak and a gasp as carbon monoxide stuffed his nostrils. He felt his flesh begin to crawl—not from fear, but from being baked. A combination of anger and remorse drove his spasming muscles.

Don't be an idiot, he heard himself bark inside his own head. *Hope is not your friend.*

Dan Morgan had gotten angry before. Too many times. But he could honestly admit that this was the first time he had gone blind with helpless rage. He staggered blindly until he hit the car with his side. He looked around wildly as his fingers scrabbled for the door handle. He saw that his back-porch door window was melting. The living room fireplace was a mound of flame. He heard his adjoining garage workshop collapsing as if Thor himself had just sledgehammered it.

The sweat and tears that managed to escape his eyes evaporated in less than a second as he fell back behind the driver's wheel, jammed it into reverse, and tromped on the accelerator. The now battered and bent classic car tore back onto the lawn as if yanked by a steel cable. He only went back far enough so the gas tank wouldn't explode and his clothes wouldn't immolate before jamming on the brakes again.

As horrifying as the last minute had been, the next few were even more surreal. Reeling from shock and exposure, he saw his horrified neighbors all around him like a small squad of concerned ghosts, as burning shreds of what had once been his sanctuary rained down around them like flaming confetti.

He sat there, staring down the shock that threatened to paralyze him. *Oh no*, he found himself thinking. *Not now. Don't have time for you now.* Somehow his agent's systematic brain recognized each onlooker...save one. Dan all but vaulted out of the car as his neighbors neared.

There was a small, shadowy figure near the bushes on the other side of the house—a figure hidden from him by the night's darkness, the flames' distorting heat waves, and some sort of black outfit, complete with visored helmet. Dan took a step toward it, a quiet prayer of "Alex" escaping his lips.

But as soon as he said it, he knew it wasn't his daughter. As he was about to take another step, he felt the hands and bodies of his neighbors close in on him. The shadowy figure disappeared behind the remains of the burning house.

Dan heard nothing the concerned citizens said, and felt nearly nothing they did to comfort and check him. Above their anxious, alarmed din, he heard a louder, commanding voice. It was his.

"Call 9-1-1," it demanded. "Now! Use your hoses to keep the fire from your roofs and walls. Steve...Steve Richards!" He had called his most trusted neighbor.

"Here, Dan," he heard the man say. "I have your dog, Neika. She staggered over seconds before it happened. I think...I think she's drugged or something..."

Dan's rage was about to engulf him again when he spotted an armored, tinted-glass SUV speeding by at the mouth of the street. He knew every vehicle owned by everyone for a mile around him. This was not one of them. And the dead giveaway was that its license plates were obscured.

"Take care of her, Steve," he seethed, already hurling himself back into his car. "See... see if they can find..."

But his wife and daughter's names were blotted out by the roar of his Mustang's engine as he reversed back across the already shredded lawn. The neighbors scattered, mouths agape, as the GT squealed back onto the asphalt, did a smoking tire turn, and shot down the street as if fired from a cannon.

It was late, so the suburban streets were fairly clear, which made sighting the unknown vehicle easier. His catching the thing, however, was not. Even from a distance, there was no mistaking it—especially for an agent whose cover was that of a classic car dealer. It was a black Grand Cherokee Trackhawk—all seven hundred and seven horsepower of it. From the shark-eye glint of its exterior and windshields, it was most likely bulletproofed as well.

He narrowed his eyes and leaned forward before shaking his head. As if of its own accord, his left arm rolled down the window, letting the night air help wake him up. It also let in the sound of sirens approaching from the opposite direction. The father and husband part of him wished he could have stayed to help put out the fire and search the wreckage. The agent in him wanted to drive his Mustang down the Trackhawk's throat.

What the hell happened, he thought, *and more important, why the hell had it happened?* His still addled mind tried to rifle through his personal list of enemies, then narrow it down to those who would be so sadistic to literally bring it home to him, but he soon decided that was a waste of time. Both lists would be one and the same, and too numerous to whittle down. There was a far more pressing issue to attend to.

He found his smartphone in his right hand, not completely remembering that he had grabbed it. He glanced at the rearview mirror to see fire trucks pulling onto his street and the flickering shadows of his demolished home. When he looked back, his eyes searched the dashboard, remembering how his family had all but begged him to have voice-activated, hands-free communication in his car, but no, he had to be the classic car purist...

His family. Had they been home when it happened? Blinking furiously, Morgan stabbed the buttons with his thumb, calling his wife's number again and again.

No answer. He remembered Lincoln Shepard, Zeta's resident communications wiz, telling him that no answer was worse than going to message. Going to message meant the phone still existed. No answer could mean the phone was destroyed...

The Mustang jumped, then shuddered as the cars went from Route Forty Two to I-93. Then it took all the GT's five-liter V8 engine and nearly five hundred horsepower to keep up with the Trackhawk's teeth-shaking roar, even on the sparsely trafficked highway. Dan watched the speedometer rise—a hundred miles an hour, a hundred and ten, a hundred and twenty...

The Trackhawk seemed to wiggle its rear at him, doggedly staying a steady four car-lengths ahead. The two vehicles stayed that way, mostly hugging the left lane, except for occasionally weaving around a speed limit idiot so closely that the state police would need a hair to measure how near they got to the slow-pokes.

A hundred and thirty... a hundred and forty...

Maybe I'll luck out, Dan thought. *Maybe there'll be a speed trap or radar surveillance to ensnare us both.* No such luck anywhere from Wilmington to Medford. *Maybe I should call the highway patrol myself,* Dan considered. But although the smartphone was still in his hand, he had more important calls to make.

He called his daughter, Alex, twice. The calls went to message. He called Shepard. That one also went to message. He called Cougar—his best friend and partner Peter Conley. Message. He called Lily Randall, he called Karen O'Neal, he even called the numbers he had for his boss Diana Bloch—something he almost never did. All went to message.

A hundred and fifty...a hundred and sixty...The speedometer trembled at the little red pin where the numbers ended. The Trackhawk was still, stubbornly, four car lengths ahead.

"Idiot," Dan seethed, shoving the phone down on the seat beside him. Why bother with the phone when he had the Zeta comm-link in his ear? It was so comfortable and ubiquitous that he had forgotten it in the literal heat of the moment. He pressed his right ear canal to initiate the connection. The resulting shriek deep in his head all but sent the car into the median.

He regained control of the car in time to avoid a wreck, as well as wrench the tiny hearing aid from his auditory canal. It flew, like a dying bee, into the passenger seat's well, bouncing on the floor mat beneath the glove compartment.

What the hell? Dan returned his full attention to catching up to the Trackhawk, only to find that despite the Mustang's slowing and wavering, the SUV was still almost exactly four car lengths ahead. *You damn bastard...*

Morgan saw they were coming into Somerville. Then it would be Cambridge, and just beyond that, Boston. Neither of them could go a hundred and sixty there, not without committing vehicular homicide or suicide. But Dan could guess. Somehow, whoever was driving that SUV would stay four car lengths ahead. Whoever it was, they were that good—so good they could destroy his home, so good they could kill...kill his...

The father and husband inside him couldn't even bring himself to say it—to even think it. But the seasoned operative could.

...wife...they could have killed my wife...

The Trackhawk took Dan by surprise by all but leaping off the highway onto an all-too-familiar exit ramp. The surprise only grew when the SUV started speeding down back streets along a route Dan knew very well.

His eyes widened as he realized the Trackhawk was moving as if the driver were a Zeta commuter. They were heading to the isolated parking garage that served as cover for the organization's underground headquarters.

Dan tried to catch up, but the '68 Mustang, as repaired and reconditioned as it was, could just not keep up, not after all the damage it had suffered at the house.

His fingers stabbed his phone's digital buttons as his foot tromped on the accelerator. He practically slammed the phone to his ear as his other hand grew white-tight on the steering wheel. He was expecting Zeta's answering message, so he could press a certain combination of numbers to get through, but that didn't happen.

The phone rang once...twice...a third time as both vehicles got closer and closer to the corporate complex that secretly housed Zeta headquarters. The closer they got, and the more times the phone rang, the more tense Dan became.

"Come on, come on, pick up, pick up!" he found himself seething, his words drowning out the ringtone. He took his eyes off the tail of the Trackhawk to see if the phone was still connected.

In that second, he felt and heard the Trackhawk sharply turn. When he looked up, its taunting tail was disappearing down an alleyway, leaving him a view of the entire parking garage that filled his whole windshield.

He heard a click on the other end of the phone.

"This is AZ27F," he snapped. "Code—"

He never got to finish his priority emergency message. The parking garage erupted like a volcano—a multi-tiered, billowing mushroom of flame engulfing the structure from its bowels to its crown.

The phone went dead.

Chapter 2

Dan Morgan didn't remember jamming the Mustang into reverse. He didn't remember slamming his foot on its accelerator. But what he did remember was whirling around as far as he could without losing his grip on the steering wheel, and driving as fast as he could—backwards.

The sound of his screeching Cooper Cobra Radial tires, complete with Outlaw II racing wheels, was drowned out by the concussive shockwave of the explosion, which was really saying something, considering the scream the car let out as Dan tried to make it retreat as fast as it had charged.

Thankfully the access road behind him was clear, not just because of the lateness of the hour, but because Zeta had purposely chosen an out-of-the-way location that was infamous for its remoteness.

Morgan kept his eyes locked on the roadway, not wanting to divide his attention or get distracted by the chunks of steel, glass, and concrete that were hurtling toward him. But, ultimately, after seeing that the road behind him was unobstructed and relatively straight, he forced himself to watch out, just in case a duck or dodge could save some part of him from being crushed by a cement cannonball, impaled by a steel spear, or decapitated by a glass ax.

But as his head turned, he spotted something far more important—an alleyway guarded by steel and reinforced concrete walls. The lessons he had learned from the escape and evasion driving courses he had taken at the CIA and Zeta came crashing back into his brain like water exploding from a dynamited dam, and the Mustang reacted to his braking and wheel-spinning like it had been waiting all its life to be used like this. If the bastards inside the Trackhawk were watching from some safe vantage point, even they might be impressed by the precise expertise of the maneuver.

One second the Mustang was speeding backward like a stone hurled from a vicious bully's slingshot, and the next it had "drifted" until it was perpendicular to the sidewalks. Seemingly just a split second before a wall of spinning, smoking shrapnel slammed into it, the Mustang shot forward into the alley mouth as if kicked. The car chunked to a stop in the alleyway like an oiled ammo magazine sliding into the butt of an automatic weapon. But Morgan didn't even have the time to exhale as a hailstorm of rock, iron, and crystal smashed and scratched the street like a monstrous cheetah's claws.

As fast as the monsoon of debris started, it rolled to a halt, quickly followed by a billowing cloud of dust that made a great smokescreen for him. In these years after 9-11, builders had been more careful about their construction materials, so Morgan felt relatively secure that he wasn't inhaling carcinogens—that was just about the only thing he felt safe about.

He took a moment to acknowledge he was alive before Jenny's guardian-angelic face settled onto his mind's eye like a lace shroud. *No, she can't be dead*, he thought before he let rage blind him again. *This time, killing whoever's responsible just might bring her back*, he lied to himself. *Maybe not*, he concluded as the dust settled, *but that won't stop me from killing whoever they are.*

Having unconsciously gone through the five stages of accepting death in two seconds flat, Morgan resisted, with consummate effort, slamming his car back onto the roadway to try finding the Trackhawk. Given the expertise of their detonation and driving, it was unlikely those obvious pros would let him catch them unawares.

Instead, he tried forcing himself to think clearly, taking his first long breath since turning the corner on his street, which seemed like a lifetime ago. And with that breath came the enormity of the situation. Someone had not just destroyed his home, but the entirety of Zeta HQ—an accomplishment that boggled Morgan's mind with its brazenness.

He imagined how the enemy could have gained access to both locations, let alone set enough explosives to do what he'd witnessed in such a way that no one, in either location, had noticed them doing it. Whoever was in that Trackhawk, or whoever they represented, was impressively capable, vindictive, sadistic, and deadly serious. And here Morgan was, alone, cut off from his team, his organization, and all their equipment.

"Where's MacGyver when you need him?" he heard himself mutter, before falling back on his training. With the silty dust of the explosion still shielding him, he slipped out of the car. He stayed outside just long enough to make a cursory examination of the area and retrieve the Beretta A400 shotgun from the trunk.

Ever since a shotgun had saved his wife's life three missions ago, they'd always kept one in the trunk of each and every one of their motor vehicles, as both protection and a good luck charm. At the thought of it, and her, Morgan's eyes grew dark once again as a heart-rending "greatest hits video" of their relationship assailed his brain like a cloud of stinging nettles. Morgan knowingly crushed them as he got back behind the wheel, shoving the gas-operated, semi-automatic, camo-clad weapon beside him on the passenger seat.

He hit the rectangular tab of the spring-lock opening of the gun box he had affixed under the passenger seat. When he straightened again, he was holding his high-strength, light-weight, stainless steel, friction-reducing, double-action, five-shot Ruger LCR snub-nose thirty-eight revolver.

Morgan looked at both weapons, feeling some of the power the explosions had taken away returning to him. He had personally chosen these guns for good reasons. The Beretta could interchangeably fire any shell, from the lightest Olympic loads to the heaviest magnums, without adjustment. The Ruger was made of aerospace-grade 7000-series aluminum, and had a shrouded hammer so there'd be no snagging on holsters or clothing. As any gun man could tell you, an automatic, no matter how expensive or well made, could jam. His Ruger revolver never did.

The thought made him feel the weight of his standard side-arm, snug in his shoulder holster. Although most of his fellow field agents preferred Glocks or HKs, Dan depended on his trusty double action, non-slip, .380 Walther PPK.

So much for his personal high-caliber equipment. As he sat there, he continued his survey, sensing his stainless steel Smith & Wesson H.R.T. (Hostage Response Team) black knife in his boot, and the Boston Leather blackjack in his back pocket.

Morgan smiled grimly despite himself, as more violent memories knowingly started crowding out loving ones. Especially gratifying was the look on his enemies' faces when they'd thought he was helpless, only to have a molded lead weight inside a four-ply, heavy gauge leather pocket smash their skulls or pulverize their bones.

And all he wanted to do was unleash all this weaponry on the occupants of the Trackhawk. But he also didn't want to commit suicide. Whoever these guys were, they had eradicated his life and career in a single hour, and more than likely, would not be impressed with his paltry armaments.

Dan gripped the steering wheel with one hand and slammed his other on the dashboard. He wasn't Zeta's Sherlock Holmes, he was their bluntest blunt instrument. It was not his job to plan, just attack. He was Zeta's human version of the steel-shank and molded lead-weighted truncheon he carried in his back pocket. He looked up as the last of the silt settled, thinking furiously, or at least as furiously as Dan Morgan could—which, on second thought, was very furiously indeed.

What crowded to the front of his mind was what Zeta had hammered into him and all the other field agents. Linc had called it the R.B. Protocol—referring to the Red Button that no one was supposed to ever push in countless comedies and cartoons. Peter Conley had called it D.A.C.—rhyming with "gack"—harkening back to the ludicrous instructions given to schoolchildren in the event of a nuclear attack: Duck and Cover. But Paul Kirby, Zeta's officious, obsequious second-in-command bureaucrat with the bug up his bum, called it the Zeta Office of Risk Management plan in case of emergencies. He would.

According to Kirby, what Morgan was experiencing now was Z.O.R.M. Ultra, i.e. the worst case scenario. The man's annoying acronyms coursed into Morgan's head like bee sting venom. The instructions had been clear: if Zeta was eradicated, his responsibility was to destroy all comm devices so they couldn't be traced by the enemy, go underground, and wait for reassignment. As if controlled by Zeta puppet-masters, Morgan's hands came up with his cellphone.

"Cell phones suck," Lincoln Shepard had told him—a sentiment Dan heartily agreed with, but for different reasons. For their internet technology expert, however, they sucked because they were so easily bugged. "Cell phones were basically made to be traced," Linc had maintained. "As ancient as they now seem, there's a reason organizations like the Internal Revenue Service still use faxes."

"They like to torture everybody with screeching dial tones?" Morgan had retorted. Dan, like every working man, was not exactly a big fan of the I.R.S.

Linc had laughed. "Actually, yes. Faxes are basically unbuggable. Even if you can find a way to hack them, the gobbledygook you get makes you slave for every translated word, and the few words you're able to decipher might not even go together."

Now, Dan thought as he wrenched the SIM card out of his smartphone, *where in this fresh hell can I find a fax?* As he crushed the SIM card, rendering the smartphone nothing more than an expensive paperweight, he remembered that some overnight delivery places still used faxes, but who did he know in Zeta who had a receiving machine, and how was he going to find their fax number? Call information? On what?

Morgan raised his head like a bloodhound at a distant, but growing, sound of sirens. He knew by the noises what was coming. First and foremost, there was a shrill, three-tone alarm. That meant police in general, and an Interceptor Utility Vehicle in particular. Dan knew the way it switched tones depended on the traffic facing it. First tone meant "I'm here." Second, more rapid tone meant "look out." The third, most piercing, staccato tone all but shrieked "get out of the freakin' way." The third tone was the one that was pumping into the night.

Following close behind were the air horn and Federal Signal Q-Siren of the Fire Department's ladder vehicles, leading a phalanx of dual-tone-sirened Emergency Medical Services Ambulances, and Rumbler-sirened Emergency Medical Service vans. The Rumbler accompanied its siren with a loud "sonic thump" that could be heard over almost anything, as well as knuckling the heart, spine, and brain of anyone stupid enough not to get out of the way.

As Morgan started his car and backed up toward the other end of the alley, he saw flashes of oscillating red, blue, and even amber dotting the street walls. Police dragnets were being tightened around the disaster perimeter, and pretty soon they'd start snaring him. Morgan's lips grew tight as he realized there were two things he most needed: a landline phone, and a good stiff drink.

Dan Morgan's eyes remained chipped glass from sorrow and frustration, but his thin lips twitched into a grief-smeared grin. He knew one place he might be able to get both.

Chapter 3

The bar had no name. In fact, Dan thought of it as The Bar With No Name. It also had no sign, no neon beer lights, and caged windows only large enough to meet minimum building code requirements. Even if there had been neon beer lights, they probably wouldn't have been visible through all the soot and dirt on the glass.

Not surprisingly, The Bar With No Name tried to sink into a neighborhood that had one of the highest crime rates in Beantown. Wedged between the airport and the harbor, the area had been created by connecting several islands using landfill.

Dan took one last look at his car parked by the curb and hoped the damage it had suffered in the last few hours would disguise its eminent steal-worthiness. He had considered leaving the shotgun on the passenger seat as a sort of warning that the owner was not to be trifled with, but ultimately thought better of it.

Instead the Beretta was in a duffel bag he carried in his left hand. The Ruger was wedged in his pants at the small of his back, and his Walther, boot knife and cudgel were where they always were. Morgan took a second to silently thank the car in case this was the last time he ever saw it, acknowledging the irony of the Cobra tires that had taken it all and kept going. After all, Morgan's code name was Cobra, and he didn't care if anyone thought that's why he had bought the tires. In reality, they really were the best ones for the '68 Mustang.

As he took his next step toward the bar, he glanced down at himself. His brown boots, blue jeans, black t-shirt, gray car coat, and driving gloves were suitably dusty and scuffed, but not so much that it might risk others wondering if he had just come from multiple explosions. By now the rest of the city would either be locked down, or about to be locked down, with visions of terrorist attacks dancing in people's heads. But, in this shrinking corner of Eastie, aka East Boston, life dragged miserably on.

As always, Morgan's eyes scoured the entire interior as he walked in—pinpointing every person, detail, and exit. Two silent Hispanics were on opposite sides of a truncated bar along one wall, while a sullen African-American prostitute and her Caucasian john were in one of the three semi-circular booths along the opposite wall. The third booth had a couple of Caucasians who were deeply committed to a hissy fit while sharing a bottle of cheap scotch.

Between them and the restrooms was what Morgan was looking for: one of the last of the pay phone booths in existence. Needless to say, the entire place stank of decaying wood, spilled rotgut, constantly replenished puke, and, somewhat incongruently, cat piss. Human piss Morgan could understand, but cat piss? What self-respecting feline would be caught alive in a place like this? For that matter, what self-respecting field operative would?

Morgan exhaled as he walked silently past the bar and booths, grateful that he had stumbled onto the place during a previous assignment when they'd needed to rendezvous with a low-grade informer. He didn't expect a "hello" or "what'll you have" from the dour middle-aged Hispanic bartender who stared at a soccer game on a small TV screen, and he didn't get any. Nor did he get any sullen stares from the other patrons. The Bar With No Name could have also been called The Bar With No Witnesses or even The Bar Where No One Cares. If the sitcom *Cheers* had been set here instead of a Back Bay bar, the theme song would've been "Where Nobody Knows Your Name."

All Dan wanted was a dial tone and a connected receiver that wasn't smeared with dog poop, and that—somewhat to his surprise and much to his relief—he did get. Morgan leaned the duffel bag in the phone booth corner as he pulled a roll of quarters from his pocket. He kept a roll of quarters in his glove compartment. Worse come to worst, they made a nifty interior-fist set of silver knuckles.

Slipping a coin into the slot, which, thankfully, wasn't damaged, he started poking the sticky, smeared, square buttons. He tried them all again. His wife Jenny, his daughter Alex, his partner Peter, his trusted fellow field agents Lily and Karen, the tech wiz Linc, and then his boss Diana Bloch. Nothing. He really hadn't expected anything else. Telemarketers had made phone calls into something to be ignored, despised, or even dreaded. Even in the best of circumstances or availability, he wouldn't connect with a phone number he didn't recognize.

Morgan seethed in the booth like a caged animal. He wracked his brain for anything to do other than marching into the street and screaming for the Trackhawk to come get him. In fact, he had been more than half expecting them to come blasting into the bar. He was beginning to wonder why they hadn't when the rising noise of the outside couple's argument reached his ears. Apparently the man was a loser and the woman was a bitch—each said so with ever increasing emphasis, probably to differentiate it from the million other times they had hurled the epithets at each other.

Mourning his love and their hate, Morgan realized there was one person he hadn't called. *Why not?* he wondered as he stabbed the memorized emergency number into the button-pad. *What've I got to lose?*

Just before he fully remembered what he had already lost, there was a click and a voice.

"Cobra!" Paul Kirby barked, somehow recognizing the bar's phone booth number on his caller ID. Did the guy have that kind of photographic memory? Morgan wouldn't put it past the bureaucrat, but whatever the man said next was almost drowned out by the couple's suddenly escalating argument.

"Hold on," Dan snapped as he turned away from the bar and jammed a forefinger in his other ear.

But Kirby hadn't waited. "...here to my place ASAP," the bureaucrat was hissing. "Zeta is under siege."

Morgan opened his mouth to demand details, but then there was a screech that made his head recoil, and the line went dead just as the man in the booth outside backhanded the woman opposite him.

When, a few seconds later, Morgan stepped out of the phone booth with his duffel bag over his shoulder, the woman was sobbing, her head down, as her bleeding nose smeared her shot glass, while the man continued berating her nagging and uselessness. Morgan's face was blank and cold as he stepped up and, without warning or pause, hit the man in the jaw with such pent-up power and hard-won expertise that the man was launched out of the booth as if by catapult, somersaulted backwards, and slammed to the floor on his face.

The woman's head popped up, bug-eyed, then whirled to look down at the man, before snapping her head back toward Dan. But he was already halfway to the front door.

He had almost made it when he stopped to catch the woman's arm as she tried to break the scotch bottle across the back of his head. He had been expecting it. He knew the old, well-worn story of the cop who beat up an abusive husband only to be attacked by the battered wife. Besides, with his peripheral vision he could just make out her attacking reflection in the tarnished mirror behind the bar.

He turned to lock eyes with her—his steel, seething, nearly tragic gaze all but paralyzing her—then slowly, purposefully lowered and turned her arm until the last of the scotch poured out into a shot glass he had palmed after the punch. Precisely, expertly, he moved her arm back up so as not to spill a drop. Then, with a split-second stare into her frightened, uncomprehending, pitiful eyes, he gunned the hooch into his throat, then tossed her the glass, which, to both their surprise, she caught.

"Thanks," he said as he quickly exited. "I needed that."

Chapter 4

Every time he went to Beacon Hill, Dan Morgan couldn't help but think that he was stepping into a Jack the Ripper movie. The swanky neighborhood's narrow, hilly, cobblestone streets had a way of inspiring that feeling. And the gas lamps that still dappled the most expensive areas in moody shadows certainly didn't hurt either.

Tonight was no exception, and Dan could add the genre of murder mystery to the cloying atmosphere. He didn't know who to expect first: Sherlock Holmes, a slasher killer with mask and machete, or death itself, complete with cowl and scythe, pointing a boney forefinger at him while intoning "you …don't …belong …here!"

But even this part of the city, like the rest of it, was effectively locked down or shut in. It seemed people were riveted to their local news sources to see if anybody was going to take credit for the building bombing. But be they twenty-four-hour news channels or online feeds, both were dealing with it the way they now always did: with exaggeration, speculation, and endless repetition that bordered on hysteria, designed to upset, agitate, and, most importantly, keep you watching.

Welcome to the Hyper Bowl, Morgan thought sarcastically as he studied the seemingly quiet area. He wondered if the cops had made the connection to the suburban house explosion yet. Probably not, but one thing was for sure: if the news media got a hold of it, it would soon be blown up—all puns intended—into the "Boston Bombing Blitzkrieg! Will you be next?!" *Things are bad enough without the leeches making it worse.*

Morgan kicked those thoughts out of his head to make room for something far more important: survival and revenge. Whoever was doing this was targeting Zeta. With the main sources of communication down, he didn't know if every field agent's residence had been attacked, or just his. In any case, from his vantage point, Paul Kirby's abode looked none the worse for wear.

The last time he had seen it was on a personal reconnaissance at the very start of his tenure with Zeta, just to know what was what and where was where. He had learned the hard way never to take anyone's words as gospel. He wanted to trust people, but when one of his favorite commanders had used his belief against him—almost setting off a coastal apocalypse, to boot—trust and Dan Morgan were now warily circling each other and not on speaking terms.

But even before all that, Morgan had tracked down his main fellow agents' residences, just in case, and just to see if he could do it without them spotting him. Actually, he never had found Diana Bloch's place, but that somehow made him feel better about following her orders. If she could hide from him, she must know what she was doing. Not Paul Kirby, however. He was the easiest to find. In fact, he not only didn't keep his place of residence secret, but actually seemed proud to let anyone know where he rested his sorry butt.

Another pang cut Morgan's heart and mind as he unavoidably remembered his wife Jenny helping their then-eight-year-old daughter Alex with her history and geography homework.

"Beacon Hill is named for the warning light that was built at the highest point in central Boston. The beacon was used to warn the citizens of an invasion."

Morgan frowned. Ironic, considering what he was now planning to do.

"It's around a sixth of a square mile along the Charles River front, with the Charles River Esplanade to the west and the Boston Common Public Garden to the north."

Coincidentally, the bar *Cheers* was based on nestled just a few hundred yards away, on Beacon Street across from the Gardens. Morgan wished he had time to get another shot of scotch there, though not in the same way he had in Eastie's Bar Where Nobody Knew Your Name.

Morgan gave a silent snort. The racial makeup of Beacon Hill turned Eastie on its head as well. Here Africans and Hispanics might get a double take from a good percentage of the Caucasians that had been swelling here for generations in their Federal-style row houses, alongside the likes of super-lawyer Daniel Webster and super-thinker Henry David Thoreau.

Just think, Morgan remembered from his overhearing the end of Alex's lesson. *All this was once a cow path.*

Once more Morgan let his rage overpower his sadness. That lesson was over. *Now it's time for some history they never teach you in Boston Public Schools*, he thought. *Or private ones, for that matter.* Because once he had found his peers' places, he had set about figuring out how to get in without tripping, or raising, any alarms.

The only one he couldn't figure out was Peter Conley's Cougar Ranch. Lily, Lincoln, and Karen's weren't easy, but they weren't impossible. But the best, most inspired infiltration he'd devised, if he did think so himself, was for the priggish Paul.

The irony was just too good. Dan couldn't get in through the wrought-iron fences, the bulletproof windows, the laser eyes, the video lenses, or even the quadruple locks. But he could get in where these lords of industry were their most pathetic: below their belts. Sure, they wanted to keep out the riff-raff, the needy, the dangerous. But there was one person they didn't want to keep out.

Their mistresses.

The rich always thought money could protect them from anything but, as usual, it turned out that their wealth *was* their weakness.

They had put in the secret tunnels and entrances themselves, so their paramours could come, or so they could go to them. The real beauty of it was that secrecy was utmost. Dan was certain that Kirby didn't even know that a previous occupant had covertly installed an escape hatch, along with an underground hallway to and from it.

Dan turned from where he had nearly scraped his car behind a dumpster nestled in an alley at the juncture of Cedar Lane Way and Mount Vernon Street. He had to lean against the brick wall, almost gasping as he remembered that Jenny had taught him this as well. Later, after Alex's homework, upstairs in the marital bedroom, it was Jenny who had filled him in on the comings and goings of the Louisburg Square society strumpets.

That woman of mine, Morgan thought miserably. *Quite the reader.* And homemaker, and wife, and mother, and companion, and partner...!

Morgan had to forcibly crush these thoughts from his mind. *Mourning, and memory*, he thought, *can wait until I feel the spines of my wife's killers snapping under my fingers...*

He concentrated instead on putting into practice the research he had supplemented his wife's stories with. Even after all these years, there was a cunningly designed series of loose bricks that had to be manipulated exactly: one in, one left, one right, then right again, down, up, up, and left. That opened a space just large enough for a dainty finger to wrap a stone ring. Morgan's muscular pinky barely made it, but his strength compensated for the grip. A panel in a recessed corner of the alley, far away from prying pedestrians' eyes, popped open as reward.

Morgan rolled his own eyes, trying to forget how long it took him to trial-and-error this entrance all those years ago. He thought he'd never squeeze through the opening, but thanked the busts and bustles of those nineteenth century women for making just enough room for the muscular likes of him.

He was certain that once upon a time there had been kerosene lamps or some such to light their way, but those were long gone. Thankfully, along with his pistols, knife, and cosh, he always carried a small all-in-one pocket tool, which included a pinprick-sized but powerful flashlight, along with a screwdriver, saw, file, hammer head, can opener, bottle opener, corkscrew, tweezer, and toothpick.

The hallway was relatively long, crossing beneath two back-to-back brownstones, but it was straight. Morgan could practically feel the cobblestones over his head, as well as the ultra-exclusive, fenced-in oval Louisburg Square park that he would never have been allowed in otherwise. But he left that behind in order to infiltrate one of the townhouses.

Not surprisingly, there was no great puzzle awaiting on the other side of the hallway tunnel. Once the great unwashed were kept out, the master should not have to unduly wait for his well-instructed mistress. Morgan pressed a rectangular panel on the middle left of a plain partition, and an entrance popped open.

Morgan was not surprised that he emerged in the townhouse cellar. The romantic rendezvous may have been desired by the lord and master of the house, but it was still important to let the visiting woman remember her lowly status that only her physical beauty belied. Fine with him, Morgan concluded. Popping up in the parlor might have been a rude surprise for all concerned.

Morgan took a breath and got his bearings. He almost laughed, remembering all the movies he had seen when a hero started calling out for their yet unseen contact. That's a great way to get killed. So Morgan moved, as silently as his boots and bulk allowed, to the cellar stairs. He thumbed off his tool light and made his way up to what he remembered was the kitchen door.

He stopped at the obstruction and listened, even though he knew that the insulation and sound-proofing were the best that money could buy. He grimaced, wondering where Kirby got the scratch to afford this. Zeta was far from minimum wage, but it's not like he could afford a mansion.

The problem with me, he thought, *is that I disliked the guy so much I didn't even bother to find out*. Morgan almost shrugged. *Well, if we survive the next few minutes*, he thought, *maybe I'll ask him.*

Morgan opened the door just enough to peer through, in case anybody was waiting. No one was. Even though his eyes had adjusted to the dark, there was recessed night lighting in the well-appointed, renovated, open kitchen, enough that he could see the room was spotlessly clean, and devoid of human presence—or maybe even human touch.

When Morgan slid in, his back against the side of a black matte industrial refrigerator, his Walther PPK, complete with silencer, had somehow appeared seemingly magically in his hand, held low to his side. He remained there, waiting, letting his senses take in everything they could. He still got nothing. If he'd had a million dollars to wager he would've bet that he was alone.

But, unlike, apparently, Paul Kirby, he didn't have a million dollars. He did have one thing he valued more—his own life—and he bet that by snaking out from the side to the front of the refrigerator. From that vantage point he could see across the cutting-edge open concept apartment from the kitchen to the dining area to the living room—all devoid of anything resembling human flesh.

Morgan did not relax. His eyes took in every surface, every piece of furniture, every houseware, every rug, every fixture. Not a single personal item anywhere: no photos, no memorabilia, no collectibles, no painting, not even a diploma. It was as if Dan had stepped into a museum diorama labeled "Disinfected Dwelling of Early 21st-Century Middle Manager Executive."

Morgan kept moving. He felt like a shark, for good and ill. While the fish was a killing machine, it also had to keep moving or die. Dan felt the same, only he wasn't in any rush. He would keep moving until something changed. With one more step, it did.

It was not a shock, or even a surprise. If he could think of any word that came close to describing it, that word would be "curious." It was as if a benign, even comforting, rainbow was in the very corner of his eye.

Dan Morgan turned his head toward the curiosity. It was in a small. rectangular, stand-up mirror in the upper right-hand corner of a writing desk by a small front window. As Morgan stepped closer he automatically decided that the window was one-way and bulletproof. He knew that kind of security measure when he saw it. But he had never seen anything like the little mirror before.

Correction: yes he had. Years ago, at The Museum of Science, planetarium, and Omnimax theater along the Charles River Dam. This had been even before the massive renovation that had started in 2013. He had gone as a volunteer chaperone with his daughter's eighth grade class. And there, among the Butterfly Garden, Discovery Center, Animal Care Center, and Rock Garden was an exhibit they called The Light House. In it, showcased as if it were the end-all and be-all of scientific achievement had been a hologram—a tiny hologram of what looked like a little rainbow man saying hello. And now, in the mirror, was Paul Kirby's face—moving but silent.

Dan Morgan stepped closer. It was Paul Kirby's face all right, existing within Morgan's own reflection in the mirror, and it was saying something over and over again. As far as Morgan could tell, it was on some sort of loop.

Dan moved his hand in front of the mirror, but the hologram did not refract on his fingers. Dan hazarded a glance back over his shoulder to see if he could spot a projector of some sort. He couldn't. He looked at his feet to see if he had interrupted a laser trip-wire. He hadn't. He looked back at Kirby's little rainbowed face, and recognized the silent words the man was mouthing.

"Destroy all comms, go underground, wait for reassignment. Destroy all comms, go underground, wait for reassignment. Destroy all comms, go underground, wait for reassignment…"

He—it—was mouthing the ZORM Ultra Protocol.

Morgan wanted to curse Kirby and all the ancestors who'd made him. Trust the bureaucrat to get him all the way out here, only to be useless.

"I got my reassignment already, butt-wipe," Dan growled so quietly even he hardly heard it. But now, he could also hardly hear something else. It was a tiny, distant splitting sound, like a strand of human hair being pulled apart.

Dan Morgan's head snapped up just in time to see, right between his eyes, a pinhead-sized hairline fracture in the one-way, bulletproof glass of the window in front of him.

Chapter 5

All hell broke loose. Quietly.

Morgan jerked his head to the left, out of the direct path of whatever it was that was somehow cracking the bulletproof glass. Something thin sizzled by his right cheek and grazed the bottom of his right earlobe.

He managed one last look at the window beyond the desk as he grabbed the little mirror with Kirby's hologram and dropped to the floor. As he landed on his back he focused on the image of the window. He saw what looked like a toothpick-sized chip—a toothpick-sized chip with a pinprick-sized hole in the middle of it.

Before he could process that, he heard another tiny hair-snapping sound to his left. His eyes snapped in that direction to see another window in the kitchen that was placed high on the wall, seemingly designed to look down on whoever might be lying on the floor. As he looked, another toothpick-sized crack appeared in that glass pane.

Morgan rolled faster than even he thought he could, hearing a small snap of the glass being breached, but this time he also heard a soft sound behind him. It was like an inhalation.

Morgan came up onto his knees to stare down at the expensive carpet where he had just been lying, but only saw the slightest ripple of something deep in the tight, padded nap there. He instinctively reached out with his free hand to see if he could feel the invader, but then another distant hair-snapping sound came to his right ear.

He spun his head in that direction to see another rectangular, bulletproof, glass eye—with a splintering mote in the middle of it—staring at him from the front hallway. Morgan launched himself backwards just in time to avoid another thin, shining thing disappearing into the back of the luxurious sofa where he had just been. But, unlike twenty-two, thirty-two, thirty-eight, three-eighty, three-fifty-seven, forty-four, forty-five, or even fifty-caliber rounds from standard guns, which left noticeable, if not gaping, holes in whatever they hit, these things hardly left a mark.

Dan didn't have time to dwell on it since his eyes were all but corkscrewing around their sockets trying to spot every possible window in the place. Not only was he apparently surrounded with assassins sporting cutting-edge silenced sniper rifles, but they were seemingly positioned on every level as well—up, down, and in the middle. All the better to puncture him with.

There was only one saving grace. If these had been normal windows he probably would have already been dead, with some sort of acupuncture-thin, scalpel-sharp shard in his head or heart. But these were not normal windows. Morgan was fairly certain these were top-of-the-line aluminum oxynitride, level ten, bullet-resistant panes, because that's the kind of security a tight-ass like Kirby would insist upon. But, as Morgan snaked to the bottom of the kitchen counter, he wished he could kiss Kirby's tight ass for giving him a split second to avoid the killer projectiles.

The expensive apartment had become a maze of subtle destruction, but instead of having to avoid laser security beams, Morgan had to duck, dodge, twist, turn, slide, and somersault to avoid getting perforated, with only his eyes and ears as warnings. Not only were they coming at him from all sides and all angles, they were coming at him from deep in the night, giving him no targets for return fire.

They were also trapping him in a cone of silence. If they had been using standard weapons, even silenced ones, they'd be making enough of a ruckus to raise an alarm—especially in such a high-security, ritzy, neighborhood. Instead, it was as if he was in the middle of a test lab, with various minor home accessories—a vase here, a clock there, a TV screen over the mantle—cracking or breaking or shattering seemingly of their own accord.

The planning for this ambush had to have been extraordinary—finding multiple vantage points without coming to the attention of private or public surveillance cameras. But even that didn't demoralize Morgan. It only made him madder. He was sorely tempted to call their bluff and raise an alarm himself. If he filled his hands with his PPK and Ruger, then opened up, the cops and private security would descend like locusts.

But as he dove from the base of the kitchen counter to the side of the refrigerator, he decided he didn't want to raise an alarm. The authorities might save him from whoever was attacking him, but they also would keep him from tracking those responsible for destroying his home, and happiness. No, he would much rather tear the heads off of "them" personally. But he would have to get to them first.

Dan took one last look at the apartment, which looked like it had been attacked by the most subtle, polite vandal ever, then all but vaulted through the cellar door. He leaped over all the stairs, to land with a satisfying thump on the basement floor. He had hardly settled before he was barreling back to the mistress partition entrance, his silenced PPK in one hand and the hologram mirror in the other.

He gave the latter a cursory glance, feeling only a slight twinge of regret, as he decided the laser projector that was creating the hologram was inside the frame, behind the reflective glass. Any other mysteries it might have solved upon further examination would have to be sacrificed for the greater good.

The greater good and regret became clear as he pressed the pop-open panel. Paul Kirby's silently mouthing, multi-colored form seemed to waver in the air of the darkened tunnel for one split second before it became a splintering, shattering pin-cushion, accompanied by what sounded like a half-dozen hydraulic pistons. The mirror danced in mid-air before bursting, spreading, and raining down in tinkling, clattering pieces.

Then there was silence, as dust clouds dissipated and the two assassins stationed there stepped forward to examine the damage.

"Seven years bad luck," Morgan murmured as he shot both shadowy figures from where he had crab-walked in the pitch blackness to the middle of the left wall.

The fact that he stayed crouched saved his life as the two attackers responded to what should have been killing shots by whirling around and opening fire again. From his vantage point below them, Dan could better examine the attackers and their weapons as he silently swore his head off. Night vision goggles they apparently didn't have, since they were peppering the wall above him with what looked like streamlined harpoon guns that had been modified for, apparently, rocket-powered needles. Whatever they were had almost no muzzle flash and a sizzling, thudding sound he'd never heard any other gun make.

Morgan could see they were wearing the same sort of dark, apparently bulletproof, outfits and visored helmets as the stranger outside his home's explosion. That all but galvanized him, Morgan moved between the two men, bringing his boot heel down on the top of the right man's foot while jamming the barrel of the Walther's silencer under the rim of the left one's helmet's visor.

With a twitch of his trigger finger he splattered the left one's skull and brains inside the helmet while using his knee as a battering ram between the other one's legs. That way he knew it didn't matter whether the bastard's jockey shorts were bulletproof or not.

Morgan didn't pause to savor the sliver of revenge he had accomplished. From the attack on Kirby's townhouse, he knew there were a lot more where they came from. He wrenched off the helmet of the one writhing at his feet before planting another PPK round between the man's pain-wracked eyes. Then he yanked off the guy's jacket before marching toward the mistress tunnel's entrance.

By the time he got there, both the jacket and helmet were on him—which was pretty much the only thing that saved him as he dove out into the alley. There was a man stationed at either end of his car, and they opened fire as soon as he appeared. Thankfully for him, they were well-trained, so they went for his head and chest. Thankfully their assault gear was powerful enough to protect him from their own hi-tech weapons.

Still, that only gave Morgan a second, but that was less than what he was planning to use. He threw his blackjack at the one furthest from him, on the left, and brought the bottom of his boot, full force, on the left knee of the one nearest him. He heard the satisfying *thunk* of leather-enclosed lead hitting the left one's helmet while feeling the even more satisfying crack of the right one's knee and leg bones under the full power of his kicking stomp.

Again, he took no pause for celebration. Morgan grabbed the club-length needle gun from the hands of the nearest one as he started to topple, and swung it like David "Big Papi" Ortiz's Boston Red Sox home-run baseball bat. When it connected with the falling man's helmeted head, it again didn't matter if the outfit was bulletproof or not.

With both assassins down, Morgan dove toward the car. No way anyone who was left would let him get to his shotgun, but if he could just carve out a few seconds of safe time he could get the car started. As if by magic, the keys were in his hand. As if guided by his wife's angelic hands, the engine roared to life. Accompanied by the heavenly sounds of the attacker's pained screeches, he prepared to peel out of the alley faster than the GT had ever gone.

But his moment of saving grace was over. To his utter astonishment, the car seemed to pump downward as if a giant monster's hand had slammed atop it. It bounced up once like a cockroach—as if the giant had misjudged the strength needed to crush it—then shook as if gripped by a seizure.

Morgan was sure he was about to be engulfed in a ball of flame, then ripped apart by a car bomb explosion, but that didn't happen either. He almost wished it had as he stared at how his beautiful car was being punctured and torn by what now seemed like both of an invisible giant monster's hands.

His windshield wasn't shattered; it was punched open by invisible fists. Morgan saw, as if in slow motion, one round piece of windshield glass shoot by his head, and then felt something resembling a concentrated tube of wind—like a savage punch that had just missed. Then, blinking, he watched as the hood of his car shredded like a piece of paper being ripped apart.

Morgan tried to get out, but the car was shaking so badly that the bouncing prevented him during his first few attempts. All the while, ragged holes were being stamped and gaping tears were being ripped in the Mustang's rapidly disintegrating body.

Morgan was astonished, not by what he was experiencing, but by how he didn't care, choosing instead to whirl around. Seeing his shotgun leaping up and down on the back seat told him all he needed to know about his attackers' arrogance.

They weren't trying to kill him. Not really, not yet. They were playing with him, like a sadistic cat with a lowly mouse. It was no coincidence, or accident, that they had kept four car lengths ahead of him during their first chase no matter what he did.

As he grabbed the shotgun out of mid-air, he saw that a small team of helmeted, assault-uniformed attackers were all around, moving slowly toward him. Each was carrying a weapon in both their hands. Some carried the needle guns. Others had what looked like a long, streamlined combination of a sniper's rifle and an anteater-snouted Taser. And then there were a few with what looked like a bazooka crossed with a t-shirt cannon. They all looked like escapees from the futuristic videogames his daughter used to play.

The attackers kept coming in a smaller and smaller semi-circle, and kept pulling their weapons' triggers, leaving more tears and holes in his once beautiful muscle car. But Morgan realized he could only hear the sound of the destruction. He couldn't even hear the weapons, other than a strange, unsettling sensation of pressure on his eardrums.

"Screw this," Morgan seethed, all but hurling himself at the driver's door. It cracked open in mid-jump, and he stumbled out into the alley like a newborn pterodactyl. Morgan slammed against the alley wall, barely keeping his balance, while the smallest of the helmeted, visored, uniformed attackers held up a fist.

The encroaching semi-circle stopped moving and firing, but Morgan didn't. He brought the shotgun around to spray them all at close range, but just before he could center his aim, the one who had raised a fist seemed to leap and spin in midair like some sort of demonic whirling dervish…a whirling dervish who seemed strangely, even sickeningly, familiar.

Much to Morgan's rage, the dervish kicked the shotgun out of his hands like an expert punter scoring the winning field goal. But it didn't stop there. The spinning kick continued as if the dervish were a prima ballerina, smashing into Morgan's head next, sending the helmet he had stolen flying at the same time the kick hurled him, whirling, into the alley dirt.

Morgan was amazed he wasn't unconscious. He lay there, head reeling, the top of his skull facing his devastated car, which was blocking entry to Mount Vernon Street. By this time, the other four attackers had semi-circled him in a curved line between him and his Mustang.

Meanwhile, coming toward his twitching feet was the kicker, who, by the way the others deferred to him, was clearly the leader of the pack. Except it wasn't a him. That much was made perfectly clear when she spoke.

"Well, well," he heard a female, accented voice from behind the helmeted visor say. "Where are my manners? You have lost your helmet, so the least I can do…"

Dan Morgan watched, still stunned, as she reached up and lifted off her own helmet. It was what he had been dreading ever since he had gone to "rescue" his daughter Alex from a Trans-Siberian Express train in the "dark territory" of Russia some time before.

The leader of this pack had the elliptical eyes, flat nose, and short hair of a white leopard. She also had the well-muscled body of a wrestler, and the smile of a dungeon master who really loved her work. She was a Serbian mercenary named Amina, and she had kicked him in the balls …twice… on that Trans-Siberian train before escaping. Morgan miserably decided that this particular rendezvous was equivalent to a third crotch shot.

Her expression was triumphant as she looked down at him while both tossing her helmet to an attacker behind her and bringing one of the snouted Taser weapons around. She pointed its wickedly tongued prongs between his eyes.

"Electromagnetic particle beam laser," she said, rolling the English technobabble around her thin lips as if savoring the finest Serbian sljivovica plum brandy. "It will make a domino-sized rectangle in your head."

Dan thought about interrupting with some pointed questions—about his house, about Zeta HQ, about how she got here, about how all this was pulled off—but the look on her face told him there would be nothing she'd like better than putting a death ray through his skull in mid-query.

"Hurry," he heard someone else tell her. "Someone must've called the cops by now."

"*Ućuti!*" she spat—Serbian for *shut up*. "The police are busy," she concluded dismissively

That told Morgan two things. She was, indeed, the boss here, but just barely. Her minions were probably hastily hired local help with a minimum of training. That also explained why Morgan was still alive. Not that it mattered, for, in the next second, Amina brought the futuristic looking rifle to her shoulder and stared sadistically down at him over its quadrilateral barrel.

With a sneer she went to pull the trigger, then seemed to get a final wicked idea. "Say hello to..." she started to say in lieu of his last words.

Dan Morgan never got to hear who Amina thought he should say hello to. Before she could finish, there was a *whomp* behind him, then the Mustang leapt into the air, and, once it was three feet off the ground, exploded.

Chapter 6

All the years of Dan Morgan's training in military and intelligence fired up his muscle memory like never before. Like many high-prepped people, he felt—even sensed—the unusual explosion a split second before it happened.

Boaz Schneider, his demolitions teacher, had called it the "Bouncing Betty Effect," referring to the World War II-era German Splittermine, which, when triggered, launched into the air before detonating.

That's what his car had done, and Morgan was not going to just lie there and let himself be perforated in the following blast. Again calling on the adrenaline-fueled speed he had experienced back in Kirby's townhouse, he instantly grabbed the still open lip of the mistress tunnel door and pulled himself into the passageway as far as his muscles would allow.

His exploding car did the rest. The door slammed shut behind him so hard it cracked in three places. Under his booted feet, Morgan could feel the steel, glass, and plastic shrapnel storming against the other side.

Double shot, Morgan thought. It had to be a double assault on the car—one to lift it, the other to detonate it.

Contrary to movies and television, cars rarely burst into flame, even if someone shot the gas tank. No, but if that gas tank were shot by a tracer bullet—a projectile with a small pyro charge in the shell—and from a great enough distance so that the round can ignite from air friction, it just might do the trick. Something sure did the trick here, and Morgan was not going to look this particular exploding gift horse in its fire-belching mouth.

His hands scrambled for his PPK, but came up empty. Sometime in this mess he had lost it and he wasn't going to go searching for it now. Instead, his hands went right for the Ruger, as he launched himself back toward the partition. No sense waiting for the smoke to clear. The more time he gave any survivors to recover, the less chance he had to stay alive.

Dan Morgan came back out into the alley, his head low but his eyes high, looking for anyone or anything who might do him harm. He saw a bunch of things at once.

First, if it hadn't already been after the hole-punching and steel-tearing assault by hi-tech weapons, his beautiful '68 Mustang GT was a lost cause. It looked like a paper model that had been torn flat, with just a few bumps of scorched upholstery still recognizable.

Second, the four assassins between him and the car were splayed like rag dolls that had been tromped on by a bully having a tantrum. Their blood and guts were mostly contained by their uniforms and helmets. Morgan was glad he wasn't the Emergency Medical Tech or Crime Scene Investigator who'd have to clean them up.

That examination took less than a half-second, after which he jerked his head in the opposite direction. Good timing. The few who had been on the other side of Amina were showing signs of life. Injured, dazed, hair-smoking life, but life nevertheless. They were trying to both get to their feet as well as raise their lasers, pin-shooters, and air cannons.

Morgan stood on no ceremony or Queensberry Rules. He unceremoniously raised his revolver, then froze. He could find no holes in their head to toe outfits. And with only five rounds in the Ruger, he couldn't afford to waste bullets on the bulletproof. He took a quick look around, and found what he was hoping for. He picked up the nearest high-tech weapon that wasn't damaged by the explosion.

Just his luck, it was the pin-shooter, which was the smallest, sleekest and least easily-damaged of the three armaments. Morgan grimaced since the polymerized metal exterior was still hot from the flames. But short of barbecuing his flesh, he wasn't about to drop it now.

If these chuckleheads could use them, so could he. Sure enough, the thing had a trigger, and there certainly hadn't been enough time to engage any safety or similar security device. Morgan pointed the barrel at them, making the rifle an extension of his arm, and let his forefinger do the rest.

The pin-shooter gave a satisfying burp, letting Morgan feel some sort of small pyro charge in the shell engage. Then, as if he had drawn a straight line between the barrel and the first target's forehead, he got a glimpse of a needle-thin missile with a shining top making the same sort of hairline fracture in the man's helmet visor that it had in the townhouse's windows. The assassin went down and stayed down.

Morgan brought his aim over to the next one trying to get up. As the smoke and dust around them cleared, Morgan got the undeniable feeling that he had stepped into a zombie killer videogame. Pin-pointing the same place on the second man's visor as he had on the first, he pulled the trigger a second time. That man went down as if yanked by a wire attached to Satan's thumb.

Now that he was prepared for it, there was no missing the needle's shining crown. *Diamond-tipped*, Morgan guessed, which explained how the cunning, seemingly rocket-powered, pins could pierce level ten bulletproofing. Despite all the man-made materials scientists came up with, diamond was still considered the hardest thing on Earth.

By then the third man was staggering to his feet, pulling up what Morgan assumed was the laser Amina had planned to execute him with. He couldn't help but let the smallest flicker of a grin play on his lips as he brought his pilfered pin-shooter to bear.

Live by the laser, die by the laser, he thought with vengeful irony, and pulled the trigger just as the man got his own death ray to waist level.

Nothing happened.

Morgan stiffened, realizing his pin-shooter was out of pins.

He looked down at it, as if betrayed, then his eyes scrambled around to try finding another. There was nothing he could see, so he looked back at the third assassin, who, by then, had reached his unsteady feet and was leveling the domino shape that served as the weapon's barrel at Morgan.

There was little else Dan could do. He hurled the pin-shooter at the man like a javelin, ducked, brought up his Ruger, and charged in a tight curve.

The assassin had to take a shaky step to avoid the spear, but that didn't stop him from firing the laser. Like a sniper's bullet that the victim never heard, Morgan thought that if he didn't feel it, it hadn't hit him. He hadn't expected to see it, but he did hear something crackling behind him.

Morgan kept running, but with his revolver in front of him. The assassin started shifting the laser's barrel toward him, so Morgan decided it was better to kiss his bullets goodbye than himself. He watched as the slugs slammed into the man's helmet and chest like fists, knocking the killer back.

Just as he managed to keep his feet, Morgan followed the bullets with himself, slamming into the man like a battering ram. The result was gratifying. The man flew back, the laser spinning from his hands.

Morgan shoved the Ruger in his pocket and caught the rifle in midair. As the man splayed out near the mouth of the alley, Morgan brought the new gun to bear, centered the domino-sized rectangle in the middle of the man's body, and pulled the trigger.

The result almost made him sick, despite having seen the aftermath of many a battlefield. The weapon opened the assassin up like a starving man tearing open a baked potato. Morgan remembered that this might have been one of the men who helped blow up his house. His gaze hardened and he marched toward the street, looking for any more like him.

He stopped when he saw a smaller, splayed, figure where the alley wall met the sidewalk beyond. Her face was ash-covered and her short hair was charred, but there was no mistaking the Serbian mercenary. The car's detonation must have thrown her like a spoiled child's rag doll.

Fine, Morgan thought as he took a step toward her. *Now she knows how it feels.* Unlike the others, he was keeping her for an intensely thorough interrogation.

But one step was all he got. As he bent to grab her, the corner of the building separating the two shattered. Morgan quickly back-tracked, bringing the rifle up as he saw what a combination of pins, lasers, and air fists could do to wood, concrete, brick, and even iron work.

He ignored the explosions to see where they were coming from. Appearing out of the shadows, fog, smoke, and dust came Amina's back-up—three more helmeted, uniformed killers, with one weapon each.

Morgan felt an urge to take them on, but he did not like the odds, nor the chances that his own laser device might hit someone other than them. Having seen what it did to its previous victim, who knew how many walls it could pierce before dissipating?

Morgan turned to run the other way. He stopped again when he saw three more silhouettes coming from the other end of the alley, each holding similar weaponry.

Of course. After what she had already accomplished on his work and life, why wouldn't the Serbian she-devil have reinforcements of reinforcements of reinforcements?

Morgan stopped again when he felt something under his foot. He almost laughed when he saw it was his Walther PPK. He hefted it as he turned toward the mistress tunnel. He hadn't even gotten a step when the passageway turned into a mass of holes, tears, and punctures.

Morgan froze once again, stepped back and put his hands up. He turned slowly to see the new helmeted trio helping Amina to her feet as the book-ending trio made their way around what was left of the Mustang, each one of them keeping the tips of their weapons centered on his face or chest. To his own surprise, Morgan found himself chuckling.

"What's so funny, *govnojedno*?"

Morgan turned his head to look at Amina, who, if he guessed correctly, just called him a piece of crap. After all, on the way back from the dark territory and his first run-in with her, his daughter Alex and partner Cougar had filled him in on some of the more colorful epithets of Serbia. Morgan looked at the mercenary's fatigued, scratched face and the way her expression mixed clear resentment with a strange, angry, respect, and he felt his grin widen.

"I couldn't figure it out, *slatki*," he said with far more humor than he felt. "Blow up my house, blow up my headquarters, sure, that I understand. But blow up my car? And right here, giving me a chance to fight back? That I couldn't figure ...until I looked at your *šarmantan* face."

His using the words for "sweetie" and "charming" seemed to affect her like gentle slaps to awaken the groggy. She shook her head, her eyebrows arching downward. "What are you talking about, *idiot*?"

That term needed no translation. "I'm talking about this little display of pique," he said back, feeling he had nothing to lose as he motioned toward the car. "The only reason I can come up with is that you wanted to destroy everything I love right in my face." He spoke slowly as if he were dealing with a rebellious teenager. "You're taking this way too personally, *slatki*."

It looked like the mercenary was going to take the bait, giving Morgan even more precious time, but then the sound of distant sirens reached all their ears. Shrill, three-tone sirens, getting stronger by the second.

Amina pulled herself free of the man who had been helping steady her. "*Idiot!*" she repeated. "I don't have time for this." She turned back to the mouth of the alley and waved her other arm dismissively. "Someone kill this *supak* and let's get out of here."

When Morgan saw her try to cover the look of consternation on her face, he realized that the car's double explosion might have stymied her as much as it had surprised him.

A man in front of him raised a laser toward his nose. Dan's eyes widened and jaw dropped.

"Here we go again," Morgan muttered, but instead of those being his last words, he watched as the man's head erupted like a watermelon hit by a sledge hammer.

Chapter 7

Dan Morgan was grateful, but he wasn't surprised by his last-second stay of execution. In fact, he had been more than half expecting it—or something like it—ever since his Mustang had leaped into the air. After all, that had obviously been no accident. Besides, he didn't need to freeze and gawp—he had seen this kind of cantaloupe-bursting eruption before, on both military and espionage battlefields.

If he had previously suspected Amina's minions were amateurs, he was all but certain of it now, as they practically spun in place, desperately trying to find somewhere to shoot back and all but ignoring the man who had just been about to firing-squad Morgan ...not to mention Morgan himself. Instead, only Morgan witnessed the executioner slowly toppling over, the smoking crater where his head had been pumping guts as his death ray slipped from his fingers.

Assholes, Morgan thought, keeping an eye on the scattering assassins. They should have finished their crony's job before stumbling around, but their stupidity was another thing he was grateful for. He only hoped they didn't start indiscriminately spraying the surrounding brownstones with laser, needle, and air-punching power.

These thoughts flashed into his brain as he lurched toward the executioner's fallen weapon. As if impelled by karma to mix bad luck with good, an assassin's foot sent it clattering away. Morgan's eyes swept the sky for the source of the head-exploding shot.

Morgan wasn't about to go chasing after the rifle, not with possible executioners all around him. And, although his fingers ached for his Walther or Ruger, he knew these guys were still wearing bulletproof helmets and clothes. He wondered if their boots were bulletproof too, but didn't want to waste a round or attract attention finding out.

Instead, he decided to continue the cycle of revenge with the nearest weapons to him—namely, what was left of his car. Seemingly as if he hadn't even paused to think about it, Morgan scooped up a twisted, jagged hunk of the Mustang's step bumper, ignored the heat burning his hands, and swung it into the head of the man nearest him, right where the guy's jawbone and throat met under his helmet. It was perfectly placed and vehemently swung—so vehemently, in fact, that Morgan felt, more than saw, the man's neck break.

By then Morgan had already moved on to the next idiot nearest him. Not being an idiot himself, he left the step bumper where it had lodged between the lip of the first man's helmet and throat. Instead, Morgan scooped up a jagged length of a windshield wiper and used it as an arrow to slam into the submaxillary triangle of the next man's chin with enough angry vengeance to lift the bastard off his feet.

Morgan took only a micro-second to "enjoy" the feeling of the windshield wiper tearing through the man's cricoid and thyroid cartilage before lodging in his hyoid bone, then moved on rapidly to grab the spare tire's crowbar where it had been spit at the base of the alley's far wall. But by then, others were noticing the swath of destruction that Morgan was leaving in his wake. His heedless, not headless, targets who had been scanning the horizon and the skies, were now turning toward him and bringing their own weapons to bear.

Morgan could tell he wouldn't get to the next guy before he brought up his needle gun, but it was too late to stop his momentum. Trying to dodge or duck would be more destructive to his bones and ligaments than just plowing on. Just as it seemed he would slam his own head into the hostile weapon, the man's helmet, then his head, tore open as if by a giant's hands.

Morgan didn't have time to thank his guardian giant before he swung the car jack crowbar through the dissipating, missile-torn, bones, blood, and brains—right into the helmeted skull of the assassin behind the sniper-shot victim, who was far more surprised than Morgan. So surprised, in fact, that he all but spun in a tight, mid-air somersault, landing on his feet like a seasoned acrobat.

That, in turn, surprised Morgan. Worse, it threw the Zeta operative off balance, and he spun to his back on the ground. Morgan found himself lying on a bed of the ruined, still smoking, still hot Mustang skeleton. From that vantage point he got a split second to restudy the situation.

The bulk of the assassins were still lurching around like homicidal zombies, waving their weapons like angry villagers storming a monster's castle. Morgan saw the man he had just crowbarred stumble and fall, slamming hard on his side, his laser rifle skittering away toward Pinckney Street.

Enough with the Mustang guts, he thought, *let me really put the rest of these babies to bed.* Inspired by the seemingly seasoned acrobat, Morgan vaulted into a crouch, then continued the motion to dive toward the fallen death ray, fully intending to grab it, somersault, roll to his feet, and start shooting.

It didn't happen that way. Just as it seemed his fingers would clamp on the rifle, a leg speared between his outstretched arms, and a booted foot connected with his chest. Morgan grunted as his rib cage seemed to compress around his inner organs. His forward momentum was halted, then reversed. He found himself flying back, just inches off the ground, before his back slammed down and he slid back into the ashen burial ground of his car.

He couldn't afford to take any time to deal with the pain, so he didn't. The difference in that half-second saved his life—again. So he was halfway up when the Serbian whirling dervish was back on him. It seemed as if the vicious mercenary had recovered enough from the initial surprise explosion to get back into the fray.

"*Želiteneštoučinitiispravno,*" he heard her seethe, "*uradi to sami.*"

If you want something done right, do it yourself.

It was lucky that Morgan's muscle memory had been so well honed by trainers and enemies alike. If he had dealt with this new flurry of punches and kicks in a fully conscious way, it was most likely that he would already be down for the count. Only in this alley fight, there would be no ten count—only a brutal, battering death.

Even Amina seemed surprised that the man managed to withstand, even avoid, her renewed assault. The Morgan she remembered was a punching bag—albeit a punching bag inside a rocketing locomotive who had just jumped down from an expertly, even brilliantly, piloted helicopter just above them.

"You're an idiot fighter," she murmured, as if trying to convince herself.

They both stilled. They seemed to be alone in the alley, in the center of some sort of mind palace coliseum. Morgan knew how Roman gladiators must have felt, standing in the center of a circle, surrounded by tens of thousands, yet still only seeing the single opponent in front of them.

Then the moment was over.

"C'mon, macho man," he heard Amina spit as she took a sharp step forward. Morgan took a mirroring step back, his back thudding against another person's spine. That helmeted assassin brought his weapon around as Amina brought her fingers forward like a lance to try tearing Morgan's eyes out. Then the assassin's helmet shattered like glass and his head practically wrenched off his own neck like another watermelon hit by another sledgehammer.

Morgan managed to avoid the mercenary's fingers, watching them get caught in the storm of blood, bone, and brains instead. Despite her ruthlessness, the mercenary couldn't help but recoil, giving Morgan another second to regain his bearings. He saw one of the few remaining assassins with his back against the wall opposite him. But as the man swung his own weapon up and around, his head, too, went the way of the watermelon.

Now pretty much everyone in the alley knew the score. Try to kill the unhelmeted guy, get your head blown off by some unseen, extremely skilled sniper.

Unable to quell a grim glee, Morgan jerked his face back toward Amina with a tight, wicked grin. But when he came at her, she responded in the opposite direction. He tried coming at her from the right, and she, again, mirrored him. He feinted to the left, but she wasn't falling for it, remaining opposite him. Just as he realized that she was purposely, and expertly, making sure that the sniper would have to shoot through Morgan to get to her, she sped toward him like a pouncing cheetah.

The next few seconds were both amazing and macabre. All Morgan thought he'd have to do was cock his head, giving the sniper a clear shot, but Amina mirrored that too. He tried twisting around, but Amina also copied that movement. And all the while, her hands and feet were stabbing out, connecting with his throat and just under his right knee.

Morgan choked and fell to both his knees. Amina was there too, aping his exact position like a sadistic nun counseling a fallen supplicant. He looked into her cruel eyes, his own eyes tearing. He didn't know what she was going to do next: cup his chin or tear it off.

"Your little sniper can't save you," she hissed into his face as a short, wicked knife seemed to appear from her left fist like a deadly snake's tongue. Normally she would've gripped the back of his neck to draw him closer to the blade's kiss, but she didn't want to risk her fingers being shot off.

"Yeah," Morgan growled back at her. "But the cops can."

That was just enough. She became aware of what he had let himself hear mere seconds ago. The sirens of the Boston Police. They were still too far away to prevent a split-second stabbing, but they were close enough to break her concentration.

Her eyes flitted away, up and to the right, and that was all he needed. His own boot knife was in his right hand and his blackjack was in his left. They met in the middle, and although the Serbian was wicked fast, she wasn't fast enough to completely avoid the double-edged coated stainless steel spear point of the Hostage Rescue Team blade, or the eleven-ounce molded lead weight encased in heavy gauge leather.

The former cut open her jaw line and the latter gave her left temple a nice wet kiss as she wrenched herself backwards. Morgan fell to his front, but kept his head up enough to witness her astonishing retreat. She slithered away on her back like some sort of possessed serpent as sniper bullets burrowed into the alley floor all around her.

Morgan dug for his own guns, but by the time the Ruger was in his left fist, the Serbian terrorist had managed to disappear around the corner of Cedar Lane Way and Pinckney Street. Morgan wanted to leap to his feet, but his body had its own ideas. He managed to get upright fast enough to judge that the police were mere seconds away.

He took a quick survey of the scene. He counted seven corpses, and any helmeted assassin who wasn't headless was long gone, along with all the cutting edge weapons.

So much for collecting extremely helpful souvenirs, he thought. *They may have been amateur hired help, but they were obviously very forcefully instructed to leave as few clues behind as possible.*

But as he was about to grab a jagged, bloody piece of sniper-shattered helmet, he heard another sound over the approaching sirens. A powerful, purring, sound. A leather-encased, helmeted figure appeared astride the black and blue two-wheeled lightning bolt that was the Yamaha R1 open-class street bike—recently declared the best on the market.

Morgan couldn't see the biker's face, but there was no mistaking the shape, poise, and attitude—nor the CheyTac M200 Intervention sniper rifle strapped across the back.

"You know," Alexandra Morgan said as she took off her helmet, letting her short, dark copper hair free, "if you had just kept your damn head down, I could've nailed her."

They both looked back at Mount Vernon Street as red, blue, and amber lights refracted off the corner walls.

Alex Morgan, Zeta's top sniper, resettled on the Yamaha's seat, and held her hand out to her father. "Now come with me if you want to live."

Chapter 8

The first hour may have been pretty rough, but the first few minutes after the incident on Cedar Lane Way were really hairy.

That's when Dan got an up-close-and-personal tour of the back streets, alleys, courtyards, cul-de-sacs, backyards, and even hiking paths of Beacon Hill—all from the rear of a motorcycle. Every few seconds, Dan thought he'd have to kiss one or both knees goodbye. He didn't worry about his elbows, however. His arms were tightly embracing his daughter's waist—just to stay on the speeding street bike.

He didn't so much mind Alex's quick, sudden turns as much as her narrow misses between parked cars, pathways, curbstones, street signs, street lights, parking meters, mailboxes, and fire hydrants as she expertly avoided patrol cars, uniformed officers, and even plainclothes people. Thankfully for them, as well as for career criminals throughout the greater Beantown area, it was deep in the night by then, and the police already had their hands pretty full.

Within minutes, they were out of the immediate area. In a gut-twistingly ironic way, Dan was almost glad that he didn't spot Amina. If he had, he doubted he could have left it at that, despite the danger that would have put him and his daughter in. But that was of little concern to the Yamaha's driver. Taking the cops' workload into consideration, Alex avoided the closest Charles River crossovers like Longfellow Bridge and Charles River Dam Road. She chose, instead, to mingle with the always plentiful traffic on the Tobin Memorial Bridge and Route 93 into Charlestown, which bookended Prospect Hill and Bunker Hill.

Along the way, Dan had to admire the modifications Alex had made to the Yamaha. Normally chopper engines were seemingly made so their riders could loudly proclaim "look at me" to anyone in the surrounding square mile, but this black and blue streaker was on its best behavior thanks to some extraordinary alterations to its muffler and chassis. No matter how high Alex revved it, it sped along with only a comforting, even soothing purr.

Also, it probably wouldn't do to sneak around the back streets of Boston with a high-powered sniper rifle wedged between yourself and your father, so, much to that father's appreciation, she had stowed it in a camouflaged sheath wedged along the left side of the clutch cover, which almost perfectly blended it into what other bikers called a "rice-burner." Dan wouldn't trade this rice burner for any crotch-rocket, flathead, or hog on the planet.

Dan had kept tight-lipped, and not just to keep his teeth and mouth free of splattering kamikaze insects. Once they wound their way into Mystic Valley, along the winding Mystic River, he moved one hand from Alex's waist to her shoulder. Grunting through the motorcycle helmet she had wisely given him—it wouldn't do to survive what they had, only to be arrested for breaking the helmet law—he gave her an address. His tone made clear that it was fruitless to argue, or even question.

Besides, if his daughter felt anything close to the mix of emotions he was feeling, she was glad that at least they had someplace definite to go. They wound their way past the Legoland Discovery Center, the Mystic River State Reservation, Hormel Stadium, Riverbend Park, and the Riverside Yacht Club until they started to creep into more eclectic neighborhoods where the Mystic River emptied into Mystic Lake.

Dan had Alex make their way into some patches of woodland until they came upon a ramshackle garage set apart from its nearest neighbor, with a dozen cars lined up around and in front of it. Dan tapped his daughter on the shoulder, so she eased her way closer. Alex understood. Her father, after all, was a classic car dealer. Whether that was his vocation or his cover was still open for debate. In either case, it made sense that he knew every car dealer, extremely large or pitifully small, in the area.

Sure enough, as she cut the Yamaha's purring motor, Dan dismounted, took a second to air out his now bowed legs, then gave Alex a "quiet" signal with his forefinger before waving her to follow him. She made her way through some Chevys, Dodges, Renaults, Fiats, Peugeots, and even a Yugo as her father wedged his way through some bushes and hanging tree branches to stand before a plain door on the left side of the garage. Alex's eyebrows rose as she noted the structure was windowless and the portal, which, on first glance, had looked worn, was actually solid and extra thick.

Dan somehow produced a key and slid it into the door's sole lock. He waited until Alex got close, then swung open the partition, allowing the two of them to slide quickly in as one. Then he shut and locked the door behind them as dim yellow fluorescent lights automatically went on overhead. To Alex's surprise, it was an office, not a garage—with the prerequisite desk, files, coffee machine, and water cooler. She took off her helmet at the same time he did.

"What are we doing here?" she wondered aloud.

"Well, I'm not going to risk going to my office," Dan replied, stepping up to a small cabinet on the wall that was filled with keys hanging from hooks. "Welcome to Yuri's Used Cars, which caters to a very specific clientele. I'll let you guess who."

Yuri, Alex thought. *Well, maybe that explained the Yugo.* "Dominicans?"

Dan nearly did a double take as he snapped up one set of keys, while replacing it with another from his own pocket. He had been expecting her to say Eastern Europeans. "And Guatemalans," he added, impressed with his daughter's knowledge of Boston demographics. "Good ol' Yuri likes serving underserved communities."

Alex waited until her father passed by her, heading back to the side door, before repeating herself. "Again, what are we doing here?"

Dan stopped by the door before looking back. "Catching a new ride."

"Why do we need a new ride?" she asked, standing her ground.

He waited for the second it took her to correctly interpret his sympathetic expression.

"Oh, shit," she said with resignation. "I really loved that bike."

* * * *

"Cops are one thing," Dan told his daughter as they eased the Yamaha, minus the sniper's rifle, into the Mystic River basin on the other side of the foliage covering Yuri's establishment. "Our Serbian hellcat is another. If I know her, she probably didn't even wait for her chin wound to be tended to before she placed, or had one of her bozos place, an anonymous call with our full description to every bear in New England."

Alex felt an urge to suggest that Amina had not set eyes on the bike before she had slithered out of the alley, but she resisted it. The odds weren't good to take the chance Amina hadn't done as Dan suggested, and they both knew it. Feeling a potent cloud of despondency settle on her, Alex trudged back up toward the car yard without a word.

The father and daughter had kept their t-shirts, jeans and boots, but had replaced their outer wear with some khaki shirts and jackets they found in a narrow locker room by a bathroom beyond the water cooler—dark tan for Alex and olive for Dan. Both were grateful they didn't have neon patches that read "Yuri's Used Cars" stitched on them.

"Yuri and I have an arrangement," Dan explained as he came up behind her. "Something happens to me, he takes over. Something happens to him, I do the same. The keys I left on the hook are his signal."

Alex glanced at her father, and he was happy to note that the gaze contained some admiration and appreciation rather than just depression or growing clinical shock.

"And the keys you took?" Alex inquired.

Dan had reached the corner of the overgrown shack, and stood beside a dull silver 2014 Ford Focus hatchback. "It's not a Mustang," he admitted, "but it'll have to do for now."

Now it was Dan's turn to give his daughter a lesson in back roads and back streets. A few minutes after they left the Mystic neighborhood, Alex took her third look into the back seat to make sure her sniper rifle was still out of sight. And her father took a third glance at her, unable to keep a smidgen of worry out of his expression. He remembered how she had looked, and, more importantly, acted when he had driven her home from her first championship junior high school volleyball meet.

It had been a heartbreaker, with her team just on the edge of victory a half-dozen times. To make matters worse, at the very last second, she'd had a chance to spike them to victory, but, in her energy and eagerness, the ball had bounced off the top of the net and gone out of bounds.

She was inconsolable, and, wisely, Dan hadn't tried to offer solace. He'd just stayed strong and ready for when she was ready to talk, but he had never forgotten her body language: head down, legs curled under her, hands cupped in her lap, eyes dead. She didn't meet all those criteria now, but it was close enough. Only this time, they didn't have time to wait.

"How did you find me?" he asked as he drove between Mystic Lakes State Park and the Oak Grove Cemetery.

The question didn't perk her up, but she didn't ignore it either. "I followed the media's lead." She shrugged. "I was going to go home, but the news clued me in that we didn't have one anymore. So I did what you probably did too; reached out to the team." She grew quiet and, for her, strangely troubled. "No answering machines worked." Remembering her actions following that discovery, she straightened in the Ford's seat and shook off her lethargy. "Of course, I checked out the situation from a distance using the CheyTac's scope."

Dan considered that carefully. The Intervention M200 had an effective range of about one-and-a-half miles. "Hell of a shot," he murmured.

"Thanks," Alex replied. "It felt …fated, you know?"

He didn't. "What do you mean?"

Alex looked out the windshield, letting the darkness and dim lights of Woburn dull her eyes. "It was like…it was like they were lemmings, or shooting gallery targets, willingly jumping into my cross-hairs. All I had to do was pull the trigger…"

Dan frowned. He didn't like the distant tone of her voice. "How did you make the Mustang jump?" he interjected.

Alex grinned as she looked to her father behind the steering wheel. "Knew I had to do something, and the CheyTac's Vector laser scope showed me one of their air cannons lying under the Mustang. Seeing what it had done to the car's hood and doors, I figured I'd give it a shot…"

"All puns intended," Dan commented.

Alex's smile was genuine. "Even I didn't think it was that powerful."

Dan sighed. "Too bad we couldn't bring any along."

"Just as well," Alex retorted, looking out the passenger window as they skirted into Burlington. "My guess is that each and every piece of their ordnance was crawling with bugs."

Of course the young woman didn't mean insects. Dan scowled. She was probably right that taking even a shattered piece would be like waving a beacon to their enemy. He shook off the thought when Alex spoke again.

"You think they're the same bunch who tried that extortion scheme on the Trans-Siberian Express?" That, after all, was where they had first met Amina.

Dan frowned. "That bunch were Neanderthals compared to this crowd."

It was Alex's turn to frown. "Maybe just on the surface, though. You know as well as I do that, other than the Serbian hellcat, the rest acted like hastily hired help. It could've been just Amina trying to get payback."

"It's possible," he replied, "but I doubt it. Those bozos didn't have the pull for this thing." Dan straightened when Alex didn't answer. Then the hairs on the back of his neck stood up and he felt a wave of goosebumps across his shoulders. That almost never happened. As his grandma used to say: *somebody just walked across my grave.*

Dan looked over to see his daughter staring back at him, something unreadable in her expression. "You weren't at your place when you saw the news report, were you?" he asked.

She shook her head, her expression unchanging. Although he saw her jaw clenching in indecision, she still made him ask rather than offering the necessary information up.

"Where were you?"

"There," she said.

"At the house?"

"No," she told him. "Zeta."

Dan didn't want to give the stereotypical response, but he couldn't help himself. "What?"

"I was at Zeta. Practicing. I like to target shoot when the place is empty." She grimaced. "No macho posturing or competition from the other fieldies."

To his growing incredulity, she tapered off.

"When?" he demanded.

"Just before," she answered, "and just after it went up. That's when I started calling everybody."

The car wavered in its lane on the Pinehurst Billerica side street, but just slightly. When he could get the words out, they were almost choked.

"Did you call Mom?" When she didn't answer, he nearly cracked the steering wheel with his grip. "You didn't call Jenny?"

"What good would that have done?" she asked.

Dan pulled over, doing his absolute best not to screech the wheels as he tucked the Ford behind the office building where the Pinehurst Drive-in Theater used to be. Once he made sure the car was in park, he shifted over in his seat to face his daughter. But when he looked into her face he remembered that she was his daughter, not just the expert sniper who had saved his life. And the expression on her face could only be described as "haunted."

He spoke softly to her. "Come on, Alex, what are you not telling me?"

Her expression changed into one of conflict, as if she knew she was wasting time, but, somehow, she had to.

"You'll think I've gone crazy," he heard her whisper. Then, only slightly more loudly: "Hell, *I* think I've gone crazy."

"Come on, hon," he said, putting his hand on her shoulder. "After what we've been through, and not just tonight, I wouldn't blame you."

That did it. Alex looked up and met his eyes.

"I heard Mom's voice," she told him. "She was the one who told me to get out of Zeta HQ and find you."

Chapter 9

As Alex's words sunk in, hope and doubt had a prize fight in Dan Morgan's brain. It was declared a split decision at best, and a draw at worst. Even so, the full import of Alex's words brought Dan's mind to nearly a complete standstill.

All he could say was, "What do you mean you heard Jenny's voice?"

Alex head went back, her eyes widening. "What do you mean what do I mean?" she retorted. "I heard Mom's voice."

He saw a glimmer of cognitive light at the end of his dark tunnel vision. "In your ear comm?" he asked. "In your head? What?"

Alex looked nonplussed, as if she hadn't truly thought about it until that moment. She froze, frowned, looked away, and thought about it.

"It wasn't the ear comm," she decided. "And it wasn't in my head. Not really."

"Not really?" Dan echoed. And when she didn't react immediately, he added, "What do you mean?"

Alex's reply had some of the same snap as before she'd admitted she heard Jenny's voice. "Dad, I've spent my life differentiating between voices outside and inside my head. For what it's worth, I could've sworn this was outside my head." She took another second to try recalling it. "*Just* outside my head. In fact, like she was right behind me. I even turned around to ask her what she was doing at HQ, but when I did, she wasn't there."

Dan exhaled, then inhaled, also looking away. He searched for any possible rational explanation, but couldn't find one.

"Are you sure it wasn't the ear comm?" he re-asked.

The look of patient impatience on her face clued him that they were back to their normal relationship. "Yes, Dad, I'm sure."

Their eyes locked, him searching, hers certain.

"How can you be sure?" he pressed.

"Because by then my ear comm screeched so loud I had to tear it out."

Dan recognized that situation, but as he opened his mouth to pounce on it, she beat him to it.

"Before I could even comprehend that," Alex insisted, "Mom talked again. Two words. 'Get out.' But she said it in such a way that I didn't argue."

Dan didn't argue either. Instead, he wondered, "Where did that come from? Just behind your ear again?"

Alex's haunted, intense expression communicated to her father that this, too, might be the first time she really faced it, so she forced herself to examine the incident.

"No. You're going to think I'm crazy, or maybe just more crazy, but I tell you, if it came from anywhere, it felt like it was coming from my..."

Alex's expression became confused again. Dan felt a pang in his heart. It so reminded him of when she was a tween, and would have silent arguments with herself before asking him about boys.

"From where, honey?" he asked. "You can tell me. Just speak the truth."

Alex looked back at him with a whole new expression that seemed to say that he wouldn't like it. In fact, the expression also said that not even she liked it.

"For the want of a better description," she told him, "from my soul."

That effectively killed the conversation. Dan blinked and leaned back. Alex looked sardonically apologetic, and even gave a seemingly instinctive little shrug. Dan shifted his body forward and gripped the Ford's steering wheel in both hands. He stared out the windshield, then put the Fiesta in drive.

As they got back on the road, scrupulously obeying every traffic law while heading northwest around Lowell, Dan tried to process this new information. It wasn't easy. Zeta hadn't recruited him because he was a strategic mastermind. They'd hired him because he was the best blunt instrument around. Whatever they pointed at he could stop, take down, or destroy, and nothing would stop him until he did.

A long time ago he had admitted to himself that he loved it. Loved it so much, in fact, that he was willing to keep his agency secret from his wife and family. And when the secrets had gotten so big and consuming that they'd practically knocked on the front door, rather than face them and deal with them, he had somehow allowed both his daughter and wife to get involved.

He glanced out his peripheral vision at the passenger seat. Alex was curled up on the seat, like a resting cat. A powerful feeling of caring punched Dan in the gut as he watched her.

He had been proud of Alex as she'd made her way quickly through the Zeta ranks—proving herself to be more intuitive, versatile, adaptable, and forward-thinking than he was. He had been proud of Jenny for accepting him for who he was, supporting him completely, and even holding her own when danger encroached. He had been as proud as a seasoned, proven warrior could be.

Until it all had blown up in his face tonight. Literally.

"Kirby had a hologram."

At first, Alex thought she had dreamed the words. But when she looked over at her father, he continued without taking his eyes off the road.

"Unlike you, Kirby answered my call," he explained. "Told me that Zeta was under attack…"

"Well, duh," Alex muttered.

"…and that I should come over immediately."

He told her the details of his trespassing, and how he had scouted his employers' homes at the start of his tenure with the organization. She seemed to approve.

"But he had a weird little rectangular mirror on his desk that seemed like some sort of alarm. It came on when I got near. It showed a little hologram of Kirby himself, repeatedly mouthing the Zeta disaster protocol. But apparently my presence didn't set off any sort of sound component."

Alex sat up and got her bearings in the darkness. On the basis of the dim lights of the quiet neighborhoods they were making their way through, Dan was still keeping to the back roads. Alex longed for her smartphone, which would have instantly showed her where they were. But if it could do that for her, it could do that *to* her …for anyone. She knew the disaster protocol as well as he did, maybe even better. She had taken the sniper rifle. She had left the smartphone.

"Hmmm," she grunted, stretching a bit. "He invites you in, but wasn't there to welcome you…"

"But our friends with the diamond-tipped, needle-thin missiles were."

"Maybe the hologram wasn't tripped by your presence. The mirror could have been two-way. Maybe he could see you through his smartphone and set off his hologram as a warning. Or even as an intro to a video link."

She looked at her father's profile as he concentrated on the dark, winding, road. "You still have it by any chance?"

"Not anymore," Dan admitted. He half-grinned, half-grimaced at the memory. "Much of it's smashed in one of the needle boys' faces."

"Too bad." Alex shrugged. "Who knows what we might've found between the mirror and the frame."

"Yeah," Dan agreed without rancor or even much regret. "That's what I was thinking, too. For what it's worth, the frame did seem a bit thicker than it needed to be. I figured there might have been a lens or bug or something like that tucked in the corners."

Alex shifted around in the passenger seat until she could face her father. "You think Kirby was setting you up for the kill?" Dan looked back at his daughter, unable to contain all his surprise at her bluntness. "I know how you felt about him, Dad," she continued. "Hell, I know how he felt about you, too."

Dan snorted. "Big fan I bet, huh?" He checked the stars and street signs, then took a left on Macintosh Drive. "Paul Kirby was never protective of anyone or anything ...except his own ass. But one thing he knew for sure. I'm not that easy to kill." When Alex remained in silent thought, her father continued. "So maybe, after our illustrious number two conspires with our enemies to destroy us, he figures he better make triple sure about me—especially when I call him from out of the blue from a long-ago rendezvous spot."

"So," Alex interjected, "you're also working from the idea that every Zeta operative's home was attacked or destroyed. Every major Zeta agent, at least."

"Except our dear darling Paul Kirby," Dan agreed. "Why else wouldn't anyone answer our distress calls?"

"And who else might be affected?" Alex mused. "Is it possible that they launched an attack on every Zeta agent in the world at the same time?"

Dan hated the thought of that, but couldn't counter it. "We would have heard about it if they did it catch-as-catch-can," he admitted. "If they were going to do it all, they'd have to do it all at once."

Alex put her hand on her father's shoulder. "You were right, Dad. Those Trans-Siberian train clowns didn't have the vision or stones for something like this. Whoever—or whatever—hired Amina to take you out cherry-picked her for the job."

"Yeah," Dan growled, "then didn't give her time to get seasoned back-up."

The two fell silent as a single theory seemed to link their brains. At the end of their last mission, the idea was floated that an anti-Zeta was sowing trouble across the globe as fast as Zeta could nullify it. That trouble would be sown a lot easier if Zeta itself wasn't around to stop them...

"Where the hell are we?"

Dan snapped out of his reverie as the last of the Dunlap Sanctuary and East Richardson Preserve passed by the Fiesta's back window.

"Get ready to cross state lines," Dan suggested as he turned right from Marsh Hill Road onto Bridge Street.

"Good thing I'm not a minor, old man," Alex said as she peered into the night to see Auto Village and Holton Street Auto Body out the passenger window. They passed a paving contractor on the left, and then they were in Pelham, New Hampshire.

The ski resorts, seacoast, Appalachian Trail, and Mount Washington Auto Road were still far away, as were Alex's favorites—the New Hampshire Motor Speedway and Weirs Beach's Motorcycle Rally. Instead, Alex examined such tourist highlights as First Chance Convenience, World Famous State Line Market, Tobacco Junction, Carlo Rose Cigar Bar, Bits & Pieces Quilt Shop, Discount Madness, Tattoo Fever, As-Cue-Rate Billiards, and Ace Discount Cigarettes.

"Time for a cheap smoke?" Alex asked sarcastically, but her father only turned onto Cardinal Drive.

"Keep your eyes on the prize," Dan growled, glancing at the auto shops that also dotted Pulpit Rock Road.

He switched off the Fiesta's headlights and turned into the driveway of the Logo Loc embroidery service building. He drove all the way through its surprisingly large parking area until he reached what looked like a small, abandoned radio station, complete with a relatively short, rusting, satellite tower nestled against and amongst a fairly thick wood separating it from Ratchets Auto Works and Offroad Supply.

Dan pulled behind a copse of trees and shrubs until the Ford was essentially masked from anyone else's eyes. He then turned off the ignition and unclipped his seatbelt.

"What have you gotten me into, old man?" his daughter mused as she did the same.

He waited until they were both completely ready to exit the car before catching her eye with a tight, mirthless smile. "Welcome to my version of a disaster protocol hologram."

Chapter 10

"Now *this* is a garage," Alex breathed as they stood inside the windowless metal doorway of a rectangular blockhouse on the edge of the parking lot's cul-de-sac.

This was a space that would have been a perfect fit for any effective chop-shop in the world. There was a single auto bay in the center, surrounded by equipment that served only one purpose: to do anything to a motor vehicle that was possible.

Alex marveled that it was the polar opposite to the usual automotive environment she saw her father in. His showroom, where he had spent all his time convincing his family he was a classic car dealer, was as bright as this was dingy, as clean as this was gritty, as open as this was claustrophobic, and as impressive as this was not. The showroom was for a car saint. This auto torture chamber was for a car zealot.

"Went looking for this place as soon as Zeta came looking for me," Dan said as he made his way through the tools and parts that seemed to litter the floor, walls, and even ceiling in an explosion pattern, the less important stuff furthest from central ground zero.

"Not when the military and C.I.A. came sniffing?" Alex wondered, picking her way parallel to her father.

"Didn't need it for them," he explained. "They were known quantities. Zeta? Not so much."

Zeta always seemed too good to be true. Ridiculously well financed. Absurdly altruistic. Willing to hire previous partners, not to mention daughters.

"When this shack went up for sale, I thought it was perfect," Dan continued. "Tucked away in a secret grove, far enough away from home and

HQ to keep secret, and right smack dab in the middle of car part central. Nothing was ever sent here, but everything could be wheeled in from the Devil's Triangle of body shops nearby. I spent every spare moment getting ready for a day …like this."

As they made their way closer to the center of the site, Alex felt herself becoming more excited. She imagined what she might discover beyond the piles of pipes, saws, drills, welders, and clamps. Visions of the sci-fi and spy movies she saw as a kid came dancing back into her brain. What would it be? An Aston Martin? Fireball XL-5? A time traveling DeLorean? The Batmobile?

Alex almost slapped herself. The strain, shock, and lack of sleep were obviously getting to her. Although she brought her brain back to reality, she didn't completely quell her anticipation. Knowing her father, and knowing what he could do once he put his mind to it, she couldn't help being a little excited.

Finally, they got within steps of a vehicle that was draped in a dark, paint-splattered tarp. It looked big enough to be the Mystery Machine from the Scooby Doo cartoons. Big enough to be the A-Team's van. Alex felt herself holding her breath as her father unceremoniously pulled the cloth aside …to reveal a dull gray 2014 Honda CR-V.

"What?" Alex couldn't help but blurt at the sight of the compact crossover sports utility van that was a favorite among soccer moms. "Not one of your cars?"

That stopped him. "What's one of 'my' cars?"

"You know," she urged. "A muscle car: a Camaro, another Mustang, even a Dodge Charger. Dodge…get it?"

"Exactly," Dan replied with sad satisfaction. He wistfully walked around the car until he was facing his daughter from across the auto's blunt snout. "Of course I wanted to use a muscle car. Of course I wanted to 'dodge' my enemies. But I had to choose the one vehicle that no one, friend or enemy, would ever expect me to be in, let alone drive."

"Choose?" Alex echoed, still reeling from the reveal. "Choose for what?"

"For just such an occasion," Dan said. "For a getaway car that no one would look twice at."

Alex blamed her stress and exhaustion for her next reaction, which even she later admonished herself for. "Well, if that was what you were going for, why don't we keep the Fiesta?"

Dan gave her a sympathetic look, obviously cutting her some slack, considering what they had both been through.

"Because," he said, beginning to move around the vehicle like a hungover, jet-lagged salesman, "the Fiesta doesn't have ballistic nylon and Kevlar steel plating, armored bumpers, three-inch polycarbonate-leaded one-way windows, and polymer, tubeless, tires that will still go a hundred miles an hour no matter how many bullets are pumped into them."

Dan gave his daughter a look that asked for forgiveness, but her surprised yet delighted return look said "carry on with style." So he did.

"I didn't just modify the engine and drive-train," he said, motioning at the hood. "I replaced it. All mechanical parts that could be switched out with electrical were. Fans, pumps, filters, piping, carburetor—all enhanced as high as they would go. Air intakes, quadrupled. Fuel system, upgraded."

"Computer performance chips?" Alex blurted.

"What do you think?" her father retorted.

"Customized to optimum performance, natch."

"Natch," he echoed. "Dual exhaust system in, catalytic converter out." Alex opened her mouth again, but Dan held up a hand. "And yes, true dual exhaust, with grates over the openings, not just split tailpipes. Unlike some people I wasn't born two decades ago."

Both father and daughter found themselves reveling in these details as a needed antidote to their growing dread and grief.

"Turbocharging, yes," he continued, ticking them off on his fingers. "Forced air induction system, yes. Nitrous oxide injection system, of course. Drivetrain and suspension maxed." He put his fists on his hips, and jutted his head forward. "Any other questions?"

Alex, being a Morgan, took a second to think about it, and with the first real smile she had in hours, shook her head. But again, her father surprised her.

"Good," he said, "because we're not done." He waved her over to the passenger window before taking his place at the driver's side. He pointed at the seats. "Not enough that the windows and car body are bullet proof. So are the seats, with both hand-stitched Kevlar and hand-made steel plates, which are also molded with ceramics and fiberglass to prevent head injuries in case of crashes."

Alex marveled at the care he had taken, and raised her hands to signal her giving up.

"Still not done." He pointed behind the front seats. Alex craned her neck to see that two thirds of the interior had been gutted and redesigned. Behind the front seats was a small padded section with a protective covering that was clearly designed for someone to sleep comfortably—much like many long-haul truckers had, except on the vehicle's floor. "Also outfitted with urinals," Dan all but snapped. "Male and female, as well as guess what." Alex's eyebrows rose and the edges of her grin twitched. "Number two?" she inquired sweetly.

"No shit," he replied, all play-on-words intended, before motioning her to the rear hatch.

When he opened it, Alex saw nothing particularly special. But then, he reached over, grabbed an all-but-invisible lip just under the bottom of the window, and pulled downward. A large recessed area was revealed, displaying a SCAR Assault Rifle, a Mossberg 500 shotgun, a Glock 17, a Heckler & Koch P30, a VIPERTEK Heavy Duty Stun Gun, SABRE 3-in-1 Pepper Spray, and enough ammo and refills to finish any job.

"Explosives, drugs, first aid," Dan said, thumbing the other wall. "That side. Don't confuse the two." Then he snapped the partition closed again and turned to his daughter.

At first she was speechless. But, as usual, that didn't last long. "You did all this," she asked. "Just in case?"

Dan exhaled. "No, not really. I did it because ..." He couldn't keep looking at her. He stared inside the enhanced, modified, bulletproofed SUV instead. "...because I was living a lie. Every time I came home, I'd tried to kid myself that we were just another American family. But then Jenny found out what I really did, and I kidded myself that the danger would never touch her. Then you saved my life with your first confirmed kill, and I kidded myself that we could work together without affecting our home life."

Dan Morgan lowered his head. "So I escaped. Here. To this. Kidding myself that someday Jenny and me ..." He had to stop, then swallow. "That Jenny and I would one day get into this thing, safe from all the world, and go everyplace she always wanted to go, and do all the things she always wanted to do..."

He stopped talking when Alex embraced him tighter than she ever had before. At first he was surprised, but then he embraced her back, remembering her as a baby, an adolescent, a tween, a teen, and now the amazing young woman she had become—little thanks to him.

It had all been Jenny. He gave Alex weapons, but Jenny had given her smarts and strength. He had taught her how to hit a target at two thousand yards, but it was Jenny who had taught her that she could be, or do, anything she wanted.

"But now what, honey?" he asked. "Where do we go now?"

Alex loosened her grip and leaned back to look into her father's eyes. He was gratified to see that hers were completely dry, and clear. Her smile was honest, appreciative, and loving.

"Funny you should ask that, old man," she said. "I think I know just the place…

Chapter 11

"Just the place" was the secluded, extremely private home of Scott Renard, the billionaire significant other of their fellow agent Lily Randall. Even though they had not been able to reach either Lily or Scott, both Alex and Dan were willing to bet this safe haven that they had visited on a previous mission—when Renard helped them rescue Lily from the wilds of Asia—would be so well-secured that it was entirely possible that even some super-secret anti-Zeta couldn't blow it up in their faces.

Only one problem. It was 3,144 miles away from Dan's secret garage in New Hampshire.

Dan exhaled slowly. "Nice night for a long drive, huh?" he asked his daughter.

She nodded, and they were off. Left unspoken was the fact that, given the state of the surveillance world, it wouldn't be wise to charter a plane, call a taxi, rent a car, or book an Uber. It would be like setting off a flare. Besides, what good would it do to spend years prepping a CR-V if they didn't put it to use?

At first it went like clockwork. One would drive while the other slept for eight hours, then they refueled and switch. It was a good system, an effective system, a workable system—until Dan's brain got too busy with all sorts of sleep-stealing thoughts. How had the enemy planted all those explosives without anyone seeing them? And, worst of all for his sleep-deprived brain, why hadn't his beloved wife spoken to him? Why hadn't she warned him?

Jenny had always told Dan never to ask himself questions he couldn't answer. She advised to only ask himself questions he *could* answer. But that was the big problem now, wasn't it? Jenny was no longer there. He had heard about parents who protected their children beyond anything else, and that was only right. He would have, and had, done everything he could for Alex.

But it was her decision to become the remarkable field agent she had become, and they had been there for each other ever since. But worse, and most sleep-stealing of all, what had happened to Jenny? Had she been in the house when it blew up? Had she been in Zeta HQ when it blew up? And how had she talked to her daughter without an ear-comm or being seen?

Even when it was his turn to sleep, Dan tormented himself with these questions. He didn't believe in ghosts, but his wife might as well have been one from the way she was haunting him now. He cursed himself for an exhausted fool.

He remembered that Dirty Harry had said in one of his movies, "a man's got to know his limitations," and Dan was proud that he knew his. He knew that he risked a wreck if he did his eight-hour shift in this enervated condition, but he also didn't want Alex to do a double, even though he knew his daughter would be more than willing.

"I don't know about you," he said once they reached the outskirts of the Osage Reservation in Oklahoma, "but I could use a shower."

They skirted the deepest recesses on the southwest edge of the Osage Reservation, and found a place that looked like even a slasher movie crew wouldn't have stayed there. Dan Morgan's rule was simple: if you could find it on Google, that meant others could too.

They drove down a dirt road amid a forest of brush to find an unlit sign: Mimi Hotel. It stood in front of a rudimentary construction of ten connected rooms with a single door and single window each.

"They call this a hotel? Even roach motels wouldn't call it that." Dan glanced at his daughter as the vehicle slowly got closer. "Think Mimi's the owner?"

Alex didn't look back at him. She kept studying the place like her life depended on it. "Prob not," she murmured. "*Mi*' is the Osage word for sun. *Mihoto* is their word for moon." Only then did she look at her father with a sheepish grin. "Learned it in a song we sang in kindergarten."

Morgan saw they were the only tenants, so he parked in front of the fifth door, then walked back to the small, dark office at the end of the structure. There, he handed two twenties over to a stoic young Osage man in t-shirt, jeans, and sandals, who went back to playing videogames as soon as he handed over the key. An actual old key—not a plastic card.

The room was as threadbare as the rest of the joint—two thin, lumpy twin beds, a bureau, a chair, a sink, a toilet, and a shower—but at least it was clean. Dan welcomed the shower, redressed in his t-shirt and khakis, and waved an "all-clear" to his daughter, hoping he hadn't used up all the hot water.

Much to his surprise, he fell asleep almost as soon as his head hit the thin pillow. And he stayed that way until Alex silently shook him awake. He heard the sounds of the doorknob trying rattling and sprang out of bed as Alex moved to the door into the next room.

Smart girl, he thought. Just like him, she had realized upon checking in that there was no back door or bathroom window to escape from in case of an attack. So, while he was showering or sleeping, she had picked the lock of the door to the next room. As Dan took up position behind the entry, Alex circled around behind the attacker, or attackers, from the next room.

Dan didn't worry about what Alex might do as the door opened and a ski-masked intruder appeared, gun outstretched, and all Dan's grief, anger, frustration, and uncertainty went from his brain, down his arm, into his fist, and almost through the guy's kidney. He hit so hard he thought his knuckles might have grazed the guy's spine.

As the ski-masked man in black went down, Dan surmised that maybe his added strength came from two things. One, he was freshly awoken from a log-like sleep, and two, he had a lot of rage that had been building since his house exploded.

Dan had taken it all out on the guy, who had come into the motel room holding a forty-five automatic, and who was clearly preparing to shoot whoever was under the covers of the lumpy bed.

Dan shoved the forty-five into his waistband. To his surprise, the attacker carried no other weapons—not a knife or a sap or a Taser—but he did have a wallet, and inside the wallet, miracle of miracles, a driver's license.

Dan yanked up the ski mask and compared the license to the man's face. Ernest Burkett did not look Osage. He was a skinhead with a broken nose, narrow brown eyes, and cauliflower ears—the kind of man who had been persecuting, even murdering, the Osage tribe for centuries. That only made things more perplexing. Dan patted him down more thoroughly for any added bonuses, like a cellphone. No such luck.

"Hey C," he called out, while stepping over the body to get a plastic cup of water from the sink. He used her code name—C for crosshairs—which they had created for just such an occasion. "Any extras?"

Dan turned sharply when he heard a *thunk* instead of an answer. He relaxed a little when he saw another skinhead—with a spider web neck tattoo, no less—cringing in the doorway, his face a mask of pain. Alex held his right arm and hand in a particularly painful judo hold. Even if he could stand the strain she was putting on his arm, the added pain she was creating in his palm and fingers precluded any attempt at movement. His free arm and hand seemed paralyzed, like a petrified tree branch growing out of his left shoulder.

"Just one," she said. "Found him skulking by the door, backing up his buddy." Spider Tattoo was trying to speak, but his brain wasn't having it. He just hunched there, struggling to breathe.

Dan brought the water back to the fallen intruder. "Ernie," Dan called, tapping him on the head with his boot. "Ernie, wake up." Dan splashed water in Ernie's face and waited, keeping his distance. Both Morgans had learned the hard way that things were not always what they seemed.

Ernest Burkett sputtered, blinked, stiffened, then groaned—and jerked his hands back toward his kidney.

"Hey Ernie," Dan said, pulling out the forty-five and pointing it at the man's head. "Who sent you?"

A few things happened nearly simultaneously in response to the question. Ernie started swearing, his friend started telling him to keep his mouth shut, and Alex used Spider Tatoo's arm like a battering ram to slam his skinhead into the door jamb.

Dan sighed and sat on the bed. "Don't have time for this, Ernie," he told him. "Last chance before it gets ugly. Who sent you?"

They'd obviously been clued in to the Morgans' presence, unless they hung out and attacked anyone who checked in. And Spider Tattoo was advising silence despite the pain he was in, so they must know who had hired them.

As he expected, Ernie was too stupid to take the hint, and instead upped the profanity—suggesting that Dan have coitus with his mother and so on. That, more than anything, convinced Dan that these two were what they appeared to be, and not some brilliant, well-disguised, well-trained assassins.

Too bad. If they had been brilliant, well-disguised, well-trained assassins, Dan might have shot one to get the other talking. But somehow he doubted they cared enough about each other to make that approach effective. So he just leaned down and quickly, precisely, expertly, broke Ernie's eye.

It is not easy to break someone's eye. It's not like an egg, where all you have to do is crack the exterior so the interior will come oozing out. The eye is a fused, two-piece unit, and to even make the brain aware of damage Dan had to strike so strongly and sharply that his finger made it through the cornea, pupil, and then, so deeply into the vitreous humor that the optic nerve was jump-started.

There are certain kinds of pain the body is generally prepared for. They're never pleasant, but they are, at least, on a scale of toleration. A scratch, a cut, even a broken bone—tolerable. Getting a finger in the eye down to the optic nerve—not so much. The brain does its own version of running around the room with its hair on fire, screaming "abort, abort, abort."

Not surprisingly, Ernie started babbling.

* * * *

The Morgans left the unconscious skinheads on the floor. Why not? The room was paid for.

On the drive out, Dan looked to see if the clerk was still playing videogames. He was.

"Maybe he fingered us," Alex speculated as the CR-V made its way onto the dirt road toward Route Forty-Eight and the Turner Turnpike beyond.

"You think so?" Dan retorted. Alex thought about it further, then frowned. "Like father, like daughter," Dan concluded.

They fell silent and thought about what Ernie had babbled. He and his partner in crime were a-holes. Well known a-holes, who hung around local dives hoping for dirty deeds to do dirt cheap.

On this particular evening, they had gotten a text on their latest burner phone with instructions to collect a man and woman at the Mimi Hotel and bring them to a hash joint on North Twenty-Five Mile Avenue in Deaf Smith County, Texas, near the New Mexico border…some 400 miles away.

Both Morgans wished they had the phone to double check this less-than-credible confession, but as was these yabbos' standard operating procedure, that phone was long gone.

"Weird," Dan concluded.

Alex cocked her head to the side. "But not the weirdest we've dealt with the last few days."

Dan had to agree. "Okay," he said. "Now we know how Bert and Ernie knew where we were, but how did the people who sicced Bert and Ernie onto us know where we were?"

"Checked the car for bugs?" Alex asked.

"It's as bug-proof as I know how to make it," Dan maintained.

Alex didn't argue. She knew her father was an expert exterminator. Not as good as his partner, Peter "Cougar" Conley, but still good enough for them to scratch a car tracker off the list of possibilities.

"Check *us* for bugs?" Alex said.

Dan grimaced. The answer to that question was anybody's guess. As long as they'd been working for Zeta, their boss, Diana Bloch, had been something of a chess master, who thought nothing of secreting all manner of cutting-edge tracking device on, or even in, her top operatives.

"What's good enough for James Bond," she'd once remarked, "is good enough for you." The Morgans remembered the scene in *Casino Royale* when 007 had a tracking device injected into his forearm. But at least Bond had been aware of it.

After the last few missions, Dan had made it clear that he didn't appreciate Bloch's lack of transparency when it came to keeping tabs on them. Diana, in turn, had made it even more clear that she was not about to risk her operatives' lives because of misplaced ego. The more ego a certain blunt instrument showed, the less transparent she would be.

"So," Dan said to his daughter. "If Zeta One stuck new bugs in us, that could mean Zeta One has been zeroed, and her tracking devices are now being supervised by others."

"Anti-Zeta?" Alex wondered, almost shuddering. "Not fun to think about, but possible I guess."

"Let's not guess if we can help it," her father suggested as he pulled onto Route Forty toward Elk City and the ominously named Dead Woman Mound. "The fact that the baddies wanted these bozos to drive us four hundred miles tells me that, just like the attack on Beacon Hill, the op was slapped together at the last minute from the only parts they had available. If they had more time, they would have set a drop-off spot a lot closer to Mimi."

Alex chewed on that rather than dwell on what they might have ticking away inside them. "Well, one good thing is that they seem to want us alive, at least for the moment. Wonder why? To kill us themselves?"

Dan Morgan exhaled through his nostrils as if trying to force a fly off his nose. "I guess we'll find out when we get to North Twenty-Five Mile Avenue," he growled. "But before we do, I've got to know one thing." He turned and looked at his daughter.

She met his gaze. "What's that?" she asked him.

"I was dead to the world. And I would've been dead, period, if you hadn't woken me. So tell me, hon, how did you know Bert and Ernie were outside our door?"

It was Alex's turn to exhale. "Easy," she replied with a mix of resignation and wonder. "Mom told me."

Chapter 12

"What?" Dan groaned. "Again?"

"Again," Alex maintained. "To tell you the truth, I was also dead to the world. Thought I'd sleep with one eye open, but just like you, as soon as my head hit the pillow, I was out like a light, and stayed that way until I heard Mom."

Dan resisted rolling his eyes as his mouth snapped open to give his daughter the third degree. She beat him to it.

"Again," Alex insisted, "not inside my head. Outside my head." She thought, then continued with even more interest. "You know what it was like?" Alex didn't wait for a reply. "It was like when she used to wake me up for Sunday soccer practice. You know, she would lean over just a little bit so her face was like two feet above me, right over my ear, and then she would speak softly and evenly so she wouldn't surprise or scare me. Worked like a charm every time. I'd wake up as if I had been beckoned by…"

Dan turned to his daughter, noting that her expression looked hesitant and even concerned. "Beckoned by what?" he asked.

"By an angel," she finished, then met his eyes. "Do you think this is just my subconscious guilt or something?"

"Well, if it is," he replied, "hone it to a fine point. It's the most helpful subconscious guilt I've ever came across." He looked back at the road, swallowing his own regret and resentment that he hadn't heard from Jenny too. "What did she say?" he asked.

"Two words," Alex told him. *"Look out."*

Dan was amazed. Of any two words Jenny could have chosen, those were the most effective. "Wake up" would have left the "why" question. "Watch out" was okay, but less proactive than "look out," which also had a nice double meaning for a field operative who often served as a "lookout" during infiltration actions.

With that out of the way, the two, no longer the least bit tired, started working out strategies for Deaf Smith County. Dan tapped into the CR-V's new engine and took advantage of the late hour—as well as advanced speed trap tech—to keep his forward momentum at a smooth ninety miles per hour, making it to the border and across the Texas panhandle in four hours flat.

* * * *

Erastus "Deaf" Smith had been the first man to reach the Alamo after its fall, and thus was given the distinction of having his name used for the "Beef Capital of the World."

Dan thought the rendezvous would be some barbecue honky-tonk where any noise would be swallowed up by loud country-western music, but as they went down Route Three-Eighty-Five at the posted speed limit, they couldn't contain their slight surprise.

The Peking Panda Palace Chinese restaurant was tucked into the north end of an arid little mini-mall at the corner of Plains Avenue next to a hair salon and pizza place. It was across from a gas station, a boutique, and a food market. It was all pretty quiet at five in the morning. Even if Bert and Ernie had succeeded in their mission, their employers couldn't have reasonably expected them to make delivery for at least another three hours, so the Morgans had plenty of time to scope out the situation.

In this case, scoping out the situation involved driving back and forth, then up and down every street in a half-mile radius. By the time they were done, Dan had judged the place as a semi-sleepy lower-middle-class 'burb with a decent mix of national chains and independent shops, fast food, gas stations, supermarkets, and a tractor supply company.

Those were mostly on the main street, surrounded by neighborhoods filled with glorified ranch-style shacks, sun-beaten lawns, and sparse trees that looked like stunted arms of the earth clawing at the sky for help.

By the time the Morgans had called a halt to their reconnaissance, they had watched most of the residents head off for work in Summerfield, Umbarger, or, if they were really lucky, the Buffalo Lake National Wildlife Refuge. To both father and daughter's pleasure, even though they were strangers in town, no one had taken a second look at the gray CR-V. To help ensure that, Dan had even installed a worn, faded license plate that didn't scream "outsider."

They staked their vantage point six-tenths of a mile away on Floss Street. Dan had found an empty lot between two small residences where Alex's CheyTac scope could make a laser line between buildings, garages, sheds, driveways, bushes, vehicles, and, in a few cases, between slats or chain links of a fence.

Feeling they had found the most effective hideout, they waited. Their patience paid off. At seven, through the rifle's scope, Alex saw activity stirring around the back, front, and inside the Peking Panda Palace.

Dan slipped on a light khaki jacket to cover his Walther and Ruger, as Alex settled into the "kill nest" of the SUV. Dan had installed sniper stations on both sides and in the rear of the vehicle—allowing Alex to lie relatively comfortably on the padded floor and poke the barrel through a slot that gave her enough side-to-side movement. Atop that was a cunning one-way glass panel that gave the shooter plenty of room to spy.

He turned to her just as he was about to exit the vehicle. "Let me know if your mom says anything more, okay?" he asked, only half-joking.

"Don't tempt her to speak up," Alex replied, hardly joking at all. "But, if necessary, a point four-oh-eight round will deliver her message, all right?"

Dan stepped out and started the long walk down Union Avenue—past Avenues D, C, B, and A—to one-forty-three North Twenty-Five Mile Avenue.

Dan had a hard time not raising his eyebrows when he entered the place. *Could it be any more generic?* he wondered.

It was a big, empty, square space, with a counter along the back wall—complete with padded swiveling stools—five basic tables dotting the floor with four makeshift chairs each. There were even a few garish paintings of ancient Peking, pandas, and Chinese palaces on the walls, looking like they'd been picked up at a local mall just yesterday.

Jenny didn't speak to him, but she still entered his mind. Back in the good old days, she'd made him watch a reality TV show with her where the contestants were challenged to create their own restaurant in an otherwise empty space in twenty-four hours.

As far as Dan was concerned, this place looked like that, only in a space that had once been a diner or something. Since he or Alex hadn't had time to check out previous occupants at the Deaf Smith County Chamber of Commerce, he saw nothing for it but to take another step in.

At this time of the morning, the place was empty—something he couldn't say about the fast food drive-in and sandwich places he saw down the street. Luckily for him, and maybe his daughter's little four-oh-eight messengers, neither the salon nor the pizza place that adjoined the Peking Panda Palace were open yet.

His entrance had an interesting effect. He saw and heard some hushed activity through the rectangular slot between the counter and the kitchen. He got the impression that the sounds were tense, but he could have been reading into that, or projecting it from his own mental state.

A young Asian woman came walking out of the kitchen. She could have been anywhere between thirty and fifty years old. She had a wide nose, thin lips, and black hair in a ponytail that bounced between her shoulder blades. She wore a starched white shirt, blue work pants, and black Chinese-style slippers with cloth uppers and white woven bottoms. Her dark brown eyes seemed lifeless, and her expression was impenetrable. At least to Dan.

"You want breakfast?" she asked as she approached, gesturing to all the empty seats. "Bun? Dumpling? Congee?"

Dan shifted away from her, heading toward a table in the center of the floor. Although she sounded as if she was making up the choices as she went along, he was not about to start asking questions.

"Dumplings sound good," he said, choosing a chair that gave him a full view of both sidewalk and kitchen, with no door or window behind him.

"Pork, chicken, beef, vegetables?" she asked, beginning to circle back toward the kitchen door.

Dan had to admit that the idea of Chinese dumplings sounded pretty good. Maybe this place wasn't a trap after all...and maybe God didn't make little green apples.

"Chef's choice," he replied, then sat down as if straddling a horse.

The woman blinked, then disappeared back into the kitchen, and the hushed voices started again. Dan couldn't make out the words but was fairly certain they weren't English.

Although he wasn't a tech fan, even he had to admit that he missed the smartphones the Zeta Protocol had insisted they trash. He was sure Linc or Alex could've shown him an app that not only would've told him what language they were speaking, but translated it as well.

The appearance from the kitchen of what appeared to be a busboy and the chef needed no translation. The chef looked older and wore a t-shirt, pants, boots, and a full apron. The busboy had a tray of dishes and cups, and was dressed the same, except his apron only covered his waist and hips. They approached Dan's table from either side.

"What kind of eggs you want?" the chef wanted to know. "Scramble, sunny, over, easy, hard?"

Dan kept his gaze between the two as the busboy angled sharply toward the table. Dan found his hand shifting toward the PPK, but then the busboy slapped down a napkin, cutlery, plate, and a plastic water glass.

"You want tea, coffee, juice?" he asked.

The two questions from two people, neither of whom waited for an answer, tipped Dan off, so he was ready when they pounced. He was already up, bouncing back from the table as if the chair had an ejector seat. His gun came out, but so did everything in the busboy's tray.

Plastic plates, bowls, and cups smashed into him, but worse, so did the pressed metal forks and knives. Dan jumped back and ducked his head, but the cutlery and the chef were on him. He felt a ladle slam into his wrist and heard rather than saw his Walther clatter across the floor. As he went for his blackjack he couldn't help but wonder why it had been a ladle and not a cleaver.

The two men were fast and obviously well-trained. Dan felt a lightning-like pain in his arm where the busboy gripped his elbow, and then felt a dizzying chop of the side of the chef's hand into his throat.

Get away from these two, his brain said. *Alex will never be able to get a clear shot.*

He remembered his hand-to-hand instructor. "When in doubt," the man had taught him, "drop."

Who was Dan to argue? He fell to his knees as if through a hangman's trap door. That move elicited a double reaction. First, a bullet hole appeared in the front window and the chef's head exploded. Second, Dan found himself looking at the busboy's crotch.

Needs a fist, his brain suggested, and again Dan didn't argue. Less than a second later, Dan saw the busboy's flushed, florid, feverish face doubling over into view, his eyes squeezed shut in agonizing pain.

Dan found himself concentrating on the busboy's sharp chin as his brain repeated its suggestion. Dan complied, with all his anger and annoyance, feeling satisfaction fill him as the busboy launched backwards, hovered in the air, limbs flailing, then smashed down on the table like a starfish dropped from a tsunami.

Before Dan could fully assess the situation, he heard rapid gunshots from the direction opposite Alex. He dropped and stared at yet another strange sight. The woman was firing some sort of semi-automatic through the rectangle between counter and kitchen, seemingly indiscriminately.

The bullets were splattering everywhere—across the walls, floor, and ceiling. There were only two places they weren't going: into the front window or into Dan Morgan. The latter target took advantage of that fact by grabbing his Walther, bending his knees, planting his feet against the wall, and launching himself, sliding, across the floor toward the kitchen door.

He came up beside it and waited for only a second as the bullets kept coming from the opening. It really seemed that the woman wasn't even trying to hit him. But better safe than sorry. Dan pumped two three-eighty rounds into the door, crouched, and rolled in. What he saw there surprised him even more. The woman was throwing her weapon away and running into the kitchen's walk-in freezer.

But that's insane, he thought. *Why go into the one place in the whole joint that has no exit?*

But his was not to reason why—his was to do and hope not to die. Dan noticed her gun on the floor; it was a Taiwanese XT97 automatic. Looking back from it, he positioned himself by the side of the freezer opening, stuck his gun barrel in, shot up, down, in the middle, then to both sides. He turned away, waiting for the ricochets to die down, then looked into the darkened enclosure.

The woman wasn't there.

Dan looked all around him, half-expecting an ambush from an unseen exit, but none came. His eyebrows knitted together, and he turned back toward the freezer.

It was wider than he thought it would be, and far from full. But there were a few bags and boxes littering the shelves on either side of the opening—seemingly filled with potatoes or meat. Keeping his PPK at the ready, Dan stepped inside for a closer look.

A "sack of potatoes" positioned on the top shelf by the door rolled off onto him. It was, of course, the woman, and she gripped him by his gun wrist and throat. But that, somehow, was not the worst of it. The worst of it was how one of her feet rested lightly on a section of his shin.

These were not grips he recognized from judo, nor did he recognize the brain-freezing, body-numbing pain that seemed to replace his blood.

"What…" he managed to say, "…are you doing?"

"Trying not to get shot by your girlfriend," she seethed into his ear, all accent gone. "Where is she?" She eased up on his leg enough for him to answer. But her grips on his wrist and neck remained the same.

"D-don't you know?" he stammered, trying to think straight.

"No!" she hissed. "We only know where *you* are. But every time you move we need to recalibrate."

"W-what?" he spluttered. "What sort of tracker is that?"

"Tracker? What tracker?" She seemed honestly perplexed.

Dan couldn't dwell on that. The pain was too great for anything but total honesty. "Why didn't you kill us before?"

"Bendan," she spat. *Idiot.* "If we wanted you dead, you would be dead. We want what you have!"

His brain reeling, his body wracked by indescribable pain, Dan asked the one true question. "What do I have?"

Rolling her eyes, the woman opened her mouth to answer—just as a gray Honda CR-V crashed through the front window and slammed into the kitchen wall.

Chapter 13

The crash shook the entire building, showing just how rushed and shoddy the construction was. Inside the freezer, Dan was safe from the glass shards and splinters, but not from the shock wave as the CR-V screeched across the restaurant floor, skidded sideways, and slid into the bar—bending, cracking, and breaking the padded swivel-top stools.

Dan didn't even see that. But he sure heard it, and, as far as he was concerned, the best thing was that it shook the Asian woman, causing her foot to slide off his shin. The indescribable pain stopped just long enough that he didn't care about the other, less all-encompassing pains at his shoulder and neck.

Even before the dust had settled, he bellowed and twisted his upper torso. Akin to a tumor being ejected from his body, the woman spun like an out-of-control water skier, then flew into the freezer door.

Dan stopped only long enough to get his breath, but by then, he was already too late to stop her. The woman all but disappeared through the crack in the freezer door. Dan blinked, then launched himself toward the door right after her. But when he thundered out into the kitchen, the woman was nowhere to be seen.

Alex was half out the CR-V's passenger door, holding the vehicle's SCAR Assault Rifle at the ready in one hand, while madly waving her father forward with the other.

"Come on, come on!" she shouted. "Got to go before the local bulls show!"

Dan didn't have to be told twice. He charged forward and dove like a seasoned acrobat through the slot between the kitchen and counter. He even twisted in mid-air and slid across both the counter and the snout-like hood of the Honda before landing on his feet next to the driver's door.

Any other time, Alex might have taken the time to applaud that impressive maneuver. But not this time. Dan threw himself behind the dashboard while Alex slammed the passenger door. Both scoured the area for anything that might stop them as he whirled the wheel and slammed the accelerator to the floor. The CR-V roared out of the ragged hole it had made, and shot up Route Three Eighty-Five like a dull gray soccer mom missile.

"Only twenty miles to I-four-oh," Alex shouted to him as the vehicle went from zero to sixty in three point nine seconds flat. "Local bulls got Chevy patrol wagons."

"We'll be out of town before they know we were here," Dan growled as he hunched down and glared toward the horizon.

"Yeah, but will our little Chinese friends?" Alex wondered, lowering the SCAR, but keeping the car's HK P30 close at hand.

"Probably not," Dan scowled like a rancher with a rancid piece of chaw. "Apparently, we both got some kind of bug up our asses. Jenny can talk through yours, and anybody can find me through mine."

"What?" Alex exclaimed, and, as they sped out of town without incident, Dan told her what the woman had said while trying to interrogate him in the freezer. Within minutes the Morgans—and the Honda—were surrounded by plains, grains, dairies, and farms.

"So they don't even know you're my daughter," he concluded as they passed a cattle herd on their left and a silo on their right. "But apparently they can pinpoint me the minute I stop."

Alex was stunned. "What kind of tracker is that?"

"That's what I said!" Dan exclaimed. "I guess as long as we don't stop, all they can do is blow up every place I visit!"

Alex looked in as many directions as she could, trying to spot any police cars but, to their surprise, saw none.

"Man," she said, speaking generally as well as specifically. "I just don't get it."

Dan did, and put dealing with these new developments on hold long enough to clue his daughter in. "Whoever these spooks are, they're way beyond the locals," he told her. "I think the cops aren't coming because these moles are cleaning up after themselves, and us." He glanced over to take in Alex's incredulous face. "I bet your bottom dollar that when the fuzz show up at the Peking Panda Palace, they'll find an empty space with not even a drop of blood on the floor, let alone brains and skull fragments. Nice shot, by the way."

"Thanks."

"No, thank you. In any case, on the basis of what we've experienced so far, I think they don't want to risk having whatever it is they want from me fall into anybody else's hands."

Alex gave out a low whistle. "That's some bet, Pop."

Dan sighed. "It's the only explanation for why we're not reenacting scenes from *Smokey and the Bandit* or *Cannonball Run* right now."

Alex stared at him in confusion. "What're those?"

"Okay, *Fast and the Furious*," Dan said, getting a look of recognition from his daughter. "Happy now?"

"No, of course I'm not happy now," she retorted, gripping the HK P30 tighter as Dan sped west onto Interstate Forty. "I'd much rather have cops all over us than Anti-Zeta."

"Anti-Zeta, huh? Dan grumbled. "I don't know...Something's bothering me, but I just can't put my finger on it..."

"*One* thing is bothering you?" Alex replied incredulously. "Well, let me know when you got it figured out, and I'll tell you the thousand things that are bothering me."

The two fell silent as Dan concentrated on getting away from Deaf Smith County as fast and as furiously as he could. At this point they were satisfied with any moment that wasn't full of gunfire or attacks, but they kept hyper-vigilant as they passed Adrian, Texas, and beyond. In fact, it wasn't until they crossed into New Mexico that Alex seemed to audibly breathe again.

When the Interstate split off from Route 66, and they passed through the relative urbanization of San Jon to the wide open plains beyond, it was Dan's turn to catch his breath. His intake was so sharp, in fact, that Alex looked over expecting to see a light go on over his head.

"What?" she asked of him.

"Alex," he replied. "You were there. You were there for all of it. Did those guys in the Boston alley seem anything like the guys in the Mimi or the Palace?"

Alex considered the question. "No," she answered. "As a matter of fact, if you, or anyone else, were to ask me, I'd say that they seemed like three completely different..."

She didn't get the chance to finish because the woman from the Palace repaid her for driving through the restaurant by slamming into the back of the CR-V. Only the vehicle she used was not disguised in any way.

The Morgans lurched in their seats, but Dan's modification of their vehicle cushioned most of the blow. He wrenched the SUV back into the lane and cursed as he stared into the side-view mirror.

"Hell, they've got a Sherpa!"

Alex wrenched around, bringing up the SCAR, and saw what her father was referring to. It wasn't a Himalayan mountaineer, it was a European four-by-four tactical armored vehicle that looked like a Humvee on steroids. She dove down to the rear sniper spot, bringing the forty-five caliber, twenty-round weapon to bear as her father tromped the accelerator and barked out advice.

"It looks like the armored variant," he yelled to her.

"Which one?" Alex barked back as she targeted the Sherpa's left front tire. She fired, aiming perfectly. Nothing happened.

"Mine variant," Dan guessed.

Alex shifted her aim to pinpoint the driver behind the thick windshield. It was the busboy. Out of her left eye Alex saw the woman in the passenger seat.

"Don't bother shooting the—" Dan started, but Alex had already pulled the trigger, only to watch the round skitter off the Sherpa's wind- and, apparently, bulletproof shield.

"I know!" Alex interrupted. "Ballistic variant!" She all but threw the SCAR away from her and grabbed the Mossberg 500 shotgun. "Let them get as close as possible without inflicting damage." Alex had enormous faith in her father's driving skills.

"Gotcha," Dan growled, spotlighting the Sherpa out the side view mirror. "Come to poppa, baby," he murmured as both he and his daughter had the same thought.

Why weren't they shooting back? Then Dan remembered what the woman had said in the meat locker. *If we wanted you dead, you'd be dead.*

"Take your time, Alex," her father hissed through clenched teeth. "They intend on keeping me alive until they get what they want from me..."

Both Morgans' minds were whirling as Alex took careful aim at the Sherpa's engine block, and Dan tried to return Anti-Zeta the favor by keeping a perfect half-car-length between the butt of the Honda and the nose of the Sherpa. He had no problem doing just that...and strangely, that worried him more than almost anything else.

Are they toying with us...?

Alex waited until the two vehicles were practically touching before she pulled the trigger and the full power of the twelve-gauge, full-bore, double-aught buckshot pounded the sneering grill of the Sherpa like an exploding cannonball.

Alex had to fall back and roll away as the buckshot spread, ricocheted, and even bounced back. For a second it seemed that the shotgun had some effect because the Sherpa fell back a bit, but then it roared forward again, shifting lanes so it was to the CR-V's right.

"You okay?" Dan shouted back to his daughter, but before Alex could answer, the Sherpa pounded its nose into the CR-V's side.

Dan swore as he regained control of the Honda, doing some fast arithmetic. Even with all his modifications, it was the Honda's five thousand pounds versus the Sherpa's nearly five tons. It wasn't hard to figure out which would win a shoving contest. Then, out of the corner of his eye, he saw the woman. She was smiling at him—without humor—from behind her vehicle's bulletproof glass.

She motioned to the highway's shoulder and mouthed the words "pull over." He mouthed two other words back at her. One that started with an "f" and another that ended with a "u."

Then he hit the nitrous lever.

Chapter 14

The CR-V lurched forward, its speed erupting from ninety miles an hour to a hundred-fifty in nothing flat. Dan felt like a mule had kicked him deep into his seat, while Alex gave a surprised little shriek as she was splayed against the back of the SUV. And she was not, by nature, a shrieker.

Dan felt his lips pull back from his teeth, imagining the king of all wolf's grins on his face as he kept the Honda straight down the lane. But the grin dulled as two more simple words entered his brain.

What now?

Sure, he could win a drag race, but the Sherpa could run at seventy miles an hour for more than six hundred miles.

Alex obviously had the same thought. She appeared beside him, clawing into the passenger seat.

"What are we going to do?" she asked. "Lead the Peking Panda people all the way to Renard's place?"

Dan thought about how to lose their pursuers without losing precious time. They were in the New Mexico flatlands now, but in just a little while they'd be entering Albuquerque, and there would be no way to go a hundred and fifty miles an hour anywhere there.

But then the decision was made for them. As Dan glanced into the side view mirror, he saw the far distant Sherpa lurch forward just as the Honda had.

"Oh my lord," Alex moaned, seeing the same thing in the passenger side mirror. "Not just ballistic and mine variants, but nitrous too."

Watching the Sherpa speed after them set off something in Dan's brain.

"Okay," he said, "if that's how you want to play…"

Something in his tone both concerned and exhilarated Alex. She knew her father better than almost anyone. She prepared herself for anything. Dan checked the road. It was empty except for them and the Renault. He checked the surroundings. Serene, beautiful New Mexican landscape. They were coursing through one of the lowest population densities in the country. Filling his eyes was the state's trademark rose-colored desert, bordered by heavily forested valleys, sweeping up into broken mesas.

"Fine." Dan sighed grimly as the Sherpa rapidly caught up to the slightly slowing CR-V. "Two can play at this game."

Dan slammed on the brakes while whirling the steering wheel. The CR-V made a screeching, smoking, seemingly impossible one-eighty, winding up facing the other way—right at the nose of the Sherpa.

He gave his daughter and the Peking Panda people less than a second to deal with that reality before tromping on the Honda's accelerator again. The specially conditioned wheels screeched and smoked once more as he shot at his pursuers, going the wrong way on a one-way road.

"Two things," Alex heard him humming as she flattened herself back in the seat. "One, they don't want to kill me..."

He hardly got the words out before the sight of the Sherpa filled their windshield. Alex managed to keep from shrieking again as she braced for impact.

But then, Dan's arms moved again, and the Sherpa was wrenched from their sight as if yanked off stage by a cable. The CR-V was launching itself off the Interstate to the countryside beyond.

"Two," she heard. "They can't drive like me!"

She held on for dear life as he rumbled across a rocky grassland toward a copse of rocks and trees.

Alex heard a clamor behind them and whirled to catch a glimpse of the Sherpa launching itself off the highway to try cutting them off. She looked at her father. He was intent, concentrating on the lack of road. Had he misjudged it this time because of pressure, repeated assaults, and lack of sleep?

She knew the Sherpa was designed as an off-road vehicle. It could navigate gradients of sixty percent. It could cross obstacles up to two feet high, and trenches three feet deep. No matter how well Dan had safeguarded the Honda, it was still basically a tricked-out family van.

They both felt the Sherpa nudge the back of the CR-V again. But this time the nudge felt different, like a sarcastic kiss rather than a warning slap. Dan concentrated on his goal, but Alex spun around in her seat to see why. Although it was small, Alex's eyes locked on a new intrusion as if it had neon arrows pointing at it.

The Peking Panda people had attached an iron hook through the rear sniper slot.

Alex snarled like a cornered cat. She grabbed the side and ceiling of the SUV and moved toward the hook before she saw a chain running from the hook to a reel attached to the Sherpa's bumper.

"Not on my watch," she hissed as she swung the SCAR onto her back with one hand and grabbed the Honda's passenger side door handle with the other.

Dan was concentrating so hard on his driving that he only became aware of what his daughter was doing when he felt hot desert sand slap the right side of his face. By then she had already swung out and up onto the CR-V's roof.

"Alex!" he heard himself blurt. "No!"

He cursed himself for the useless exhortation and redoubled his attention to his driving. It was especially important now, lest he become responsible for knocking her off the vehicle.

Alex saw what was going on as soon as she flung herself onto the roof. Holding herself splayed there, she watched the busboy nimbly scramble back across the Sherpa hood toward his passenger door. He had crawled out to grab the hook—usually used to pull other vehicles out of mud or water—and locked it onto the CR-V.

The Asian woman was behind the wheel, and the cunning, triumphant look on her face told Alex everything else she needed to know. Once the busboy was safely back inside, the woman would brake, and the Sherpa's five tons would anchor the Honda like the iceberg had anchored the *Titanic*. The Honda would stop as if hitting the Great Wall of China, only it wouldn't crumble and shatter. It would wrench and leap up, all the glass shattering while hunks of plastic and metal would rip off like bitter tears. Then it would come slamming down, shattering some of the Morgans' bones, but, as their pursuers hoped, probably not killing them.

Alex only had seconds, and she took them. Skittering across the CR-V's roof from cab to stern like a cross between a squid and a spider, she grabbed the back lip of the SUV's rear hatch with one hand, and wrenched the SCAR around with the other.

For a split second, her eyes locked with those of the Asian woman. As Alex returned her attention to the matter at hand, her mind recognized the Asian woman's changing expression. She knew what Alex was preparing to do, and was not going to let it go unanswered.

Alex had less than a second. She rammed the muzzle of the eight-pound, short-stroke, forty-five caliber weapon against the nearest chain link and pulled the trigger—just as the Asian woman slammed on the Sherpa's brakes.

The SCAR's forty-five caliber rounds were faster than the woman's leg muscles. The lead came shattering out at six hundred rounds per minute as the driver's slippered foot tromped down on the armored vehicle's stiff brake pedal. If anything, her braking helped the chain link snap, and snap it did—so sharply that even Dan heard it from the front seat.

Three things happened then. First, the Sherpa continued its skidding and squealing stop. Second, the chain whipped upward, the right side putting a pock mark in the Sherpa's hood, and the left side stinging Alex's right arm. And third, the CR-V's left tire went over a well-worn rock.

Unladen, the CR-V had a ground clearance of seven point eight inches. But this bulletproof, super-powered monstrosity Dan had created was anything but unladen. The snapping chain hadn't really hurt Alex, but it stung just enough to wrinkle her concentration. When the SUV bounced, she lost her grip on both the SCAR and the rear lip of the roof.

Dan felt it. Worse, he saw it out the side-view mirror. His daughter Alex bounced up into the air, tumbled at least four feet to the left, then came dropping down. He didn't see her hit, but the Asian driver and busboy did.

She may have snarled like a cat, but she didn't land like one, which in the long run was a good thing. Thankfully she had gotten a lot more training than just sniper practice, and the first thing they were all taught in self-defense was how to fall. The rest of the lessons had been supplemented by experience, especially recent battles on, in, and around a Trans-Siberian Express, which had been going a lot faster than the off-road slowed SUV.

The woman in the Sherpa watched Alex use a cactus like an awning, then twist and somersault onto creosote bushes before rolling across burrograss that both slowed and cushioned her fall. The man in the Sherpa watched the SCAR assault rifle slam on and skitter across the ground some thirty feet away.

Dan slammed on his brakes, and watched as brown and red dust clouds billowing up and showering down on the semiarid plains. He grabbed the P30 automatic and jumped out of the still shuddering CR-V, intent on racing to his daughter's side. But as soon as his boots hit the tobosa grass he froze. Alex was not where he had seen her land.

His eyes shifted over toward the Sherpa. The Asian woman stood outside the driver's side door, holding the SCAR rifle. A small, knowing, even sympathetic, smile played on her cruel lips. The busboy was kneeling in front of their vehicle's bumper, holding the broken but still long chain in his fists. Dan knew the chain was still long because most of it was wrapped around Alex's throat as it stretched her across the busboy's lap.

"You," the woman said to Dan, "we will not kill." She motioned toward Dan's daughter and the busboy. "I cannot say the same about her."

Dan felt the urge to charge, but he fought it, knowing that he would not make it in time. Either Alex's neck would be snapped or there was still a bullet in the SCAR's magazine. Even if there wasn't, he was certain his daughter's skull could be broken with one swipe of any of their arms. He felt a second urge, to try shooting both the woman and her busboy, wild west style—but he wasn't exactly feeling like the Duke or Dirty Harry.

"All right," he said, sounding more tired than he had in years. "What do you want?"

The woman motioned for him to drop his weapon and approach. "What we have always wanted," she said. "For you to come with us."

"You will leave her be." It wasn't a question or request.

The woman looked like she wanted to show what a poor bargaining position he was in, but then gave an eminently pragmatic shrug. "We have no use of her, so we will not take her." She motioned again, in the expressive way she had—first to raise his hands, and again, to approach.

Dan Morgan dropped the P30 on the desert floor, then raised his hands. He took his first step toward them.

"Okay," he said. "I guess we'll all be finding out exactly what's going on with…"

He never got to finish his sentence because the Sherpa's windshield started cracking with needle-sized holes, the Sherpa's right side began to get torn apart like paper, and the Sherpa's left side began sprouting punctures as if being punched by an invisible heavyweight champion.

Chapter 15

The Peking Panda woman and busboy only had a moment to react in utter surprise and confusion before Alex Morgan jammed the VIPERTEK heavy duty stun gun against the young man's arm with one hand, and shot the woman full in the face with the SABRE three-in-one pepper spray in the other.

Fifty-three thousand volts pumped through the busboy's nervous system, making him dance like a spastic puppet, while the combination of stinging pepper, facial-burning tear gas, and ultra-violet marking dye made the woman lurch back as if being yanked off a galloping horse by a hangman's noose.

Alex had pulled both out of her jacket as soon as her captors were distracted by the vicious, new, unexpected ambush. The Peking Panda people had been so busy grabbing her and dragging her back to their vehicle that they hadn't bothered to search her. After all, they had already collected the SCAR assault rifle, hadn't they?

As soon as Dan saw Alex had her own rescue well in hand, he scooped up the P30 and fired in the direction the needles, tears, and punches had come from while backtracking as fast as possible. Alex managed to re-pocket the small stun gun, but had to drop the pepper spray in order to grab the SCAR, which had fallen from the screeching woman's hands as she frantically clawed at her eyes.

Alex took one step toward the CR-V when a hailstorm of needles sent her slamming back against the Sherpa's hood. Swinging the SCAR around to target the newly arrived, but still as yet unseen enemy, she found herself staring at the Peking Panda woman, who had somehow managed to open up her livid eyes to stare back.

Alex saw the other's surprise, agony, and sudden fear, then watched as the woman's head peeled opened like a pineapple chopped by an invisible machete.

Alex's own head snapped forward so her eyes locked with her father's. There she saw anger, frustration, and, worse, helplessness, as he kept firing to the right, left, and above her, simply trying to find a target. It was no time to have a chat about plans or strategy. As the Peking Panda woman's half-headed body collapsed in on itself, burbling guts out onto the grassland floor, Alex whirled around, then sprung up onto the Sherpa's grill.

Dan felt the instinctive urge to shout "no" at her again, but recognized it as a knee-jerk parental response. He let the seasoned agent inside him elbow aside the father and take over. Alex was right. There was no way she could get to him without being hit by diamond-tipped needles, lasers, or concentrated air punches. And the only thing between her and those things was the Sherpa. More specifically, the center of the Sherpa, since the edges of the vehicle were being demolished all around her.

Dan backed up toward the CR-V as he watched her scramble over the middle of the Sherpa's hood. Since he had made it back to the Honda without getting punctured, chopped, or air-punched himself, he decided that he was out of effective range. So he used this supposed safety zone to reach inside his vehicle and grab at the other weapons that were left: the Glock 17 and the Mossberg shotgun. As he reemerged into the sun, he shoved the handgun into his belt and brought the shotgun up.

Over the thirty-inch barrel, he saw his daughter trying to figure out a way to get into the Sherpa without getting perforated. The doors were open, but each of the portals was being pounded by the hi-tech weapons—most likely being wielded by the helmeted, bulletproof baddies they had met in the Beacon Hill alley.

Of course she wanted to break through the windshield, but she had found out the hard way that it was amply bulletproofed. Both father and daughter knew there wasn't time to wait. She'd have to risk swinging inside, hoping she didn't get too badly punctured, pulverized, or sliced.

Dan decided for her by bringing the Mossberg up. Both the Glock and shotgun had an effective range of fifty yards, but the handgun had slugs, while the shotgun had shot. In other words, the Glock had a single finger. The Mossberg had a whole hand.

Alex's concerned face snapped up after the first shotgun blast. To any innocent observer, it would look like a father was shooting at his daughter. Alex knew better. She saw what he was trying to do, and started planning on how to take advantage of it. Rather than run into the needles, high intensity light, and concentrated air tubes himself, he was sending little steel, tungsten, plastic, bismuth, and tin friends to knock them away just long enough for his daughter to slip by.

Both were worried, as well as not worried, about the timing. Her swinging into the Sherpa's cab between shots had to be exact, but when to try doing so was severely limited. That was because the shotgun only had five shells in the magazine before it required reloading, and besides, by the time he had used four, the helmeted scumbags would probably be onto the ploy and take the steps necessary to perforate them both.

Alex had enormous faith in her father's aiming skills. They had stood side by side in shooting galleries and battles alike. He might not be as good a shot as she was at this stage of life, but she knew she could literally bet her life on him.

She did. Dan blasted a second time, scattering whatever junk the others were hurling at her, so she threw herself into the Sherpa's cab like a hyper-fast caterpillar—right before he blasted a third time. Then both Morgans jumped behind the wheels of their respective vehicles and tromped on the accelerators.

The Honda and the Sherpa leaped forward, tearing up the creosote bushes under their special metal-ringed, run-flat tires that had lived up to their reputations. Alex felt the Sherpa slip, as if she had hit a foot-long patch of ice, but before she could worry about it, she heard the sickening sounds of flesh tearing. She didn't bother to check that she had run over the busboy. She had bigger concerns to feel bad about.

A big black tactical vehicle came roaring out from behind a rocky bluff some two hundred yards away. To put it more accurately, it came erupting out *over* the bluff to crush the prairie floor on high-payload, military-grade tires. Gunning its engine, the thing came speeding at them as the Morgans all but stood on their accelerators.

Dan knew what it was: a Guardian MAX, made by the International Armored Group. He ought to know; it was built on a Ford HD truck chassis, and if there was one thing he knew, it was Fords—certainly a lot better than he knew Hondas. These damn Guardians could be armored up to NATO's highest level of protection for occupants of light armored vehicles and, with their six-point-eight-liter V-ten engines, could eat up the distance between them like a Florida alligator ate retirees' poodles.

It also could seat five, which probably meant Amina, a laser rifler, a diamond-tipped needle shooter, a hole-puncher, and a driver. Five against two—not terrible odds, but far from great ones considering the condition of the Honda, Sherpa, and their drivers, not to mention their ability to return fire under these circumstances.

Dan stopped himself from thinking about what was behind them, and started thinking about what was ahead. They were in the mouth of one of New Mexico's infamous "staked plains," which could be the most rugged stretch of land in the state. These mesas usually led to canyons, but first wove through twisted, curving tunnels of rock that opened and tightened up again with unguessable regularity.

He pictured the seventy-three inch wide CR-V getting through a narrow pass as the eighty-seven-inch-wide Guardian MAX LTV smashed into it. That was the way to go, but the Sherpa had to be dealt with first. The killers in the Guardian seemed to feel the same way. From their vantage point, the Honda was hiding behind the Sherpa like a freshman behind a senior, so they took it all out on the latter.

Through his side-view mirror, Dan could see the gun slots open up on the MAX's sides and three different weapons appeared. As they tried pelting the Sherpa's rear with needles, air punches, and high-intensity light, it looked as if the Renault was wiggling its ass at them—until Dan realized that effect was caused by already broken pieces swinging in the wind.

Once more, Dan wished he had a cellphone or Zeta ear-comm to communicate with his daughter, or at least that he had been smart enough to grab some walkie-talkies. But he'd just have to depend on their familial bond, and hope that the acorn didn't fall far from the tree.

As Dan headed toward a twisted, curving opening in the rocks at the edge of the basin they were speeding across, Alex came hurtling toward him, seemingly unable to prevent what the Sherpa had done twice before—rear-end the Honda. But within seconds, Dan saw the method to her madness, especially when he saw her ram the barrel of the SCAR onto the Sherpa's passenger side window.

"Dear God," he breathed. *She couldn't be thinking of doing what I think she's thinking of doing, could she?*

It was exactly what he would have thought of trying if their positions had been reversed. Both knew that if she had managed to get ahead of the Honda, that would have exposed it to unsurvivable hammering from the MAX. There was really only one thing left to do if they wanted to trade certain death for possible suicide.

But was she as good a driver as him? She was as good a sniper—better, in fact—so it was time to stop worrying and start helping. As she emptied the remainder of the SCAR's most powerful rounds into the Sherpa's passenger-side windshield, he saw her silently screaming face, but also a growing crack in the windshield glass.

He couldn't decide whether to breathe a sigh of relief or hold his breath—knowing that when a windshield is labeled "bulletproof," that usually actually meant resistant to certain calibers, as well as to distant shots, not point blank ones. In any case, attempting what Alex did should not be tried at home.

Dan kept one eye peeled on the rear view mirror so he saw Alex start pounding the center of the crack with the gun barrel and, when that wasn't as fast or effective as she wanted it to be, neatly and nimbly flip the gun in mid-air so she could grab the barrel and use the butt as the club—while still steering the Sherpa with her other hand. Dan saw her wince from the barrel's heat, and winced with her, remembering how that felt. But he also knew that she, like him, would not let go. Instead, she started swinging the seven-pound weapon like a cleaver, hitting crack central every time.

Dan shifted his eyes down to where the driver's side latch for the CR-V's rear cargo door was. He was certain that Alex had seen it after all those hours in the Honda's passenger seat. His eyes snapped up just as the SCAR butt broke through the Sherpa window. Then she started chopping with it, making as big an opening in the windshield as possible. Normally, once a windshield's integrity was compromised, the entire thing would fall out like a dropped net, but bulletproof glass was made of stronger stuff, so she only managed to make a gap of about two feet.

It would have to do. Dan watched Alex slam down on her accelerator again, gripping the steering wheel with both her white-knuckled hands. He waited until the cab of the Sherpa filled the Honda's rear view mirror like an IMAX movie, then yanked the rear hatch latch.

The tail door popped open, then, because of the rough road, almost immediately bounced back to lock again. Cursing in tense rage, Dan yanked the latch release a second time, then hurled the twenty-five ounce P30 at the door.

His aim was perfect. The gun punched the bottom of the hatch like an angry fist, sending it swinging up. As it rose, it revealed Alex oozing through the break in the Sherpa's windshield like a python being called by a snake charmer's *pungi*.

Dan clamped his hands on the Honda's steering wheel to make sure the vehicle was in front, then gently braked until the Sherpa's snout was practically inside the CR-V's cargo area. Alex scrambled over the Sherpa hood, got her feet under her, and tensed to make the jump from one vehicle to another.

Of course, the Guardian MAX took that moment to catch up. Almost at the exact millisecond Alex's toes were about to leave the Sherpa's steel, the MAX rammed into its back, turning Alex's jump from a smooth dive to a flailing spin.

Dan bellowed like a wounded elephant as he watched his daughter's arms and legs bend, thrash, and flounder, her twisted body seemingly frozen in mid-air in an endless, agonizing eternity in the space between the two vehicles.

Chapter 16

Morgan was halfway out of his seat to try grabbing Alex in mid-air when the Guardian finished the job.

He should have known better. The Guardian rams the Sherpa, the Sherpa unavoidably lurches forward, ramming whatever is in front of it, which was, in this case, a much lighter, much smaller soccer mom van.

The three machines looked like a vehicular Russian nesting doll, then Alex was thrown into the back of the Honda's seats. Dan felt the stomach-churning *thud* of his daughter's limp body in his very soul, then had to grab the steering wheel before he lost all control.

The Guardian's nose went down, sending the Sherpa's tail up, the shock wave trying to do the same to the Honda. Dan wrestled the wheel while trying to press the accelerator through the floor boards, his eyes searching both the windshield and rear-view mirror for any sign of escape, or his daughter.

Instead he saw the Sherpa, like a drunken frat boy, shudder and weave. Then, like an angry dragon, it nosed into the rear opening while clawing at the bumpers. The MAX hit it again.

The Sherpa rammed its nose into the ground this time, sending it ass over teakettle into the back of the CR-V. Both the back bumper and the entire rear hatch door were torn off with a metallic scream, sending metal and glass spinning in all directions.

The Honda was shoved forward, its rear wheels leaving the prairie ground, then slammed down again. The CR-V lost little speed because although Dan had not been smart enough to remember walkie-talkies, he had been smart enough for four-wheel drive. Once the rear wheels reconnected with what served as their roadway, the CR-V tried to make up for lost time, which was vitally important because, in the interim, the Sherpa had turned violently abusive.

Rather than somersaulting, smashing down, and coming to a smoking, wrecked stop like a good boy, the Sherpa slid to the side, tripped over some rocks, and rolled. The Honda was being followed by a combination stream-roller and thresher.

To Dan's infuriated eyes, it was like an up close and personal bird's-eye view of the record-setting Aston Martin roll in the aforementioned *Casino Royale*, although 007 hadn't had his unconscious daughter sliding inexorably toward the thresher's maw.

The next few seconds were the hairiest Dan had ever experienced. He had to accelerate madly to keep from getting ground up by the Sherpa's smashing, but he also had to brake to keep Alex from falling out and unavoidably getting chewed up.

He had to speed up, watching Alex tremble back toward the open maw, brake to jerk her back from the abyss, speed up again as more hunks of the Honda's rear opening were snapped off, then brake again to save his daughter—all in perfect rhythm and with expert timing.

The Sherpa's rolls slowed, just in the nick of time for Dan to see an opening in the mesa rocks barely wide enough for the CR-V to squeeze through. With something like pleasure, he yanked the Honda's steering wheel to the right, sending Alex slamming into the SUV's side wall, and shot through the opening. The tight squeeze sent sparks and scraping sounds everywhere, but then, helping Dan believe in karma, the Sherpa landed, slid, and spun, miraculously slamming across the opening like a closing door.

Dan almost laughed with relief as he saw the Sherpa-sealed entrance to the mesa maze in his rearview mirror. He looked forward to make sure there was nothing he might crash into for the next dozen yards, then reached back, grabbed the nearest part of Alex available—her sleeve—and hauled her between the CR-V's front seats. He looked down at her, intending to spend only a second, but in actuality waited as long as it took to assess her condition. She was completely out and badly bruised, but breathing steadily.

His relief was nearly dizzying, and he gave thanks as he returned his attention to what served as the road ahead. He wasn't sure whether it was his gratitude or the area's actual scenery, but the badlands he now found himself in were fascinatingly beautiful. The multi-colored cairns sloped up from inches to hundreds of feet, each in its own weird and weathered shape. The washes twisted and turned like labyrinths of rainbow-splashed pastels.

Then the thirty-second vacation was over as he heard an explosion behind them. His eyes snapped up to the rear-view mirror, no longer blocked by a rear hatch, to see the Guardian shredding open the Sherpa obstruction like a starving man tearing open a burrito. The MAX barreled through the wreckage and charged straight at the Honda.

Dan jammed the pedal to the metal. With no rear hatch, bulletproofing made no difference. But all the time and labor he had expended on bulletproofing the seats paid off in spades as he heard, but did not feel, needles snapping behind them.

He was sure the air fists were out of range, but the lasers didn't care about any stinking bulletproofing. So it was back to square one, only with a Guardian instead of a Sherpa, and minus one advantage. They might not be able to drive like he did, but they sure as hell didn't care about keeping him alive. He had to wonder again why the Peking Panda people had, but then he started playing the CR-V's wheel and pedals like a virtuoso.

The Guardian didn't care. Dan would slip around a cairn, but the Guardian smashed right through it. He snuck into another opening too small for the MAX. It smashed into it until it wasn't too small anymore.

That gave Dan an ever-increasing lead, but still the MAX didn't care. It was fresh, probably fully fueled, and not missing any doors or weapons. Dan was back down to his Walther, Ruger, blackjack, and boot knife. He drove fast and thought furiously, but every idea he got—like playing joust or chicken with the thing—he knew the MAX would smash through. It was like David versus Goliath again, only this time David was crippled and Goliath was wearing armor and carrying a flame-thrower. A slingshot just wouldn't cut it.

The Honda turned a final mesa corner, and emerged once again out into New Mexico's wide open spaces. The MAX, of course, smashed through the stone gateway, reducing it to pebbles. The two vehicles sped out across a rolling basin of soft grass surrounded, as if in mother nature's coliseum, with a circle of gypsum dunes, canyon pines, white fir, and desert wildflowers in yellow, white, pink, and scarlet—all of it bordered by mountains, topped with a painfully blue sky and pure white clouds.

Dan Morgan felt like a cockroach on a wedding cake—a true trespasser into a sacred place. The needs or wants of the a-holes pursuing them meant little. He glanced at the sleeping face of his daughter, then chewed at his lower lip.

"Well, gonna die anyway," he muttered. "There are worse places to do it."

But that didn't mean he was giving up. He drove until the Honda ran out of gas, which was three-quarters of the way across the huge basin.

The Guardian, not surprisingly, seemed to distrust the stop. It slowed, then circled the CR-V. It had only completed one circuit, from twenty yards away, when it opened fire.

Dan grabbed Alex and dragged her with him to the floor under the dashboard as needles, concentrated light, and air fists started sticking, slicing, and smashing all around them. Glass, metal, plastic, and cloth rained down on the Morgans. After the barrage stopped, Dan heard a voice.

"*Krelats*," was what was said, but its meaning was clear, especially from the mocking, Serbian-accented voice that spoke it. *Imbecile. Buffoon.*

Dan knew his Serbian nickname when he heard it. Not bothering to remove his guns, sap, or knife, he sat up, letting all the chips of the Honda fall where they might. Then he stepped out of the SUV. The Honda was quite the worse for wear. The engine was smoking, the windows looked like an acupuncturist had gone nuts on them, the body side moldings looked like "roommate wanted" tear-off ads at a college student center, and the doors looked like the Incredible Hulk had been using them for punching practice.

Dan looked from his labor of love to his new labor of hate. Amina had not taken off her helmet this time. She had replaced it with one that had a flip-up visor, so fairly total protection was just one finger-flick away.

"You don't, by any chance," he inquired, "want me to go anyplace with you, do you?"

She looked at him with sneering derision. "No," she said, but then seemed to consider the possibilities. "I may decide to take along your darling daughter, however. I have friends who are relatives of the people she killed on the train who might like to spend some ...how do you say...'quality time' with her."

Dan almost charged, but decided to avoid a summary execution for as long as possible. He saw, beyond the woman, three more helmeted, uniformed people, their visors down, holding their high-tech weapons at the ready in the doorways of the Guardian.

"Speaking of quality time," he changed the subject with seeming nonchalance, while feeling acidic bile in the back of his throat, "nice wheels. Considering Guardians are only available to law enforcement, government, and military, you wouldn't mind cluing me in on who gave it to you, would you? For old time's sake?"

It was Amina's turn to almost charge, but she managed to control herself, with obvious effort. Then her sneer returned.

"No," she said, "not for old time's sake. But maybe, perhaps, for, how you say, a going away present. Or, how we say, *ДеamxВucx*. A last wish."

She charged. His Walther was out before she got within three feet. He was expecting to be mowed down, but hoping he could bring her with him. The other Anti-Zeta hired help was obviously sternly instructed. They didn't even bring their weapons to bear as, suddenly, Amina wasn't in front of Dan's gun anymore.

Her foot seemed to come out of nowhere, kicking the PPK from his hand before a second foot swiped across his jaw like a nine-iron. Dan staggered as Amina landed on her feet, a dismissive grin on her face.

They stayed in place, considering one another in the glorious natural amphitheater and sky dome all around them.

"Well," Dan said, spitting blood from his mouth as he got up, "at least I know now why you wear that helmet." He leaned toward her. "You don't want to show off that scar I gave you, do you? Too bad. I bet your little train friends would find it very pretty."

She seemed to fly through the air at him, foot first. He made a grab for it, but her hands grabbed at him as well, and for a few seconds, she rode him like a monkey on a tiger. He punched her square in the chest, feeling only Kevlar. Though his strength got her off him, she landed holding his Ruger and blackjack.

"So now, *supak*," she said as she tossed the revolver and cosh away. "Maybe now you know why I stopped you here." She put her empty hands out to encompass all the beauty around them. "I stopped you here because, boot knife or no boot knife, this is where I'm going to beat you to death."

She took a purposeful step toward him, her brain clearly writing a check she was certain her body could cash, but then the Guardian MAX sunk a foot into the ground, its roof accordioning the windows like a beer can crushed by an invisible giant.

Dan gaped, and Amina whirled around, as a cone of thunder slapped onto the MAX, making the weapon holders grab the sides of their heads and drop, spasming, to the ground.

Dan felt an up-rushing of wind and looked in that direction as, out of a fluffy cloud, came what looked like a big, black, metal hermit crab, with blunt wings instead of legs. In the middle of those wings were what looked like huge room fans facing downward. As Dan watched, the crab-shaped thing floated down as if on the strings of a celestial marionette. Three wheels folded out from its underside, and the thing landed fifty feet away.

Dan spun again as he heard tortured wheels ripping up the ground. He was just in time to see the hammered Guardian speeding in the opposite direction. He was hoping the hermit crab thing would utterly destroy it with a death ray or whatever, but no such luck. He decided just to be grateful for this seemingly divine intervention as he collected his blackjack, Ruger, and Walther.

By that time, a hatchway had appeared, seemingly magically, on the side of the hermit crab's head, and a familiar face popped out of the opening.

"Hey Cobra," said Dan's veteran military and intelligence agency partner, Peter "Cougar" Conley. "Need a lift?"

Chapter 17

First things first: Alex.

She was lying in a clear-topped capsule tucked in the back of the hermit crab-shaped plane's oval, off-white, seemingly porcelain interior—resting comfortably, if the serene expression on her face was any indication.

"We've already done an MRI, CT Scan, a full range of X-rays, and even Ultrasound," Conley assured him.

"We?" Dan echoed, not taking his eyes off his daughter.

Conley made a general encompassing motion with his right hand to indicate the plane in general and, specifically, the medical capsule—medcap for short—that Alex was lying in.

"She's got a little internal bleeding," Conley informed him, "a hairline fracture about the size and width of a fingernail clipping, a nice collection of bumps, bruises, and cuts, but nothing permanent." He put a reassuring hand on Dan's shoulder. "With a little R and R she should be good as new."

As much as Dan tried to concentrate on Alex's face to pick up anything only a father might notice, he couldn't help letting his gaze slide off to take in the jet's extraordinary interior. The place was so sleek and elegantly designed that he wouldn't have been surprised if Conley had called it an iPlane.

The cabin was not divided into different areas by walls or doors. It was one big oval area, with the only indication of front, back, and sides being the placement of the piloting, passenger, and storage sections. Dan knew there had to be spots for the lavatory and galley, but he hadn't been able to spot them as yet. Instead, he saw six other compartments spaced on either side of where Alex lay.

"What is this?" Dan asked his partner. "A flying hospital?"

It was an understandable guess. Although Conley had assured them that they were at least thirty thousand feet in the air he could sense no evidence of it. He had concluded that only the sick or the injured would get that sort of treatment.

Conley noted where Dan was glancing. "Oh, I get it," he realized. "No, buddy, those are dream caps." When Dan looked nonplussed, Conley elaborated. "Sleeping quarters, with no diagnostic equipment, anti-magnetic screens, or radiation shielding like the med-cap has."

Dan wrested his eyes away from his daughter and looked at his taller, slimmer, and blonder friend, who had always reminded him of a cross between Jimmy Stewart and Clint Eastwood.

"Thanks, man, you pulled my fat out of the fire once again."

Conley dismissed it with a grin. "My pleasure as always, buddy. It's not like you haven't done the same for me." He nodded at the med-cap. "Or her."

For the first time in days, Dan Morgan let out a relaxed sigh, and took the time to study his surroundings for something other than threats. His eyes scoured the ship's controls, which looked far more like a videogame room with an overactive thyroid than any cockpit he'd ever seen.

"Brother," he breathed, putting his hands out. "I always thought you could fly anything, but this...!"

Conley stepped beside Dan, and replaced his hand on his shoulder—only this time the grip was more preparatory than reassuring.

"Who said anything about me flying this thing?" he told Dan. "I only came along because we were afraid that if you didn't see a friendly face on our landing, you might start shooting. And we couldn't risk you damaging this baby."

Conley walked to an ergonomic seat that looked like it had all but grown from the floor covering—a floor covering that seemed like a combination of the most expensive carpet crossbred with memory foam—and sat down.

"But," Dan stammered, "if you're not flying this thing, who is?"

"Come on, buddy," Conley chided, his grin getting ever wider. "Can't you guess?"

"Good morning, Mr. Morgan," a familiar voice said, coming from everywhere and nowhere. "Welcome to Flying Fox One, or, as we like to call it, Palecto."

Conley rolled his eyes, still smiling. "Actually, only he likes to call it that."

"Renard?" Dan exclaimed to the empty air.

"Who else?" Conley interjected. "You think I can afford something like this?"

Dan tried to comprehend it, but failed. He looked to his partner and just said, "Palecto?"

"Don't ask," Conley suggested. But it was too late.

"The Torresian flying fox," came the disembodied voice, whose name, Renard, meant "fox" in French. "Initially described as a separate species from genus Pteropus, belonging to the megabat suborder Megachiroptera—the largest bats in the world."

Watching Dan chew on that, Conley leaned back and crossed his legs. "Wow, Lily," he breathed. "How do you stand him?"

"As you well know," came the voice of Lily Randall, their redheaded Zeta colleague and Scott Renard's significant other, "he's not like this all the time." Cougar and Cobra could imagine her fixing the tech billionaire with a warm smile. "But I have to admit he's justly proud of the craft that saved your ass, Dan."

Conley got up from the chair. "Yeah, to be honest, Danny boy, he's got good reason to be." The lanky pilot pointed at the flight section of the curved ovoid wall. "That's not a videogame console with delusions of grandeur. That's a videogame console with deserving grandeur."

Cougar ticked the benefits off on his fingers.

"Vertical takeoff and landing, advanced radar and sensors, amazing maneuverability and supercruise speed…"

Dan knew that meant it could maintain sustained supersonic flight while most aircraft could only intermittently reach those speeds.

"…and to top it all off," Conley concluded, "the megabat connection is apt, since this baby flies blind to any other aircraft." He turned back to Dan. "The FX-1 makes Stealth Bombers look positively 3D."

"And that's not even mentioning its data fusion capabilities," came a third voice Dan instantly recognized as that of Lincoln Shepard—Zeta's resident computer master and king nerd. Lord knew Dan had heard him in his head through the late, lamented Zeta ear-comms often enough. "Or its advanced avionics, net-centricity, situational awareness, human-system integration…"

"Linc?" Dan interrupted. "What? Are you all there?"

The voices fell silent until Karen O'Neal, Linc's fellow I.T. expert and girlfriend, spoke up.

"Not all, Cobra," she said. "But we'll just have to do for now."

Dan was unfazed by the short Zeta roll-call. He was just pleased that there was anyone else at all.

"Yes, you will," he assured the voices. "You will, with bells on. But where's there?"

Conley clapped Dan on the shoulder a third time, and motioned at the empty space in front and above him.

"They were holding off on doing this next magic trick," Cougar explained. "Linc was afraid you'd get all scared and start gasping 'ghost.'"

"I was not!" Linc's disembodied voice complained.

But before Dan could comment, Scott Renard's face appeared in the empty air in front of the two partners. It was not ghostly at all, or flickering in any way.

"Welcome, Dan," he said. "Good to have you back."

Then the others—Lily, Linc, and Karen—appeared over his shoulders. They couldn't contain themselves. They all started laughing, even celebrating, together in the empty, open air. But they all knew the respite had to be short-lived.

"Okay, okay," Dan said, as if quieting an unruly class of geeks. Even he had to admit how amazing it was to interact with a bunch of associates floating in the air in front of him. "I've got questions. Who's got answers?"

The others looked at one another before Lily took over. "We all do, Dan," she said. "You've got"—she looked at Renard, who held up his forefinger—"one hour. Rest, eat, freshen up…"

"Not necessarily in that order," Linc interjected before Karen backhanded him on the arm.

Dan could now clearly comprehend how grateful they all were to be alive and together, after the monumental and devastating attack.

"You'll need to hit the ground running," Lily continued with not a shred of humor. "Debriefing upon your arrival. We've got a lot to do and very little time. As much as I hate to admit it, it looks like the destruction of Zeta HQ was just the tip of the iceberg."

Chapter 18

Given what he and Alex had been through, rest was probably out of the question, so Dan didn't try. But, also given what they had been through, Dan decided to prepare a retroactive last meal for himself as a reward.

Not surprisingly, Palecto's larder—once Conley had shown him behind a virtually invisible partition made of the same sleek, cool-to-the-touch material as the rest of the interior—was well-stocked, high end, and ridiculously pretentious.

Once Dan also got help on how to use the seemingly magic cook top, indistinguishable from the rest of the smooth counter surface and activated by smartphone-surface-level touch, he made filet mignon—charred on the outside, mooing on the inside—crispy potato chunks—fried in both duck *and* bacon fat—and fresh garlic-almond string beans.

The latter wasn't his choice. Garlic and almonds were the only way the green beans came.

"Now I'm sure my cholesterol can be tested like fine wine," he cracked as he approached Conley, who stood between the controls and Alex's med-cap.

Cougar had shown him where the new clothes were, so after an invigorating shower in a state-of-the-art stall—complete with high monsoon shower head, pulsating back jets, a steam generator, and even a foot massage mat—he eschewed the accompanying drying chamber to use the softest and most absorbent towel he had ever experienced, then picked out a brand new wardrobe.

Now Cobra and Cougar truly looked like partners. Both wore extremely comfortable, dark gray, long-sleeve shirts, matching pants, and zip-up collarless jackets. Dan didn't have to say a word about them. His expression, mixing incredulity with suspicion, made Conley chuckle.

"Don't knock 'em until you walk a mile in 'em," he said, mixing clichés. "Anti-odor, breathable, releases heat in the warm, retains heat in the cold. Also surprisingly helpful in camouflaging concealed weapons."

Dan looked doubtfully at his friend, but raised his eyebrows when Conley pulled one side of his jacket aside to reveal a full shoulder holster rig underneath, complete with Cougar's current favorite sidearm, a Smith & Wesson 9 Pro.

But instead of dealing with these things directly, Dan merely muttered, "Breathable?"

Conley chuckled while dropping his jacket flap. "That means your sweat not only doesn't stink, it doesn't even show."

The footwear both wore was also very comfortable, but obviously durable—multi-use slip-on shoe-boots that seemed to adjust to their feet with every step, which was helpful as the front of the aircraft seemed to turn transparent.

Dan fought the urge to grab onto something, but recovered his equilibrium as he joined his friend by his daughter's med-cap.

"You are such a cowboy," he muttered as a way of dodging his discomfort with standing in mid-air as the world beneath him seemed to get larger. To recover from all the high tech and high comfort surprises, he concentrated on what he was seeing.

"The most secluded place in the King Range Mountains of California's Lost Coast," Conley said as green and brown mountains played with black sand and gray rock beaches, while myriad shades of blue warred between the California sky and the Pacific Ocean.

Alex might have known what Conley was talking about, but Dan didn't. "'Lost Coast'?" he echoed.

As the Flying Fox sank closer to the mountains and tree tops, Conley explained. "So rough and rocky that roads would be too expensive to build or maintain," he explained. "Virtually nobody but hikers have come anywhere near here for nearly a hundred years." He pointed one way. "Sinkyone Wilderness State Park." He pointed the other. "King Range National Conservation Area." He pointed straight down. "Fox Burrow."

Dan didn't follow his friend's finger with his eyes, just in case the floor turned translucent too. Instead, he looked up to the mid-morning sky as Palecto floated down until the view was swallowed by mountainsides and pine, spruce and cypress trees.

As with the takeoff and flight, Dan hardly felt the landing, but turned when the same nearly invisible hatch Conley had originally stuck his head out of re-opened. In came two young people in hospital scrubs on either side of a gurney. They only had eyes for the med-cap and Alex.

Lincoln Shepard was behind them, followed by Karen O'Neal. They wore the same shirt, pants, jacket, and slip-on shoe-boots as Cobra and Cougar. Linc remained the same teddy bear of a man, only now even more so, thanks to a bushy beard.

As far as Dan was concerned, Karen was still a vibrant, whip-smart young woman with only two flaws. One, her hair was not as blonde as it used to be, and two, she had chosen to love Linc when, of course, she was way out of his league. But Dan never had, and never would hold that against her.

Seeing them in the flesh made him feel great. He held out his hand to Linc, but the tech guy ignored it, enveloping Dan in a bear hug instead.

"Oh thank god, Cobra," he said. "You would not believe how hard we tried to find you."

"Hey, hey, sure I would," Dan started, but stopped when the two orderlies wheeled Alex by them.

Before they were even completely past, O'Neal took the crook of his arm. "Come on," she said, giving Linc a look that said "first things first."

They all followed the orderlies out of the aircraft. Dan had to keep himself from stopping to take it all in. The Flying Fox had seemed to become part of the surrounding hangar, having landed in a berth that was obviously designed just for it.

Although Dan managed to keep moving, he couldn't stop himself from looking up, just as a cunningly camouflaged netting moved into place to obscure their landing vent. Obviously it was not just regulation netting material. It looked something like the stuff that had been on the aircraft's floor.

With one step, they were in a specially made hangar. The next, they were in a rustic lodge hallway. The next, they were in one of the sleekest, most advanced hospital rooms Dan had ever seen. They let him watch Alex be transferred to one of three intensive care unit beds, then O'Neal touched his elbow again as doctors and nurses started their examination.

"She's in good hands," she assured Dan.

"Great hands," Linc added. Then they all returned to the hallway of the rustic lodge.

Dan shouldn't have been surprised by any of it. After all, he had seen one of Renard's other wildly expensive mountaintop houses, but this one had the extra edge of being built in a wilderness, and probably a state and nationally protected wilderness at that. Remembering how many hoops he had to jump through just to renovate his workshop garage, Dan could hardly fathom how many hurdles Renard must have leaped to get this thing done. He remembered the ruin his workshop garage was now in, and that not only brought him back to the present; it reminded him that while he was Dan Morgan, Scott Renard was Scott Renard. Genius or money could overcome most anything, but genius *and* money could probably surpass everything.

O'Neal seemed to read his mind. "Took Scott decades to pull this place off. Some grateful high rankers had to look the other way, but the high rankers who replaced them don't even know it exists. We all want to keep it that way."

The four Zeta operatives turned a corner, stepped into the Fox Burrow main living space, and everything was forgotten for one stunning moment. The area was a gigantic triangle of stone fireplaces, wooden beams, and floor-to-ceiling, wall-to-wall windows displaying a glorious, even breathtaking view of the California coastline, the Pacific Ocean, and the King's Range Mountains that was not available to anyone else on the planet.

Dan had to mentally wrest his senses from the sight to stay on track. Helping was the feeling of Peter Conley's hand back on his shoulder once again.

"Yeah," Cougar whispered to him as he passed. "I had the same problem the first time I walked in here." Then Conley moved on to the center of the space, which had been subtly designed as a figurative and literal focal point.

Above what looked like a table made from an ancient redwood tree trunk was a holographic image of a turning Earth. On the other side, his face seen through the slowly revolving planet, was Scott Renard, wearing what had come to be known as the "Steve Jobs look"—black shirt and pants.

Seated beside him was Lily Randall, wearing the same things the other Zeta operatives wore. Seated opposite each other at the three and nine o'clock positions were men who weren't wearing the Zeta outfits. But they were men Dan recognized.

One was ex-military, nicknamed Hot Shot, and the other was the geek of all geeks known as Chilly. He made even Linc look like an investment banker. They were Renard's best hackers and dressed accordingly—Hot Shot in olive khaki t-shirt and pants, Chilly in shorts and a *Zootopia* t-shirt.

"Hey guys," Dan acknowledged them as he neared, but they didn't react in the slightest. They only had eyes and ears and fingers for their laptops.

Dan glanced at Linc, who met his gaze as he sat next to Karen at the one and two o'clock spots. He pursed his lips, lowered his eyes, and minutely shook his head in a "don't bother them" motion.

Dan noted his partner pulling out a chair at the seven o'clock spot, while motioning for him to try the five o'clock position. Again, Dan should not have been surprised that the chairs—which looked like they had been made from the same redwood—were extraordinarily comfortable.

With a single look at them all, he knew that he was back to being part of a true team. Not one leader and a bunch of subordinates. It was a group of eight leaders, all with their own specific areas of expertise.

"On the night of April twenty-sixth," Lily began, "an unprecedented attack was launched on our organization. An attack of extraordinary scope, whose purpose, apparently, was to effectively destroy Zeta in a single stroke." The young woman paused to look at the others. "In at least six instances, that attack failed."

Then she focused on Dan. "We'll fill you in on how we survived ..."

"We were at a Comic Con," Linc interjected. "As Link and Zelda."

Although O'Neal slapped Shepard on the arm again, Dan barked out a laugh—the first laugh he'd had in days, for which he was extremely grateful. He could just see them as the lovers from the beloved videogame *The Legend of Zelda*, as well as understand why any of the hateful, short-sighted, tunnel-visioned Anti-Zeta wouldn't have seen them.

To his pleasure, everyone, save Chilly and Hot Shot, laughed as well, although Dan thought he noticed the latter hacker give a small smirk ... but that might have been at something he saw on his screen.

Dan looked back to Lily as she spoke again, but before he did, he noticed the hackers' extraordinary rapid eye movement. Whatever the two were doing, it was intense and continual, explaining why they weren't reacting to anything else.

"Okay," Lily continued, "we'll fill you in on more of how we survived, but the rest of us know that already."

"Gotcha," Dan interrupted, then filled them in on everything that happened since he'd arrived at his house, which seemed a lifetime ago. He spoke with excruciating but exacting detail, so they could glean as much about their enemy as possible. He also couldn't help asking a question or two.

"I can't tell you how they did it," Scott Renard answered the first one. "I can only tell you how I would have."

Dan pushed himself away from the table to get a better view of the man. *This ought to be good,* he thought. It was.

"Knowledge is doubling every year," Renard explained. "For good and ill. The same research that went into developing, say, the Flying Fox aircraft or the medical advances we're using to help your daughter heal, is also being brought to bear on weapons of war. Where, just a few years ago, you'd need dozens of explosive devices to bring down a building the size of Zeta HQ, now the same might be accomplished with one device per floor, or even just one device …if you understand the building's structure."

"How do you mean?" Dan wondered.

"Well," Renard continued, "just like the human body, buildings have weak spots. A good, and terrible, example was the World Trade Center. Any layman watching couldn't understand why a building that tall, with just one hole at the top, would collapse entirely. That was why some were so certain it was an inside job—a conspiracy that involved dozens, if not hundreds of devices secretly planted throughout. Now, while the new World Trade Center can't be brought down by any one device short of a nuclear one, Zeta HQ might have been."

"Might?" Dan pounced on the word.

"Might," Randall interjected. "With the building already down, and the enemy still at large, it's difficult to collect the necessary intel to know for sure."

"Yeah, Dan," Conley drawled. "Your Serbian frenemy was pretty obviously recruited by whoever we're dealing with because she loves you so much." Dan grimaced, but Conley ignored the reaction and continued. "But we think the others always stay helmeted because if we saw their faces, we might recognize or identify them." He glanced at Lily. "Our guess is that they're loose cannons from all over the world …and probably some likely suspects we've worked with, or worked against, in the past—like Amina."

Conley turned toward Renard, who tapped the table, and Amina's revolving head appeared, floating in the air between them. Dan noted that it was pre-scarred Amina.

"Amina Novakovic," Lily said. "Five feet, seven inches tall, a hundred and twenty-eight pounds…"

"Of solid muscle," Dan interjected, making Conley chuckle once more.

"Born in 1987," Lily continued, "so she was four when the Croatian War of Independence started…"

Conley's smile disappeared. "Just in time for the atrocities between Croat and Serb," he said. "With the Muslims, and Amina, in the middle." He glanced at Dan. "A lot of anger and hate there …to be taken out, apparently, on anyone she can get her hands on."

"Lucky me." Dan looked at the others around the table. "I mean that. Luckily, I have some guardian angels who went way out of their way to find me. And speaking of that, what did you do to her and her buddies? In New Mexico, I mean."

Both Conley's and Renard's faces grew assured smiles.

"Oh, you mean what did Palecto do to them?" Conley replied, only to turn his head toward O'Neal. "You better explain, Karen," he said. "It's too much for this old gunslinger to fathom."

"D.E.W.," she said. "Morning dew." She looked at Dan apologetically for her self-aware play-on-words, then translated. "Directed Energy Weapon," she told Dan. "Uses invisible things we take for granted, like microwaves or particle beams, tightens them to their most powerful, and employs them as clubs or swords or whatever." She continued with satisfaction. "But we like to use sound."

"Okay," Dan interrupted, holding up his hands in surrender. "You're losing me."

Renard tapped, then slid his finger across the table top, and a video of military and law enforcement tests appeared in the air between them. Dan watched as test subjects and objects were damaged or knocked down by ...nothing he could see.

Dan cocked his head to the side. "Still lost."

"Okay, Danny boy," Conley chimed in. "Let me put it into words you might understand. Palecto took an anvil made up of solid sound, and dropped it on the Guardian MAX like it was an open accordion. Remember how it sunk and the top folded like a fan?" He waited until Dan agreed before continuing. "That's the sound of power."

Renard's forefinger tapped the videos off. "Yes," he said, "hard to fathom, but believe it or not, you're sitting in a great, and again, a terrible example." He motioned toward his hackers on either side of the table. "Though Fox Burrow is both visually and electronically camouflaged, and appears, on the surface, to rest in one of the most beautiful and secure locations in the country, it is, even now, being bombarded by digital attacks, as if every hacker from Afghanistan to Zanzibar has been given one assignment, and one assignment only."

He pointed at Dan Morgan.

"To get you."

Chapter 19

Before Dan could react, Conley, Randall, and O'Neal had a race to see who could stand up first. Cougar won, but Karen got the reason why out of her mouth quicker.

"Alex is awake."

The debriefing was adjourned just long enough for everyone—save Chilly and Hot Shot—to get to the intensive care unit. It then reconvened around Alex's bedside.

As they entered the bright, friendly environment designed in white with turquoise accents, they saw Alex sitting up in a sleek robotic bed, wearing a U-neck t-shirt of the same material they all wore, save Renard. Dan glanced at two computer tablets that flanked her—attached by medi-pads at her wrist, throat, forehead, and chest—before turning his full, smiling attention on her.

"Looking good, Hot Shot," he said with relief. That got a smile out of her.

"Looking hot, good shot." Cougar said, coming up behind Dan. That got a laugh out of her. Then the others gathered around for hugs and welcomes.

When she stepped back, Karen noticed that Linc looked like he'd been thinking about saying the same "looking hot" line before he was beaten to it. But they both knew that Cougar was really the only one who could've gotten away with it.

Meanwhile, Dan opened his mouth to say more to his daughter, but then his eyebrows rose and he snapped his head to face O'Neal.

"Hey, how did you know she was awake?"

Karen merely tapped her earlobe with a forefinger.

"What?" Dan complained. "You got new ear-comms?" He turned to Linc. "Toss me one."

The I.T. wiz looked sheepish. "Not that easy, Dan," he said apologetically. Alex proved she was fully awake by being way ahead of her father. "Zeta HQ was destroyed, remember?" she told him. She looked at all the over-the-cutting-edge equipment around her before returning her attention to him. "They probably got next-gen Fox-tech now, right?"

Lily smiled as her boyfriend approached Dan.

"We'll install one in both of you before you leave," Renard promised.

"Leave the mountain?" Dan wondered, not wanting to wait that long.

"Leave this room," Renard corrected. "Unlike the Zeta ear-comms, which I always considered bulky, the next-gen R-comm needs a short procedure to install." He waited a beat, then mentioned, "I didn't name it, by the way." He glanced at Lily, who by her proud expression, took the credit.

"Bulky?" Dan echoed. The last ear-comm they got looked like a flattened lima bean. "What does this R-comm look like?"

Linc gave Dan a sheepish look. "What can I say?" he conceded. "When he's right, he's right."

"The R-comm looks like nothing, Dan," Conley informed him, before reconsidering. "Actually, it might look like a blackhead ...if you put it under a microscope."

"But ...R-comm?" Dan echoed.

Renard's expression acknowledged it might not be the most elegant of names. "I wanted to call it 'Entendre,' which is French for 'Understand,'" he explained, "but marketing said no way. They came back with 'Extender,' which I thought sounded like a male enhancement drug, so..."

"So," Lily took up, "saner, more brand-conscious, heads prevailed."

Dan looked at the others. "So it does everything the ear-comms did?" he wondered aloud.

"And more," Lily added, in a softened tone that gave him the impression that she was trying to save an old man's sanity. "It also translates every major first world language..."

"And many of the second world ones," Linc interjected.

"...including multiple dialects of Mandarin, not to mention both the male and female idioms of Japanese." She looked up, literally and figuratively, to her boyfriend, Renard.

He smiled down at her, then turned his head back toward Dan. "It can be adjusted to any country you visit."

Dan's expression told them they were wise to approach it in the way they did. "What?" he said. "How does that work?"

The others looked to Renard, who continued. "They speak their language," he said, "you hear yours. Honestly, you'll have to experience it for yourself."

Dan was going to cut the conversation short before it degenerated into complete marketing speak, but then looked from Renard to Alex, and back again.

"Wait a minute. You hear a voice in your ear?"

"Dad..." Alex started.

"No, wait," he told his daughter, then turned back to Renard. "You hear someone else's voice in your ear?"

Renard put his hands up to signal patience. "While you were telling us your story in the salon," he explained, "I texted the physician to thoroughly check Alex for any sign of anything like the R-comm anywhere in her body."

He looked toward the head of the bed, to a tall woman in a lab coat who had a name tag that read "Dr. Whittaker." She shook her head "no."

Dan didn't bother trying to get details of the equipment used. He was already certain it would be way beyond him.

"I'll admit I'm as perplexed by Alex's inner voice as you were," Renard confessed. He held up an apologetic hand as Alex opened her mouth to remind them it wasn't an inner voice. "Please forgive me," Renard continued. "I meant to say Alex's advising voice. But, in any case, the science of nanorobotics is advancing faster than almost anything else, while, at the same time, it's far more secretive than anything else because of the weaponization potential. It's possible that technology could explain what she heard."

Dan didn't want to parrot unfamiliar words yet again, but couldn't help himself. "Nanorobotics?"

"The creation, and introduction into the human body, of absurdly small robots made of molecular components," Linc told him.

Dan rolled his eyes at his I.T. friend. "And you think that makes it clearer to me?"

Alex laughed, and put her hand on her father's arm. "Dad," she said warmly. "Remember when we saw that movie *Osmosis Jones* when I was a little girl?"

"Yeah," Dan replied. "I thought it sucked."

"It did suck," Alex agreed, "so you made me watch *Innerspace*, which didn't suck, and then *Fantastic Voyage*, which was cheesy but also didn't suck."

"Yeah," Dan said, more calmly. "I remember."

"Well," Alex concluded, "nanorobotics is like that, except real."

Dan looked to his daughter, then Renard, then the others. "Okay, okay," he said. "So she could have a little speaker inside her that someone can talk to her through?"

Even Linc looked skeptical, but he said. "It's possible, I suppose."

Dan threw his hands into the air. "Will someone give me something to shoot, please?"

Conley laughed, while Randall looked pensive, and Renard re-approached the field operative.

"Alex's voice could be from a microscopic speck anywhere in her body," he told him. "And manifest itself in such a way that it seems outside her ear..."

"Or from my subconscious guilt for not being there for Mom when she needed me most," Alex interrupted regretfully.

Dan turned to her. "If that were the case, young lady," he said with stern kindness, "then she sure as hell would be talking just outside *my* ear, not yours."

The others shuffled around, trying to figure out how best to assuage both their colleagues' consciences, but Renard took the lead.

"Look," he lectured them both, "the subconscious mind is an amazing thing, but I have yet to hear of one that is able to spy on approaching attackers...twice." He looked at the others. "Someone is ahead of us, but someone is also after us, and the sooner we deal with that, the better."

Turning from their expressions of agreement, Renard faced Alex. "As for your inner or outer voice, I can only advise one thing." He took a second to include Dan. "Listen. Listen carefully."

* * * *

The R-comm installation was as promised—short, and as sweet as Dr. Whittaker could make it.

As far as Dan was concerned, all she did was stick a thing that looked like a cross between a Q-tip and a tweezer into his audio canal, then stepped back so Scott Renard and Lily Randall could step forward.

Renard spoke in French. Dan heard it as a soothing rumble in the background, while in the foreground he heard, "The Guardian MAX was found. Or at least its charred skeleton."

"Behind an abandoned gas station in Pecos Village," Lily Randall told him in English as she stepped up. "Twenty-five miles west of Santa Fe."

Dan was impressed. He could hardly tell one of those was spoken in a foreign language.

"Now all I have to do is learn every language, and I'll be good to go," he said to Renard.

"I don't suppose Amina or any known wanted terrorist was also spotted in the area," he said to Randall.

Neither needed to answer. Instead, Renard sat on a wheeled stool and rolled between the two beds on which Alex and her father lay.

"Lily used an emergency device I had given her after her rescue from China," he explained, filling in some backstory the others knew, but the Morgans didn't. "She informed me of the assault on Zeta and the destruction of your HQ."

"'Informed,'" Lily scoffed. "Screeched like a crazy lady, more like."

Renard observed her coolly. "You were remarkably composed," he assured her. "Considering the situation."

"Where were you?" Dan inquired of her.

"Driving away," she said.

"I don't suppose a voice told you to get out?" Alex said.

"No such luck," she answered with a sympathetic smile.

"Plenty of such luck," Dan interjected, nodding toward Renard. "With friends like him, who needs fairy godmothers?"

Lily chuckled, looking gratefully at the billionaire, then sheepishly at Dan. "Yes," she concurred. "And, like you, by the time I got to my apartment, it had been firebombed."

"Which I had advised her not to return to," Renard said. "I instigated my own disaster protocol, sending Palecto to collect everyone it could."

"He even flew it in person," Lily interjected with a certain sense of appreciation. "Usually, he does it from wherever he is," she told Alex. "By remote control." She looked to Dan. "That's how he got you out of New Mexico."

"I begged him to let me give it a try," Conley called from the far wall. "But he said, 'maybe next time.'" He stared at the tech master. "I'm holding you to that, Foxy."

Renard nodded, then shook his head, as if he couldn't decide which tack to take. "It's a glorified drone," he contended modestly.

"So you collected Lily, Linc, Karen, and Peter?" Alex asked, getting them back to the matter at hand.

Renard chuckled. "Not Mr. Conley," he revealed, looking over at where the man in question leaned against a med-cabinet.

"Cougar's got his own disaster protocol," Dan informed his daughter. "It's hard to destroy a home that can't be found."

"Yeah," Conley chimed in. "But as soon as the Zeta ear-comm started screeching, I started trashing stuff and headed west."

"We found him at the house where we first met," Renard explained, looking at the lanky pilot in admiration. "*Inside* the house, with his SubSonex personal jet in the driveway."

"That was fun," Conley remembered. "Getting there, and getting inside." He grinned at his partner. "No lasers, needles, or air cannons for me, Cobra."

Dan looked back at their benefactors, and noticed that Lily was affixing him with a serious, even somber stare.

"Kirby and big boss Bloch are still in the wind," she told him.

"Diana Bloch may be still in the wind," Dan Morgan replied. "But she is *not* the big boss. Remember?"

Dan's words sank into everyone present like honey into hot tea, and as if by a cue whispered into their ear by a mother's voice, they all started moving.

Chapter 20

As much as Alex wanted to hop out of bed and go with them, Dr. Whittaker made her see reason and remain resting—the best, but not the easiest, thing to do.

Dan left a little paternal and personal concern behind with her, but then focused forward, following Renard, Randall, Shepard, and O'Neal. Conley, not surprisingly, covered the rear in general—and Dan's rear specifically—as the parade passed by the table, fireplace, and windows into a space that was as futuristic as the salon was rustic.

Dan stopped short, forcing Conley to bump into him before sidling by.

"Yeah," he drawled into Dan's ear as he passed. "Had the same reaction the first time I came into this room too."

As the others spread out a bit, Dan endeavored to take it all in. Although no one had opened or shut a door, going from one room to the other was like stepping from noon to midnight. Somehow, even the light that was beaming into the salon stopped dead at the entry to this space.

From Dan's perspective, it felt and looked like going from Renard's heart to his brain. While the salon was designed to be as welcoming and comfortable as possible, with all the senses engaged, this control center was seemingly designed as a sensory deprivation tank, only with the water replaced by data.

It was illuminated by subtle recessed lighting as well as at least two dozen monitor screens of various sizes expertly placed around the ovoid room. It was shaped similarly to the Palecto's interior, but while the Flying Fox's resting place seemed like a womb, this seemed like a black hole. Even the monitor screens seemed muted.

As Dan took a step further into the space, he noted that no matter where he looked, his eyes were captured by a specific section of screens, allowing whatever was on those screens to share, support and monopolize a specific subject, be it news, sports, entertainment, communication, or surveillance. It was confusing, constantly changing chaos to Dan's eyes, but not, apparently, to anyone else's. While Conley went to a small spot at the exact opposite of the entryway, the others moved to spots that seemed to be reserved for them. They settled into them, standing, leaning, or sitting with content comfort.

"Cobra," Lily called softly to him.

Dan looked from the void to where she stood on one side of a large central screen. She motioned for him to approach, and as he did, Renard's head seemed to appear on the other side of the screen. His black clothing had all but disappeared into the rest of the room.

"You were right," Lily told Dan. "Diana may be our boss, but, to paraphrase ex-President Truman, the buck doesn't stop there."

Dan kept himself from twitching as a third head appeared between Randall and Renard—a floating head of a thin man with thick, swept-back hair, whose expression mingled serenity, strength, sardonicism, and a certain slyness. It was a head that seemed as real as either of the others in the eerie light.

It was a face Dan recognized. It was the head of the man he and all the others knew only as Mr. Smith. Originally, he was known to the Zeta operatives as the man who had recruited them to the organization. But as time—and trouble—went on, it became pretty apparent that he was more than just a secret agent scout. Much more.

Now they all accepted that he was the literal and figurative figure head of the Aegis Initiative—an organization that had turned out to finance Zeta and, as Dan suspected, had its fingers in all sorts of international pies.

Everything was a conglomerate these days, Dan thought annoyingly. *A conglomerate that lived by the golden rule: he who has the gold makes the rules.* It had also become obvious that when push came to shove, Mr. Smith called the shots at Zeta.

Dan had never been completely happy about that. If he was to be under anyone's thumb, he wanted it to be just one thumb. It was bad enough that Paul Kirby was trying to wrest control, without two more leaders in line to muddy the waters.

At Zeta, Mr. Smith's rule was law. But this wasn't Zeta.

"You'll never guess what his first name is," Dan heard Conley comment from the far wall.

Dan's eyes were as narrow as his smile was thin. "John," he surmised. Conley cocked his head to the side with a bemused smirk. "Right the first time."

"And wrong," Renard added, sharing a glance with Randall, who gave him a look that said *"pray, continue,"* as well as communicating her gratitude that she didn't have to be the one who spilled Zeta secrets. As Renard's fingers tapped into the darkness below the floating face, Smith's head turned in place.

"He's had at least three names that we're aware of," Renard mused. "Maybe four."

"Or more," Linc interjected, more than happy to spill what were once secrets.

"We can only guess at his childhood and family," Renard continued, "but the first time we were able to spot him in history, despite remarkable efforts to avoid detection, was as Thaddeus Jeffries, a linguistics fellow at Middlebury College in Vermont."

Smith's head winked out, replaced by a grainy, blown up college yearbook photo showing a tall, thin, thick-haired person seemingly in mid-move, as if trying to get his face behind another student's face in front of him.

"The next time we found evidence of him," Renard continued, "was when he was a forensic accountant by the name of Warren Pendleton at the Advanced Intercept and Recovery Company in New Haven, Connecticut."

The yearbook photo was replaced by a newspaper crime scene photo digitally focusing on a tall, thin, thick-haired man in a three-piece suit behind two cops talking to two plain clothed detectives. The man had his head down and was studiously looking into a wallet.

"Advanced Intercept and Recovery?" Dan echoed.

"Private investigation company," Renard elaborated, nodding at the floating picture. "Pendleton, aka Smith, was looking through a corpse's billfold for clues. Apparently his ability to, as they say, 'follow the money,' was unparalleled."

"We assume this was about the time he decided to streamline and simplify his pseudonym," O'Neal added from her position at a computer screen next to Linc. "Thaddeus and Warren could be a lot more easily found than Smith, who could weave in and out of engineering, mathematics, scientific research, history studies, statistics, engineering, and entrepreneurial positions like smoke."

Dan made a doubtful noise. "I think I'd remember John Smith more than Jeffries and Pendleton."

"Yeah," Conley concurred, "but that's you, Dan. I don't think you're what anyone would call normal."

It was meant as a compliment, and Dan took it as such before turning back to Lily. "You think he did all that?"

"Looks like it," she answered.

"And probably more," O'Neal chipped in. "Near as we can tell, he only stayed at any one position until he got so good at it that he made himself indispensable. Then he was gone." She stared at her screen. "Usually no more than eighteen months."

Dan gave out a low whistle as Renard took the story back again, illustrating Smith's bio with incriminating photos as he went along.

"As we got closer to the twenty-first century, the man now known as John Smith seemed to focus his intentions, moving more and more into corporate and government finance. He seemed intent on trying to remain as anonymous as possible until word of his expertise became too widespread. He stepped into the edge of the spotlight as a personal consultant."

A business card appeared in mid-air in front of Dan's face, as if an invisible hand were holding it up to him. On it were five simple letters, S-M-I-T-H, and a series of numbers he couldn't identify.

"What is that?" he wondered aloud. "It's not a phone number or address."

"That's the beautiful cunning of it," Linc enthused from his screen. "Apparently each card that was bestowed had to be deciphered. Break the code and you could contact him ...or he would contact you."

"That one's longitude and latitude," Conley explained from his vantage point. "Show up at the spot, and you get access."

Dan restudied the card. "But there's no time designated."

Conley grinned. "Turns out you could show up anytime ...except one second too late. That was when the great and glorious Smith would decide you had taken too long or were trying to bend him to your own will. In either case, you weren't smart enough to deserve an audience with the wizard of Oz."

"The guy's got style," Dan muttered. "I'll give him that." He turned back toward Lily. "How did you get all this? I got nothing every time I tried checking him out."

Lily looked, in turn, to Karen. Karen looked up at Dan. "Algorithms."

Dan threw up his hands. "Of course." The science nerd had tried explaining them to him during what had turned out to be Zeta's last b.e. mission—Before Explosion. "Data tattling on other data, right?"

Karen smiled on the unique Dan-view of the extremely complex situation. She opened her mouth to go into even more detail on the advances she,

Linc, and now Renard had developed since last time, but then her eyes sparkled and her mouth closed.

"So now we know," Dan summarized. "Mr. Smith is not Mr. Smith, or maybe he is, but whether he is or isn't, how does that get us any closer to whatever or whoever attacked Zeta HQ?"

Lily Randall stepped up. "Our immediate superiors are still in the wind, Cobra," she reminded him. "We can't find Diana Bloch. Believe me, we've tried. But I think we can find S-M-I-T-H."

She looked back at Renard, who said, "Chilly. Got a sec?"

The burly, bespectacled, bearded hacker entered the room. Dan's face showed some concern as he passed him.

"Won't Hot Shot need you if the invisible assault is as bad as your boss said?"

Chilly moved coolly past Dan. "Nah," he said casually. "Not for a bit."

Linc snorted, but when no one else joined in, he elaborated. "Get it? Bit? Abbreviation for 'binary digit.' Get it?"

Karen rolled her eyes affectionately. "Nerd humor," she told the others. "Ignore him."

By that time Chilly had reached his boss's side. He was apparently used to the way Renard's dark clothes blended with the data room.

"Mr. Morgan makes a valid point, Chilly," Renard said in the company's way of communicating "at ease."

Chilly cocked his head and shrugged. "We've gotten ahead of the attack curve and made some dead bugs, Trojan horses, byte backs, malware mirrors, web worms, cache twenty-twos, and an ABEND algorithm that should hold them for"—Chilly checked his watch—"a half-hour or so before we have to update and counter any attempts at superseding or infiltrating the code." He met Dan's eyes. "Besides, Hot Shot'll signal if he needs back-up,"

Most of the rest of the agents reacted as if the hacker had been speaking Swahili, but Linc was laughing so hard he had tears in his eyes. "ABEND," he chortled at O'Neal. "Get it? The old IBM error message? Abnormal end? Oh man, that's good."

"Yes, yes, Linc, I get it," she whispered to him. "It was good. Now shut up and listen, okay?" O'Neal was happy he hadn't gotten into a monologue deciphering all of Chilly's hacker wordplay about bugs, bytes, malware, worms, caches, and even the term "back-up"—although even she had to admit they were all pretty darn clever.

"Good," Renard told Chilly. "While you were doing that, we've been trying to track down this Mr. Smith. Got anything?"

Spoken like a true cue, Dan thought.

Chilly considered the question for a second, then spoke up. "Yeah, I think so."

Linc, although he admired the Renard hackers and truly appreciated Chilly's pun-laden update, had still always harbored envy. "Hey, if we've been breaking our bones trying to find Bloch and Smith, what makes you think you can do it?"

Chilly turned his impassive, calm blue eyes on the I.T. guy. "Because he sent us a card, man."

"What?" Linc exclaimed, leaping to his feet. "What card?"

Chilly moved the fingers of his left hand in the air and they watched as a net of data fell over them. They all stood in it like hikers lost in a Himalayan sleet storm, but then Chilly started shaping it with his right hand's fingers. One by one, pieces of data dropped, flew, flicked, or condensed away until a roughly rectangular pattern took shape.

Renard's smile got wider and wider as his eyes got brighter. "Oh, the clever devil," he breathed. He turned his smile onto Randall. "And here we thought *we* were so smart. But I don't think we found anything that he didn't want us to find."

"Of course," Randall realized, before looking at the others while the data continued to winnow and fluctuate. "He wouldn't try reaching out to us with any of Zeta's clearly compromised contact routes. If he wanted to drop us a clue, it would be through outside sources."

As Dan watched with ignorant fascination, he couldn't help but wonder. "But why him? Why not Diana? Why didn't she try?"

"Maybe she did," Lily answered without taking her eyes off the changing, shifting data. It was like watching Michelangelo chipping away at a block of stone until all that was left was his most famous sculpture. "Maybe we were too stupid to find it."

"Or maybe," Karen suggested, "the Zeta communication channels were too corrupted to allow any messages out."

Dan noticed how she, as well as all the others—including himself—scrupulously avoided even mentioning the most obvious possible reason Diana Bloch didn't get a message to them: that she was dead. But then he stopped thinking about anything except the card that was taking its final shape before their eyes. Even he, with his self-admitted Paleolithic approach to modern technology, knew that this process was staggeringly complex and involved billions of seemingly disparate pieces of information.

To his surprise and Linc's delight, they all heard a small pinging sound when it was done.

Floating in front of their faces, somehow, was a card that was a virtual twin to the one that had been there just a few minutes before. Only this one had five different letters and seventeen different numbers.

"Is that even English?" Dan wondered, concentrating on the letters.

"Nope," Linc said, who had come over from his screen to stare at the floating data as if they were dancing gems. "Definitely not."

Dan looked at the others with impatience. He couldn't help but feel time slipping out of his grasp. And the more time passed, the more powerful their enemies became …and the farther the people who had destroyed his home could run.

"What now?" he demanded. "Are we back at square one?"

"Definitely not," repeated Renard, who had joined Linc and Chilly to stand in a triangle around the floating card. He, like them, seemed mesmerized by the genius it took to pull this off.

Dan wasn't mesmerized. "So, what do we do?"

Cobra's question managed to distract Renard, who turned to smile with revelation at the operative. "Do?" he echoed. "We do what Mr. Smith would want us to do."

Dan thought Renard would tell him, but when, like some people who know too much, he didn't, Dan asked the obvious with barely controlled anger.

"And what is that?"

Renard's reply was so blissful, even Lily had to wonder if he wasn't stoned.

"Why, follow the money, of course."

Chapter 21

"You okay?" Conley asked, rousing Dan from his stupor. He raised his head, blinked, and tried to stay awake as the others kept working on translating the card.

First they tried to figure out what language it was in, and, since the planet Earth has more than seven thousand languages—many more if you include dead ones—that wasn't as easy as it sounded.

Renard narrowed it down to a mere three thousand by figuring Smith would want the most indecipherable language, especially to Americans. That sent the search to Asia, but just when Dan thought they were getting somewhere, Linc spoiled the party.

"Papua New Guinea alone has more than eight hundred languages," he informed Dan.

So the search continued. Dan admitted he was not helping by glaring at the I.T. experts, so he joined the rest of the team in the salon, where they were trying to formulate a plan of attack. At least stepping out of the control room, back into the literal and figurative light, made Dan feel better.

"Once we have a location," Lily said, "we'll go in and fan out…"

"Nope," Conley said casually, beating Dan to the punch.

"What do you mean, 'nope'?" she demanded as Conley looked at Dan—like a jazz musician handing off a solo to the drummer.

"With Bloch still M.I.A.," Dan told the redhead, "we need someone in control. Someone not at risk in the field." He saw that Lily was already accepting the logic of his statement, but he finished the thought just in case. "Let us go in," he said, motioning to himself and Conley, "while you handle the big picture."

She couldn't argue with that, so, as she brainstormed with O'Neal about every possible contingency, Cobra and Conley walked across the room.

On the way, they passed Hot Shot, who was still communing with his lap top while all ten fingers seemed to be jitterbugging on the keyboard of their own accord. Dan glanced at the computer screen, half-hoping to see a videogame of solitaire, but he was happily disappointed to see it was still all digital gobbledygook.

The two field ops entered the mansion hallway shoulder-to-shoulder.

"Where are you going?" Dan asked his partner.

"Prepping the Flying Fox so that when immediate departure becomes imperative," Conley answered smoothly, "immediate departure will be possible."

Dan thought about asking for details, but then accepted he really didn't care. That was how much faith he had in his friend. If the thing needed beagle blood to fly, then Cougar would have it filled with beagle blood by the time Dan got back.

So, instead of asking stupid questions, he peeled off once they started passing the I.C.U.

Alex was sitting up, but she was still in the recovery bed, with Dr. Whittaker keeping a calm, friendly, watchful eye nearby. His daughter hadn't exactly perked up when Dan walked in. In fact, he seemed to have interrupted some sort of internal discussion she was having with herself. If he knew her, himself, and the entire Morgan family, it was probably centered around the "to get up and report for duty or not to get up and report for duty" conundrum.

He let her continue as he pulled up an ergonomic chair designed to match the futuristic bed and the rest of the fixtures and sat beside her. They both stayed quiet as he tried to figure out the best way to tell her that he was probably leaving very soon and that, given the situation, she shouldn't go with him.

As he opened his mouth, she turned her head to face him, and had beaten him to it.

"Bon voyage," she said.

That surprised him. "What?"

She pointed at her ear. "R-comm," she explained. She then motioned at Whittaker. "The doctor gave me one too." The tall, dark blonde physician gave Dan a small, waving, smiling acknowledgement. "Just in time for me to hear about Smith's calling card."

"Yeah," Dan replied. "About that..."

"Good hunting," she interrupted. "Nothing I'd like better than to have your back, but I don't want you worrying about whether I have a concussion or not." Before he replied to that, she muttered, "and I don't want to be worried about that either."

Again, he opened his mouth to comment, assuage, commiserate, sympathize, or something, but then Linc's voice appeared in both father and daughter's ears. And just their luck, the I.T. wiz was affecting a pretty bad English accent.

"By George, I think we've got it."

Both father and daughter imagined O'Neal slapping Shepard on the arm again.

Dan got up, putting a reassuring hand on his daughter's shoulder. "I promise you one thing," he told her, annoyed at having to rush the declaration. "I'll get the ones who killed ...destroyed our home."

The flickering of Alex's eyes clued him in that she hadn't missed his sudden decision to change the direction of his accusation. Neither of them was ready to accept the possibility that Jenny had been in the house when it exploded.

Feeling frustrated and awkward about the bobbling of his promise, Dan headed back to the I.C.U. door. "No matter what," he concluded, then double-timed it back to the control room.

He reentered the darkness to find Chilly, Renard, and Shepard—the latter looking like a cat who had eaten an entire pet store of canaries.

"What?" Dan all but spat at them.

The others deferred to Linc, since he had apparently been the one who had found the key. "Like I told you," he began, "Asia has thousands of languages, but we were concentrating on Japan, because it's an agglutinative, mora-timed language with a lexically significant pitch-accent. But we decided that was too obvious for anyone as cunning as your Smith guy."

Linc took a micro-second to breathe, then plunged back into his spiel. "Yeah, so which language wouldn't be as obvious? Not Chinese. That would be way too obvious, no matter how many dozens or even hundreds of dialects there are. Well, how about one that has a pre-historic dialect, a four-tongued historical dialect, and a present-day five-tongued dialect with a full fifty-seven variants...?"

"Cut to the chase!" Dan bellowed.

Linc had reacted as if Dan had slapped him in the face with a fish. "Taiwan," he had blurted.

Dan had been expecting Linc to apologize or defend or allude to the various science-fantasy languages he had learned or developed for his card and video game playing friends, so when the man had instead burped up the result. Dan tried to comprehend it.

"Taiwan?" he repeated.

Before Linc, Chilly, or even Renard could respond, they all heard Conley's voice in their R-comms.

"Ready for takeoff when you are."

* * * *

"The Taiwanese language is so complex and evolving, every generation sometimes can't understand the previous one," Linc informed Dan on the way to the Flying Fox's arrival and departure bay. "There's even one form that is entirely poetry, like Shakespeare, but so complicated from so many perspectives that some poets can't understand the beginning of their epic poems by the time they finish. *That's* the one Smith used."

Dan stopped in his tracks to pinion Linc with a suspicious glare. "So how did you know it?"

Linc had the decency to blush. "Because it's the one they use in Taiwan's major contribution to world pop culture," Linc had confessed. "Their centuries-long puppet theater, movies, and TV shows."

"Of course," Dan responded, throwing up his hands as Renard had caught up to them, and put his arm around the I.T. man's shoulder.

"Does Mr. Smith know his audience or what?" the tech billionaire enthused. "How many people who are gunning for us do you think would know about a Taiwanese puppet show language?"

Dan chuckled despite the seriousness of the situation. He had to admit that the only plain sight this could have been hidden in was Linc's. Dan, too, then clapped Linc on the shoulder, eliciting a thankful smile from the I.T. guy.

As the trio entered the aircraft bay, they found the rest of the team waiting for them, even Chilly and Hot Shot—although the latter had tablets near at hand. As Linc went to accept congratulations from his fellow Zetas, Renard laid a hand on Dan's arm, signaling for him to hold back for a private tête-à-tête.

"I'm fairly certain you were shielded from the people who are chasing you when you stepped into Palecto," Renard reminded him. "That protection continued, even doubled, as soon as you landed here."

"Fairly certain?" Dan asked.

"As certain as I can be," Renard admitted.

Then that was probably fairly certain indeed, Dan thought.

"But once you leave here or disembark from Palecto…," Renard started.

"All bets are off?"

"No, all bets are *not* off," Renard retorted, pointing at Dan's right ear. "The R-comm will keep you securely in touch, but be advised that it also includes a new facial recognition software scrambler that should keep you safe from even the most advanced surveillance systems."

"Should?" Dan pounced on the word.

"Remember my speech about knowledge doubling every year?" Renard replied. "I was being modest. By the time you arrive in Taiwan, it could be doubling every fortnight—especially in that region. Every time we try to predict what China and Japan can do, by the time we decide, they've already done it." Renard shook his head, giving time for Lily to approach.

"But don't worry about all the cloaking devices we'll keep giving you," she suggested, walking with them toward the Flying Fox. "Worry about why they're still looking for you. We sure are."

Dan exhaled with a grim grin. "It's okay, temp-boss lady," he assured her. "They shouldn't worry about looking for me. They should worry about what'll happen to them when they find me."

Renard and Randall exchanged an intrigued, curious look as Alex approached, accompanied, as always, by Dr. Whittaker, just to be on the safe side. A good sign was that Alex was wearing the newly de rigueur Zeta outfit of shirt, pants, jacket, and boots.

The daughter leaned on her father and whispered. "You find Smith. I'll find Bloch."

The two Morgans looked at each other with complete trust, care, and conviction; then Dan made his other farewells and boarded.

* * * *

The takeoff was smooth and, within the ship, as silent as ever.

Dan stretched out in his seat. "What's our ETA?"

"You've got a good twelve hours," Conley assured him. "Raid the ice-box, double check the ordnance I chose, and maybe even get some shut-eye. I got a funny feeling you'll need it."

The weight of the last few days climbed onto Dan's back like the entire cast of a German opera.

"Good idea," he sighed, stood, and headed for a dream-cap. He had only gone two steps, however, before he stopped and turned back to Conley.

"What about you?" Dan asked him. "Want me to spell you awhile?" Conley looked at his partner with an incredulous expression. "Yeah, I want you to spell me, 'cause I'm fully committed to crashing this baby into the South China Sea. Wow, you really are tired, aren't you?" Conley laughed at Dan's muzzy expression, then waved him away. "No, really, Cobra, sweet dreams. You wouldn't believe the auto-pilot on this thing."

Dan took another step, but stopped again when everything he had survived since turning the corner of his home street fast-forwarded through his brain. "Really?" he asked Conley.

Conley turned, his expression changing from concern to sympathy. He was sorry to admit to himself he knew exactly how Cobra felt. "If you wake up to find my head has exploded," he assured his partner, "then you'll know, won't you? Now go to sleep and dream of the fragrant island."

Chapter 22

The first attack occurred two hours, thirty-seven minutes, and twenty-two seconds after Dan Morgan had exited the Flying Fox.

Prior to that, he had gotten a lovely nap, an invigorating cleaning, a swell meal, and enough intel on Taiwan from Randall, Renard, and O'Neal—whom Conley referred to as "the Law Offices of..."—to fill his head to the bursting point.

What Dan had retained from the barrage was that "the fragrant island" was actually the nickname—or maybe the translation—of Formosa, which was what the ninety-mile wide, two hundred and fifty-mile long island had been called before 1895, or maybe 1912, when the constant squabbling between China's Qing Dynasty and Japan had settled.

Even Dan knew that the Chinese squabbling was still going on, although the Japanese squabbling had effectively ceased in 1945. O'Neal let him know that the aboriginals, who had been on the island for thousands of years, had no say in anything, despite the fact that about five hundred thousand remained in a general population of around twenty-four million.

Dan had tuned out around then, letting the flow of facts and statistics wash over him, until he'd tuned in again when he heard information that had something to do with him.

"We're having Cougar drop you off in the middle of a coconut palm jungle between the Eluanbi Lighthouse, the Kenting Meteorological Radar Observatory, and Kenting National Park," Lily Randall informed him. "If he handles the landing just right..."

"I'll handle the landing just right," Dan heard Conley mutter. "Don't you worry your pretty little heads about that."

"...you should be unobserved."

There was that pesky word "should" again.

"It's the Taiwanese equivalent of the King Range Mountains' Lost Coast," Renard added. "From there," Randall continued, "make your way to Pingtung County, Hengchun Township. We'll have a local op rendezvous with you."

An unusual silence followed that statement. Dan waited a full five seconds before inquiring further.

"Do I get a name, description, or specific location?" He was distracted by the way Cougar's shoulders were hopping, as if he were silently laughing. Then he realized why. "You don't know who the local is yet, do you?"

Dan let his own silence linger as he accepted, considering the situation, that this was the best anyone, including himself, could do.

"We're not sure any Zeta-friendly, truly trustworthy contacts remain in the country," Randall slowly related. "We've been reaching out as best we can since you left, but so far..."

"I've even been scouring my staff in the region," Renard interjected, inspiring Dan to remember that, amongst all the other intel they had pelted him with, Taiwan was a hub for computer research, development, and manufacturing. "But I want to make sure whoever I ask is capable of facing the kind of danger this will no doubt entail."

Dan opened his mouth to suggest the tech boss forget it, but then closed it again. Given the situation, he really didn't have time to create a contact of his own. Better someone than no one, but if he had to go in solo and mostly blind, he would.

"Unfortunately I have my own assignment, Cobra," Conley said. Dan was tempted, but knew he would never ask Cougar what it was. But Cougar would also never leave his partner hanging. "I'll be putting our Peking Ducks in a row," he murmured mysteriously before returning his full attention to the landing.

"As soon as we secure and vet a contact, we'll let you know," Randall assured him.

"No worries, Cobra," a distracted O'Neal chimed in. Dan guessed it was she and Linc who were doing most of the securing and vetting. "We're getting close. The timing should be perfect. By the time you get to the meeting point, the sun will probably be up and your contact should be arriving."

Before Dan could ask the meeting point location, Conley interrupted.

"Drop your socks and grab your Glocks," he cut in. "Time's up. We're landing."

Everyone, Dan included, was grateful for the interruption in the rain of new "shoulds."

The complexity and finesse of the landing were incredible. Conley had to swoop out of the sky over the South China Sea, with a minimum of sight time, and get in so low and so fast over the top of the jungle's coconut palms that even the tropical birds might have thought they imagined it. Then he had to precisely place the Flying Fox just over a clearing amongst a copse of perfectly shaped trees that the on-board computer had found. But Dan had expected nothing less.

"Take a walk," Cougar said to his partner and passenger. "Say hello to your contact for me." The sardonic smile on his face reminded Dan that they had both been through worse.

Not much worse, Dan thought as he grabbed the dark gray backpack Renard had designed, and headed for the hatch, *but worse...maybe*.

Dan had already slathered himself in a Renard-approved combination sun and insect repellant, because Linc had informed him that the dengue fever-carrying mosquitoes were as big as wasps and the wasps were as big as hummingbirds. He grabbed the handle of a special corded wire just inside the hatch door, and hopped out. The corded wire was elastic and designed for this kind of exit.

It lowered Dan down like he was a floating aerialist at a circus, then stopped him just an inch from the ground. Palecto had already measured the distance and programmed the cord before Dan had touched it. Dan let go, and the corded wire rolled back up, and then into its slot by the door, like a self-retracting metal tape measure.

Dan stood in his dark gray t-shirt, pants, boots, and jacket, waited, and watched as the Flying Fox shot straight up into the nearest cloud almost as fast as he could blink. It may have started northwest after that, but Dan wasn't sure.

The temperature was comfortably warm, and so far he had arrived on one of the fifteen non-rainy days of the month. Dan took a second to look at the coconut palms, evergreen laurels, Chinese cryptocaryas, and Japanese blue oaks before Linc spoke in his ear.

"Turn left around twenty-five degrees...nope, too far...Yup, that's it. Walk forward."

* * * *

Taiwan was brown and green and gray and about as rocky and hilly as a country bisected by a mountain range and mostly covered with forested peaks could be. But as Dan entered his second hour of walking, he began to see populated life at the end of the arboraceous, vertiginous tunnel. Off in the distance, he thought he could see a few twinkling lights, but as much as he wanted to check them out, his inner Linc kept him moving southwest.

"Just another mile or so," he said, "and you should start skirting some fishing villages."

Sure enough, about fifteen minutes later, Dan took his first step onto something other than grass and ground. It was a cracked concrete path that had seen plenty of use in its time.

"Know who I'm meeting yet?" he murmured, careful to keep his lips as still as possible in case he was being watched.

"It's tricky," O'Neal said tiredly. "We want our friends to hear us, but not our enemies. We think the word has got out to the right sources, but so far, no definite replies."

"But you're in the rendezvous area," Randall advised him. "Only a few miles from Coastal Highway One-Fifty-Three, so explore. Act like a tourist."

That was easy. As soon as Randall finished talking, Dan turned a corner on the path, and saw, stretching out below him to the coast, a small, quaint, cove village of well-built pine, bamboo, and concrete structures nestled around a simple one-lane circular pathway. It was still early, but he could see two men with nets and one with a spear heading for the lone dock.

From his vantage point, Dan could see that all activity seemed to encircle a stone, cement, and wood structure closest to the concrete wall separating the village from a splotch of a beach. Hefting his knapsack, he headed in that direction.

As he neared, a five year-old girl and her dog noticed him, but if they found it odd that an American had appeared out of the jungle this early in the morning, they didn't show it. As he continued toward the central structure, they went back to studying what appeared to be an abandoned shedded snake skin. Dan had seen birds and even squirrels on his walk, but thankfully no snakes, boars, bears, or monkeys, all of which the country apparently had in abundance.

As Dan got closer, the wind off the ocean gave him a refreshing spray. He stopped and appreciated it. When he opened his eyes again, he saw three young ladies and one old woman emerging from a door at the back of the main building. They all fanned out across a concrete patio. The three young women wore loose dark pants and sandals with roomy white shirts and carried fishing poles. The older woman wore an old sleeveless muumuu.

As the old woman began pulling plastic tables and chairs away from the far wall at the rear of the patio, the young women headed for the beach, looking Dan over. As they passed him, he could see them start to talk and laugh amongst themselves, doing everything but pointing at him. Well, at least somebody acknowledged his existence. As before, he decided to take the chattering as a compliment.

He watched as the young women spread out across the small, narrow, beach. One took a position on the far right, another on the far left, and the third in the middle. They all cast off and started fishing as if they had done this a hundred, or even a thousand, times before. Dan only turned when he heard a hoarse voice behind him, and then a quieter voice in his ear.

"You hungry? Want to eat?"

Dan turned to see the old woman beckoning to him from the edge of the patio. Although Palecto had given him a pretty spectacular Denver omelet, that had been some time before his hike through the coconut palms. He opened his mouth to say "sure, why not," but closed it when he remembered that the old woman didn't have a translating R-comm. At least, he certainly didn't think so. He smiled instead, hoping the repast would fill the time until someone—anyone—contacted him.

The old woman gave him some guava juice and then what she—and the R-comm—called high mountain tea. When it came time to order the main meal, she had brought out a well-worn piece of plastic with various fishes pictured on it.

She pointed at the first one, and looked at him with expectation. Dan just looked back in confusion. She pointed at the second one, then looked at him again. Again he hesitated. She pointed at a third fish, but instead of looking at him, turned and pointed at one of the young women. Dan got it.

Fish for breakfast? he wondered. But then he felt the crisp, salty air again, saw the blue waves, and appreciated the style of the young women.

Well, at least it would be fresh, he thought. *When in Taiwan*, he supposed, *do what the Taiwanese do.*

He pointed at the second fish without even knowing what it was. Within twenty minutes, the milkfish was caught, steamed, and on a plastic plate in front of him. It, like the juice and tea, was delicious—when Dan could get a piece of it into his mouth without bones.

In fact, everything was fine until two hours, thirty-five minutes, and three seconds had passed since his entry into the jungle. That was when the two men with their nets, and the one with the spear, returned from the dock.

So soon? Dan thought. *They couldn't have caught their fill for the day.*

As the trio casually approached the restaurant, Dan pushed the plastic chair back from the plastic table, which made a squeaking, juddering sound. He remained seated until one of the net men, wearing a worn t-shirt and shorts, came up the left side of the patio, while the other, wearing a bathing suit, came up the right. The third one, the spearman, wearing a wetsuit, asked the old woman something with forced camaraderie.

"Need any more fish for today?" the R-comm translated for Dan.

But it wasn't the words that made Dan stand up. It was the old woman's reaction. She looked at the spearman with disdain bordering on anger, while her eyes held not a shred of respect.

That was all Dan needed to know, already feeling the juice, tea, and fish begin to boil in his gut. His timing was terrible. He had waited too long. Even at his best, he couldn't take all three down before they used their weapons. And as they kept sidling toward him, he recognized something else in their eyes. It was the same thing he had seen in the eyes of the waitress and busboy back in New Mexico.

I have got *to stop going to Chinese restaurants*, he thought as he went for his Walther.

But, as he feared, the one closest to him threw his net, and, just Dan's luck, the man threw it perfectly. The surprisingly heavy clinging web slammed onto him, throwing off his aim and sending him staggering back. He spun, throwing up his free arm, and managed to avoid getting ensnared.

Okay, his mind barked, *he's without his immediate weapon. Take him down, or shift aim to one who still has their weapon?* The nets were bad, but the spear was worse. His arm shifted toward the third man, but as that guy ducked down, the second one threw his net, and the first, now net-less one, charged Dan.

These guys were fast. The PPK bullet just grazed the spearman's slicked-back black hair, but it succeeded in getting the attention of the little girl, her dog, and the fisher women. They watched as the second net slammed into Dan a blink before the first man did.

This time the net went completely over him, and the first man was on top of him. The only thing that kept Dan upright was the fact that he was much bigger, taller, and more muscular than the attacker. Even so, he staggered back while the table, high mountain tea, and milkfish went everywhere.

Dan lucked out. His feet hit a dry spot on the cement floor. The attacker wasn't so lucky. He slipped and went down. He tried to take Dan with him, but the Zeta op's luck held as the attacker's fingers hooked only the net, going some distance at pulling the thing off Dan, who did the rest, hurling it atop the attacker as he shifted just in time for the second man to leap onto him like a splayed starfish.

This man had more of a head start than the first, so despite not being as tall and strong as Dan, his weight was enough to bring them both down onto the cement floor. Dan had learned as well as anyone how to fall without hurting himself, but the man's clawing fingers sunk into the crook of his right arm as the attacker flailed and kicked. There was a dull thudding sound, and a flash that came from between them, and then the second attacker was dead weight atop him.

The first attacker scrambled up as the spearman raced forward, the point of the blade directed right at the widest part of Dan's chest. With all his strength, Dan launched the limp, bleeding, body of the second man off him. It was a great throw. The probable corpse collided with the spearman, sending them both back.

Dan sprang to one knee, bringing his smoking Walther to bear, when the first attacker, also scrambling up, swung a plastic chair with all his might. But he was smart enough to aim at Dan's gun arm, not his face. The PPK got caught in the sharp, hard rungs of the chair back, and was pried from Dan's fingers as surely as if the man had used a vise.

As before, the gun went off, the bullet taking the second man's left ear, eye, and most of his nose with it.

Dan heard the chair hit the patio ledge, and his gun clatter behind him amongst the other plates and cups. As the rest of the second man's head turned, and his body followed to flop onto the patio floor the way the milkfish had flopped on the sand, Dan shifted to face the remaining attacker. Unfortunately he had already noted the man's speed.

The third man pushed the spear tip behind Dan's rear leg, tripping him. As Dan fell again, the third man flipped the weapon, and stuck the spear tip inches from Dan's eyes. Dan wanted to bat the spear away, but the angle was too severe and the spearhead was too close. He looked up to see the surviving attacker staring down at him with rage, just before he started seething.

"They're dead!" the R-comm translated the spearman's words into Dan's head. "You killed them, you foreign devil!"

The man looked up in despair for a second, giving Dan hope he could take advantage of it, but the spear only stabbed closer. It was just millimeters away when the third man, his face twisted in regret and hate, leaned in even closer.

"They said don't kill you. They said grab you, keep you for them. For money! So much money! They said no problem, but now my friends are dead! So I will do to you what you did to them!"

Dan was ready to grab at whatever part of the spear he could get before it nailed his skull to the cement. No matter how the old woman had looked at the guy, Dan already knew that he wasn't an amateur spearman. He wouldn't pull the weapon back before thrusting it. So they would just have to see who was faster: the trained agent or the lithe, wiry spearman.

Dan never did find out, because a breath later an upturned eye, double shank, fifty-millimeter, five-gram fishhook sunk through the spearman's cheek and, like the prize catch of the day, he was yanked back and away.

Dan jumped to his feet as the young woman who had caught his breakfast expertly used the spearman's head like a medieval mace against the concrete lip of the patio. The old woman and other fisher women winced at the sound of a bone cantaloupe breaking open. The little girl and the dog stared with wider eyes than they had used for the snake skin.

The young woman who had caught the milkfish stood looking down at her spearman catch just long enough to make sure he wasn't moving, then turned her head to the American.

"Dan Morgan, I presume?" she said in nearly perfect English.

Chapter 23

Her English wasn't quite perfect since she had tongued over the "r" in "presume." She also rolled her tongue over the "let's" in "Let's get you out of here."

Dan was more than willing to go, but he'd only gotten a few steps before he looked back. The old woman, the two other fisher women, and even the child and her dog were gathering around the corpses with what appeared to be curiosity.

"Uh, shouldn't we…?" Dan started.

"The villagers will clean up," the milkfish-catching woman said without slowing her pace as she led Dan through the concrete building. "They have no love for mainland spies."

"That's who they were?" he asked, noting the sparse, plain, but clean and well-made room's few simple furnishings.

"Of course," said his rescuer without slowing or looking back at him. "We don't have much violent crime here. But fraud and mainland moles are pandemic."

Dan studied his rescuer as they neared a side door. It was tougher to judge her shape in her loose-fitting, untucked shirt and baggy pants, but her face was fit and nicely shaped, if unmemorable.

The better to slip in and out unnoticed, Dan thought. *Perfect for an undercover operative.*

He put his other questions on hold as she pushed open the side door and they emerged into the parking lot. It was shaped roughly like the patio, but emptied out onto a concrete road, which wound up into wooded hills. Again, the ocean air was refreshing on his face, but it had taken on some strength during their quick march through the building, and he noted that the sky was graying and the tree tops were swaying.

She marched over to a compact dark blue hatchback. As she curtly waved him over to the passenger seat, he noted its make and model. CMC Zinger MPV—China Motor Corporation compact multi-purpose vehicle. No foreign cars for this girl. This was one of the few vehicles made in Taiwan.

The interior was fairly standard for this brand of vehicle, with more plastic than wood or leather. Its two outstanding features were its twenty-four hundred c.c., hundred and thirty-six horsepower motor, and that it smelled, unsurprisingly, of fish.

"In Japan this sort of car is known as a space wagon," the girl shared as she started the engine while Dan hunkered down in his seat. "Probably because there's space for my stuff and it also looks like it came from space."

It wasn't until she had driven a few dozen yards that he opened his mouth again. "How did you find me?"

The young woman concentrated on the road, but answered without pause. "Tell your superiors I got their signal, but I couldn't answer in case we were being bugged."

"And you just happened to be there?" Dan asked skeptically.

The woman sniffed. "It's where I work. What you might call my cover." It seemed she was going to leave it at that, but then she sniffed again, a little more forcefully. "And give your superiors credit. The meeting place was not picked by accident."

Dan pictured the way the fishing village was designed, and acknowledged what was pretty obviously the only real meeting place within it. Then he heard Linc snicker deep in his ear, followed by Randall's soft voice.

"We have to be careful, Cobra. Don't know who's listening and how much they're hearing. Less said the better for now."

And of course you rely on my skill, Dan thought but resisted replying.

Instead he studied the area and the driver more scrupulously. The beaches, fishing coves, and palm trees rapidly gave way to two-lane highways and blotches of civilization. He knew he had arrived when he spotted a Starbucks and McDonalds, along with a snorkeling center, a diving club, and even a combination motel resort and cocoa center.

The driver tossed him a stained, floppy bucket hat. "Don't be obvious about it, but try not to be seen."

Dan saw the sense in it, so he pulled the small hat as tightly over his head as he could and slumped down in the seat so he didn't tower over the driver.

"You think the fishermen had back-up?" he wondered.

"Those three?" she scoffed. "I doubt it. I actually think they spotted you by total accident. You heard what that spearman said. 'So much money.' Apparently, there's been a price on your head for some time. And given that you, a big fish—if you'll excuse the expression—just happened to march into a relatively small pond crawling with bored snoops, well...?"

Dan mulled it over, but couldn't quite make it work. "Is it really that bad here?"

"It's great here," she retorted, "but this is an island you can cross in a six-hour drive one way, and a three-hour drive the other. And it's also an island that another country of one and a half billion has coveted for seventy years. Do the math. A billion Chinese who need something to do. Why not pepper them all over a little island their masters want under their thumb?"

During her speech Dan had kept fiddling with the hat and his posture to try ensuring no one else would spot him.

"Do you think this hat makes me blend in," he complained, "or yells to everyone 'look at the big American ape'?"

The driver glanced over, then jerked her eyes back to the road. But she couldn't keep her laugh in. It was a charming, warm, human sound that made Dan feel much better.

"Plop it over your eyes so it looks like you're trying to sleep," she suggested. "That will explain to any looky-loo why it's obviously not your hat."

Plop? he thought. *Looky-loo? Did this girl grow up on American television?*

But he did as she recommended, regretting that he could no longer study the area.

She seemed to read his thoughts again. "You're not missing much," she commented. "Just lots of rocks and trees."

But that gave him time to catch up on some other things he wouldn't mind knowing—like his savior's name, for one.

She laughed again. "I'm Lo Liu." She pronounced it Low Lee-yuh.

"Lowly?" he replied, trying to pronounce it correctly.

She laughed a third time, but with an undercurrent of sadness, as if she'd had to deal with many a mispronouncing English-speaker over the years.

"Call me Lulu," she suggested.

Dan wanted to work on saying her actual name right, but knew he really didn't have time. "Thanks," he told her, "my name is ..."

"Bond, James Bond," she quickly interrupted, laughing once more, but with more self-awareness than sorrow. "Oh, I know your name, Mr. Morgan. Remember, I used it at the beach."

Dan mentally kicked himself. "Of course," he acknowledged. "But that was right after you hooked and gutted a big one. I think you could forgive me if I was a bit distracted."

She gave a relieved smile. "And I hope you will forgive me for my brusque bluntness."

"No apology necessary," he maintained. "Your English is very good. Maybe better than mine."

Her smile widened, but he didn't see its sardonicism. If he had, it might have reminded him of Peter Conley's resting face.

"Thank you," she said instead. "Because I bet your Taiwanese sucks."

This time Linc laughed aloud inside Dan's ear, but the comment didn't faze Morgan.

"What Taiwanese?" he answered, and they both laughed.

That cemented their relationship, so he learned more as she kept driving. Although she looked eighteen, she was actually ten years older.

"How did you get involved in this game?" he asked her as they passed through Checheng Township.

Out the corner of his eye, Dan saw more hot springs, grasslands, forests, a prominently advertised peeled mung bean dessert palace, and yet another riotously colored temple. Apparently, since Taiwan was so drably colored itself, all the temples and many of the restaurants and hotels looked like a rainbow had thrown up on them.

"Can't you guess?" Lulu answered with more mischievousness than maliciousness.

Dan was going to plead ignorance, but it all made sense to him: what he was doing here, what she was doing here, and why they had met so fortuitously.

"Smith," he said.

She repeated, "Smith."

The car stopped. It took Dan by slight surprise, and he chastised himself for letting his guard down as he sat up and popped the hat off his eyes.

"We're here," she said.

It seemed to him that they were in the middle of nowhere—not quite the coconut palm forest, but nowhere near Checheng either. Still, Lulu was already heading for a break in the trees. As Dan got out of the car, he looked closer to see a wooden and bamboo gateway, nicely blended into the trees so it almost looked like a part of them.

"Where's here?" he wondered, following her down a steep stone pathway.

"My family's legacy," she told him as they neared a heavy, thick, wooden doorway with a single vertical pole for a latch, and a narrow, opaque glass panel parallel to it. Like the gateway, the door seemed to blend in to the hillside all around it. Lulu took out a key and plunged it into a small round lock between the pole and the glass.

"Welcome to Gaoxing Didian," she said, but with more sadness than pride.

He followed her into a small, humid foyer lit only by sunlight, facing a simple rectangular counter. On either side were triangular windows looking out into forests of fir, ficus, bamboo, and, of course, palm.

Lulu pointed upwards. "Mudan Township." She pointed right. "Manzhou Township." She pointed left. "Shizi Township." She passed the desk to another door that was a smaller twin of the one they'd entered by. "And, in the middle of it all, our little 'Happiness Place.'"

Pushing open the door behind the counter, she walked down a tile path between mostly open-air compartments. The humidity was much stronger in this larger space, because each compartment had a square pool of steaming hot spring water. There were six in all, three on each side.

"My parents were smarter than I ever knew," he heard her say as she headed to another heavy, thick, wooden door at the other end of the compartments. "Because there are three major words for happiness. 'Xingfu,' which means long-lasting happy family life, is best. 'Kuaile,' which means someone who is truly forever happy, is next."

She reached the furthest door and held up another key. "And then there's 'Gaoxing,'" she said. "The least long-lasting happiness." She pushed the key into the lock. "A temporary moment of happiness, really, often due to the influence of material possessions." She turned her head to face Dan. "My family seems to have the curse of second sight."

Lulu turned the key, pushed the door open, and stretched out her arm, beckoning Dan to witness what she revealed.

Beyond the door was a small temple that was traversed by a small white path, flanked by eight long tables—four on each side—instead of pews. At the end of the path were two simple ancestral altar shrines, containing traditional ancestral tablets behind incense pots.

The tablet in the left shrine featured a black-draped photo of a man. The other one had a white-draped photo of a woman. It was easy for Dan to guess they were Lulu's parents.

But the altar shrines were not nearly as distracting as the rest of the space. Covering every table and every wall were at least six computers, countless papers, print-outs, pictures, maps, and graphs—all acupunctured by push pins with different colored tops.

Dan looked back at Lulu with concern, but the only expression he could see on her face was one of dedicated certainty.

"I know I'm going to regret asking," he said, "but what is this?"

Lulu sighed. "And I know I'm going to regret answering," she replied. "But I bet you've probably already guessed. You're pretty good at guessing. It's my investigation into the murderer of my family."

Dan looked down at her. "Smith?" he asked.

Lulu looked up at him. "Smith," she answered.

Chapter 24

They had plenty of time to talk on the five-hour drive.

Lulu could have shaved at least an hour off the drive if Taiwan wasn't Taiwan. But Taiwan was Taiwan, and she explained why as they first drove fifty miles straight south, then twenty-five more miles straight east.

"They could and should have named this country 'Seismic City.'" She made a waving motion that was meant to incorporate the entire island. "All seismic faults."

"And that means earthquakes, right?" Dan asked. He was still in his dark gray outfit, but was relieved he didn't have to make the whole trip slouched down with a tiny hat pasted on his temple.

"Boy, does it," Lulu concurred. "Like three hundred a year." She chortled at Dan's eye-widening reaction. "Take it easy, Cobra," she advised. "They're not all '*Land That Time Forgot*' level. Those only happen once every twenty years or so. The last big one was in 1999 on September twenty-first. Killed almost three thousand people, no matter how prepared we thought we were." She glanced at him again. "You got your 'nine-eleven.' We got our 'nine-twenty-one.'" She let that settle in before continuing in a lighter tone. "The latest U.S. Geological Society 'seismic hazard map' declared that nine-tenths of the island has their highest 'most hazardous' rating." Her expression became meditative. "Due for another biggie any time now."

Once again, Dan was reminded that, for all intents and purposes, Lulu had been raised with the pop culture and slang of America and Japan.

"So, what are we doing?" he asked her. "Driving around major fault lines?"

She considered the comment with downturned lips. "Basically, yes. If we drove no more than twenty miles north from the west coast where we were, by the time we hit Fangliao Township, we couldn't get across the island short of stealing a plane."

Dan wished Cougar would chime in about then, but the pilot was still AWOL from the R-comm.

Lulu made a chopping motion from straight up to straight down. "Taiwan is bisected by mountain ranges—like two wrestlers not willing to give an inch. In between them is the Taroko Gorge."

"It's like Taiwan's Grand Canyon," Dan heard Linc whisper deep in his ear.

"It's like Taiwan's Grand Canyon," Lulu said.

Dan grimaced. Linc chimed in, but Conley didn't. Life wasn't fair.

"Any way you look at it," Lulu continued, unaware of the voices in Dan's head, "we can't get from one side of the island to the other by car except by the Shuishalian or the Nanbu Cross-island highways, both of whose entrances are way up north. So better this little southeast detour than slogging over to those things."

"You're the driver," Dan commented, knowing all this chatter was just her way of putting off the inevitable.

He turned his eyes toward her, and tried to remember what had seemed to be a teenager in a loose white shirt and dark pants. Now she was dressed to blend in with any young professional on her day off: a dark blue, long-sleeve, light-weight U-neck top, dark tan casual slacks, and dark blue slip-ons—all under a light-weight, dark tan, three-season windbreaker. She made it look fashionable. Now her black hair was pulled back into a ponytail, and she wore glare-reducing sunglasses through which her deep brown eyes could still be seen.

He let the silence linger a second more, filling his eyes with the green, brown, and gray scenery, then opened his mouth to say something along the lines of *oh, look at that elephant in the room*, when she beat him to it.

"I was fifteen years old," she said, keeping her eyes on the road. "You know how fifteen year-old girls can be?"

Dan rolled his own eyes, almost chuckling. "Boy, do I," he said with empathy, the fifteen year-old Alex coming into his mind in sharp focus. "But silly me, I always wanted to believe that Chinese teenagers were different."

Lulu sniffed in thankful derision. "Oh, yes, the old *gweilo* fantasy of the polite, quiet, subservient Asian."

"*Ge-why-low?*" Dan interrupted instead of challenging her on her stereotypical preconception, especially since that stereotypical preconception was, in his case, right on the money.

"Foreign devil," she translated before plunging back in. "Well, Cobra, I'm not Chinese. I'm Taiwanese. Taiwan is still an independent democracy.

And like all teenagers in all free countries, boy, did I take advantage of it." She exhaled, her eyes misting. "My parents' only crime was trying to keep me safe and happy. But I treated them like aged, ignorant, idiots."

Dan understood. "Like teenagers everywhere—from Asia to America. And beyond."

Lulu took little solace in Dan's well-meant disclaimer. "You have your nine-eleven," she said with heavy sadness. "We have our nine-twenty-one. But I have my own, personal four-fourteen." She took a deep breath and plunged into the memory.

"That night, thirteen years ago, I decided I was going out, no matter what my parents said, and no matter how much they needed my help. Our resort was more crowded than usual—a whopping great four guests—but nothing was going to stop me. I got in my lowest cut, highest hemmed outfit and headed for the door. When I went out, passing someone coming in, my parents were alive. When I came home, they were dead."

She looked at Dan with haunted but still hard eyes. "Five hours, Mr. Morgan. All it took was five hours."

"What happened?" he asked.

Lulu returned her attention to the road, her entire demeanor changing. She went from a lost, regretful young daughter to a hardcore, fervent avenger in two seconds flat.

"An accident," she scoffed. "Like I told you before, we're not a country with many violent crimes. If they had been shot, or stabbed, or strangled, the whole country would've stopped dead—if you'll excuse the expression—until the killer was caught. But they weren't shot or stabbed or strangled. According to the final police report, my father had slipped, hitting his head on the side of a hot spring pool, then his top half had slipped into the water." She looked back at Dan. "They weren't sure what killed him first: blood flooding his brain, drowning, or being scalded to death." She turned back to the road. "My mother died from a fall...supposedly running to get him help. They found her at the bottom of a ravine."

Dan was smart enough not to even inquire into the chances of the police report being true. "The man you passed on the way out," he said instead. "Smith."

"Smith," she agreed.

"How did you know it was Smith?"

"I didn't. Not then. I accepted it was a man who called himself Mr. Smith after six years of research."

"How do you know he killed them?"

"I don't," she said in a tone that was anything but an admission. "But he was the only one with a fake name. He was the only one who couldn't be found. He was the only one who wasn't questioned. He was the only *gweilo*."

Dan wanted to start barking at Randall and Shepard about how they could have teamed up with this tragic obsessive, but he stopped himself, remembering her admonition to have a little faith in his superiors.

"So," he said to her instead, "you've dedicated your life to finding and proving it was him."

"Darn tootin'," she replied in a sardonic drawl. "And everyplace I found evidence of him stank with death." Lulu sat up straighter behind the wheel, trying to change back into the young professional. "Quite the mover and shaker, your Mr. Smith," she continued.

"Not my Mr. Smith," Dan said, also choosing to stare out the windshield.

"Oh," she said. "You're just following orders, huh?"

Dan winced. "I deserved that. But keep in mind, I'm looking for him too. And not to give him a pat on the head."

"So why are you looking for him?" she asked.

Dan answered honestly. "To find out why our headquarters and all our homes were destroyed. To find out why I've been chased halfway around the world. To find out what is going on."

Lulu surprised him by turning off Route Nine at the juncture of Nanxing Road. And by saying, "Well, why didn't say so before? I can tell you all that."

Chapter 25

Dan remained surprised as she drove into Fuli Township in Hualien County, a sleepy little parish on the east coast, a quarter way up the island. All it looked good for was to link one major trucking thoroughfare with another that was several hundred yards ahead.

But the surprises kept coming for Dan when Lulu turned left and pulled in beside a multi-colored, neon-lit glass booth containing a young woman in a flaming red, lace-up, midriff and cleavage-baring top and hot pants sitting on a padded stool.

"Betel nut beauty," Lulu explained as she unbuckled her seat belt and opened the driver's side door. "Don't dawdle," she suggested as she got out. "Or stare."

Dan emerged onto a small main street of eight buildings with either thatched, corrugated steel, concrete, or shingled roofs. Then, as he speechlessly followed Lulu around the side of a small shop behind the neon-lit glass booth, he heard Linc speaking quickly in his ear, as if reading a disclaimer for a prescription medicine commercial.

"Also known as Shuangdong or binglang girls, they sell betel nuts to truckers, who chew them like American truckers chew tobacco. Started in the 1960s as a marketing ploy at one betel nut stand, then caught on. Now these kiosks are everywhere along roads in rural, suburban and urban areas…"

"Shut up, Linc," Dan hissed between his teeth.

"You say something?" Lulu asked without slowing or turning around.

Rather than answer, Dan caught up with the young woman as she pressed yet another key into another lock on another door while grabbing yet another handle alongside. With a twist and a push, she ushered Dan inside.

It was the dimly, fluorescent-lit back room of the Taiwanese mini-convenience truck stop store out front. Big oil-drum-sized cans filled with tea leaves, cigarette packs, and betel nuts—which looked like chestnuts with glandular conditions—all but filled the space, save for a few narrow curving paths.

Another woman, wearing bright pink short-shorts, low-cut tube top, and skyscraper-high heels sat on a closed can, smoking a cigarette. Since she looked thirty years old, Dan guessed she was in her forties, or beyond.

She said something in her native tongue, which the R-comm told Dan was "Hey, Lulu."

Lulu began twisting some cans around to make more room. "Hey Zen Shoo," Dan heard in his head. "Your shift soon?"

"Yeah, I guess."

"Mind relieving Quac now?"

The betel juice beauty frowned, pinched a piece of tobacco leaf off her tongue, stood, dropped the cigarette, then ground it under her stiletto heel. To Dan's eyes, it was quite a performance.

Without another word, the person the R-comm called Zen left the room, passing a balding man who had poked his head in.

"Oh, Lulu," he said. "It's you. I was expecting you closer to dark."

"We made good time, Foo," she told him. "Everything ready?"

He looked apologetic, even obsequious. "Almost," he admitted, his hands up in the universal position of helplessness. "Like I said, thought you were coming later."

Lulu stopped long enough to pinion him with a baleful stare. "Okay then, Foo. *Will* it be ready?"

He nodded like a bobble head on a mechanical bull. "Yes, Lulu, of course, Lulu."

And before she could melt his head with her stare, he was gone, back into the main rest stop store.

As Lulu returned to her redecorating, she took a second to see how Dan was doing.

"Friends of the family," she told him as she returned to her can shifting.

Beginning to get a re-glimmer of why the remaining Zeta had reached out to this extraordinary young woman, Dan stood up. "Can I help?"

Lulu seemed a bit surprised, then relaxed, as if Dan had passed an unnecessary, even petty test.

"Yes, as a matter of fact," she said. "You could."

She directed him in her manipulations until they had created a little amphitheater of the oil-drum-sized cans.

"We've got a network of small businesses," she explained during the maneuver. "United in trying to keep our little country free of outside influence..."

"And finding Smith," Dan added.

She lowered her head, then looked up at him craftily. "Beyond the death of my parents," she said, "our Mr. Smith always seems to be at the very center of international influence. Wouldn't you agree?"

She reached behind some more barrels and pulled up a plain old laptop computer, which she then set on a barrel top, facing him.

"Sit," she offered, waving at a can a few feet from the computer screen. He did so as she punched a button on the keyboard and the screen lit up. On it was a list. A long list.

"There are more than five hundred intelligence agencies in the world," she said, scrolling down the list. "India alone has twenty-seven." She looked back from the screen to stare at him. "And all of them, apparently, are after you."

Dan made a harrumphing sound. "Tell me something I don't know."

"Okay," she replied. "Remember the spearman?"

Dan straightened.

"Apparently, he wasn't quite dead yet," Lulu said pleasantly. "So my boss lady had a little chat with him." Lulu stared over Dan's head, clearly picturing something extraordinary. "You should see that woman filet a milkfish. I've never seen anyone more deft with a knife."

Dan found that his mouth was dry. He cleared his throat. "And?"

"Seems he said you have something they all want," she told him. "Something you don't know you have."

Dan went over everything he had experienced in the last few days, then went over it again. "Any idea what that might be?" he wondered aloud.

"Oh, sure," she said with a humorless smile, "and I think you and your superiors have some ideas too. But ultimately, it doesn't matter."

Dan was honestly taken aback. "How can you say that?"

Her smile took on some mirth, and she gave the smallest of shrugs. "All that matters is that everyone on this list wants it, and somehow, miraculously, knows you have it." Her voice took on the tone of a wide-eyed teacher lecturing a group of credulous children. "Now how could something like that have happened? Who on Earth could have slipped something into your drink and told all of them"—she pointed at the laptop screen—"about it?"

The young Taiwanese and the seasoned American operative locked eyes. They gave each other a look they both recognized. They had seen that expression on each other's faces at least twice before. From that moment on, they would refer to it as the "Smith Face."

"That's what I'm here to find out," Dan said.

"Then you've come to the right place," Lulu replied while pressing another button.

The screen changed to a slide show of images. He recognized location photos of the Boston Commons, Washington D.C.'s Lincoln Memorial Reflecting Pool, New York City's World Trade Center Memorial, London's Hyde Park, Zurich's Grossmünster Church, Moscow's Red Square, Mumbai's Siddhivinayak Temple, Beijing's Forbidden City, and an impressive skyscraper that looked like an architectural bamboo reed against the sky—all of which Dan recognized, save for the final one.

"What was that last place?" he asked her, figuring it would be important to know, if not now, then soon.

Her expression held surprise, but then changed to a sort of realization. "Taipei 101," she explained. "Formerly known as the Taipei World Financial Center, which, for six glorious years, was the planet's tallest building until Dubai's Burj Khalifa beat it."

"Thanks for the tour," Dan commented as his mind whirled without success.

"It wasn't for your entertainment, Mr. Morgan," Lulu assured him. "You've personally met the man, correct? I mean, face to face, right? Unlike me, which was face to profile."

"Yeah, I met the man," Dan said.

Lulu pressed another keyboard button. The pictures played again, in the same order, only this time, each was treated with a digital close-up on a specific person in each of the crowds.

Dan saw Mr. Smith nine times. It was never a clear, direct shot, but it didn't have to be.

"Wonderful things, security cams," Lulu mused. "So thorough. So hackable."

"Over how long a time were these pictures taken?" Dan asked with an edge of urgency.

She gave him a *you're-not-as-dumb-as-I-was-afraid-you-were* smile.

"Two weeks," she told him. "And the last shot was forty-two hours ago. Whatever he was doing in each of those places, it was a surgical, hit-and-run strike. And I think, and I think you think, it was leading up to today. Now."

"How did you focus in on those pics?" he wondered. "I—I mean we—have been trying to track Smith for years and got nothing."

Lulu sat on a closed can opposite him. "You had lots of other things to do. I didn't. And I had a dozen years head start."

"But, still…"

"This is Taiwan, Mr. Morgan," she sighed. "The country that a certain big mommy wants to make sure is always under the radar. Why do you think you recognized all those other world landmarks but not Taipei 101? So while the rest of the world overlooks us, or purposely looks the other way, we're free to develop all manner of helpful stuff, including facial recognition software and behavioral algorithms that make even Apple and Microsoft look like Dick and Jane."

Dan had stopped trying to identify all the young woman's pop culture allusions, but there was one word she used that all but slapped him.

"Algorithms," he repeated, eyes narrowing.

Lulu went on. "Yep. Helpful, insidious things. Like our own cells. One second they're creating us, the next second they're destroying us. All depends on whether they're used regeneratively or degenerately."

Dan waved the digression away, choosing instead to stand and stare down at her, his fists clenched. "Where is he?"

Before she could answer, Foo re-entered the back room, holding a garment bag in each fist.

"Ready," he interrupted with a big, relieved smile on his face.

Lulu looked at Dan, held up a forefinger, and went over to retrieve the larger of the two garment bags. She laid it atop three closed cans in front of Dan and, with a look to make sure he was paying attention, unzipped it all the way down.

Inside was one of the most impressive, striking tuxedoes he had ever seen.

"Had it made as a cross between the Brioni and Brunello Cucinelli cuts," she murmured. "Turned out pretty well, don't you think?"

Dan Morgan usually thought of himself as fairly balanced, but all the twists and turns this trip was taking had him wobbling. "How much was this?" was all he could think to ask.

She smiled. "Normally around a hundred and twenty thousand dollars," she calculated, then amended it when she caught a glimpse of his surprised face. "Oh, sorry. That's Taiwan dollars. Around four thousand U.S. dollars."

"That's not much better," he said. "Where did you get the money?"

Her smiled widened. "Didn't need it. Best tailor in Taichung is a friend of the family." Her expression became curious as she tried to read the look of stupefaction on his face. "Well, if you think the suit's something," she assured him, "wait 'til you see the shoes."

"What," he demanded, "is all this for?"

Lulu stepped back to take the other garment bag from Foo's hand.
"What do you think it's for?" she replied. "You want to know where Smith is, don't you? Well, one thing I can tell you for sure, he's not out front in the neon booth with Zen handing out betel nuts."

She pulled down the zipper of the second garment bag to reveal a beautiful evening gown.

"Suit up, Mr. Morgan," she advised with a big, evil grin on her face. "We're going to a party."

Chapter 26

The shoes really were something. So dark it was like looking into a black hole, and so comfortable it was like wearing an expert foot massager's ever-moving fingers. After trying them on, Dan understood something he had never understood before: why any man would ever pay thousands of dollars for shoes.

He covered his impressed surprise with another question. "Did the guy who made these also make the tux?"

Lulu looked at him as if he had mistaken Chinese dim sum for Japanese sushi.

"Of course not," she replied, while putting on her own gold-stitched evening slippers. "Making clothes and shoes of this quality are two completely different arts."

"Let me guess," Dan interjected while letting his eyes move up from her shoes to her dress. "Friend of the family?"

"Of course," she said with a grin. "And my eyes are up here."

Dan mirrored her grin as their eyes met. But prior to that he had taken in her transformation. She was wearing a dark blue, ankle-length cheongsam dress with a high neck, a tear-drop eyelet atop her cleavage, a side-slit down from her mid-thigh, and a subtle black lace stitching of a rising phoenix that wove up and around the entire garment.

She, along with the dress, was stunning, but there was no way Dan was going to tell her that.

"I think it would look better in red," he said instead.

"Red is the color of wedding dresses in this part of the world," she informed him. "And we may be doing many things this evening, Mr. Morgan, but getting married will not be one of them."

She saw a cloud pass his face, and realized she had hit a sore spot, but did not call attention to it. Instead, Dan tried to defuse the moment.

"You wish," he replied with a mock sneer. "What did you do to your face, anyway?"

He thought he was being playfully insulting, but Lulu let him know there was method to her makeup.

"Good call," she told him. "It's the latest fashion for models in China, Japan, and Korea: to make them look like plastic or porcelain dolls. Some women spend thousands on surgery. I wasn't about to go that far, even for Smith." She stood, checked that her hair was still solidly affixed in a braided bun, and did the same ogling of him that he had done to her. "And you clean up real nice. Ready?"

He was, and they left the shop by the same door they had entered. Dan wondered how they would both look in a CMC Zinger, but like so many things on this mission, he never got the chance to find out. The Space Wagon was gone. In its stead was a black car Dan instantly recognized as a Porsche 718 GTS.

Three hundred and sixty-five horsepower popped into his mind. *Zero to sixty in four point four seconds. Top speed a hundred and ninety miles per hour. About eighty thousand dollars...*

"What?" he asked Lulu in amazed admiration. "A friend of the family didn't have a Pagani you could borrow?"

She didn't even look at him as she circled to the passenger door. "A little too showy," she said. "There are only four Paganis in the country, and everyone knows their owners."

"I did good?" Foo asked her from behind the steering wheel. He was wearing a chauffeur's jacket and hat.

"You did fine," Lulu assured him as she prepared to squeeze into the tiny space behind the seats.

Dan held up his hand to stop her as he walked over to the driver's side door. He was going to ask her what the Taiwanese word for 'out' was when he realized the R-comm might drown it out during translation anyway. So, he just motioned at Foo with his forefinger in what he hoped was a universal sign of "come here."

Foo looked at Lulu, who was standing beside the car, framed in the passenger side doorway.

"What if we need the car from valet parking for a quick getaway?" she asked Dan.

"What, we're going to wait for him to drive up?" the operative exclaimed. "If all five hundred agencies are gunning for me, let them see me live this large, okay?"

Lulu took a second to consider it. "Okay," she said, then shooed Foo out from behind the wheel.

Dan took his place in growing anticipation, then remembered where he was and what they were doing.

"Where to?" he asked the beautiful "jade vase" beside him.

She told him where and how before his foot hit the accelerator. She may have asked if he wanted a betel nut for the road. But it was drowned out by the screeching of tires and the splash of gravel across Foo's chauffeur uniform.

* * * *

Dan made the twenty-mile trip to Hualien County in ten minutes flat. It would have been even faster if he hadn't had to slow for the final stretch of farm-lined country road.

The sun was going down as they approached, so he was able to see the mountains with seemingly endless green slopes on either side. Then she directed him to turn left at a break in some hedges as the sky began to be dotted by thousands of stars. The sports car moved along a narrow, winding gravel driveway.

"Too much to ask where we are?" he inquired.

Lulu was peering through the windshield, seemingly looking for any signs of trouble.

"It's a family resort named after the patriarch, who never chose an English name," she told him. "So its title would be meaningless, but you have to see it to believe it."

"It doesn't look like much now," Dan commented, making sure he stayed on the gravel, rather than the bowls of grass all around them.

"We came in the servants' entrance," she explained. "The head of housekeeping and food services are ..."

"Yes, I know," he interrupted. "Friends of the family."

The car made it out of a glen, and moved out onto a plateau overlooking the entire property. Dan had to stop the car in a cloud of gravel just to take it all in.

"Eighteen hundred acres," she told him, also staring at the expanse. "Right smack dab in the middle of a neo-volcano. Part resort, part museum, part farm, part orchard, part wildlife sanctuary. Parrots, pheasants, cranes, peacocks…"

"And that's just the party guests," Dan commented as he started driving the car slowly down the gravel again.

Lulu laughed nervously at his joke. He could feel her tension rising the farther they went. And since she had shown no sign of tension before, he knew things were getting more than spearman serious. She seemed to try to deal with it by becoming a tour guide.

"One million hand-planted trees," she said as if a recording were playing out of her mouth. "The milk produced by the farm here is sold in 7-Elevens and Starbucks…"

"Where are we going?" he interrupted her seemingly unconscious drone. "The barn?"

"No," she replied, getting ahold of herself. She pointed out the right side of the windshield. "We're going there."

Spread out in the distance were three extraordinary structures in a rough frowning formation. On the right was a banquet hall, adorned in royal purple, complete with Mediterranean domes, pediments, and porticoes. On the left was a hot spring spa seemingly made as a tribute to Noah's Ark and the Japanese Royal Palace, complete with a *torii* gate, bamboo paneling, and multi-colored lanterns.

And in the center was a huge reception hall that nearly defied description. Dan would not have been able to, but Lulu tried.

"Taiwan has been occupied by the Dutch, Spanish, Chinese, and Japanese," she said. "There are aboriginals still living here. This …this …place was created with all of them in mind."

Dan believed it. It looked like Eastern, Western, American, and Asian influences were fighting each other to a standstill. Out front there were Buddhas, Taiwanese folk gods, rearing bronze horses, Greek gods and goddesses, and even a marble dinosaur adorning the junctures of a giant garden which wouldn't look out of place at Versailles. And it all was lit so brightly it probably could be seen from space.

"We're going there?" Dan echoed in disbelief.

"In a manner of speaking," Lulu said. "At least at first…"

By the time Dan pulled the car along its circular driveway in front of the main entrance to the reception hall, both occupants of the Porsche 718 were back to relatively normal. A handsome man in flowing Chinese robes opened the driver's side door. A beautiful woman in the feminine equivalent opened the passenger's side door. Neither valet reacted to

Lulu. Both reacted to Dan—with recognition, frozen features, and up-raised eyebrows.

Their faces returned to placid servitude, and they quickly retreated as another beautiful woman, who was even taller than Dan and even more plastic looking than Lulu, appeared at the bottom of the reception hall steps. This hostess was also wearing resplendent ancient Chinese robes that gave the local temples a run for their rainbow money.

"Mr. Morgan," she said. "You are expected. This way please."

The woman acted as if Lulu didn't exist, but Dan didn't. He waited until she had reached his side before following the hostess.

They all entered what appeared to be a massive hunting lodge, with huge beams, fireplaces, gigantic furniture ripped from trees, and a big menagerie of taxidermied animals—as well as many more animal heads mounted in every open wall space. Dan wouldn't have been surprised to see the spearman's head tucked in the crook of a vaulted ceiling.

Amid all this was, apparently, the cocktail party of the year. Dan took a second to take it all in, as well as study the faces of every party guest he could see. There was every color, sex, size, and shape, adorned in everything from silk pajamas to highly decorated military uniforms. But there was not a single person he recognized.

By the look on Lulu's face, she couldn't say the same. But before he could inquire, their hostess spoke up again, although her tune was exactly the same.

"Mr. Morgan," she repeated with just a mite more urgency. "You are *expected*."

Dan looked at the woman's seemingly still plastic face, and just managed to note a vibration deep in her almond eyes. He looked from her to Lulu, who appeared positively ultra-human in comparison. She cocked her head, then put her hand out to communicate "you first."

The plastic hostess glided down the center of the opulent, lofty space, making sure her American male charge was close behind. After what seemed like an extended hike, they reached the other side of the salon, where there was a small set of thick, heavy, red curtains. Although no guards were stationed there, both Lulu and Dan noted several Chinese robed men who had "the look," conveniently positioned nearby.

Their hostess moved between the curtains, holding them just wide enough for Dan—and therefore more than wide enough for Lulu—to slip through. They now all stood in a sumptuous study, empty of any people other than themselves. On four sides was a two-story library. In front of them was a gloriously built and accented desk. Behind it was an equally impressive chair. And behind that was a spectacular fireplace large enough for Dan to step into without slouching.

Their hostess went to the other side of the desk and beckoned at Dan to join her. Although it was clear that the hostess didn't include Lulu in the invitation, he looked at her first. Lulu's expression was both perplexed and determined, but also seemed to suggest: *when in Taiwan...*

They both moved over until they were between the chair and the fireplace. The grate was empty and clean. Although there were smoke stains on the stones, it was obvious that no fire had been lit for quite some time.

The reason for that became all too apparent as the seemingly solid stone that served as the fireplace's back wall opened to reveal an elevator. Dan stepped back, but then the hostess's cold, perfectly smooth, hand was on his arm.

He looked over at her, and saw even more in her pleading, insisting eyes. "Yeah, yeah, I know," he told her. "I'm expected."

He turned his head toward Lulu and gestured for her to come along, but then the hostess's hand gripped his arm. When he looked back, her head was shaking "no."

Dan returned his gaze to Lulu. She looked angry and frustrated, but also resigned. She was about to signal him that he should follow the rules when she dropped her hands.

"Wait a minute!" she blurted. "Just because she's a Westworld robot doesn't mean we have to be."

"Damn straight," Dan responded with relief. "Come on, let's see where I'm expected."

The hostess gasped, taking a step back while putting one dainty hand in front of her mouth. Both she and Dan were then surprised when it was Lulu who said "no."

He looked at his Taiwan contact, who had her fists on her hips, and her shaking head down. "No," she repeated. "We may not be robots, but we *are* puppets. And we all know who the puppeteer is, don't we?"

The breath came out of Dan's nose like fire from a dragon. He wanted to turn to the hostess and demand safety for his companion. He wanted to turn to his companion and spout some nonsense about her making sure to be here when he got back. But as soon as he considered it, he shut his mouth, knowing both were empty wastes of time.

He didn't even say "I'll be back," because everyone would think he was ripping off Schwarzenegger. All he did was nod at Lulu, then step into the elevator.

He didn't have to press a button. The door closed automatically, and as it did, he thought he heard someone say, "Before you embark on a journey of revenge, dig two graves." He couldn't tell if it was the hostess, Lulu, or some sort of weird elevator music.

Ultimately, it didn't make any difference. In a day of surprises, the puppeteer had saved the best for last. The elevator descended for eighteen seconds, then stopped. When the doors opened, Dan Morgan looked out at the most amazing casino he had ever seen.

Chapter 27

Dan Morgan had seen casinos all over the world, but nothing had come close to this towering rock triangle, not even the Macau or Dubai megalopolises, for two reasons. First, gambling was strictly illegal in Taiwan, and second, none of the other ostentatious monuments to chance were built inside a supposedly dormant neo-volcano, as Lulu had casually called it.

So these were true all-or-nothing gamblers in the most daring and therefore exciting place in the world. Just by entering, you were making two ultimate bets. One, that you wouldn't be arrested, and two, that the volcanic hands of God would not slam together to make you part of the magma.

Dan thought that maybe the people here would react the way the valets upstairs had, or the way wild west saloon patrons did when a gunslinger came through the swinging doors. In other words, everyone would stop, turn their heads, and stare. But he knew better. These were gamblers betting against the house, law enforcement, and mother nature. They wouldn't care if Buddha himself had shown up.

That was not to say that no one noticed him. On the contrary, several opulently suited servants moved into place on the sides of a central path, while another tall, glorious plastic doll hostess in ancient Chinese robes glided up to the bottom of a short stairway that led to an entire bank of elevators. Apparently there were hidden entrances all over the reception hall, not just in the combination study and library.

Otherwise, it was just a casino, albeit a supremely expensive one, made of track lighting, carpet, furniture, and machines. For all the attention the gamblers paid to the towering, craggy, multi-colored magma above them, it might as well have been made of plaster by amusement park engineers.

The new hostess led Dan past opulent and well-designed sections for poker, blackjack, craps, roulette, bingo, keno, and baccarat. Around the base of the triangular wall were the slot machines, as if those players should go first in the case of an earth upheaval. Given that this was Asia, there were even sections for pachinko pinball, mahjong, and fantan, which could be called Chinese roulette.

But there were no restaurants or shops. This was a place only for betting your money, and possibly your life.

The striking hostess kept her head down, moving past all of these distractions. As Dan studied everything, everyone, and all possible escape routes, he realized that the hostesses were doing what he had thought Lulu might do: playing the demure, humble, chaste Asian girl that *gweilos* like him might have hoped for.

Dan's concentration was shaken by the secret casino's most central and unusual feature. The hostess led him past a huge fountain right in the middle of the space, situated under the apex of the highest point of the natural interior's spire. He hadn't noticed it when he had entered because, at that point, it had been a placid pool.

As they passed, as if the hostess had an "on" button in her hand, the lights and waters of the fountain sprang to life, sending dancing jets of liquid into the air.

Good God, Dan thought. *I've fallen asleep in the Happiness Place. Lulu will be waking me up any second...*

But she didn't. Instead, the hostess led him to a beautiful lacquered door on the far side of the casino. It was one of three such doors positioned there, obviously as excavated spaces within the excavated space. The hostess stopped, turned toward him, and bowed. Her intention was abundantly clear. He was expected. It was up to him now.

Lady or the tiger, Dan thought. *Only one way to find out...*

Dan opened the door and stepped in. The door closed silently behind him.

It was neither the lady nor the tiger—although it might have soon proven to be multiple tigers. Inside the room was a large round table, around which eight men sat. Dan recognized seven of them.

Sitting in front of where Dan stood, his back to him, was Smith, in a severe black suit, white shirt, and slim black tie. Seated to Smith's right was General Deng Tao Kung, a Chinese military and intelligence strategist with whom Zeta had what could be termed a "frenemy" relationship.

To Deng's right was Alexi Ademenko of the Russian Foreign Intelligence Service. To his right was Hayao Misumi of the Japanese Defense Intelligence Headquarters. To his right, there was Tomas Blanco of the Argentinian

National Directorate of Strategic Military Intelligence. To his right, was Fahad Gadai of Pakistan's Inter-Services Intelligence organization. Next to him sat Vihaan Khatri of India's Defense Intelligence Agency.

The one next to him—a very thin, sunken-cheeked, white-haired Asian man in a long white robe, black slacks, and Chinese slippers—was the one Dan didn't recognize.

"Ah," Smith said without turning his head. "Good timing."

He gestured to the one Dan didn't recognize, who was obviously the dealer, since he started mixing up a pile of thirty-two long black dominoes that had white and red dots on them. As Dan watched, the old white-haired man piled the domino tiles into eight face-down stacks of four each. He then leaned back and looked at the other players expectantly.

That was when Dan noted that each of the men had stacks of eight-sided, multi-colored coins in front of them—black, white, red, green, silver, and gold. Gadai had the highest stacks of coins. Smith had the lowest. As Dan watched, each man picked up some coins and placed them into an etched circle in front of them. Only then did the old man slide one of the piles of four dominoes to each of the men, before pulling one pile toward himself.

The men then turned over the four dominoes and started arranging them in front of themselves, placing two in etched squares labeled "low" and "high." When they were all finished, they compared their tiles to the old man's. Some smiled, others didn't, as the old man shifted coins toward the winners and away from the losers. Smith didn't smile, and Dan watched as the coins he had put in the circles in front of him were taken away.

It went like that for the next few turns, until Smith's coins were nearly gone. It was an eerie experience, since the gamblers were essentially silent. Dan wondered if they even knew each other's languages. He noticed that their faces, except for the old man's, were becoming more greedy and hungry-looking. Each had leaned forward, and were betting more aggressively.

The old man motioned at Smith's almost depleted stack, and signaled that this could be the last round. He shuffled the domino tiles and made another eight stacks as the others went all in—seemingly uniting to wipe out Smith. But not all the other players had the coins to effectively do so. If Smith lost this round, only Gadai and Blanco looked powerful enough to emerge as victors. It all depended on how the domino tiles fell.

Except, unlike the other rounds Dan had witnessed, the old man didn't choose which stacks went to each player. Instead, the old man motioned to Smith, who, as the poorest person, got to choose his stack. Smith was just leaning in, his arm outstretched, when Dan stepped forward and gripped Smith's sleeve.

The people at the table started to complain or rise until the old man put out his own thin arms. Then he looked at each one and said something in each of their languages, which shut them up and sat them down. Then he turned and smiled at Smith, and perhaps also at Dan.

"Pot's prerogative." He too, like Lulu, tongued over the "r."

Dan didn't question the statement, just looked down at Smith, who looked up at him, his arm unmoving. Dan pulled at Smith's sleeve until his hand was over another stack of four tiles.

"Do you mind?" Dan said to his boss of bosses.

Smith took that stack without question, and everyone but him started organizing their dominoes. Smith, however, was too busy staring at the tiles Dan had directed him to, and letting his lips stretch into a disbelieving smile.

Moments later, all hell broke loose.

Chapter 28

"Do you have any idea what you did?" Smith asked Dan as the two watched Gadai, the last of the players at the table, march angrily out of the room.

The Pakistani, like the rest of them, had looked ready to denounce the validity of the game, but they had clamped their teeth and jaws after one seemingly serene glare from the old man. Then they had stalked out in their particular nationalistic ways. In other words, only Misumi was polite about it.

When Dan did not reply, Smith continued. "You hit a Heaven and Earth combination. The odds of it are thirty-five thousand nine hundred and sixty to one."

"And," he heard the old man's voice, "only possible in this particular game of my own design—Pai Gow Ultimate."

Dan turned to face the old man, who was looking into his eyes.

Smith made the introduction. "May I present Feng San Wu," he said deferentially. "The owner of this establishment."

If Smith deferred to the man, the least—and smartest—thing Dan could do was the same.

"An honor," he said. He didn't think a handshake would do, so he bowed slightly.

The old man seemed to like that. "The man who moves a mountain," he said, "begins by carrying away small stones."

Smith's smile widened. "Shifu Feng likes to quote Confucius. He even named this establishment after him. 'Confucian Games.'"

"Ah," Dan repeated, realizing then it was probably the old man's recording he'd heard when the elevator doors had closed. "Where the elite meet to get beat?"

The old man seemed to like that too. He laughed and put a hand on Dan's shoulder as he led their way out of the room.

"'The superior man is modest in his speech, but exceeds in his actions,'" the old man murmured, making a feeble gesture at all the activity in the dangerous, illegal compound. "'By nature, men are nearly alike,'" he continued. "'By practice, they get to be wide apart.'" He ambled toward the fountain between the two Zeta men, and Dan saw conflicting things in his watery but alert eyes.

"You know," he mused, "my people were so desperate to gamble that they created a betting ring to wager on the life expectancy of terminally ill patients. Police reports surmised that the patients' families went along in order to pay for the funerals. I realized then I should create this place." He raised one arm toward the spire. "Up there, the beauty of nature." He lowered his arm. "Down here, the baseness of nurture. They are not so different, Mr. Morgan." He held his palm up. "They turn and flow into each other, like day into night." He turned his hand to show his knuckles.

"Like yin and yang, right?" Dan offered.

The old man beamed. "Exactly." He gazed across the sea of gamblers, and suddenly looked tired. "Like the brain and the body. Humans cannot exist without both. And I dedicate my life and my wealth to serving both." He finished his musing with another Confucius quote. "'I slept and dreamt life is beauty. I woke and found life is duty.'"

At first Dan thought the man had said "doody" but realized that he'd said "duty." Dan thought that the quote would work very well with either word.

"If you'll excuse me, gentlemen," Feng said, and he was quickly flanked by three beautiful hostesses who, while they didn't touch him, stayed close by as he moved back toward the private rooms.

Dan watched him go, hearing Smith speak beside him. "A remarkable man. He sees to every special game of chance personally, and no one doubts his word." He then leaned closer to Dan's ear. "So tell me, Cobra. How *did* you hit the Heaven and Earth jackpot?"

Dan turned back to Smith with an expression that was as hard as the magma around them. "Because I didn't give a damn about anything but my wife's murderer."

The words hit Smith like a glass of ice water. His diffident expression became serious. Then he motioned for Dan to follow him, and turned to step into the fountain.

Dan straightened in surprise, making him hesitate just long enough so that Smith moved out of grabbing range. Then he rolled his eyes in exasperation, and followed his superior into the water. He wasn't surprised when the liquid was warm. They were surrounded, after all, by a volcano and hot water springs.

As he neared Smith, he watched and waited to see who would react first—security or the gamblers. But neither did. Security just looked blankly through them, and the gamblers didn't look at all. Apparently security had orders to let the *gweilos* do whatever they wanted, and the gamblers had bigger fish to fry, or lose.

In just a few seconds Dan and Smith were up to their knees, with the closest fountain jet no more than five feet away. At that point, it was like standing next to a fire truck with all their hoses on full. But, even so, when Smith spoke, Dan somehow heard him.

"I don't care how good anybody's surveillance devices are," Smith said. "No one can hear us in here when the water's running. Not even the R-comm, I bet."

Dan didn't let the self-aware comment faze him. "Look," he seethed. "I don't care about your stupid games. I only tracked you down to find out who attacked us and destroyed my home."

"And I was only forced to run and arrange this stupid game for the same reason," Smith assured him. "Zeta Tech had completed the Threat Assessment Software, and, as you may remember, it revealed the existence of a widespread organization that had the exact opposite goals from ours. You called it Anti-Zeta. I, naturally, call it Alpha."

"And you didn't tell us about it?" Dan asked incredulously.

"Too late," Smith said. "Happened too fast. Oh, I had perceived a developing situation for some time: disgruntled, power-mongering Zeta contributors who didn't fully appreciate our peaceful intentions, but that's par for the course. Every government and religion works fine until you put more than one person in it."

Dan waved Smith's disclaimer away. "But other than wanting to destroy us all, what does that have to do with this?"

Smith, infuriatingly, held up a finger and, seemingly infected by Shifu Feng, quoted Confucius. "'Nature's secret is patience,'" he intoned. "Alpha finding out about TAS was no surprise. Zeta was most likely riddled with double agents. So, naturally, Alpha wanted the Threat Assessment Software for themselves, and if they couldn't get it, they wanted to kill everyone who knew about it."

Dan threw up his hands. It was the only thing he could do besides throttling his superior. "This is where I came in," he growled warningly.

Smith matched his look of intensity. "And this is *why* you came in," he said pointedly. "Because the moment their slaughter started, I saw no choice but to let every intelligence organization in the world know about TAS."

Dan couldn't keep himself from looking back at the private room. The other gamblers in that room had represented the countries with the greatest intelligence apparatuses, manpower, and finances—ninety espionage organizations between them.

"So, obviously," Dan said, waving an arm toward the Pai Gow room, "they wanted a piece of it."

"Obviously," Smith agreed. "So I said 'put your money where your mouth is.' And, as I expected, they loved that."

"You were playing for the software?" Dan asked.

"Even better," Smith countered. "They were playing to win *you*. I was playing to keep you."

"What?"

Smith's grin was torn between triumph and cunning. "Yes, all these ducks," he revealed to Dan, "were informed that TAS was in the hands of our most capable and violent operative, but if he died, TAS would be lost."

Well, at least that explained why anti-Zeta, a.k.a. Alpha, wanted to kill him, while all the others wanted to capture him.

Dan had to take a step back. He tried to resist, but he couldn't help himself. He started patting his limbs to find any sort of tell-tale bump.

"Where is it?" he demanded. "How did you plant it on me?"

Smith tried his best to look apologetic, but failed. "I don't know," he said honestly. "I had to leave that up to Diana. I was already halfway around the world, getting all these ducks in a row."

Dan took a threatening step toward Smith, but just as he started raising his fist, he found himself barking out a laugh. "Oh, I get it," he chortled. "That's what Feng meant by 'pot's prerogative.' *I* was the pot."

Smith smirked. "Yes. And, thanks to you, Zeta gets to keep TAS. For the moment."

Dan stiffened in the fountain despite all the hot spring water around them. "Yeah," he growled. "All bets are off now, aren't they? It's open season again, right?"

Smith cocked his head to the left. "Most assuredly. We are safe while under Shifu Feng's protection, but once we leave here…"

"What are we up against?" Dan asked, his mind working furiously.

"Alpha is now in the open," Smith informed him, "but that may make them even more dangerous. Now they'll try to make alliances to get TAS and wipe out Zeta, while I do somewhat the same."

"Somewhat?" Dan echoed.

Smith lowered his chin, his eyes flashing. "Offer TAS to the country that will promise resources to help us stop Alpha."

"Dammit, Smith," Dan snarled. "You make it all sound like a game."

The Zeta boss opened his arms to encompass all the gamblers around them. "It very well may be, Cobra."

"No," Dan Morgan said into his superior's face. "It may have gotten my wife killed ...and maybe some other innocent people ...thirteen years ago." He looked at Smith. "Did you kill Lo Liu's parents?"

He had pronounced the young woman's name perfectly.

When Smith remained silent, Dan asked another question. "You know who I'm talking about, right?"

This time Smith didn't hesitate. "Oh, yes. Given her remarkable tenacity, I would be very poor at my job if I didn't know who you were talking about."

"Did you kill her parents, or have them killed?"

"No," Smith said flatly. "No, I did not. And you know that's true, don't you?"

Dan had only to think about it for a second. It may have been somewhat reluctantly, but he nodded.

"As for your wife, Cobra," Smith continued, leaning down to look him in the eyes. "They must have thoroughly checked the wreckage of your house by now. That will tell the tale. But as you well know, Zeta's regular channels of communication have been hopelessly compromised, so none of us can find out from here. That is something you have to do, and with all speed, yes?"

Dan met his boss's eyes with angry acceptance. "Yes. And you?"

"Me?" Smith retorted with mock affront. "I have plans."

Dan looked at his superior in a way Smith did not like. "Want to hear God laugh?" Cobra asked him point blank. "Make plans."

"Confucius?" Smith asked, stepping back.

"Woody Allen," Dan replied, grabbing Smith's tie and leading him like a dog out of the fountain.

When they both could hear something other than the water and each other, Dan twisted his forefingers in his ears—as Feng and his three hostesses approached, the latter carrying fluffy towels and very fancy cordless hair dryers.

"Testing, testing, one, two, three," he said. "Cougar, you read me?"

The pilot answered. Apparently whatever radio silence Lily Randall had ordered him to follow had been lifted.

"Wet and soggy," he said in Dan's ear, rather than "loud and clear."

"Need a lift," Dan advised. "And bring the Peking Duck along."

"Roger that," Conley snapped. "Wheels up."

Dan let go of Smith's tie, took a towel, and turned to the boss man.

"Lulu keeps investigating her parents' deaths, right?"

"I welcome it," Smith said.

Dan believed him. He took a step toward the elevator, but turned back. "And nothing happens to her, yes? I know some people who would be very upset if something happened to her."

Smith chortled. "So do I," he reminded Dan. "I daresay she can take care of herself, Mr. Morgan. Especially now, since she has a Cobra as a friend of the family."

Dan smirked, then headed back to the elevators. But as he turned to take what he hoped was a last look at the casino, he saw General Deng saying something in Smith's ear. Then, as the elevator doors were closing, he saw Feng himself appear in the diminishing opening.

As those doors closed Dan heard the old man quote Confucius one last time, as if he had heard every word Dan and Smith had said.

"'Those who know the truth are not equal to those who love it.'"

Chapter 29

When Dan returned to the study-cum-library, only the hostess was waiting for him. But before he could go ballistic, she smiled in a way she hadn't before. It was a knowing, human smile, not a trained, plastic one. But the tune she sang was the same, albeit much sweeter.

"You are expected," she said, motioning toward a side door behind a circular stairwell—not back to the curtains through which they had entered.

Something about her tone and demeanor told him that he shouldn't fight her on this. And, sure enough, when he emerged from the side door, he stepped out into the reception hall's palatial kitchens, which were, in their own way, as impressive as the Confucian Games casino. Spectacular stoves lined each wall, with massive prep islands of wood, marble, quartz, granite, and soapstone lined up in between.

They could have made airplanes or luxury liners in the space, but instead they were making amazing food to serve, everything from ice cream sandwiches to chateaubriand for every visitor to the resort. A small army of international chefs attacked woks, pans, pots, and machines to realize their creations.

As Dan surveyed the food factory, he saw a squadron of waiters, waitresses, maids, and butlers in a clump in the corner, all staring in one direction as if they were betting on a cockroach race. Dan moved unerringly toward the assemblage, already certain what, and who, he would find.

Sure enough, there was Lulu, sitting on an empty overturned vegetable crate, her cheongsam dress unbuttoned and open. Underneath she wore black, second-skin tricot knit microfiber workout shorts and a matching low-cut Supplex/Lycra sports bra that left little to the imagination. Unlike the shirt and slacks he had first seen her in, there was no disguising her strength and fitness now.

"About time," she said when she saw him. "We running or walking out? As you can see, I'm ready for either." Her slippers—not surprisingly, considering her cleverness—would work for either outfit.

"A little of both," Dan informed her. "Let's say a healthy, non-obvious trot."

"Out the guests' or servants' exit?" Lulu asked as she stood and started re-clipping the cheongsam.

"Take your pick."

She started unbuttoning her dress again while talking to the others. "Mao-shan," Dan heard in his head, and the R-comm had no other translation.

"What's that?" Dan asked as one of the maids tossed Lulu black tights and a long-sleeve turtleneck that glowed like silk and was thin as a hair.

"You heard of ninja?" Lulu asked as she slipped both on with ease.

"Sure," Dan said.

"Mao-shan are their Chinese predecessors," Lulu said, taking a larger-sized turtleneck and tights from a butler and holding them out to Dan. "You're all wet."

Dan looked down at his tuxedo, thinking of his approaching chauffeur. "No thanks," he told his Taiwanese contact. "I think this'll do. Wet or not."

He waited until Lulu gifted her dress to a like-sized waitress, and turned toward the servants' exit, all but blending into the darkness.

"I got to find out about these mao-shan," Dan commented as he joined her.

"You don't find mao-shan," Lulu advised him, scanning the area behind the reception hall. "They find you. Head for the garage?"

Dan shook his head. "What's the most remote, unused part of this place?"

Lulu looked up at him. "Edge of the Rift Valley," she answered, pointing northeast. "We better get going. Quite the hike."

They set off without another word. Once they passed the buildings, zoo, farm, and orchard, the park became notably more wooded, surrounding the two with cotton trees and scarlet flowers.

The grass and ground became more inclined and Dan spotted several different kinds of deer peering curiously through the night at them. They were obviously not used to being hunted, since although the elk were still stand-offish, they didn't bolt at first sight.

Dan enjoyed the silence and serenity, knowing he'd probably get neither again for the foreseeable future, then said the magic word.

"Smith."

Lulu let it hang in the warm night air for a beat. "Smith," she then echoed.

"I'm surprised you didn't try to get to him, despite your seeming willingness for me to talk to him first."

"Come on," she grumbled. "Get real. You were expected, remember? I'd have as much chance getting to him in that place as a snowflake in a supernova." She looked at the sky with a certain grim longing. "He's probably long gone, even now."

"He says he didn't kill your parents."

"And you believe him?" Her words, coming from the darkness, carried only curiosity, not accusation.

"Yes," Dan said. "And you should too."

There was another pause. Longer this time. When her next word came, it was as hard as diamonds.

"Why?"

"Because," Dan answered with the same logic and conviction he had felt when confronting Smith in the fountain. "If he had, you'd also be dead by now."

The silence fell again like a tsunami of tar. They kept walking for another minute or two until Dan looked up, discovering the jaw-dropping infinity of stars sparkling above them like a billion quasars. He had never seen a night sky so massive and clear.

It threatened to be so overwhelming that he was either going to fall onto his back and stare, slack-jawed, or start talking again.

"Think about it. Smith knew you were tracking him, and he knew why. If he was guilty, what's the point of keeping you alive? To taunt you like a cat playing with a mouse? Smith may be many things, but..."

"All right, all right already," Lulu interrupted from the darkness. "I know, I know. Why do you think I wasn't arguing?"

"He said he welcomed your continuing investigation..."

"He better," Lulu replied. "'Cause I'm not stopping. He may not know which of his many ...*associates*"—she said the word as if she were saying "vermin"—"did the deed, but I bet he knows that one or more of them did."

"And he's leaving you to find out," Dan finished her thought. "Now that's Smith all right. If he had to set right everything his ...associates did wrong, he'd have no time to move the likes of you and me around like..."

Dan was prevented from saying "pawns" or "puppets" by a sudden downdraft of air so powerful it brought them to their knees.

"Niubi!" Lulu hissed, while Dan heard the literal translation for the exclamation of amazement in his ear: "Cow vagina!"

Cow vagina, indeed, Dan thought as he peered up through slit eyelids at the underbelly of the Flying Fox slowly making its descent through a grove of bombax trees that seemed purposely pruned to make a perfect camouflaging shape for the aircraft.

He grabbed Lulu's shoulders and propelled her outside the grove until the stealth jet could make its silent landing. Then he accompanied her back just as the hatch opened and Peter "Cougar" Conley stuck his head out.

"Going my way?" he inquired.

* * * *

Dan brought both up to date as Lulu wandered Palecto's interior, trying very hard not to look impressed. Conley, for his part, was trying to do the same, but with regard to Lulu's manner and outfit rather than Palecto's accessories.

"So he's been making us all dance in the name of some amorphous larger picture?" the Taiwanese op declared.

"I *like* dancing," Conley commented, taking his usual position against the far wall between the lavatory and galley. He looked to Dan. "That's what I thought we were hired to do."

"And dance damn well," Cobra agreed. "Especially when the enemy is watching and listening."

Lulu didn't argue the point. "Yeah, all right," she grudgingly agreed. "I'm just *yanfan*, and Cobra knows why."

Cougar chuckled when their R-comms translated her term as "pissed."

"So do I," Cougar reminded her, pointing at his ear. "And I don't blame you."

Lulu looked from one to the other, then stood straight and put her fists on her hips.

"Yeah," she said, "right. And when do I get one of those? I had to trash my Z-comm when it started screeching."

Dan stood, his hands up in submission. "Next time you're in Orange County, I know a doctor who would be happy to oblige."

Lulu batted Dan's arms away, but with a grateful smile. "Don't patronize me, Cougar. You know my hands are full here."

Dan glanced at Cougar's quizzical expression.

"You know," he said as way of explanation. "Friends-of-the-family issues."

"Gotcha." Conley looked at Lulu. "Can we drop you off at the garage?"

Lulu went from looking petulant to looking excited. "Can you?" she responded excitedly as well as doubtfully, thinking of all the possible disruptions and witnesses. "I'd love to fly in this thing."

"Watch me," Conley answered.

* * * *

Naturally, Cougar's landing was nothing short of brilliant, hiding in clouds until he could drop down silently behind a copse of conifers just fifty feet from the garage. If any valets saw anything, they didn't raise an alarm. Besides, Dan truly doubted it, since given the jet's pitch blackness, the only thing anyone would notice even if they were looking directly at it would be a series of Palecto-shaped swathes of stars blocked from view.

When Lulu stepped toward the hatch, she was wearing the R-Zeta uniform of dark gray, lightweight, moisture-wicking, odor-fighting t-shirt, pants, slip-ons, and collarless jacket over her sports bra, workout shorts, and Chinese slippers.

"One step closer to that R-comm," Conley commented. "Keep up the good work."

"Deal," she told the pilot before turning to Dan.

They said nothing, but saw in their eyes the tasks ahead: Dan finding out what had happened to his wife, and Lo Liu finding out what had happened to her parents. And both knew they wouldn't do anything to screw up each other's mission.

The Taiwanese aren't huggers, and Dan could sense that. But when Lulu raised her right hand and held it there, he gladly gave her a high five.

"Good hunting," he told her.

She smiled at the aptness of his comment, then hopped to the hatch door.

"Ready," she told Cougar.

He pressed a spot on a white, smooth, console, and the hatch slid open, then slid shut again. Lo Liu had disappeared between the two actions. But before she did they both heard the same thing.

"*Ao bai goulai chi tou.*"

It took even the R-comm awhile to figure out that obscure Taiwanese saying, so it wasn't until the Flying Fox was out over the Philippine Sea that they both heard the translation.

"Come and play again," was the best the R-comm could do.

"Quite the cutie," Conley judged in retrospect. "No Peking Duck, of course, but still…"

Dan stood up, stretched, and yawned. "Yeah, too bad we probably won't see her again." He stopped in mid-stretch and turned back to Conley. "Where are you hiding the Peking Duck anyway?" he asked his partner.

Conley concentrated on the controls. "Not welcome on the fragrant island," he said cryptically. "But ready and willing when able."

Dan nodded with more understanding now than he would have had before his visit to the island.

"Where to?" Conley asked him before he wandered off too far.

"Home, James," Morgan replied, making his way toward a dream cap. "We got our work cut out for us."

Chapter 30

The first thing Dan Morgan's Andover, Massachusetts neighbor Steve Richards heard was Neika barking. When Richards sat up in bed, he looked to where the dog was collared out in the yard.

As much as he had tried to make the German Shepherd understand that she was welcome in the Richards home, the loyal canine had refused to budge from her self-appointed place keeping watch over the burnt-out patch of grass next door. Richards was just about to lie back down, hoping to ignore the sounds, when the barking continued.

That's not like her, he thought and sat up again, eyes wide open. He craned his neck toward the window and, to his surprise, saw what looked like a dark gray ghost shambling through what remained of the Morgan house next door.

Richards was up and on his feet, grabbing for his robe, and heading for the stairs in the space of two seconds. In the space of ten seconds he was in the yard and un-clipping Neika from her leash. In the space of thirty seconds, he was catching up to the dog as she was hopping and licking all over the "ghost."

"Humph," Dan Morgan said in apologetic tones as he scratched the dog with a big smile on his face. "I should've seen her first, of course. But I thought she would've made even more noise if I had."

"Silly man," Richards murmured, surmising why Morgan was here. The fact that he hadn't seen his dog first, and had chosen to arrive in the middle of the night told him that much. "You won't find anything," he advised his neighbor. "The cops and firemen didn't. Missy thought that was good news," he finished, invoking his wife's name. Unlike him, she had grown up with dogs, so Neika would've had to howl like a werewolf to wake her up.

Dan looked up from Neika's calming face to his neighbor's caring one. Both the neighbor and the dog could feel the waves of sadness coming off the man.

"Now I know why 'it seems like a lifetime' is such a cliché," Dan mused, looking around at what had once been his home. "Because it really does seem like a lifetime ago that I was here."

"Seems that way to me too," Richards admitted, looking around the neighborhood, which, happily, had gone back to being quiet and peaceful very quickly after that terrible night.

Dan looked up at Richards. "They really didn't find anything, or are you just being nice?"

"Or worse, they found something and thought it best not to tell me," Richards countered, before shaking his head. "No, I have friends at both the cop shop and the firehouse, Dan. The latter think it was a torch job and the former are keeping the file open while they look for you …and your family."

The words made it clear. No bodies were found in the wreckage. The expression on Dan's face, when he raised it back to meet his neighbor's eyes, was both hopeful and haunted.

"So that's it, huh?" he said hollowly, having to make sure. "Nothing?"

"Nothing human," Richards assured him.

That got Dan to his feet, Neika circling her master's legs. "What does that mean?"

Richards' expression was knowing. "That means the authorities found no clues to follow. But that doesn't mean I didn't." Chuckling at the look on Dan's face, Richards turned toward his own garage, and beckoned Dan to follow. "Come on. I got something I think you should see."

* * * *

It was a key. A key in a small, strong, titanium box Richards had found under some charred planks, melted plastic, and pulverized bricks. It was a key Dan recognized.

Much to his excitement, he had thanked Richards profusely, then, somewhat to his frustration, asked if he was willing to keep Neika for just a little while longer.

"Of course," the neighbor had replied. "She's a gem. You know that. But I'm not the one you should be asking."

Richards had looked down at the dog, who had already realized what was happening—and had seemed none too pleased about it.

Dan had realized the truth of his neighbor's statement and had kneeled down to lovingly grasp Neika's head and look into her clear eyes.

"I'm sorry baby," he had told her so quietly only she could hear the words. "Nothing I'd like better than to take you along, but the people I'm dealing with would like nothing better than to kill you just to see my reaction. So stay here with Steve for just a little while longer, okay?"

Then Dan had said their command code word for "be a good girl" and left with so much regret that he hadn't been sure he could ever return to this street without feeling it.

The next stop was the remote storage facility he had found to keep his secrets. He had chosen the place not just because it was isolated, but also because the units were individual boxes unattached to each other, as well as out in the open air rather than inside a building. It was also accessible twenty-four-seven, so a renter didn't have to rub shoulders with other renters during normal hours. In other words, exactly the sort of place most modern types would steer clear of.

Jenny had discovered its existence on one of his most recent missions—the mission that had put her in harm's way …the mission she had shotgunned her way out of.

The key in the little titanium box someone had hidden in their house before it had been attacked was a dead ringer for the one he had on his own storage unit. But when he tried it on his laminated, stainless, titanium, uncuttable lock, it didn't work. It wasn't a key for his unit.

Dan tried the key in every lock, moving in ever-decreasing squares, starting from the first unit closest to the corner of the barbed wire fence. The storage unit establishment was about an acre big—more than forty thousand square feet—but Dan just kept going until the key fit in another laminated, stainless, titanium, uncuttable lock. He turned it to the right, and the bolt snapped open.

Dan almost laughed. Of course it was the unit directly behind his. It was also the same size as his. Dan left the key in the lock, then slipped his hand inside his dark gray jacket until his fingers were resting on the butt of his Walther PPK. Leaving them there, he used his free hand to slip the lock off, grab the now open latch, and lift the corrugated steel, garage-like, door up and open.

The lamp lights along the outer fence were enough for him to see what lay within. Inside the storage unit were not weapons or files or codes or jewels or money or even passwords. Instead it looked like a museum of his life.

There was the first checkers set his mother had given him. There was the old-fashioned coffee grinder his father had given him. There were lovingly detailed classic car models he had made as a tween. There were the wrestling cups, boxing medals, and football trophies he had been awarded as a teen. There was Jenny's and his wedding album. There was even the "embrace the pain, love the pain" pillow Jenny had stitched for him as a joke on his fortieth birthday.

It hit him, in the words of another cliché, like a thunderbolt. This was the ephemera of his entire married life—not his family life. All traces of Alex were M.I.A., removed when their daughter got her own place. It was his and Jenny's life, all collected in one place …one place that wasn't their home.

Dan blinked, realizing all this was not just his life in souvenirs. This was not a museum of the Morgans, secreted away just in case something bad happened. It was clear and present evidence that, somehow, Jenny had known that their home would be destroyed, and had moved all of this into the storage unit before it could happen.

Dan remained in the open entry of the storage unit, trying to find anything that would help him believe that his theory was not the case. His gaze flitted from memory to memory until it settled on a gleaming eight-by-ten gunmetal frame. He tried to see what was inside the frame from where he stood, but a lamp light from the fence created a glare.

Dan took a step closer, letting the corrugated metal entry slide down. The shadow from the descending door again obscured the picture from view. With another step, Dan saw it was a photo of two people. Another step revealed to him that one of them was Jenny. She was smiling, looking honestly happy. She had her arm around the other person's shoulder. But when he took another step closer, a different lamp light at a different section of the fence blotched out the other person's face.

It wasn't him in the photograph. The person wasn't tall enough. Those weren't his wide shoulders. Dan angrily took another step closer, causing the corrugated metal door to screech down even further, plunging the room into gloom. Dan spun to stalk back to wrench it open so it would stay open, but someone beat him to it. Dan froze as the corrugated door began to rise again, ever so slowly.

As it did he pulled his Walther from its shoulder holster, and held it loosely at the ready. He watched as two strong hands kept lifting the storage unit door, until the lamplights from the fence poured in again, blanketing the front of the visitor's face into darkness, while surrounding the head with glowing yellow light.

"Hey Cobra," the visitor said with a voice Dan recognized. "Long time no see."

Chapter 31

The person who re-opened the storage unit door didn't step into the light. He stepped into the gloom, so that the darkness inside the storage unit and the yellow light outside it balanced just enough for Dan to make out the person's face.

Dan made a noise between a sigh and a snort but, quite noticeably, didn't put his gun away.

"Diesel," he said.

Diesel was one of the core back-up ops Zeta used, especially whenever the Morgans were involved. He had been the hot-shot sniper before Alex had come into her own, but had also been useful as a driver. Hence, Dan figured, his code name.

"Cobra," the big, crew-cut man repeated. "How's it hanging?"

Dan ignored the very small talk, and answered the question with another question. "Been waiting long?"

Diesel jammed the corrugated door back up into the open position, making a big point of showing how strong he was, and stood his ground.

"Long enough," he commented. "But you know how it is for us field guys. Get an assignment, do an assignment, get another assignment."

There was no love lost between the two. They'd had to face each other as combatants twice during their last assignment, and both times, it was Diesel who'd come out worse for wear. As they watched each other, Dan got the sudden mental image of two jousting horses facing off, snorting and hoofing the ground, champing on their bits until they got the signal to charge.

"Yeah," Dan drawled. "I know how it is. So what's the assignment anyway?"

"Take a wild guess," Diesel said, stepping back and aside. As he did, Dan saw he was wearing full assault team gear. "Find you, bring you in for debriefing."

"Where to?" Dan asked, unbudging. "A crater where Zeta HQ used to be?"

Diesel grimaced. "Naw, AZ43-I set up a temp command post nearby." He had used the internal designation for Paul Kirby. "We knew you'd show up here sooner or later."

Dan raised his head. "A temp command post?" he marveled. "Why not your place? You live around here too, don't you?"

Dan watched Diesel's eyes. They seemed unfocused for a second, but then relaxed.

"Hell, Cobra, you wouldn't want to see my place. Looks like a tornado hit it." He waved Dan over in a convivial manner. "Come on, let's get a move on. The sooner we team up, the sooner we can go after whoever did this."

Dan's smile was wide and tragic. "Right you are," he said, then got close enough to put his gun in Diesel's face, but not so close that he left the protection of the storage unit. "Your place looks like a tornado hit it, huh?" he spat. "Well, my place, and all the other loyal Zeta ops' places, look like a bomb hit 'em."

"Hey, hey, hey," Diesel complained, his hands up. "That's what I meant, Cobra! You know that's what I meant."

"No, I don't," Dan seethed, motioning with his gun. "Weapons off and down, very slowly."

Diesel, like a deer in headlights, did as he was told, but his deer was a pleading one.

"Come on, Cobra," he said, gingerly putting his nine millimeter automatic onto the ground just outside the storage unit entrance. "You're not going to shoot me…"

"Not in the face, no," Dan agreed. "But it might be interesting to see if a Walther round can penetrate riot gear leg padding."

"Easy, Cobra, easy," Diesel went on, his eyes darting as he rose, hands still raised to his ears. "What do you want from me?"

"A leader," Dan told him. "A leader to follow all the way to Paul Kirby. Then we'll all have a nice talk."

All Diesel's obsequiousness left him. He even dropped his hands to his side with a knowing smile.

"You know that's not going to happen, Cobra. So let's stop fooling around and deal with this like men."

Dan scoffed, standing his ground and not lowering the Walther. "When did you turn, Diesel? When did they get to you?"

The big man gave a little nod, then shook his head slightly as if having an internal battle between yes and no.

"You that slow, Cobra? Right after Bishop admitted he was a double agent, of course." That had happened on their last mission together as well. "And if you were smart, you'd turn too. Why the hell keep working for this penny-ante, screwed-up ..."

In mid-word, Diesel dove faster than Dan thought he could. But he didn't dive for his nine millimeter, he dove at Dan, betting that the military-trained agent wouldn't or even couldn't shoot anyone who had fought alongside him full in the face.

And he was partly right. At the last second, Dan had shifted his aim for Diesel's leg, but only because he wanted someone to interrogate later. In any case, unlike at the Pai Gow Ultimate table, this time Dan Morgan came up snake eyes. Turned out the assault team padding could handle a PPK round, especially a glancing one.

Next second, Diesel's fists were smashing into Dan's wrist and face, sending the gun flying back into the picture frame, and Dan flying back into the table holding all his classic car models. As they cracked, broke, splintered, and shattered, Dan, as much as he tried not to, couldn't avoid a split-second feeling that a sliver of his childhood had been destroyed, giving Diesel just enough time to take advantage.

He grabbed at Dan's throat with one hand and at his eyes with the other, sending them both back into the display case full of Dan's football, boxing, and wrestling awards. The nearly five hundred pounds of solid male muscle smashed into it like a wrecking ball into a house of cards. But rather than feel like he'd lost a part of his youth, Dan felt all that athletic accomplishment and knowledge flowing back into him.

As Diesel tried to get him onto the ground, Dan remembered his military jiu-jitsu teacher bellowing at him at the beginning of his lessons.

If he gets you on the ground, you're done!

Dan, feeling like he was floating in slow motion rather than falling quickly, planted one anchoring foot, grabbed Diesel's nearest gripping pinky, spun on his anchoring leg, and twisted Diesel's last finger as if trying to yank a pull-tab off a beer can.

It was Diesel below him, heading to the ground on his back, with his face twisted in pain from the lightning bolts his pinky was hurling into his brain. As they both slammed to the storage unit floor, Dan remembered what his jiu-jitsu teacher had said at the end of the lesson.

If you get him to the ground, finish him!

So Dan's knee was up between Diesel's legs and his forearm was down across Diesel's throat. But Diesel's leg was up as well, with just enough time to get his knee on Dan's chest. With a mighty surge, he propelled Dan off just enough so the groin shot and larynx-crushing didn't have their full effect.

Neither man waited to catch their breath. Dan tried to leap in mid-push, to bring both feet down on any part of Diesel he could reach, while Diesel rolled and vaulted up. They crashed into each other in mid-air, sending checkers and coffee grounds everywhere around them like some sort of comic book "pow!"

Both Dan and Diesel brought their fists around, only Diesel needed his other hand to steady himself on the checkerboard. But Dan's other hand was free. He used it to chop into the elbow of Diesel's punching arm as his meaty fist connected with Diesel's cheek, nose, and the lower part of his right eye.

Dan's right foot hit the ground just as his fist connected, giving him the anchor needed for power. His other foot went back like a discus thrower, with Diesel's head becoming the discus. The ex-Zeta driver shot backwards, smashing into a set of Royal Limoges fine porcelain tableware Jenny's parents had given the Morgans in honor of their engagement.

As the plates, bowls, and cups spun, flew, and smashed, Diesel flailed out for anything he could find. Dan dove after him, but both stopped dead as they found themselves in a crouch, facing each other, their boot knives in their right hands.

Dan had his Smith & Wesson gut cutter. Diesel had a Kershaw that Dan laughingly recognized as the "4007 Secret Agent Fixed Blade." It was actually called that, and the fact that it was the one Diesel had chosen told Dan all he needed to know about the Zeta wannabe and traitor. Still, it was a three-ounce, nine-inch, black oxide steel blade with a rubberized handle, and could cut him just as well as a knife named Spectre.

The two men stayed where they were, both looking for an opening that wouldn't result in a gushing vein. Diesel's face was twisted in derision and daring, while Dan's features remained placidly serious. He remembered his knife fighting teacher's first words.

There are three rules of knife fighting. One, don't get in a knife fight. Two, didn't you hear the first rule? Don't get in a knife fight! And three, if you're stupid enough to get into a knife fight, accept the fact you're going to get cut. Just make sure that your cut isn't fatal.

And then the man had taught them every trick in the book to ensure that. And one of the primary rules was to make sure the opponent's knife had something to cut other than your flesh.

Dan's free hand swept out, searching for anything that wouldn't bring him within Diesel's reach. Diesel, knowing a good idea when he saw it, did the same. As soon as their hands found something, they charged each other, the blades low, plunging, slicing, and plunging again like pistons.

What Dan had grabbed by happenstance was his thick, heavy, wedding album. What Diesel had grabbed, because it was the only thing left he could find, was the "embrace the pain, love the pain" pillow.

The knives flashed out like saw-scaled vipers—the snakes that kill more humans than any other. Diesel's blade sunk into the wedding album like a spike, and stuck there. Dan's blade went through the pillow like it was cloth and feathers, which it was, then sliced open Diesel's arm from the end of his elbow to the tip of his pinky.

Diesel tried so hard not to scream that he nearly cracked his teeth. He managed to hold onto his knife, but couldn't prevent himself from dropping back to the floor as if in the middle of an epileptic seizure.

"Remember, you bastard," Dan barked as he stepped back. "You can't spell Diesel without D-I-E."

Dan tried to keep a careful watch on the man. After all, although painfully wounded and spurting blood, he was still a figurative and literal backstabber. Even so, the man's pathetic contortions and pitiful noises aroused both sympathy and disgust. After all, the man had once been a fairly dependable fellow fighter. Dan tried to remember if Diesel had ever saved him.

That was a mistake. When he looked back, Diesel had managed to use the remaining splintered table to block Dan from seeing him reach behind his back with his uncut hand. The knife was no longer in it. Instead, there was a Beretta Nano—a nine-millimeter automatic designed for concealed carry, stopping power, and never getting stuck in a holster, boot, or belt. And despite his knife wound, the gun was steadily pointing in the middle of Dan's face.

Diesel let Dan see his pained, victorious, mocking smile, and started to say "never take your eyes…" when his gun hand exploded off his wrist, taking the Nano with it.

A stunned second later, Diesel was back writhing and howling on the ground, unable to use one filleted hand to stop the bleeding of the other bloody stump. A second after that, Alexandra Morgan came marching in, slinging a McMillan CS5 "Stubby" sniper rifle, complete with suppressor, over her dark-gray garbed shoulder.

She took one glance at her father before stepping over to where Diesel contorted, pulling a med kit out of the messenger bag slung over her other shoulder.

"How are you?" her father asked with honest interest.

"Better than him," Alex told Dan with not much irony as she brought out a tourniquet, bandage pad, crazy glue applicator, and painkiller syringe. "Cougar picked me up right after he dropped you off." She took a second from her medical ministrations to point at her ear. "Listening to your escapades was better than any iTunes playlist."

Dan came around the other side, kneeled, and gingerly picked up the blood and gut-flecked Beretta and boot knife between his thumbs and forefingers.

"What's the crazy glue for?" he wondered.

"You think I'm going to stitch that cut up?" she retorted. You've seen my sewing skills. Besides, we don't have all day."

Dan watched as Alex held the sliced flesh together with one hand and smeared the glue on it with the other. Soon, his attention wandered to the nearly hysterical, bleeding betrayer.

He couldn't help thinking about a scene in one of his favorite Westerns when a character advised, *if you're going to shoot, shoot ...don't talk.* But he didn't say it aloud because he wanted Diesel to talk, really badly.

"Got any truth serum?" he asked his daughter.

"Do I got truth serum?" she answered. "Does Yogi Bear love picnic baskets?" She glanced up at Dan. "That was the purpose of this exercise, wasn't it?"

"Not entirely," he reminded her. "But it's a good start."

"And for a finish?" Alex inquired as she reached for a second syringe.

"Find AZ43-I, *and* AZ04-D," he said.

"Well, I don't know about your favorite Beacon Hill buddy," she said while administering a narcoanalysis injection. "But remember what I promised when you left for the fragrant island?"

"I do indeed," Dan answered, an expectant, relieved smile growing on his face.

She looked ready to reveal the results of her search, but was then distracted by the way Diesel stiffened.

"First things first," she reminded Dan, nodding toward Diesel, who seemed to be drifting into a state of hypnosis, a coma, or both.

As they waited for the drug, or mortality, to take effect, both Morgans found themselves looking at the wreckage all around them.

"My, my, my," Alex tsked. "Look at the mess you've made of your life."

Dan didn't know whether to laugh or cry until his eyes settled on that pesky picture that had bothered him when he'd first entered. The one that now lay on the storage unit floor, its gunmetal frame bent and its glass cracked.

Dan leaned over and peered at it, hoping the damage didn't obscure the other person in the shot. It didn't. Dan Morgan looked down to see his smiling, happy wife, with her arm around the shoulders of AZ04-D herself—Diana Bloch, Zeta's head of operations.

Chapter 32

When Dan saw what was on the back of the picture, he all but forgot about Diesel.

They didn't get much out of him anyway—not even his name, rank, and serial number. Nor did Dan expect them to. If ever there was the personification of a "need-to-know agent," it was Diesel. Anyone, Alpha or Zeta, could throw him farther than they could trust him.

Dan figured Diesel was just one of many biodegradable operatives Alpha had assigned to watch for Cobra at any number of his haunts and hangouts. Even the idea of following Diesel to get to Paul Kirby was a nonstarter. Just about the only thing the wounded, drugged prisoner coughed up was that he was ordered to wait until Dan walked in front of him before trying to kill him.

They left the handless man at a hospital after anonymously informing the Boston P.D. that he was one of the men responsible for the Beacon Hill bombings. The Morgans had little doubt that even if Diesel had been in one piece and at full strength, a lowly assistant district attorney would be able to nail him for decades, if not centuries, behind bars. And if he tried to invoke the name of Cobra as some sort of state's evidence, Alpha or Zeta could flip a coin to see who would serve Diesel his own death penalty.

Once Diesel was out of their sight, Dan forgot him. They were too busy with the six letters and fourteen numbers on the back of the photograph.

"Six letters?" Lincoln Shepard exclaimed in their ears from back in the Fox Burrow. "Are you sure?" The Morgans' ominous silence was all that was needed to make the I.T. wiz backtrack. "I just thought maybe all the destruction inside the storage unit had smudged the writing or something..."

"No smudging," Dan assured him. "No mistake."

Speaking of haunts and hangouts, they had collected Yuri's Ford Focus Hatchback from Dan's secret garage and decided the best place to drive it was The Bar With No Name, which, conveniently, was open twenty-four-seven. That was also the best place where a father and daughter in dark gray outfits could disappear into a booth and seemingly talk to themselves.

Thankfully the squabbling couple Dan had met there before were nowhere in sight, although Dan couldn't help but wonder how they would have reacted if they saw him again.

"Well," Peter Conley drawled in their ears from his undisclosed location, "the fourteen numbers are most likely longitude and latitude again. Read 'em to me, and I'll work on that while you brainiacs work on the letters."

"Back to square one," Linc moaned after Dan read the numbers.

"I don't think so," Lily Randall countered from over Linc's shoulder. "Smith said that it was Diana who planted the TAS on you, right, Dan?"

Dan and Alex shared a look over their beers, then the young lady returned to ravenously attacking the surprisingly good huevos rancheros.

"Right," Dan said.

"So, as with everything before, Smith and Bloch were working together," Randall surmised.

"Yeesh," Karen O'Neal chimed in from her station in Fox Burrow's information center. "I can't even begin to imagine what complex convolutions that brain trust could think up…"

"No worries," Alex assured them between bites. "They both knew that they still had to make it clear to the likes of us."

"And only us," Randall reminded them. "Not Alpha. So I'm guessing, and hoping, that this code is in the same Taiwanese puppet theater language."

"It's not," Dan informed them. "These letters look completely different than the other letters."

"Dad blast it," Linc complained.

"No, it makes sense," Randall suggested. "Once we revealed the Taiwanese puppet language key, Bloch and Smith couldn't have been sure that one of the double agents wouldn't get word of it."

"Read them to me," Linc asked. "We'll take it from there."

Dan stared down at the back of the picture, trying to ignore his daughter's eating noises. "I can't," he confessed. "They're some sort of hieroglyphics."

His daughter stopped eating and there was a silence along the R-comm.

"Well," Linc continued. "Can you take a picture and text it to me?"

"Of course they can't," O'Neal interrupted. "They trashed their phones as soon as the Zeta Disaster Protocol was invoked."

"Yeah, yeah," Linc agreed. "Of course."

"The R-comm wouldn't happen to have a video component you didn't tell us about, did it?" Dan inquired to the air.

"Sorry to say, no," Renard answered without shame. "Facial recognition scrambler, pulse rate monitor, location finder, yes. Camera, no."

Silence descended as each remaining Zeta agent racked their brains for an answer. Even Dan tried, only to be interrupted by his daughter clutching his arm. He looked over to see her shining eyes, which were wet and bright with realization and memory.

"Dad," she said, knowingly using that term instead of Dan or Cobra. "When I was a little girl, Mom and I had our own unique language. So we could communicate and no one else would understand us."

"A written language?" Randall quickly asked.

"Yes!" Alex answered. "Every day she'd include a note in my lunch box. It started as a game, but became a habit all through kindergarten and grammar school." Alex looked down at the wreckage on her plate. "But I stopped when I got to junior high. I was too cool for that..."

Dan saw his daughter blush, and his heart went out to her. But then, his hand did too, holding the picture.

"I guess it's about time you looked at this too, huh?"

She did, and within a minute she had the translation. The six letters were B, I, G, D, I, and G. When that was done, Conley informed them that the latitude and longitude was a spot surprisingly close to The Bar with No Name.

Breakfast forgotten, the Morgans were out of the booth and the bar faster than Diesel could've pleaded the fifth.

* * * *

"The Big Dig," Dan muttered in the dawn's early light, while looking at a locked chain link fence surrounding a refuse-strewn patch of broken concrete and metal near the Seaport across from Logan Airport. "Started way before you were born," he told Alex, who was already trying to figure out the best way to get inside without alerting any passing authorities. "It was supposed to make car travel easier."

"Doesn't look so big to me," she commented, trying to see if any street kids had beaten her to making a slice in the fence.

Dan yanked the chain links far enough from the right wall of a building that he could slip between the two. "Took twenty years longer than it was supposed to, cost triple what it was supposed to, put a bunch of people in jail, and killed an innocent bystander when a hunk of it fell on them." He grimaced at his daughter as she slipped in behind him. "Your tax dollars at work."

"So why are we here?" Alex wondered as the two moved quickly into the shadows created by an unfinished elevated roadway and the side of an unfinished abutment.

"This is where the longitude and latitude numbers pinpoint," Dan reminded her, checking the area for any curious on-lookers. He could see none.

The two stood facing the corner of a wall, with crumbling concrete to their right and rusting steel to their left.

"So what now?" Alex wondered.

"I'm surveying maps," O'Neal informed them from thousands of miles away.

"And we're hacking security cams in the area," Renard added.

"But it looks like you two are the key," Randall reminded them.

"If it were me," Linc sad. "I'd start digging around like a rabid dog."

Dan's brows knitted. "This was a fairly dangerous place even before the Big Dig screwed it up even more," he mused, looking down. "It's mostly landfill, with subway tunnels, utility pipes, demolished house foundations, and even parts of sunken ships stuck in it."

Dan was about to throw his hands into the air and go back to the bar for another beer when Alex took three steps to the right, two steps back, then dropped to her knees. Dan caught up with her just as she wiped some dirt off a metal plate, then yanked it up to reveal a half-circle sewer entrance.

"Damn," Dan growled. "That thing must weigh a…"

By then Alex had gripped the center of the half-moon top, and pulled it upward, revealing a pipe. It went down and off out of sight like a water-park slide, but was just big enough to fit them if they went one at a time. Alex looked up at her father with bright eyes.

"How the hell did you know that was there?" he asked, just as he realized the answer.

"Mom told me," Alex Morgan said.

There was no doubt or delay after that. Even if Dan had wanted to go first, just in case, he was too slow to stop his daughter, who hopped over the opening and slid down, her arms above her head. Dan followed quickly, his arms crossed in front of him.

The pipe brought them down twenty feet, then curled up just enough so they could land on their feet in the darkness.

"Damn," Dan repeated as he pulled his ten-in-one tool from his pocket. "I feel like Maxwell Smart."

"Who?" Alex asked, doing the same.

"Google it," Dan suggested as he brought the tool's high-powered, highly charged flashlight up to reveal an abandoned underground construction site. "If we get out of this."

"Yeah," Alex responded, pointing her all-in-one tool's flashlight in the opposite direction. "I sure can't Google it now. I bet there are no bars down here. Right, Linc?"

Linc didn't answer.

"Linc?"

Again, he didn't answer. She didn't bother going through the roll call.

"You're kidding," Dan said. "Even the R-comm doesn't work?"

The two looked at one another, and saw in each other's faces that even so, neither considered leaving.

"Your mom told you, right?" he said to her as a way to start their search.

Her eyes were still bright. "And I quote: 'Three right, two back, wipe pull, pull.'"

"She saying anything now?"

To his surprise, Alex answered with a huge smile. "One word. 'Cold.'"

Dan's eyes widened. He wasn't sure whether to accept what was happening, or worry that his daughter had gone crazy and regressed to childhood.

"Really?" he exclaimed. "A game of hot and cold? Now?"

Alex and Jenny had driven him crazy with that game twenty years ago, running all over the house trying to find something the other had hidden by telling the other whether they were hot—close—or cold—far.

Alex giggled. "Really. Now," she told him, happy to cling onto anything positive in this situation. "Come on, Dad," she urged. "Let's get hot."

So they tried. Alex marched fearlessly forward through the eerie, twenty-foot-high and fifteen-foot-wide tunnel while Dan took a more careful approach.

"Seems like they're using the abandoned I-six-ninety-five project as a hiding place," he muttered. "I don't know if it's crazy or genius. Probably both."

"I-six-ninety-five?" Alex repeated.

"Yeah," Dan explained as they went farther and farther away from their starting point. "It was supposed to pass west of downtown, connecting Roxbury, Brookline, Cambridge, and even Somerville, but after destroying hundreds of homes, and threatening thousands more, it was canceled." He waved his flashlight beam across the circumference of the tunnel. "And abandoned. They didn't have the time or money to dismantle it."

"'Warm,'" Alex said.

Dan did a double take. "Warm?" The look on his daughter's face reminded him of the look on his wife's face when she'd told him she was pregnant. "Then let's go."

They moved with more certainty and speed through the tunnel, seeing more broken tools, vehicles, rebar, and even tracks. They were getting into the devised, but abandoned, plans to extend several subway lines. Dan saw broken, faded signs that featured flecks of red, blue, green, and silver. He seemed to remember talk of an Arborway Line Restoration, but that, like the rest of it, was gone and buried.

"'Hot,'" he heard Alex say, as the sound of her footsteps quickened and the shaking of her flashlight beam grew more agitated.

"Careful," he called to her before remembering that was exactly what he used to say to her when she ran too close to the stairs during the game play. Just like then, she ignored him.

He looked after her, seeing puddles of mud and sludge on the ground—evidence of leaks. The Big Dig had been rampant with them, causing millions of dollars in damages to steel supports and drainage systems when the salt water of the Atlantic Ocean had mixed with the fresh water of Boston Harbor for a corrosive cocktail.

"Careful!" he called again, louder this time.

But Alex was beyond caring. "'Burning hot!'" she cried, and turned a corner ahead.

Dan heard her shriek, and then he was beyond caring too. He charged forward with abandon, reached the spot where she'd disappeared, and slid around the corner like a drifting hot rod.

He didn't shriek, but he did drop—between a set of tracks. He hadn't fallen like Alex, so he stood behind her, one booted foot on either side of her dark gray-covered haunches. They both stared up, amazed, by what was on the platform above and across from them.

They were in a nearly renovated subway stop, and, on the platform, was what appeared to be a hastily put-together but effectively workable, office, complete with desk, chairs, computer, drafting table, refrigerator, and water cooler. Even the station lavatory, locker room, and shower seemed to be working.

And sitting behind the desk, looking calmly down at them, was Diana Bloch.

"What took you so long?" she asked.

Chapter 33

"You're kidding," Dan Morgan demanded. "Right?"

Diana Bloch was not wearing dark gray. She was wearing cooling-tech, sweat-wicking, UV and odor-protecting dark blue pants that could be unzipped above the knee to make shorts, an aqua-blue long-sleeve hoodie, a black vest with multiple pockets, and what looked like a combination of black socks and slippers that had a fairly aggressive tread.

"Yes, I'm kidding," she said in a way that sounded like she wasn't kidding.

Dan and Alex vaulted to the platform. Even though they were certain no electric power was coming from the city, they still avoided any metal rails, especially since the entire office area was dimly, but clearly, illuminated by something.

The father marched up to the desk while the daughter examined the setup with a certain wonder.

"And I shouldn't punch you in the mouth, why?" he asked her, also seriously not serious. "And don't say it's because you shouldn't hit a lady."

"Wouldn't think of it," Bloch told him. "I gave up my 'dainty lady' status long before I joined the CIA." She stood and faced Dan. "You shouldn't punch me in the mouth because my split lips and broken teeth might make my answers unintelligible."

Alex came to both people's rescue without guile. "This is amazing," she said sincerely to Bloch. "How did you set it up so fast?"

"Fast?" Bloch echoed in her usual supercilious way. "My dear girl, I've been preparing this little getaway from the moment I heard about all the nooks and crannies the collapse of the Big Dig's Inner Belt project left in its wake. Oh, I thought, what possible use could I put all those lovely hiding places to?"

"As far back as 1974?" Dan marveled.

Bloch gave him a sad, yet still withering look. "Yes, as far back as that, Cobra ...when I was still in the Office of National Intelligence." She looked over to Alex. "I took the office's name seriously." She returned her attention to Dan while pointing at her forehead. "After all, the most powerful muscle in even an un-dainty lady's body needs to be stronger than the biggest one in a mouth-puncher's."

It was Dan's turn to feel his face flush. "You looking for an apology?" he asked her.

She stared back at him. "Only if you hadn't found me." Then she turned her head back to Alex, motioning at the hide-out. "This all came together the moment I received Smith's first tentative feeler about joining Zeta."

"Why then?" Dan said, more interested.

She took a position between the two Morgans, so she could look at either or both at the same time.

"Because, as soon as I was recruited I saw the cracks in Zeta's foundation—and started planning ahead accordingly."

"Cracks?" Dan repeated, finding himself forgetting his anger, since he had felt somewhat the same way when Smith had started trying to recruit him.

Bloch had a special subtle skill at doing that—deflecting anger. As she continued, he realized she had been able to do it with any emotion, which she always managed to fold into her own plans, to power her own goals.

Bloch looked at Dan with a certain camaraderie, even conspiratorially. "Yes, Cobra, cracks. You saw them too, but I'm guessing you chose to ignore them, because it was like a dream come true for you, yes?" Dan's expression became ruminative as his boss continued. "All the power, few of the rules. Seemingly unlimited expense account, truly evil targets, unsullied by base politics..." Bloch returned her attention to Alex. "What's that adage again? 'If it seems too good to be true...'"

"'It probably is,'" Alex finished for her.

Bloch came around the desk, nodding sadly. "So, little by little, bit by bit, month by month, year by year, I had things moved, powered, protected, shielded, and prepared for the day when this sanctuary would be needed."

"What?" Dan exclaimed. "So you just ran away and hid while the rest of your agents' lives got destroyed?"

"Dad...," Alex began, but stopped when she saw that Bloch's face hadn't taken on any regret, remorse, or even indignation.

"No," he spat. "She has to know the effect of her actions." He marched up to Bloch until his chin was at her forehead and his hands were near her throat. "So while you were safe, my house was a fiery hell-hole. My dog was drugged. My wife …!" His fingers began to tremble. "I don't care about anything until I get my hands around the throat of the one responsible for my wife's…"

"Death?"

Bloch had said it. Dan looked at her in utter disbelief, convinced, maybe for the first time, that only this hidden mastermind could have the knowledge and experience to betray Zeta …all because she was rankled at being under Smith's command.

But before he could act on his conclusion, he heard his daughter's voice.

"Dad?" He looked over at Alex, who was watching him with love and sympathy. "Mom says stop."

"God damn it!" he exploded. "When will you realize this is all in your head! It's all…"

"It's not, Cobra," Bloch interrupted as she moved back toward her desk. "I was only telling you all this to give her time to get safely back here to ground zero."

"Her?" Dan echoed, not daring to hope.

"Yes," Bloch said, sitting down. "You can't get revenge for a body that's not dead yet."

And, with that, Jenny Morgan stepped out from the tunnel her husband and daughter had entered by, wearing much the same outfit as Bloch.

About a minute into the family's joyful, tearful reunion, Dan realized Bloch had gone back to her desk to give them enough room.

* * * *

"It took some effort," Jenny told Alex once they had all calmed down. "The nano receiver Diana managed to give you only worked within a certain range. That's why I wasn't talking to you all the time." She gestured toward Bloch. "Once she identified a threat, we had to race there, hoping to warn you in time."

"How did you 'give' me the thing?" Alex asked. "The same way you gave Dad the Threat Assessment Software?"

Bloch sniffed. "I wish it had been that easy," she explained. "Although it's as small as a pore, I couldn't slip it into your water bottle until I could make it bind to your cell surfaces through proteins marked with sugar molecules."

"Stop, stop," Dan surrendered, waving his hands. "Say it in English, please."

Alex laughed. "I drank it, but I didn't poop or piss it out." She looked to Bloch. "Is that close?"

"Close enough," the woman agreed with a sardonic smirk. "Rest assured you'll …evacuate …it out eventually."

"You're kidding," Dan said in disbelief.

"No, I most certainly am not," Bloch replied.

"Will I poop or piss out the Threat Assessment Software?"

They all laughed, despite the circumstances.

Bloch gave him a knowing, somewhat sadistic grin. "How can you evacuate something you never ingested?"

It took a second, but Dan's eyes widened and his eyebrows rose. "Are you telling me…?"

Bloch interrupted with another question. "How do you think we identified the threats Jenny warned Alex about?"

"…I never had it?" Dan finished.

Bloch's cunning smile widened. "If Smith said you had it, who would disagree? Certainly not most of the world's intelligence organizations. Besides, like Sureshot's little nano visitor, it only needed to be there for a relatively short amount of time." She shrugged while pointing at him. "Or, in actuality, not be there."

Dan waved his hands again. "Wait a minute, wait a minute. Time enough for what?"

All hints of humor left Bloch's face as she leaned forward and stabbed her forefinger into the desk.

"To borrow another evacuation term, to flush Alpha out." Her eyes bore into Dan's. "But even before Alpha reared its ugly head, I knew we had to do something to make your wife safe. The fact that your daughter was Zeta but your wife wasn't made her a ridiculously dangerous liability, with no real way to protect her."

Dan wanted to counter that he could protect her, but he knew by her close call during the last mission that was no longer the case. Maybe it never had been.

So, apparently, did Bloch. "Mrs. Morgan proved herself against the seeds of Alpha during your previous major mission, and in no uncertain terms. Then, when the growing Alpha threat started showing their true objective—to wipe us all out in one surgical strike—I knew the most vulnerable target would be your wife. I wasn't going to let that happen."

"Why didn't you tell me?" Dan complained.

Bloch looked at him with narrow eyes and narrow lips. "Oh, come now Cobra," she chided. "I needed a blunt instrument, and *no one's* blunter than you when you're enraged."

Dan marveled at his boss lady, realizing that she had somehow wounded and inflated his ego at the same time.

"At great risk," Jenny told her family, "Diana made sure I was safe."

"After all," Bloch added, "who had the greatest reason of all to serve as a literal and figurative guardian angel to her family?"

Dan looked to his soulmate with the most relieved, loving smile he'd ever felt, but it was tinged with a renewed sprinkle of ego. "But if you could only talk to one member of the family, why not me?" he asked, only half joking.

All three women reacted with varying degrees of mirth.

"Now, honey," Jenny soothed him. "I figured of the two of you, you didn't need it as much as Alex…"

"And because," Bloch interjected, "of the two of you, you usually have your hands full, while Alex waits for just the right moment…"

Jenny, being the ever wise, faithful, generous wife, brought Dan's attention back to her. "Besides," she said to him, "Alex would never accuse me of nagging…!"

The long-time married couple smiled warmly at each other, until Jenny saw Dan's smile disappear.

Then the agent known as Cobra yanked his Walther PPK out of his shoulder holster under his dark gray jacket, pointed it at Diana Bloch's face, and pulled the trigger.

Chapter 34

The thirty-two caliber automatic pistol round just grazed Diana Bloch's earlobe.

Bloch had started ducking to her right the second Dan's hand had moved under his jacket, and she continued to drop, her right hand snaking under the desk to grip her Canik Elite automatic, which was in a holster attached to the side of the desk leg.

As the Walther bullet sped past her ear, she had the wicked-looking red-and-green fiber optic front sight of the Canik pointing back at Dan's face as she pulled her single action trigger. Her nine millimeter round almost trimmed the middle of Cobra's sideburn.

Both their bullets went by the still-moving Zeta ops, and continued on to their intended targets: people in visored helmets and assault gear coming in from the hole in the wall Alex had fallen through, as well as the furthest opening of the planned subway tunnel.

Dan knew their targets wore bulletproofing, but Diana didn't, so the lead from his Walther smashed into the needle gun the first attacker was holding up, and her Tungsten missile slammed into the middle of the second attacker's visor.

The effects were impressive. The PPK bullet ricocheted off the needle rifle, sending it down, while the Canik bullet sent the second attacker's head snapping back as if hit by a shot put. The first attacker's needle went into his own foot, and the second attacker's concentrated light beam sliced a divot in the tunnel ceiling.

Like night cockroaches caught in a kitchen light, the attackers seemed to freeze while Dan and Diana seemed to move in slow motion. But then the shock snapped as more helmeted, visored, assault-geared attackers started pouring in from both openings.

"Goddammit!" Alex hissed as she sprung to her feet, pulling out not one, but two Sig Sauer P320 nine-millimeter automatics—one in each fist—from under her dark gray jacket.

As they rose, both Dan and Diana used their left hands to push Jenny down under the desk while their gun-filled right hands pointed at their attackers.

Then all three Zeta ops opened up. Dan used his Walther's remaining five rounds to destroy the first attacker's needle gun power unit, sending up a spray of diamond-tipped missiles in a mirror ball pattern.

Bullet-proof or not, the tactical gear material was not strong enough for something that small and fast, so the first attacker, as well as the three men beside and behind him, went down screeching, grabbing at their limbs and bodies as the needles made them look like a porcupine had rolled across them.

Alex, in the meantime, had marched forward, both guns straight out in front of her, and made perfect targets out of the three men falling over each other to get to the platform from the tunnel opening. Alex's rapid-eye movement was astonishing as she used her guns—personally chosen for speed, power, and accuracy—to find the attackers' weak spots as they appeared to her.

One looked up, leaving a quarter-inch gap between visor bottom and shirt top. Alex's bullet found it. Another twisted down and to the left, creating a space between their boot and pant leg. Alex's bullet found it. The third pushed their laser rifle up, trying to nail Jenny under the desk, but created a gap between his gloves and sleeves. Alex's bullet found both. And all without pausing between trigger pulls.

Meanwhile, Diana crouched among the three Morgans, and filled whatever gaps they left. First, a shot into the cracked visor of the second attacker, shattering the thing. It might not have killed him, but it did blind him. He started wrenching off the helmet as Diana shifted her aim to a fifth man trying to climb over the writhing, porcupined attackers. As he looked up, Diana pounded a round under his chin, then shifted back to put a bullet between the eyes of the one who had yanked off his shattered helmet.

Two things happened simultaneously. First, another attacker launched himself over the men whose throats, ankles, and wrists Alex had shattered, bringing a concentrated air cannon to bear on the Morgans. Second, Dan scrambled to cover Jenny.

Dan found himself shouldered out of the way by his own wife, who came barreling out from under the desk carrying a sawed-off black synthetic Beretta gas-operated semi-auto A400 Xtreme Plus twelve-gauge shotgun that had been sheathed there.

The man with the air cannon did a double take as he noticed that the middle-aged woman had a hand cannon on her hip, but by then it was too late for him. Just as the attacker was pulling the trigger to try making a hole in her daughter and husband's sides, Jenny unloaded the two ounce ball of buckshot point blank into his chest.

The pellets did not penetrate his bulletproofing. They didn't have to. The power of them crushed his sternum, the shattered bones tearing open his heart like claws. The man was thrown back, as if by a wrecking ball, to crash into the next two attackers.

As Dan gaped at that, he noticed Diana running in the opposite direction while throwing her Canik at him.

"Catch," she advised as Jenny and Alex kept firing, facing opposite directions, side by side. "It's got eleven left in its belly to your Walther's zero."

"Are you running again?" Dan blurted despite himself as he snapped the Canik out of the air.

"Hardly," Bloch sneered as she reached the opposite end of the tunnel. "Cover me."

Dan gave a quick look over his shoulder to see the Morgan women keeping the wolves at bay. But, as he turned back he saw more and more of the attackers crowding the two openings. There was no one crowding the opening Diana was running toward, because it seemed to have been blocked off by a cave-in.

As he watched, Diana stopped and spun, producing a hammerless FN Mk2 semi-automatic revolver from under her vest, then shooting an attacker who was sidling past the desk.

"I said cover me!" she snarled as Dan stepped up and pumped the Canik into the man's back.

Dan whirled to make sure no one was getting through the Sig Sauer or Beretta cracks, but even as he brought the remaining ten rounds of the Canik to bear, he saw it was a losing game. At their best, even if they had ammo and time to reload, all four guns had forty more shots, tops, while the attackers had bulletproofing, lasers, diamond-tipped needles, and seemingly unlimited air at their disposal. Unless Bloch had a cannon somewhere secreted around, they'd either have to make a break for it, or go down trying.

Diana didn't have a cannon. She had something arguably better. As Dan stepped up to join his family, laying down a wall of lead, he heard Bloch bellow.

"Eyes shut!"

All three Morgans took a knee, squeezing their eyes shut as tightly as they could. Even before their eyelids were completely screwed down, there was an ear-pounding sound, like a flashbulb magnified a hundred times. Dan felt a needle speed by his nose and felt the heat of a laser beam by his cheek, but then, for a blessed second, nothing more.

"Come on!" he heard Bloch roar.

When Dan opened his eyes he saw the attackers rolling around on the ground, kicking, their hands clamped to their visors.

"Dan!" he heard his wife screech, then turned to see her and his daughter jumping into what looked like a cross between a dune buggy and an all-terrain vehicle, only with train wheels sitting on the rails instead of tires or tracks.

He leaped into the back with Jenny as Alex brought up her Sig Sauers next to Bloch behind the controls.

"Hold on!" Bloch hissed, then slammed her palm on a large red button where normally a car horn might be.

Dan hated it whenever a movie hero used the now useless cliché of "hold on," but in this case, he was taken by surprise when the low-slung vehicle shot forward like a cheetah on crack.

"Be ready," he heard Bloch's words howl by them as the vehicle flew through the unfinished tunnel on seemingly worn tracks. "They could be anywhere along the line."

Sure enough, Dan saw one helmeted attacker try to target them, but they sped by him so fast, Dan didn't even have time to target him back.

"What the...?" Dan blurted.

"Same concept as roller coaster electromagnetic launchers," Bloch said while checking in all directions as they sped past abandoned construction equipment. "The tracks were already laid. Shame to waste them." She turned to look at Dan. "The Big Dig used these things to travel between construction sites."

"At these speeds?" Dan blurted as he pushed his arm straight over Bloch's left shoulder to shoot her Canik at a laser rifle sniper crouched at the crook of a tunnel.

Bloch laughed as she went back to scanning the area as they sped by, with the Morgans doing the same.

"What did you do to them back there?" Jenny asked Diana breathlessly.

"Flashbanger," Bloch explained. "Blinds, deafens, disorients. Cheapest, easiest, most effective defense. Had a line of them set up like a moat wall above the place I hid this electrocar."

"Good thing they were just more local hired help," Alex growled.

"How do you know that?" her mother asked.

"I was a much better shot than any of them," her daughter replied.

"Yeah," Dan agreed. "Some of them acted as if they had never fired their weapons before."

"Damn Alpha sending all their dupes first to find our techniques, strengths and weaknesses," Diana griped, "before taking us on themselves."

"Fine, but how did they know where to send the dupes?" Alex wondered angrily, her trigger fingers itching to take down as many as she could.

"Good question, that," Dan grunted, checking behind them.

Diana opened her mouth to comment, but closed it to think instead. The car sped along the track for a few seconds in relative silence, until they all saw light ahead.

"You sure you weren't followed?" Bloch asked.

"You know we weren't," Dan answered. "The only people who knew we were coming here were…"

"Get ready to jump!" Bloch interrupted. "And hit the ground run—"

The electrocar smashed into another seemingly rusted gate, hurling it open and sending the train wheels onto gravel, dirt, glass, and overgrown grass. They now found themselves at the opposite end of the abandoned lot Dan and Alex had entered by.

"Go, go, go!" Diana yelled, already running for the fence. "Until we get into the city, we're sitting—"

Before she could finish the warning, needles, light beams and invisible air fists were splattering, slicing, and pounding all around them, shot from the tops of the buildings and walls that closed in the vacant lot. At least the needle and laser rifles could be spotted by flashes and light, and all three Zeta ops targeted them back, while Jenny was smart enough to use the remaining shotgun rounds to deflect the diamond-tipped missiles.

But an air punch wrenched the Beretta from her arms. She spun, grunting, but Dan caught her and propelled her along as Alex put a Sig Sauer slug into the air cannon's barrel. It exploded in the shooter's arms, sending him cartwheeling through the air, then off the roof, to splatter on the ground.

Dan got his wife back running, then gritted his teeth as he felt a needle rip across his thigh. It didn't stop him, but it slowed him for a second, until his wife tried to return the favor by helping him forward.

"Jenny," he groaned, "no."

A light burned across her shoulder and his chest. It was a good thing that these attackers were amateurs. If the sniper had been a pro, the light would have chopped them open like death's scythe.

Alex shot into that barrel too, but instead of decapitating the sniper, it merely made the rifle explode, burning off his face and four of his fingers.

They all kept running as fast as they could, but the shots were getting closer and closer all the time. Even if the attackers were amateurs, they'd lock in their range eventually, and long before the Morgans and Bloch could reach the fence, get over it, and cross the street into the protection of alley walls. They couldn't even dodge or take protection against one wall. The snipers on the other walls would just make mincemeat of them.

Dan was about to demand they all get into a circle and take on the snipers the way wild west wagons got into a circle to take on bandits. Maybe then they might be able to take down the amateur hired help before they were all too badly wounded or killed.

Morgan's last stand was canceled when they all felt the powerful downdraft Dan had already felt with Lulu in the Taiwan forest. The helmeted men who weren't blown off the walls then dropped one by one as if by God flicking his forefinger into each of their heads. They all spun off their posts like toy soldiers swatted away by a bored bully.

Shielding his eyes, Dan managed to look up to see Peter Conley's "Peking Duck"—namely, Danhong "Dani" Guo, an ex-finance ministry agent for China who had been "Smithed" and, truth be told, "Cougared" into Zeta—holding what looked like an H-shaped double barreled rifle that sent laser-targeted lances out of both cylinders as fast as she could pull the trigger. As Dan watched in amazement the lances didn't fly straight. They curved in the air, going wherever they needed to impale their targets.

With the addition of the Zetas' other handguns, the Alpha hired help was down and done within ten seconds. Ten seconds later the Flying Fox had landed in the field, and Dani was helping Jenny on board.

"We need to check all these bodies for clues," Bloch mused as she surveyed the human wreckage.

"Good luck with that," Dan informed her, joining her in the survey after collecting a fallen laser, needle, and air rifle. "I can guarantee there'll be no other physical evidence, and all any wounded survivor would know is that some anonymous stranger paid them big money to go to a specific place and kill whoever was there." He motioned to a few crumbled corpses. "Be my guest if you want, but the only other trustworthy partners are a few thousand miles away."

Bloch gave him a piercing stare. "You think?" she asked tellingly.

Then they were both distracted by a rising noise coming from the tunnel the electrocar was wedged in. All the Alpha hirelings who had been sent inside were now squeezing and crawling out, bringing their guns to bear.

"Oh, great," Dan growled, turning to call on Dani and Alex.

"No," Bloch advised him, one hand up as she rummaged in her vest with the other. "Wait."

So Dan waited, keeping a watchful eye on the Alpha thugs gathering in strength all around the electrocar.

"Uh, Diana...," Dan started as the enemy started pointing, yelling, and running toward them.

But then Bloch held up something that looked like an automatic car lock device, and pressed a little square button on it.

Every Zeta not in the aircraft hunched over instinctively as the electrocar exploded with the force of Satan's fist.

Dan straightened, knowing that whatever Alpha wasn't killed instantly by the detonation had had their internal organs pulverized by the shockwave. He looked down at his Zeta superior, who stood surveying the body count blithely.

"I, for one," she told him, "took to heart the advice of a British peer." She turned and walked calmly toward the open hatch of the Flying Fox, where Dani, Alex, and Jenny were waiting. "Never let them see you bleed, Cobra," she told him when she joined the others in the jet. "And always have an escape plan."

Chapter 35

Landing Palecto at Fox Burrow the second time was different than the first time.

This time there was no just dropping down, stepping out, and walking in. This time the occupants had to wait to be thoroughly scanned, med-checked, and debriefed before they even got to the hatch. That meant that each had to spend a few minutes in the med-cap on board where they were x-rayed, ultra-sounded, cat-scanned, and digi-probed in ways they could only imagine.

After all that—"And not even a lollipop," Alex had groused—they moved to what Conley called "the biz booth." Dan and Alex hadn't even known the thing existed until Conley pressed yet another invisible latch line on the curved wall.

They reminded Dan of a scene in the movie *2001: A Space Odyssey,* when the lead scientist talks to his child from a space station orbiting the moon, except the image here was much clearer and the sound much better. Every person now on the Flying Fox got to spend a few minutes seemingly having a pleasant, innocuous talk with strikingly realistic holograms of Lily Randall and Scott Renard.

"It was like 3-D Face-Time without an iPhone," Alex had commented on that one.

In any case, as everyone waited for everyone else to get vetted, Dani had plenty of time to explain the new weapon she had used against the Boston hired help—the double-barreled, H-shaped cannon that had swatted the bad guys off their walls like flies.

"It's a hand-held version of the railgun the Chinese Navy revealed awhile back," the striking, willowy Chinese woman said. "Like the electrocar you escaped the underground in, it uses electromagnetism to launch a projectile at more than five thousand miles per hour."

Jenny needed a second to visualize that, but it didn't faze her daughter. "But those weren't simple projectiles you were firing," Alex said.

That brought a smile out of Dani. "No," she agreed. "This new iteration adds a digital component. Rather than just firing simple unthinking shells, this device has a targeting computer than can communicate with the missiles themselves, allowing each to pinpoint a different target in succession."

"Expensive bullets," Alex commented.

Dani shrugged. "China can afford them."

"You mean those big bullets can think?" Jenny asked.

Dani gave a little, charming, laugh. "Not quite," she answered. "But close. The weapon sends out a wide beam that maps the targets—targets I can edit so no innocent bystander is hit—"

"So you better be quick," Alex interrupted.

"Yes, that would be best," Dani told her. "But the weapon will wait, and adjust while it continues to keep remaining targets marked even if they move—until the trigger is pulled."

Alex gave a low whistle. "So you don't need to be an expert marksman, but you do need to have quick hand-eye coordination."

Jenny looked to her daughter with concern. After all, Alex was now Zeta's hot shot sniper and this weapon could make her obsolete—the way she had made Diesel obsolete. "Does that bother you, dear?"

Alex laughed, putting her arm around her mother. "Are you kidding?" she told her. "What do I like better than target shooting?"

"Videogames!" Jenny laughed.

As the ladies took some quality time, Dan sidled over to Conley, who was in his usual position—arms folded, ankles crossed, leaning against the Palecto bulkhead in a space that was exactly equidistant from everyone else.

"So what's with Renard's version of the T.S.A.?" Dan grumbled. "Might as well get some airport security to do strip searches in a windowless room."

Conley snorted. "Things are heating up, Daniel," he told his partner with a sardonic look. "Or haven't you noticed?"

"Considering what I've been through the last few days," Dan replied, "it feels like I've been doing laps on a track of burning coals."

"Yeah," Conley drawled, "but aren't you getting tired of more and more people knowing exactly where you are?"

Dan straightened, then looked at the rest of the people inside the Palecto cabin.

"Yeah," he said, with realization. "Bloch said I don't have the Threat Assessment Software on or in me, so what is everybody using to track me?"

"Good question," Conley mused, drawing out the first word. "One that Renard's and Bloch's T.A.S. would love to know the answer to."

Bloch herself emerged from the Biz Booth, a look of determination on her otherwise stiff face. As if on cue, the cabin hatch unsealed with an audible *woosh*. The Morgans, Conley, and Guo followed Bloch, who marched into Renard's hidden home like she knew it well. Maybe she did.

Dr. Whittaker was waiting for them outside her office. She smiled, pointed at Bloch's right ear, and crooked her finger. "Your turn," she said.

But it was never that easy with Diana Bloch. "Just a moment," she said, before turning to Dan. "For better or worse, I knew how the Zeta ear-comms worked. But I have no idea what the security level is on these." She turned back to Dr. Whittaker. "Get Mr. Renard for me, please."

"No need," they all heard, turning to see Scott, as well as Lily Randall, inside Dr. Whittaker's examining area. "Welcome back, Ms. Bloch."

Bloch shifted her attention to Lily, all but ignoring Renard. "You and I need to have a little talk," she said flatly before turning back to the others. "With all due respect, a private talk."

Lily's face went from being welcoming to deadly serious. "Yes, ma'am," she said without an iota of self-consciousness before also looking at the others. "Please wait for us in the salon," she told them.

"It shouldn't take long," Bloch added as she closed the door in all their faces—including that of a blinking Dr. Whittaker.

It didn't take long. In fact, by the time Whittaker had finished installing an R-comm in Jenny's ear and they'd made their way to a reunion with Linc and Karen, then all settled in to admire the scenery out the huge windows, Renard, Randall, and Bloch swept in, the latter motioning everyone toward the info center.

"How are you reading me?" she asked under her breath so everyone could hear her in their heads. Apparently the R-comm had passed even Bloch's heightened sense of quality control.

"Loud and clear," Jenny and Linc said in unison, making nearly everyone smile.

"You owe me a Coke," Jenny told the I.T. guy as they followed their leaders into the darker room.

"What does that mean?" Linc whispered to O'Neal as they took up the rear.

Karen shook her head. "Darned if I know," she replied.

"Guess we'll have to ask someone older," he concluded as Bloch took up a position in the middle of the area, opposite Renard.

A hovering, rotating planet Earth appeared between them as if seen from space.

"What is the status of the hack attacks on Fox Burrow now?" she asked, her manner, position, and tone making it clear to everyone that the boss was back in town.

Renard's fingers twitched and little ripples, like pebbles thrown in a pond, appeared all over the globe, then sent out arcing lines that converged on a spot in Northern California. Within seconds it looked like the flight routes of the most successful airline ever. Within a minute, it looked like a ball of yarn, with the planet underneath.

"Well, they haven't diminished," Renard commented, "if that's what you're wondering."

Dan wasn't wondering that, but he couldn't help wondering where Chilly and Hot Shot were. They certainly were nowhere in sight.

"But," Renard continued, "in terms of their intent, that seems to have shifted slightly since Cobra's little odyssey began."

"How do you mean?" Bloch asked.

Renard looked to O'Neal, signaling everyone that this was her area of expertise. He was too busy running his multinational company to deal with such minor dangers.

"They've become less focused, more diffuse," Karen informed the others. "Before they were like fly fishermen, trying to hit a single trout. Now they're like net trawlers, trying to catch as many fish as they can, so they can worry about finding the exact one they're looking for later."

All her talk made Dan think of Lulu. He wondered how she was doing...

"Cobra!" he heard.

He snapped out of his memory, then snapped his face toward Bloch. "Yeah?"

"I said, does that ring a bell to you?"

"Yeah," he repeated, without giving a hint that his mind was wandering on anything else but business. "Smith said that the game would now change."

"How so?"

"That they'd be less interested in me specifically, and more interested in creating alliances that would be more powerful than any alliances Smith could set up."

"They?" Jenny echoed.

No one looked at her askance, or with anything other than respect and professionalism.

Bloch agreed. "Zeta's enemy specifically, and America's enemies in general," she explained. "Alpha still wants to destroy us, but not specifically over the TAS anymore."

"Yeah," Conley drawled. "Now they just want to use it as their ticket to ride."

Jenny looked from Cougar to Cobra with just a little confusion.

"Telling other powerful intelligence organizations in unfriendly countries that they can get their hands on it," Dan explained to her.

"So they can team up to destroy us," Alex added.

"And the CIA, the NSA, the FBI, Homeland Security," Randall reminded them all, "and anything else they can catch in the blowback."

"Oh, dear," Jenny blurted.

Conley looked at the others. "Couldn't have said it better myself."

Jenny followed his gaze to look at the others herself. "What can we do?" she asked without insincerity.

"Excellent question," Bloch retorted without facetiousness, then looked into each Zeta face. "Any answers?"

Dan looked at the others as well, but spoke while he was doing so. "I don't know if any answer we can come up with is workable without knowing what Smith's got in mind." Dan gave that just enough time to sink in before he added the kicker. "Or what Paul Kirby is doing."

The mention of that name was like dropping a stink bomb into the room. Dan did his best to dispel the odor.

"Diesel tried to shoot me in the head by using the name of Paul Kirby as bait," he detailed. "Hell, Paul Kirby used Paul Kirby as bait at the very beginning by answering his goddamn phone and demanding I come to his Beacon Hill abode for what turned out to be a nasty little ambush."

"Not so little," Alex murmured. "But plenty nasty."

"You got any idea of his twenty?" Dan asked Bloch, using trucker lingo for "location."

Bloch, apparently, knew what he meant, but she made them all wait while her eyeballs shifted and her eyebrows knitted.

"Not," she answered, "at the moment."

Dan's chin raised as he let his top teeth tap on his lower teeth. The rest remained silent, watching the two of them as if they were in a tennis match using balls made of bombs. It was, seemingly, Bloch's serve.

"I think," she continued, "our Mr. Kirby..."

"*Your* Mr. Kirby," Dan corrected.

Bloch acknowledged the interruption, but let that ball go by. "*Zeta's* Mr. Kirby," she corrected before continuing, "may be looking for safe passage and sanctuary."

"And is willing to accept it from anyone?"

Dan was kind enough to phrase it as a question rather than a statement.

Bloch allowed him to score the point. Her head down, her eyes softly closed, she replied.

"That," she said, "is possible."

The silence was longer than ever before. Alex, for one, was concerned it might last forever until the only person with the position and knowledge to break the stalemate took action.

"And what," Jenny Morgan asked, "can we do about *that?*"

The others may have regarded her question as an unsolvable riddle, but Diana Bloch reacted to it as if it was manna from heaven.

"What we can do about that," she emphasized, putting her fists on her hips and leaning forward until her head came through the floating, rotating planet Earth, "is to catch up with Smith again while creating the most enticing, beautiful, secure safe passage and sanctuary the world—and Paul Kirby—has ever seen."

Chapter 36

It may not have been the most secure safe passage and sanctuary Dan had ever seen, but it sure was in the running for the most enticing and beautiful.

Dan managed to tear his eyes away from the seven-story, rectangular central plaza with a gigantic clock whose swinging pendulum was four stories high, all crowned by two-story stained-glass murals that encircled the entire two million square foot building.

These murals did not picture religious or even historical themes. They pictured scenes from the works of Alexander Pushkin, whom many considered the greatest Russian poet of all time.

Dan didn't know that, of course. He had been told this information by his guide—a guide he was very familiar with by now.

"Really?" he asked Valery Dobrynin, an ex-KGB frenemy who had proven invaluable on a recent mission, and was proving so again. "A toy store?"

"Really," said Dobrynin, looking happier than Dan had ever seen him. "And not just a toy store. *The* toy store. The largest in the world." The little Russian looked around, trying—and failing—to take in all the glowing, golden interior with its balconies, mezzanines, inlaid flooring, neon, and so much else. "At least a hundred separate stores, featuring every variation and genre of toy, a separate floor for just games—board, video, arcade, and otherwise—one whole floor for an international buffet …"

"All right already," Dan said. "Not here for a tour."

He was already somewhat overwhelmed with what had happened that morning. This toy store—The Central Children's Store at Lubyanka Square—sat smack dab in the middle of Moscow, between the Bolshoi Ballet, Saint Basil's Cathedral, Red Square, and, as Dan had put it when Bloch had originally presented the operation, "the effing Kremlin."

Dan still didn't like to swear in front of his wife and daughter, although Alex could curse any sailor under any table.

Cobra was not only a bit dazed by the sites he and the little Russian had walked by on the way here—Dobrynin nonchalantly, Morgan not so much—but by the speed at which "Operation Janus" had come together.

Right after declaring that they should create safe passage and sanctuary for their Zeta's errant second-in-command, Bloch had taken up a position away from O'Neal, Chilly, Hot Shot, and even Renard in the Fox Burrow information center, and they all had typed and talked furiously with the goal of reaching Smith or Kirby—not necessarily in that order. But all too soon afterwards, Bloch, being Bloch, had come up with so much more. According to her, Kirby had reached out, and was willing to negotiate a return to the fold.

"He's frightened and doesn't know whom he can trust," Bloch had informed them.

"Join the club," Dan had muttered. "At least on that second thing."

Then, faster than anyone, including Bloch, was comfortable with, Operation Janus was a go.

That was fine as far as it went, but the next problem was that Zeta would have to go to Kirby, who was, as it turned out, in Russia. That choice bit of intel created a little stir, some looks between Zeta agents, and a lot of tongue biting—except in one notable case.

"Good luck with that," Dan had told Bloch before standing up to leave.

"Not so fast," Bloch had replied, unruffled. "I also would have turned him down flat, if it wasn't for one thing."

Bloch knew Dan too well. She knew that would stop him, as well as make him turn back to face her.

"Okay," he had said. "I'll bite. What's the 'one thing'?"

"Oh," Bloch had said with mock innocence, clearly resurrecting their previous verbal tennis match. "I misspoke. I meant to say 'one person.'" The look she had given Dan at that point could've frozen butter. "I believe he's managing your classic car dealership, isn't he?"

Dan had nearly stuck his nose in Bloch's face, planning to make it crystal clear that Valery Dobrynin would be dead meat the second his ex-KGB handlers knew he was back in town, but Bloch had already been way ahead of him.

Seems the agent that those who knew him best called *Tarakan*—the cockroach—had been nursing acute homesickness for some time. And when cockroaches are homesick, they don't just pine or moon, they send out feelers.

"You little *sukablyad*," Dan had said, using a handy and versatile piece of Russian profanity when Dobrynin came out of the Palecto hatch some hours later. "Shouldn't you be dead?"

"Many times over," the little man had agreed as they headed for the planning room. "Only this time, apparently, the Alpha-ites thought it only necessary to destroy your home and secret headquarters—not your place of business." He glanced up at the man who had made his defection possible and had given him his new American job. "By the way, had a lovely chat with Yuri after we nearly shot each other in surprise. Turns out we have a lot in common."

"Great," Dan had said. "If we survive this suicide mission, you and he can partner up."

Dobrynin had given Dan an apologetic smile, already knowing that Kirby and Tarakan's own Russian Intelligence superiors had made it abundantly clear that only the two of them, of all the Zetas, could enter Moscow to negotiate. But before then, there was one more outlandish thing they had to do, and it had been waiting for them in the planning room in the form of two makeup chairs and two makeup masters.

The art of movie special effect makeup had been all but eliminated by the advent of digital visual effects, but the great makeup artists had not lain down or stood still. Renard, being a huge fan and friend of those brilliant technicians, had been almost giddy with excitement to get a few into his house to work Dan and Valery over before their flight.

"It's not enough for you to have face recognition software scramblers in your R-comms," he had commented as a thin, older, balding man who had four fingers on one of his hands worked on Dobrynin.

"Yes," Bloch had said, standing by as a younger man with a widow's peak haircut and goatee worked on Dan. "What if one of Valery's old friends happened to see him, but hadn't known of his free pass?" She looked at the Russian. "Acquired at great expense and sacrifice."

"*Da*," Dobrynin had added without moving his head. "You know as well as I do, Cobra, that Moscow is crawling with ex-KGB just looking for a fight."

"Not to mention FSB, SVR, GRU, and FSO," Dan had almost moaned, assuming that, to pull this off, Bloch had called in every favor she had ever made in her life—as well as some she probably hadn't even made yet.

Any other thoughts he had were wiped away when the makeup man had stepped back and Dan had looked into the face of a stranger in the mirror. He knew it worked for not just him when Jenny and Alex had been called in, and hadn't recognized him either. But they had certainly recognized his voice.

"Janus have anything to do with Judas?" Dan had asked Jenny as the entire remaining Zeta crew and Renard headed back to the Flying Fox. Jenny had shaken her head. "Roman god of duality," she had told him, her past as a teacher and reader coming to the fore again. "God of beginnings, endings, and everything in between. Pictured as two-faced so he can look at the past and future."

Dan had given Bloch and Dobrynin a meaningful look before Cobra, Conley, and Tarakan had made their good-byes to the others, and re-boarded the supersonic stealth. Six hours later Palecto was in Russian Federation airspace, and Dobrynin knew just where Cougar could drop them off.

"Stalin City," the little man who was unrecognizable as Valery Dobrynin had said to Cougar and Cobra as the former had brought Palecto swiftly down amid a grove of oak trees just southwest of Moscow University. "No buildings or any permanent structures are allowed here."

Dan, wearing a dark olive suit and dark blue shirt, had followed behind Dobrynin as the little man, now wearing a black shirt and dark gray suit, had hopped out and scuttled to what looked like the top edge of a sewer entrance hidden amidst gnarled, cross-linked tree roots. To Dan, it looked like the Russian equivalent of the entrance Jenny had led Alex to in Boston.

As Palecto had shot into the clouds like God's yo-yo, Dobrynin had slipped down into the opening, and motioned for Dan to follow. Within seconds, they were standing in what looked like an abandoned subway tunnel, only in much better condition than the one under Boston.

"Deja vu," Dan had muttered as he had followed Dobrynin, who had not even stopped to get his bearings.

"You know Stalin was paranoid, yes?" the Russian had asked.

"Is the Pope Christian?" Dan had replied, his eyes scanning the granite and concrete-colored, moderately well-lit, tunnel, empty of anything but subway tracks and wires attached to the walls and ceiling.

"No, he's Catholic," Dobrynin had corrected before continuing. "In the twenties, Stalin wanted a top secret escape route in case of coups. Later, he was worried that he would wind up like Hitler—trapped in a bunker—so he expanded this on an epic scale. Then later than that, he worried that he'd be hit by a nuclear bomb, so this was enlarged again. So now it's big enough that the Politburo can survive down here for even years if necessary."

Dobrynin had looked up at Dan with a grin. "But, so far, not necessary, so no one comes down here. Still, top secret, and a good place for executions or hikes into the city."

Dobrynin had known where to enter, and he had known where to exit, bringing Dan up via a grating near the Kiyevsky Railway Station, just west of the Moskva River. From there it was only twenty minutes by subway to the Revolution Square station, and then a ten minute walk—past a Chamber Music Theater, an Audi dealership, Dolce & Gabbana, Tom Ford, Alexander McQueen, and Yves Saint Laurent shops, a Spanish tapas joint, Greek gyros, Chinese dumplings, Japanese sushi, and even a place called Wine and Crab—before they'd arrived at the toy palace, which looked from the outside like a grand, romantic train station decorated for Christmas.

After trying to take it all in, Dobrynin had given in to Dan's seeming depression.

"Very well. The tour portion of our adventure is officially over," he assured him. "But really, if you were choosing a public meeting place, wouldn't you choose something like this?"

Dan was trying to study every possible hiding, escape, and attack place, forcing him to see the method in Kirby's madness. But the accent, for him, was on the madness, not the method.

"No, I would not," Dan told his guide. "I would never choose a place that depended upon the enemy's unwillingness to hurt children."

Dobrynin exhaled, acknowledging Dan's point with a worried look of his own.

"Come," he said. "We are to meet on the top floor."

"Of course we are," Dan muttered, still trying to lock as much of the surroundings as he could into his mind's eye, as they made their way through the throngs of children, teens, and adults to one of many silver escalators.

As they rose, Dan saw a working circus carousel surrounded by dolls and model kits, an entire wing of building blocks, and a jungle of stuffed animals of every size, until they reached the buffet. It was decorated with zeppelins—small, medium, and large—made of wood, plastic, rubber, and steel, all flying or floating or bouncing just over their heads.

As Dobrynin led Dan to a corner table overlooking the intersection of Pushechnaya and Rozhdestvenka Streets through large, wide picture windows, they both got their bearings. The desserts and drinks were to their left. More tables, banquets, and booths were in front of them. And beyond that were many more food stations boasting the best surf and turf of Asia, Europe, and Mother Russia.

Dan kept an eye out for any sign of anything, but his eyes couldn't help settling on one of the small tables nearest him. At it sat a man, a woman, and a little girl. The man looked to be in his forties, wearing jeans, jacket, a t-shirt and a glowering expression, as if telling anyone in sight, *mess with me at your peril.* The woman looked to be in her thirties, wearing a worn but clean wraparound dress, flats, and a somewhat worried expression, as if saying to everyone in sight, *please don't do anything to me or my family.*

But the little girl looked to be under ten years old, wore bright new shorts, sandals, and top, and had a smiling, open, carefree expression that said, *everything is awesome.*

Dan realized that these three represented the last fifty years of Moscow's history—just as Paul Kirby, wearing a dark tan suit over a light blue shirt and tie, appeared from behind a cashier's station and started walking toward them.

Dan tapped Dobrynin's leg under the table, and when the Russian looked up at him, directed a glance in Kirby's direction. Dobrynin shifted as naturally as he could to seemingly look at the desserts and drinks just as the fortyish man at the nearest table started to get up. As he bent to get his feet under him, his jacket flapped open and Dan could see a brand new Lebedev PL-15 pistol in his shoulder holster.

Dan went for his own Walther as he also got his feet under him, but it was too late. Just as Dobrynin scrambled around, going for his own PSM pistol, the fortyish man stood, pointed the Lebedev, and shot Paul Kirby point blank in the chest.

Chapter 37

He should have known. The bang, being that the PL-15's ammo was not subsonic, was one of the loudest Dan had heard in years, but the blood bursting from Kirby's shirt made an even louder noise in Dan's mind.

"Get to Kirby!" Dan barked at Dobrynin as he bolted up and started to bring his Walther to bear. But, seemingly, in the very middle of the movement, Dan jammed the PPK back into its holster under his jacket, and charged like a minotaur entering a labyrinth.

Because, in truth, that is just what the Zeppelin-decorated restaurant at the top of the gigantic toy store had become—a maze of screaming women and children, all trying to get blindly away from the loud bang and spurting blood.

Even halfway through his gun-drawing motion, Dan knew that the odds of cleanly hitting the assassin were thousands to one—especially when the shooter was crouching behind the panicking woman and child who had been at his table.

The assassin's wife and daughter? Dan didn't care—there was no way he was going to shoot through or past them to get to the killer. Instead, he plowed into the alarmed throng like a bull in a china shop. He discovered within just a few steps, however, that the china won, unless he planned to break every dish, stem, handle, and spout.

Dobrynin had thrown himself onto the restaurant floor as soon as the shot went off, and from there, under the table, he saw Dan struggling against the human tide to get his clawing hands on the man. But the man who had shot Kirby had jumped up onto the padded bench behind the table, and was running atop it to get either to the stairs, the kitchen, or any emergency exit.

Tarakan acted like his nickname and started crawling under the tables and behind the banquettes to get to the place he had seen Kirby fall. Meanwhile, Dan had also seen what the shooter was doing and, as he tried to wade against the tide of humanity, grabbed a metal dessert plate, hurling it at the man's neck.

He silently thanked all those games of Frisbee with his own wife and daughter many years ago as the steel disk whanged into the killer's throat. The shooter went from running to slipping in an instant, and slammed onto his side atop the padded bench before toppling over backwards behind it.

Dan, still trying to run, stepped up onto a chair, then onto a table, and then leaped over a bunch of fleeing people, one shoe sole just grazing the top of an old man's head. Dan landed on another table, and as his weight started toppling it, he slid across the surface and jumped to the bench the killer had been running across. As Dan looked down, he saw the shooter slithering, sliding, and trying to crawl along the bench base toward his previous objectives.

Dan went for his gun, then stopped again as the killer wrenched himself between the legs of another woman trying to escape. So, instead of shooting at the killer, Dan stepped up onto the top of the bench and ran across it, keeping watch on the killer like a harpooner gauging a swimming whale off the port bow. The second the way cleared, Dan jumped with all his weight, aiming his feet at the shooter's torso.

The shooter rolled on his side and scissored his legs, bringing another man and his two sons down over and around him, as Dan just barely managed to avoid crushing one boy's hand and the other's knee. Growling like a frustrated bear, Dan grabbed at any limb of the shooter he could reach, but by then, the assassin had put three more people between them as he scrambled to his feet. Dan, seeing no way to catch up, threw himself back over the bench, landed on his feet on the seat, and ran the way the shooter had before getting hit by the dessert plate.

By then, Dobrynin had managed to come out the back side of the banquette, parallel to the one Dan and the shooter had been using. That put Valery at a ninety degree angle from where he had seen Kirby fall, but Kirby had fallen near the middle of the floor and Dobrynin was against the far wall. Looking for any way through the hysterical mob, Dobrynin glanced up. He vaulted onto a chair, jumped onto a table, and leaped at the strongest Zeppelin in range.

It was a steel one, and to the Russian's relief, it carried his weight until Dobrynin could scramble to a larger wooden one next to it. From there, with his hands gripping the wood and his feet resting on the steel, he looked down to where he remembered Kirby falling. All he could see were the bobbing heads of terrified diners, waiters, busboys, and even chefs. Then, out of the corner of his eye, he saw other heads bobbing, but in a different direction.

Idiot, he thought, the epithet needing no translation into English. It was mall security, choosing to try swimming against the tide. *They weren't spawning salmon*, Dobrynin thought. *They would fail.* But they did give him an idea. He hung from the furthest zeppelin he could reach and waited until there was enough space below him. Then he let go, landed amid the agitated bystanders, and let them move him in the right direction.

By then Dan had managed to catch up to the shooter, who was still trying to push through everyone else to get to the stairs. Dan slammed into him like he was back to being a college footballer, sending them both just beyond the stairway entrance. Not surprisingly, there was a little space there, since none of the panicked populace wanted to wander anywhere that wasn't close to an exit.

Without a word, the assassin went for his gun, obviously hoping to blast Dan in the chest or head. Growling, Dan grabbed the man's wrist with one hand and his elbow with his other, then twisted until he heard a cracking snap.

He heard a pained howl before realizing his mistake and feeling its result at the same time. With both his hands occupied, Dan had left the shooter's other arm free to inflict damage, which it tried to do to Dan's face. But, at the same time he was twisting the killer's arm, he was twisting his own body, trying, and mostly succeeding, to move his head far enough away from the punch to minimize the damage to his face—and to the makeup.

Even so, he did see a star or two, which he used as inspiration to lash out at the shooter's nearest knee with the sole of his shoe. Because he was partially blinded, however, his heel only glanced off the man's thigh. But it was enough to send them both stumbling back. Dan fell against the side of the mob, who, like fans at a crowded rock concert, sent him back onto his feet. The shooter, however, fell against another table and chair. With his remaining good arm, he grabbed the seat and swung it at Dan with all his might.

Still wanting to protect the innocent bystanders, Dan grabbed it rather than ducking. As soon as he did, the shooter vaulted over the side of the stairway, and crashed, feet first, onto the crowd on the stairs. Dan heard the bystanders yell in pain and surprise, then shoved himself to the side of the stairway in time to see the people the shooter had fallen on collapsing like ten pins. The shooter took one look back up at Dan, sneered, then rolled, stamped, and stood on the fallen and falling innocents before racing out of sight.

"Damn!" Dan seethed, looking everywhere to find a way to get after the killer. His eyes swept across, and then back, to Dobrynin, who was standing in the rapidly emptying area where Kirby had fallen. The Russian looked back at Dan, then looked down at the empty, blood-stained, floor, and raised his hands in the universal sign of "don't know." Then, seeing Dan's desperate expression, Dobrynin's face became equally intent, and he jabbed his forefinger repeatedly in the opposite direction, across the restaurant.

"The mezzanines," Dan saw the little man mouth. "The balconies!"

Of course, Dan realized, running away from the rest of the panicked crowd. The mob thinned so rapidly in that direction that Dan was soon sprinting at full speed, coming out into an open hallway that he had seen upon first entering the expansive building. That gave him an almost total view of the entire store, as well as most of every stairway and escalator.

Spotting the shooter was no problem. He was the one person who didn't care who he hurt while trying to get away. Dan's trigger finger twitched again, but the odds of hitting his target at this range with the short barreled, non-laser-sighted Walther, was ridiculous.

If I ever get out of this, he thought as he started running toward that area, *maybe I will let Alex choose a more modern sidearm for me*. He only wished she were here now. She could have given the man a third eye without touching a hair on any innocent bystander's head.

But she wasn't here, so Dan ran around the balcony corner until he came to a mezzanine opening. From that angle he could see that the shooter hadn't spotted him yet. Dan was sure the killer was certain that Dan was still behind him, trying to catch up. Dan hunched down, approaching the bannister overlooking the atrium. From there he could see where the assassin was likely to run—right through the stuffed animal section of the store.

Okay, Dan thought, running in that direction. *Alex might've nailed him from a hundred yards, but could Alex have done this…?"* Dan leaped up onto the bannister and hurled himself through the air.

It was a perfect arc. Dan left the seventh floor mezzanine, sailed down, and flew through the sixth floor mezzanine opening, onto a huge pile of stuffed animals—just as he remembered Alex had been a high school track star. Even so…

The surprised shooter saw Dan go sailing past, then couldn't stop himself from slowing and looking back as the stuffed animals flew in every direction. But then he spun back straight and started racing again as Dan came plowing out from an exploding pile of nearly life-sized baby elephants, big apes, and giant teddy bears.

Dan had nearly caught up at the top of the next elevator, but he slid as two other men, of about the same age and temperament as the shooter, came at him from both sides. Dan didn't see a knife or gun, so he didn't care what their hands and feet did as he planted his elbow in the middle of one man's face and his fist into the throat of the other man.

Although their fists glanced off Dan's left ear and right shoulder, he was too pumped up to feel it. He did hear his subconscious snarl "hired help," however, as he charged down the escalator after the assassin. But the assassin looked back and sneered again, just as two more men of the same age, build, and temperament appeared to flank the end of the conveyance.

The shooter ran through and past them as they waited for Dan. But Dan didn't wait for them. He vaulted over the side of the escalator, landed on his feet, and pulled out his PPK as they ran around to stop him.

"*Spasibo*," he said—thank you in Russian—as he shot one, then the other, in the chest. *At least*, he thought as he put the Walther away and continued after the shooter, *the PPK's reduced caliber won't cause any collateral damage on innocent bystanders.*

Dan made it back to the mezzanine ledge just in time to see the shooter slowing from a run to a walk as a small army of mall security men poured around the corner in the opposite direction.

Stop him, Dan yelled at them in his mind. *Get him, get him, get him!*

But they didn't. Obliviously, they let the shooter walk amongst them in the opposite direction, paying absolutely no attention. But the shooter wasn't oblivious. He turned his head yet again to look back up at Dan, and gave him his widest, smuggest, most assured, and most evil grin.

Okay, Dan thought. *These bozos were obviously more hired help. So chalk this one up as FUBAR, find Valery, and get the hell out of town.* But as much as he tried to accept the logic of his thoughts, the shooter's grin kept sticking in the craw of his mind's eye.

Dan looked wildly around. He could see by the layout of the building, and by the shooter's attitude, that he would get to the bottom floor, walk casually across the foyer, and step blithely out the front door—right under the gigantic, multi-story-high pendulum beneath the huge mall clock.

Dobrynin saw Dan running toward the clock from his vantage point on the seventh floor. "No," he said, then started repeating it a little louder each time as Dan got closer and closer and closer. "No, no, no, no, no!"

Then Dan jumped again. He grabbed onto the very top of the pendulum, making it swing wildly. Somehow, miraculously, he held on as seemingly every single person in the toy mall—including the shooter—froze, gasped, or shouted. The pendulum swung back, and, rather than get thrown off, Dan slid downwards. He slid down four floors as the shooter started running for the front door.

Dan saw the man speed beneath him, and then he let go. He dropped twenty feet, moving slightly to the side, which saved his legs, and especially his ankles. He hit the floor while on the move, somersaulted, and came up on his feet like they had taught him in the paratroops. Dan suffered more aches twisting around and changing his direction than he did hitting the ground. He slammed open the front door mere seconds after the shooter.

What greeted them on the wide streets and walls of the Imperial Russian, Petrine Baroque, Muscovite, and Constructivist architecture was the Moscow version of a disaster protocol. Screaming sirens heralded the arrival of blue-striped white VAZ-2170 police cars, PAZ-3205 police buses, OMON SPM-1 riot vans, and red Russian State Fire Service trucks, as well as about a half-dozen officers on horses accompanied by another half dozen who were barely controlling German Shepherds, Giant Schnauzers, Dobermans, and Labradors on leashes.

The R-comm in Dan's ear just kept bellowing, "Down, down, down on the ground! Hands on your head! Now! Now!"

Dan ignored them just long enough to tackle the shooter, taking special care to cup the back of the man's head so he could smash the assassin's face into the sidewalk.

Then, apparently, the entire first operational regiment, the Zonal center for police dogs, the Directorate for Public Order, and the Riot Police Unit were all over him.

As they wrenched his arms up his back, clubbed him, then cuffed his hands, fingers, and ankles, he spoke only for the R-comm's benefit.

"Well, that went great. I'll let you know how the gulags are…in about fifty years."

Chapter 38

"Gulag?" Valery Dobrynin snorted. "You shot two of their citizens and crushed the face of another. You'll be lucky if they don't shoot you, *then* hang you."

Dan was not nervous for four reasons. One, the Russian Constitutional Court had banned capital punishment in 1999. Two, a makeup-less Valery had been waiting for him after the arresting officers had also removed Dan's facial disguise, seemingly as evidence. Three, Valery was waiting for him in a pristine gray and tan interrogation room rather than a dungeon. And four, the only thing he had heard in his R-comm after his arrest had been Lily Randall's voice saying three words.

"We're on it."

Dan Morgan leaned back in the simple black padded chair, and studied the black handcuffs and silver finger cuffs that still imprisoned both his thumbs and forefingers.

"Then why aren't we separated in the bowels of Stalin City," Dan inquired mildly, "with FSB guns pressed to the back of our heads?"

Dobrynin twitched at the mention of the Russian Secret Police, inspiring Dan to turn toward him with a raised eyebrow.

"What are you doing here anyway? I thought you'd be well on your way to the Baltic by now."

Dobrynin shrugged. "I wanted to back you up, and give you information on Kirby's body ...or the lack of same."

"Then why didn't you just say it?" Dan wondered, turning in the chair to face Dobrynin. "And why didn't you just tell me about the balconies and mezzanines rather than mime everything? I would've heard it through the R-comm."

The little man sheepishly shifted in his own seat. "I forgot I had it," he admitted. Dan almost laughed at him, despite the situation. "Really," Dobrynin stressed, facing Dan. "I mean, I'm not used to it, and it's so ...so ...nothing."

"I know, Val, I know. To tell you the truth, I sometimes forget it's in there too." Dan put his cuffed hands onto the plain table in front of them. "So, tell me now."

Dobrynin glanced nervously at the one-way glass taking up most of the wall in front of them. "But...but won't they hear?"

"Like they don't know already," Dan scoffed. "How many surveillance cameras do you think there were in the toy mall? I'd guess at least six hundred—six for each storefront."

"Seven-fifty minimum," Dobrynin murmured. "You forgot the restaurant and staff areas."

"There," Dan concluded. "So?"

Dobrynin took a final furtive look at the glass, then slid his chair closer to Dan's. "Kirby's corpse was gone—completely gone—when I got there."

"Any blood trail? I mean, if he was dragged, or knocked away by panicking people."

Dobrynin straightened in his chair, blinking. "Come to think of it, no."

"What does that tell you?" Dan asked.

Dobrynin's face took on a feral ferocity Dan had come to appreciate. "That tells me that there had to be at least two other conspirators present to take the body away." He looked at Dan with dawning realization. "Just one wouldn't do, unless he carried him in his arms like taking a bride across the threshold. And we would have seen that. There would be a blood trail in any case."

"Yeah," Dan said. "How many executions in a public place you know of that have an exclusive clean-up crew waiting?"

Dobrynin pondered on that. "What does it mean?"

It was Dan's turn to glance at the one-way mirror, while he raised one eyebrow. "That's what we should find out any time now."

Dobrynin opened his mouth to raise a question, but Dan held up his cuffed hands, doing his best to make a *wait-a-minute* motion. Then he lowered his hands, re-shifted in his seat, and watched the door. Dobrynin looked at his associate, frowned, then turned to do the same—as the latch turned and the door opened.

In walked a very unhappy police chief in a light blue shirt and dark gray uniform, flanked by two men in suits. The man to his left was shorter than Dobrynin, with a cannonball head, a partially burned-off left ear, and a body seemingly made of one solid, coiled, muscle.

The man to his right was Smith.

The man to his left moved his arm so it tapped the police chief. The police chief started in place, then bowed stiffly toward Dobrynin and spoke.

"I want to thank you," Dan heard in his ear, followed by Dobrynin's translation, since it was obvious he'd forgotten he had the R-comm again. "For your help in bringing to justice two Chechen rebels, as well as several other terrorists, including a Serb and a Siberian."

Dan hoped that was true, but given that Moscow had long been a target for Islamic, separatist, and even neo-Nazi terrorists as well, the authorities had a list to choose from. In any case, the words were a verbal version of a "get out of jail free" card.

"Your assistance in this matter," the police chief continued stiffly, "has been of great importance to the Russian people in ridding our great nation of agitators who seek to—"

The man to his left tapped him again, shook his head curtly, and then motioned slightly to Dan. The police chief cut off his speech, turned toward the door, and waved several officers in. Dan recognized them as the men who had wrist- and handcuffed him. They shuffled forward to uncuff him, one on each side.

As they did so, the man to the police chief's left leaned down and spoke to Dobrynin. "And thank *you*, comrade," he said, "for helping us curtail the insurgence of Alpha from our great nation."

Dobrynin's expression looked as if he were staring into the face of God, but it was diminished by Dan elbowing him.

"Ask him if they tested the floor for Kirby's blood."

Dobrynin's frozen expression still managed to convey that he didn't want to. Nevertheless, he did, in as quick and deferential a manner as he could.

It was the man with the burnt ear's turn to grow still, then obviously ponder the suggestion. He didn't answer. He merely gave a slight nod as if saying, *good idea.* Then he looked at the three policemen with an expression that communicated that they had better have any necessary tests done by the time they saw him again or else *they* would be shot, then hanged.

He straightened as the police scurried away, and wiped off the jacket of his suit with both hands, as if ridding it of crumbs.

"Now, if this minor misunderstanding has reached its satisfactory conclusion," he said in perfect English, "please follow me. We have a car waiting to take you to your destination."

The car was waiting for them at the back, private, exit—one obviously used by personages the police didn't want anyone else to know about—and was not a riot van. It was an Aurus Cortege, the official model of the Russian government's state garage.

As Dan approached, he judged its pedigree. Six-point-six liter V-twelve engine, eight hundred horse power, armor plating, bulletproof glass, at least five tons. Its brand name consisted of the first syllable of the Latin word for gold combined with the first syllable of the mother country.

Then, Dan realized why they had kept him waiting in the interrogation room for so long. The forces-that-be had been waiting for night to fall.

The man with the burnt ear left them at the vehicle, after shaking Smith's hand. The three stepped into the expansive, expensive rear seats, then an innocuous, anonymous young man in a suit got behind the wheel and started the engine.

"Do you know who that was?" Dobrynin blurted with excitement, then snapped off the words after Smith's right hand shot up as if it were trying to cut the Russian in half.

Smith, Morgan, and Dobrynin remained stone silent during the rest of the ride to the southwest of Moscow University. They remained stone silent as they walked through the tunnels of Stalin City. They remained stone silent as the Flying Fox dropped out of the inky sky. They remained stone silent as they climbed aboard.

But as the hatch sealed and Palecto shot back into the atmosphere, Dan beat everyone to the punch with his first words.

"They weren't Alpha."

Chapter 39

"More hired help," Dan groused as Conley guided the Flying Fox southeast over Kazakhstan. "I'm beginning to think Alpha is just a call center with a very long list of every thug in the world."

"What makes you think they were hired help?" Smith wondered, watching Dan as he washed off the last of his makeup disguise.

"Would you use an old pistol if you had needle, laser, or air guns at your disposal?" Dan countered as he reached for his freshly laundered and pressed dark gray Zeta suit. "Sure, they obviously were instructed to make some sort of definitive statement that none of us were safe anywhere …" Dan stopped and turned toward Dobrynin, who was wolfing down a chateaubriand for two. "Did we ever find out who the woman and little girl were?"

Dobrynin stopped in mid-bite, looking as if the cook of the manor had turned the kitchen lights on to catch him stealing a midnight snack. "The ones at the shooter's table?" he inquired around the meat. Dan pulled the t-shirt over his head. "Hostages," Dobrynin said after laboriously swallowing his latest mouthful. "According to the police statements General Sannikov had them send me…" He glanced at Smith. "That's the man who came in with you."

"I know," Smith said.

"Of course," Dobrynin agreed. "Of course you do."

Smith glanced at Dan. "Alexey Demyan Sannikov. Head of Directorate 'A', also known as Alfa—the counterterrorism task force of the Federal Security Service."

"Also known as the FSB," Dobrynin burbled.

Dan and Smith looked back at the chewing Russian at the same time and said in unison, "I know."

Dobrynin hastily went back to stuffing his face. He may have mumbled "You owe me a Coke," but Dan couldn't be sure.

"Apparently," Smith told Dan patiently, "the man showed the mother and daughter the gun and forced them to sit with him."

"Well, that explains the woman's expression," Dan mused as he slipped on the dark gray slacks. "The little girl must've thought it was a game."

"Some game," Dobrynin muttered.

"Yeah," Dan agreed, hefting and studying his Walther PPK. "I realize wearing visored helmets in a toy store would be something of a giveaway, but Alpha couldn't be bothered to outfit their hired help with bulletproof jackets? I only shot those two in the chests to prevent any innocent bystanders from getting hurt by ricocheting bullets and shards of skull."

Smith went on. "Yes, our guess is that Kirby, or whoever was running him, chose the toy mall because they thought you wouldn't start shooting in there. Apparently they thought that would make it easier to kill you."

Dobrynin sat up, chortling. "They don't know him very well, do they?" He smiled at Smith. "They do now, *da*?"

Dan ignored the compliment. "So," he continued, putting the PPK down and picking up the jacket. "It's me again. I gather Alpha and company don't necessarily believe you when you maintain I don't have the Threat Assessment Software on me."

Smith sighed. "Cobra, the people I deal with don't believe anything I say. They don't believe anything they say. They don't believe anything."

Dan was frustrated as he picked the Walther back up. But he still didn't shove it into his shoulder holster. "Linc," he said to the air. "The new ordnance ready?"

There was no answer.

"Linc?"

Still no answer. The three Zeta ops on board converged their gaze onto their recruiter. Their recruiter stretched his arms and legs in a self-conscious way.

"Lincoln Shepard will not reply," he said calmly. "Nor will Lily Randall, Karen O'Neal, Scott Renard, or any of his staff. We are cut off from them."

Dan looked pointedly at his PPK, eliciting a smile from Smith.

"That won't be necessary, Cobra," the tall, older, man said affably, though his eyes were as cold as dry ice. "You see, I couldn't help but wonder if perhaps the opposite forces were tracking you through some other method. A method a bit more …old-fashioned, shall we say?"

"I knew it!" they all heard Conley exclaim from the piloting position. They all turned to face each other as the lanky helmsman snapped his fingers. "Yeah, Dan, remember when we were bellyaching about all this new nano nonsense we had to try figuring out? I was beginning to think they were tracking you with radioactive lint or something."

Dan let his mind wander back to everything that had happened to him and his family since he had turned the Mustang around the corner of his street. He remembered how he'd felt when he saw the power of the bombs, the hologram, and the weapons. He realized how they had made him feel he was dealing with something he didn't know or understand.

"You mean…," he started.

"Well, let's put it this way, Cobra," Smith said, bending down to put his elbows on his thighs and his chin on his fists. "If you wanted to track someone close—say, your wife. Not nice, I know, but say you had to for some reason. How would you do it?"

Dan stood straight, picked up his gun, and stuck it in his shoulder holster. "I'd go to her best friend and convince her to inform me of her every move."

Smith smiled, his eyes crinkling, and leaned back, his arms wide. "There we go," he said. "You and Diana even discussed it after the Boston T-party."

Conley guffawed at the play-on-words Smith had made from the similarity between tea and "T" for Transit, which is what Boston called their subway system.

Smith returned his attention to Dan. "How *did* Alpha know you were in the bowels of Boston …unless someone told them?"

The already quiet Palecto interior got even more quiet.

"Smoke and mirrors," Smith told them. "Since we're dazzled by the lasers, we stop thinking about the traitors, and moles, and sleepers, and, to borrow another Revolutionary War term, the turncoats."

"Is that why the R-comms are cut off?" Dan asked.

"Oh yes," Smith informed them. "Linc and Lily made some believable excuse, backed by Scott and a few others. Rest assured our communication devices will be back on by the time we land."

"Shepard, Randall, and Renard," Conley rumbled from the pilot's post. "That leaves…"

"Open your mind, Cougar," Smith suggested as he concentrated on Cobra. "Someone told Alpha who was coming and going, as well as how many and where. So Diana and I gave different information to the only ones who knew all that. Information designed to point directly at them depending upon the result of their appraisal."

After that bombshell, quiet reigned supreme inside the Flying Fox. Even Dobrynin forgot to chew.

"So," Dan said. "You know who it is?"

Smith agreed. "Thanks to you, and Tarakan here." Smith acknowledged Dobrynin. "We know. But Alpha doesn't know we know."

Dan started to smile, but then the smile faded. Whether Alpha was a call center for thugs or not, they still wanted every Zeta dead. "So what are we going to do with that information?"

Smith motioned for everyone to sit down. "We are going to have a Zeta summit," he told them as they took positions around him. "A top-secret summit for every remaining member of Zeta to make a last stand—secure in the knowledge that Alpha could have no idea where or when it's taking place."

Cobra and Cougar shared a glance, knowing full well that they were walking into an ambush inside an ambush, and everyone had better be ready for it.

"And where and when *is* it taking place?" Dan asked.

Smith looked at him. "As soon as we land," he informed them. "In Taiwan."

Chapter 40

Dan looked at Smith in disbelief and a little concern when he saw where Conley was landing. It was in a perfectly trimmed section of the bamboo forest, shaped exactly like the Flying Fox, just outside *Gaoxing Didian*. Lulu's Happiness Place—the place where her parents had died.

"Why didn't you tell me we were going here?" Dan asked his boss of bosses.

Smith didn't look at him as he replied. But at least he did reply. "Old habits die hard for a reason, Cobra," he said. "The more I know, and the less others know, the better it's been for me." He looked over at Dan with a grim smile. "Just like the mystery of death. Everyone finds out eventually."

Valery Dobrynin, meanwhile, marveled at the cunning expertise of the landing spot. It was placed in a cove, essentially hidden from view of the densely wooded hill the hot springs resort spa nestled upon. And it was expertly groomed to leave a flat surface that was exactly big enough for Palecto to slip in like a glove. Once the stealth craft landed, it was basically invisible to everyone unless they swung directly above it.

"Been busy while we were in Russian stir, huh?" Dan asked the Zeta pilot as Conley made the exacting, tricky landing like he was slipping a coin into a jukebox.

"Got to do something while you're shooting up a toy store," Cougar quipped.

"And while Alpha might do many things to us," Smith added as he prepared the hatch for disembarking, "waiting isn't one of them." He punched the prep button on the lowering handle so it could measure the distance to the ground. As it calculated the occupants' weights and heights,

Smith looked back at Dan. "Would you care to go first in case you'd like to gauge our hostess's mood?"

Dan was going to defer to his superior, but then thought again. "Might not be a bad idea," he judged. As he stepped in front of Smith, he gave him the disclaimer. "She might control herself, but I can't say the same about any of the family's friends."

The hatch slid open and Dan stuck his head out into a semi-circular bamboo tower that left just enough room for his body. It was like a tailor-made airport exit crafted by an artisan. Looking down from there he saw Lo Liu waiting under the wing, wearing her "work clothes" of loose white shirt, black pants, and Chinese slippers, her hair in a tight ponytail.

Dan exited the way he had upon first landing in Taiwan, the handle bringing him gently down, then rolling silently back up. As Dobrynin prepared his descent, the American and Taiwanese agent locked eyes.

"You okay?" he asked.

She smiled thinly, but her eyes didn't. "Like you said, I'd be dead already if he wanted that." She looked up to try to catch a glimpse. "So I'm willing to give him the benefit of the doubt …for now." She raised her hands to steady the Tarakan as he undulated down to the ground. "Especially after he called me while you were *zanyat*."

At least Dan knew the R-comms were back on because he heard "*occupied*" while Dobrynin was smilingly saying to her, "Nice Russian."

She smiled back. "*Yaznayunemnogo.*"

"*I know a little bit,*" Dan heard.

Then they all waited for Smith. He landed before her, with an honestly considerate expression.

"I'm sorry I waited this long to come back," he said.

Her expression was noncommittal. "You've been busy," she offered, then turned away while patting one of the bamboo stalks. "But if you had come back before this, you would have probably been impaled on one of these babies."

Smith straightened, impressed, and smiled at Dan as Conley softly appeared among them. They all followed Lulu to the seemingly impregnable bamboo wall, but just as her nose touched it, she sidled left, revealing an optical illusion opening. As they wound their way toward a stone path southwest of the spa, they discovered that the entire copse was the bamboo equivalent of a hall of mirrors. Every path seemed like a dead-end until you were almost upon the turns.

Soon they were at the road, and then the gateway Dan remembered from last time. But it wasn't until they were inside the spa that Dan saw they weren't alone. What was left of Zeta—Linc, Karen, Lily, Alex, Jenny, and Diana, as well as Zeta's compatriots Scott, Chilly, and Hot Shot—were already there, and were all wearing the dark gray outfits in seeming solidarity. Besides, the advanced material was about the only thing that took the area's humidity in stride.

"Ready?" Smith asked. Both Diana and Lulu nodded. "Lead the way," the man invited.

Diana and Lulu exchanged glances, then the latter stepped forward as the former motioned in deference. The rest followed her through the waiting room and into the spa. Dan noticed that all of the six square hot spring pools were capped with a textured teepee-like cover that made them all look like rustic sensory deprivation chambers. They certainly lowered the temperature in the usually steamy room.

Then they were past, and into the temple. Dan was just a bit surprised that the walls and parts of the ceiling still remained covered with Lulu's research. He was not surprised, however, that the parental shrines were exactly as they had been. The only thing that had changed, in fact, was that the long tables were now shifted a hundred and eighty degrees so they made one long counter, around which thirteen simple chairs had been placed.

Diana took the nearest chair just inside the door. Smith walked all the way to the head of the table and sat on the end, framed by the pictures of Lulu's dead father and mother. The others took places around the sides. All except Lulu, who leaned, arms and ankles crossed, at the side of the door.

Smith waited until both Chilly and Hot Shot, sitting across from each other on either side of Diana, had put their laptops on the table. Hackers waited for nothing, even life-or-death summits. Once they were deep in liquid crystal war, Smith stood on no ceremony.

"So," he said. "What do you do now?" He waited, taking time to look into every face around the table before continuing as if he wasn't expecting an answer. "Zeta headquarters is destroyed." He looked down the expanse to Diana.

She took her cue. "Since that time, every major fire and explosion investigation organization has pored over the site, trying to find the origin, cause, and arsonists. That includes the National Fire Protection Association, the National Association of Fire Investigators, and the International Association of Arson Investigators. When last we could check up on it, they had yet to find anything definite."

Smith made a humming sound. "So, a new explosive, perhaps," he surmised, then looked back at the table. "All of your homes are destroyed, correct?"

He looked at each Zeta operative as they nodded, until he got to Conley.

"No way of knowing," the secretive pilot rumbled.

"For all intents and purposes, then," Smith suggested. "So, you have no headquarters and no residences. The majority of remaining field operatives have taken refuge with Mr. Renard, who has kindly offered his sanctuary and assistance way beyond the call of duty."

Scott sighed. "Least I could do, considering what you've done for this country …I mean America."

"So," Smith mused. "I repeat. What do you do now?"

Diana was ready this time. "The same as the other fire investigation organizations. Find the origin, cause, and attackers." She ticked them off on her fingers. "Origin and attackers, this organization we're calling Alpha."

"The opposite of Zeta," Smith interjected, unable to quell a small ironic smile.

"The cause," Bloch continued, "their desire to destroy us so they can succeed in their desire to destabilize alliances and foment disorder."

Smith grimaced. "Really?" he interrupted. He looked around the table again with a bemused look on his face. "So where's the profit in that? Fun, yes, but no organization as apparently powerful as Alpha can continue to exist without taking advantage of the disorder and destabilization it creates."

Randall caught his eye. "Follow the money, you mean?"

"Always follow the money," Smith agreed. "I do it out of habit now." He stretched a hand out toward Bloch. "When Diana alerted me to this disaster, it was the first thing I did."

Dan saw that several people, most notably Renard, looked furtively around to see if anyone else was noticing them looking furtively around.

"Did you find anything?" Bloch asked.

Smith straightened and clasped his hands like a pastor surveying a wayward congregation. "You ever notice that when a fire starts in someone's home, the first thing they do, after panicking, is to reach out to the most important thing to them? You get to find out what people find most important if you pay attention to that. Sometimes it's money. Sometimes it's someone. Sometimes it's a treasured keepsake…"

"Where is this getting us?" Renard asked, taking on the tone of a corporate leader who wanted to make sure a meeting ran right.

"To the truth," Smith answered.

Renard, having faced the most powerful businesses in the world, was unfazed. "And that is?" he asked.

Smith, who had faced the same people, as well as those much worse, was equally unfazed. "I'm glad you asked that, Scott." Smith placed his hands on the table and leaned down. "Alpha could not have destroyed your headquarters and your homes without help. Someone in this room betrayed Zeta. Someone in this room has been informing Alpha of your every move."

"Who?" Diana Bloch demanded.

Smith sat down. "Could be anyone who's been hiding pay-offs." He looked at each face around the table. "It could be anyone who is at the crossroads of all the information that goes in and out of Zeta." He smirked as they all looked at each other with suspicion. "You're already narrowing the suspects, aren't you? You're all realizing who's been holding your lives in their hands—"

"This is nonsense," Renard exploded, bolting up so fast he sent his chair crashing down behind him. It knocked some of Lulu's findings around, and the Taiwanese woman went scurrying to collect them while giving Dan an incredulous look. "This is getting us nowhere," Renard continued railing, pointing angrily at Smith. "All you're doing is turning us against each other!"

"All right, all right," Bloch interrupted, standing up herself. "Enough drama, Smith. You've had your fun." She looked at each of the people at the table. "Let's take a break to calm down."

"We don't have time to take a break!" Randall insisted, looking at her tech boyfriend with doubt for the first time in months. "If someone has been informing on us, Alpha could be moving in right this very second!"

"Well, let's take a break anyway," Bloch ordered. "And when we come back in a few minutes, let's dispense with the nonsense and come up with some effective plans, shall we?" The woman shook her head and left the table.

The rest of the group also rose with varying degrees of worry and relief. Dan caught Lulu's eye again, and this time her expression clearly communicated: *you gweilo are nuts.* Dan couldn't help but agree as he rose, exchanged a doubtful look with Conley, then noticed Hot Shot murmuring in Renard's ear. Renard listened absentmindedly before turning to talk intensely lwith Chilly.

Dan kept watching as Hot Shot approached Lulu and said something. The young woman pointed off to the living quarters, then went back to tidying up her evidence. For some reason, Dan kept watching Hot Shot, who went off, obviously to the bathroom.

As soon as the hacker had left the room, Diana, Jenny, Alex, Smith, Renard, Randall, Linc, O'Neal, and Lulu completely changed. They moved like a tidal wave toward the hot spring pools, taking everyone with them as fast and as quietly as they could go.

As soon as they entered, Bloch pointed Dan, Jenny, and Alex toward one. Conley was brought by Linc and O'Neal into another. Valery was brought by Lulu into a third. Renard and Randall went into the fourth. Shepard and O'Neal went into the fifth. Bloch and Smith went into the sixth.

Dan looked everywhere for Dani, but she was nowhere to be seen, and before he could say anything about it, his wife and daughter all but dragged him into the hot spring pool teepee, which, he was relieved to discover, was stone dry. Dan watched as Alex pulled the latch of the textured tops closed and latched it into place. From the outside, the covering looked like canvas. From the inside, it looked like Kevlar.

"Holy...!" Dan started before Jenny pressed a finger against his lips, then embraced him before pulling him down to the cement floor. Alex gripped her parents from the other side, just like she used to when she was a little girl.

A small army of helmeted, visored, bulletproof-uniformed Alpha agents who had surrounded the spa during the last ten minutes opened up as one with their diamond-tipped needle, laser, and air cannon guns.

Chapter 41

For more than a solid minute, tiny titanium missiles with diamond chip heads, hypersonic-intensity light, particle, electromagnetic, and microwave beams, and air cannons with the power of firehose water pounded the Happiness Place. It was the longest sixty-three seconds Lo Liu had ever experienced.

While none of the people inside the hot spring pools saw it, they all heard as the needles tore open wood, the beams sliced through stone, and the air smashed glass all around them. They did see, however, things bouncing and sliding off the pools' Kevlar caps.

Had to be some combination of bulletproof and super strength material, Dan thought. *Maybe developed in Zeta or Renard labs.*

In any case, he watched and listened as *Gaoxing Didian* was torn apart around them. As it was, Dan remembered the construction of the hot spring room. Lulu's parents had built it to be the safest place in the spa, with no heavy beams or rocks perched precariously over the bathers.

But the attack just kept going. Dan remembered what just a few Alpha weapons had done to his Mustang in that Boston alley, and imagined how much damage what sounded like many more were doing to the quaint spa. He could practically see, through the sounds alone, the foyer and temple getting torn apart.

He saw Lulu's parents' shrines being ripped apart by monsters' scratching, tearing, punching fingers. He saw the glass and wood of the picture frames shredded and hammered. He saw the photographed faces ripped, crumpled, torn, and scattered. He saw all of Lulu's gathered evidence being erased as if a giant were repeatedly stomping on it.

He listened as the sound of shredded wood, pulverized stone, and shattered glass diminished until the only noise that was left was of the weapons themselves. Yet still the attack continued, as if the attackers were just too pumped by the easy destruction they were wreaking.

Dan couldn't help but wonder if the weapons would lower enough to reach the pool walls. But then he remembered their design. The only thing above the bamboo jungle floor was the spa's walls and windows. The attackers would have to stand over the pools, pointing down, to reach the occupants. Dan moved his hand beneath his jacket and gripped his Walther. He wasn't about to let them catch him unprepared.

The weapons slowly stopped pumping their needle, light, and air missiles into what had once been a resort. Dan started vaulting to his feet, pulling his PPK out, when the hands of his wife and daughter grabbed him, and yanked him back down between them with a strength he never knew they had.

"Wait for it," Alex whispered.

For an agonized few seconds, a smoky silence descended on the little ruined resort as the circle of helmeted, visored, uniformed attackers cruelly, sanguinely, and ravenously surveyed the destruction they had caused. For another endless second they gazed at the devastation, before one lone Alpha agent, near the middle of the circle, took a single step forward.

Then the jungle erupted around them.

It was a second circle of needle, light, and air destruction. A second circle outside the first circle the helmeted attackers had created with their own bodies. A second circle that didn't spread out all their shots. The explosion of dozens of missiles, beams, and punches came all at once like a crop circle of scythes tearing down anything before it—including those who'd thought they had impenetrable clothing, helmets, and visors.

"That new ordnance you asked Smith about?" Dan heard Linc say in his ear. "It's ready."

Dan heard Linc's voice, but it didn't drown out the sounds of screams from outside as he remembered the needle, light, and air weapons he'd collected off the fallen hired help in Boston. The weapons he had handed over to Zeta and Renard's research and development to see if they could improve them. Apparently, once they saw how they worked, they easily did.

"Now," Alex told him, getting up herself as she pulled out her double Sig Sauer P320s.

Dan followed his daughter out of the makeshift but extremely effective bunker, seeing Conley, Valery, Lily, and Lulu doing the same, each holding their weapon of choice. In the latter's case, it was an ancient Taiwanese farm tool—a short nunchaku-sized club attached to a longer spear by a short chain. It had once been used to beat wheat, but when it was used to fight back an invading Japanese army, it had become a foundation of the eighteen legendary weapons of kung-fu.

Smith and Bloch also emerged, but rather than brandish weapons, they pointed the others in different directions, making a quick, effective circle so no Alpha attacker could escape. No one had to find a window or door. They had all been reduced to slivers. Dan and Alex went out where the foyer used to be, finding a staggered line of crumpled bodies. After they made sure no one was in any condition to fight back, Jenny appeared behind them to pull away, then pile the fallen, damaged weapons where a crawling, bleeding, Alpha agent couldn't reach them.

As Alex took the lead, Dan looked up to see an actual line in the trees where new weapons, adapted from the ones he had collected in Boston, had been set to do the most effective damage. Through a gap in the bamboo, he focused on just one. It looked like a slightly larger version of the kind of ankle monitors cops put on suspects under house arrest. Only these were strapped to bamboo tree trunks, designed to bathe ambushers in destruction.

"It wasn't easy," Dan heard Renard in his ear. At first he thought it was from the R-comm, but when he glanced left, he found Renard nearby. "But it wasn't impossible. The tech was brilliant but simple—like many new advances—and thankfully we had many cutting edge batteries already in production for our digital devices. Coming up with enough new needles was the biggest bump—these aren't diamond-tipped, I'm afraid..."

Dan looked down at a writhing helmeted man and kicked him unconscious. "Don't think you'll be hearing any complaints," he muttered to the tech genius.

Renard didn't seem to hear him. He was looking off at a portion of the bamboo forest that was shaking as if a bear were moving in on a campsite. "Well, maybe not the biggest bump," he admitted, moving in that direction as the other Zetas finished their sweep. "The biggest bump was keeping all this from a certain employee..."

Some bamboo trees on the inner edge, closest to the section of the spa that had been the family quarters, opened. Hot Shot came out first, his arms behind him, looking pained. Right behind him was Danhong Guo.

"Look who I found," she said with a grim, satisfied smile.

She turned him to show everyone that the hacker was pull-tied with plastic, as well as cheaper but more secure Chinese Bri-Circle handcuffs around his wrists. Vicious Chinese thumb-cuffs trapped his fingers, but what completed his captivity were riveted, rounded Chinese leg irons, which had, over the years, gained the accurate nickname of "death shackles."

Dan appreciated that the Chinese woman was taking no chances, remembering stories of how it was easier to bury executed prisoners with the leg irons than get them off them.

"He seemed to think he could get by me," she continued as Smith, Bloch, and even Chilly came up to them.

Dan may have wanted to join the crowd, but like the rest of the field ops, he knew where his priorities lay. Still, he kept his ears open.

"But he was trained by the American military," Dani continued, "while I was trained by the Chinese." She looked at the informer with a sadistic smile. "And that made all the difference."

Hot Shot looked like he wanted to say something, but just ground his teeth instead.

"He looks none the worse for wear," Bloch commented at his unmarked face. "Too bad."

Dani sneered. "My father taught me Guo family fist," she informed the Zeta chief. "We don't damage our fingers and toes on skull bones." She poked her prisoner at a certain place under his right shoulder blade. "Right, Hot Shot?" Everyone saw the man twitch as if Dani had stuck a live wire onto him.

Although virtually everyone looked ready to chew the hacker's face off, only Chilly stuck his jaw at his former partner's nose. He looked like he was about to unleash a torrent of invective, but all he said were three words. Yet those words were dripping with derision and disgust.

"Not cool, man."

Renard put his hand on Chilly's shoulder as Dani and Conley yanked Hot Shot away.

"Didn't matter how much I paid him, or depended on him," Renard explained to the fellow hacker, who seemed more insulted and mortified than anything else. "He wanted to become his own boss ...and to do that he thought he had to tear me down first." He looked after Hot Shot sadly. "I've been seeing the signs for a while, but I never thought he'd go this far..."

Smith joined the two, putting his own hand on the tech genius's shoulder. "Good performance in there, Scott," he said. "If I didn't know better, I would have said you were the traitor with the guilty conscience."

Renard just grinned wanly at the master recruiter. "Thanks. Thought you overdid it a bit, though."

Smith let that pass, and turned as the rest of the Zeta agents slowly joined them—save one. They all looked off to the circular killing field all around the wreckage of what was once the Happiness Place to see Dan

Morgan going from body to body. He wasn't checking their wounds. He was pulling off their helmets to look at their faces.

Lulu came back from where the temple had once stood, fragments of her parents' shrine photos littering her open hands. But even she looked up to witness what Dan was doing. And as she watched, slowly and in growing numbers, the friends of her family—the ones who had been vital in creating the landing spot and getting the trap set up—appeared from the foliage and forest to join her.

By the time Dan had completed his check, almost two dozen Taiwanese had gathered around the girl. As Dan approached them, his face a stone mask, he recognized her fellow fisher-women, the Betel Nut Beauties, and the rest stop manager.

"She's not there," Dan said, breathing hard.

"Who's not there?" Linc asked.

"Amina," Alex correctly guessed. "Amina's not here." The sniper turned to the others. "And she wouldn't have missed this for the world."

Before anyone else could hazard a guess, explanation, or question, Valery Dobrynin stood stiffly erect and couldn't help but touch his ear with his forefinger—cluing everyone in that the Russians also had their version of the Zeta/Renard ear-comms.

"It's …it's Sannikov," he stuttered in amazement before turning to Dan. "They've done the blood tests."

"Was it Kirby's?" Dan asked urgently as he stepped up to the little Russian.

Dobrynin kept his finger on his ear, listening, then looked up at Dan, his big, glowing, wavering eyes wide. "It wasn't even human!"

Even Dan reacted to that bit of news, looking back at all the others, who were staring in shock at him and the Russian.

"They …they are still not sure if it is pig blood or even …even …"

"What?" Linc exclaimed.

Dobrynin almost whispered the next words. "Stage blood."

Dan snapped around to Renard and Smith. "Seems two can play at this special effect makeup game," he snapped. "The entire execution was a set-up. A fake!"

Even Bloch was thunderstruck. "But…why?" she stammered.

Smith stood up straight, his eyes troubled. "Smoke and mirrors," he said slowly. "More smoke and mirrors." He looked to the others, specifically Shepard. "Why does any magician create a distraction?"

"To keep your eyes off the real trick," Linc answered instantly.

Smith looked to the Taiwan skies, shaking his head as a wolf's grin slowly grew on his face. As always, Bloch and her agents were fascinated by how the man reacted to things that would horrify anyone else.

"Oh, God bless them," he sighed. "Here we thought we were setting them up, and all the time, they were setting *us* up." He motioned at all the fallen bodies around them. "Just chaff," he tragically presumed. "Just pawns, sacrificial lambs..." His eyes stopped when he saw Lulu. "Like your parents," he breathed, falling solemnly silent as a realization struggled to take shape in his mind.

"But why?" Randall echoed her boss, trying, like everyone else, to figure it out herself.

"And where is the real trick taking place?" O'Neal wondered.

"Wherever it is," Linc told her, "odds are it's taking place right now."

"It could be anywhere in the world," Dobrynin blurted. "How can we...?"

"Get Hot Shot," Bloch demanded. "He's going to get the interrogation of all interrogations..."

As they were all talking, only Dan noticed that the old woman who had been his server at the fishing village restaurant had made her way from the road, through the bamboo forest, and to Lulu's side. Dan moved quickly toward them, hoping the woman could do her knife magic on Hot Shot the way she had to the spearman, but as he approached, Lulu's face changed to anger and fear. Before he could say a word, she told him why.

Dan turned and spoke above the others.

"It's all been a diversion," he boomed. "A decoy. Alpha wanted to keep us busy while they pulled off the destabilization of all destabilizations!"

Chapter 42

"The Confucius Casino is under siege?" Bloch exclaimed as they double-timed it back toward the Flying Fox.

"No," Dan answered, glancing at Lulu to make sure his terminology was correct. "It's locked down."

"Locked down?" Linc echoed as he struggled to keep up with the others, both physically and emotionally. "You mean, no one can enter or leave?"

"Worse," Lulu explained from where she was having her family friends unstrap the adapted Alpha weapons from the bamboo tree line. "Secretly, it's been taken hostage."

"Secretly?" Randall asked with conviction rather than disbelief. "How so?"

"One of my hostess friends managed to get a message to Madame Wu," Lulu said, "before all communications were cut off. A butler, at great personal sacrifice, managed to crawl out the top of an elevator, climb up the shaft, and pull open the doors in the meeting hall to tell her what had happened."

By then Lulu had left her friends to complete the weapon collection, and joined the Zetas as they moved quickly back to Palecto.

"What happened?" Conley urged from over his shoulder.

"An elite squad circled the gamblers and threatened death if they moved," Lulu explained. "An elite squad in visored helmets, carrying three kinds of rifles the butler had never seen before."

"*Derrmo*," Dobrynin cursed in Russian. The R-comms translated it, but the Zetas needed no translation since they all felt the same.

"Since then, no one has been able to enter or leave the casino," Lulu concluded.

By then Danhong had caught up from where she had been supervising Hot Shot's imprisonment in a hot spring pool.

"'At great personal sacrifice'?" she wondered.

Lulu turned to her. "He's dead. From wounds suffered by needles, deep cuts, and internal bleeding." She looked over to Dan. "His internal organs had burst."

Dan motioned for Lulu to take the lead as they moved into the bamboo maze, but waited when he saw Bloch stop short, with Linc, Karen, Lily, Jenny, and even Chilly behind her. Bloch shared a look with Smith, and then the Zeta boss led the others in another direction.

"Where are they going?" Dan barked, taking a step after them before he felt Smith's arm across his chest.

"In the right direction," Smith assured him, and motioned for him to quickly follow Lulu. After a jaw-jutting moment, Dan did so, followed by Smith, Renard, Dobrynin, Alex, and Guo. Conley didn't have to follow. He was already in the lead. Bamboo maze or no bamboo maze, Dan knew his pilot partner could find an aircraft blindfolded with both hands tied behind his back.

Everyone boarded as quickly as possible, while Lulu informed Conley of the casino's location.

"Confer quickly," Conley suggested as he programmed the location into the aircraft. "This is going to be fast."

"As you say, a hop, skip, and jump?" Dobrynin offered, trying to lighten the mood.

"As I say," Conley said to the little Russian with a grim grin, "No skip or jump. Just hop." He looked over his shoulder. "Ready?"

But Smith was already deep in conference with Dan while Danhong was intently communing with Alex.

Renard came to stand beside Conley, put his hands where the interior wall sloped to a gentle bump, and said two words to the pilot.

"Punch it."

Sure enough, the Flying Fox went up as if via supersonic slingshot, then came down like God's yo-yo, to hover over Feng San Wu's family resort reception hall in what seemed like ten seconds flat.

Renard made it look as if the floor had turned to glass so they all, after a second of regaining their balance, could see the resort below them with crystal clarity. Dan was not surprised that the place was not crawling with local militia or cops. It was, however, crawling with employees and gamblers' significant others. But every person down there had a vested interest in not alerting the authorities to the existence of the casino.

And, it seemed, every gloriously dressed person on the lawn outside the reception hall was looking up at them with expressions that combined wonder and desperate hope. He had only turned away when he nearly tripped on Lulu.

"That's everyone from inside the hall," she whispered to him. "I called ahead to make sure."

"All evacuated?" Dan asked.

"All evacuated," Lulu answered.

"Good," Renard interrupted before catching Smith's attention. "Agreed?" he asked somewhat innocuously.

"What's to agree?" Dan said for the master recruiter. "Alpha only wanted us to think they were after the software. What they actually wanted was us out of the way so they could do whatever the hell they're doing in there."

Smith breathed deeply. "Agreed," he said to Renard. But the tech billionaire was taking no chances if he could help it.

"Ready?" he asked with an expression that said it wasn't just a formality. In fact, he waited until he got a nod from every single person on board.

"Set," Renard continued, his fingers dancing on the smooth hump that circled the ship's interior.

Dan saw something that looked like a wave of sparkling water fly out, down, and over the reception hall. He also heard Renard muttering.

"Remember when I told you that buildings have structural weak spots? Well, even ones built over dormant volcano peaks do. *Especially* ones built over dormant volcano peaks..."

Smith interrupted to hustle Dan and Alex over to opposite places on either side of the pilot area. Dan looked at his daughter with concern since he didn't remember a hatch on that side of the ship. But he couldn't get Alex's attention because she was still in deep discussion with Danhong, who was handing her the H-gun.

Smith broke his attention.

"Setting the drop handle for 'free-fall,'" he warned, his arm in front of Dan's face. "It will lower you until it senses the ground, or floor, whichever comes first."

Before Dan could react, Renard's voice cut back in, only this time he was talking only to Conley.

"Hit it."

Conley slapped his palm on a different part of the controls. Dan felt the ship lurch, as if it had just let out a monstrous burp. In a way, it had. Dan then totally remembered what had happened to the Guardian MAX assault vehicle when it had almost caught up with them in New Mexico.

The same thing happened to the reception hall below them. A gigantic sonic hand slapped down on it, crushing the ceiling and sending the walls splattering outward.

The resort's employees scattered, looking like multi-colored insects making a break for the hills, as what was left of the building sagged.

"Blast it," Renard seethed. "We're not strong enough." He turned his head toward Smith. "The flooring has got to be specially reinforced. Add that to the centuries-old dried lava cap, and we won't..."

"Belay that doubt," Conley interrupted. "Here comes the cavalry."

Dan looked off in amazement as, rising above the surrounding mountains and trees, was a second Flying Fox.

After several blinks, Dan noticed Conley and Renard smiling at him, the former with certainty and the latter with relief.

"Well, how did you think the others got to the spa before us?" Conley asked.

"And did you think I only had one?" Renard added. "Well, I only had one at Fox Burrow...!" He turned toward the second Palecto with pride. "And this one is militarized..."

Before he even finished the sentence, what looked like heat waves erupted from the other craft's underside, its sonic beams smashing into the reception hall floor like a big brother rushing to rescue its sibling.

As they watched, two large sections of the reception hall floor caved like a table top punched by a karate master's fists.

Booming out over even that was Renard's voice.

"Go!"

Hatches appeared, then opened on either side of the ship. Dan and Alex Morgan grabbed the handles of the automatic landing devices and jumped.

Chapter 43

From below it looked like both sides of the volcano peak had broken into shards. The Taiwanese people, well prepared for earthquakes, moved away quickly as the jagged stalactites crashed into the fountains with splashing roars.

Every eye was looking up, so no one missed the sight of two people in dark gray doing a controlled fall through the holes—one hand up, holding a handle-ending cord, and the other hand down, filled with some weapon.

Within a second, everyone could see it was a man on the left and a woman on the right. The man was dropping much faster, seemingly spotting everyone below him individually, while the woman's eyes were intent on a rectangular bump in the center of her unwieldy weapon, the thumb of her hand moving almost impossibly fast.

From Dan's point of view, it looked like he was rapidly landing in enemy territory, with frightened gamblers' faces and blank-visored heads inexorably pin-pointing him. He had the element of surprise, but he also had only his Walther PPK—no matter how much Alex and Bloch had pleaded with him to use a handgun that had more in its magazine.

"Six rounds hitting their target is better than fifteen missing," he had answered.

But now even he knew that the element of surprise could only keep him unperforated just so long. And by the number of visored, helmeted faces converging on him, six rounds, even perfectly shot, would be far from enough.

Come on, Alex, he thought. *Come on, come on, come on...*

Needle, laser, and air gun barrels were rising to his level. He kept dropping, seemingly to meet the weapons halfway. He brought the PPK up, targeting the closest needle gun, remembering how it had burst in the Boston underground. He hoped he could do the same before his body was cleaved and punctured or his internal organs were hemorrhaged.

As his feet neared the top of the fountain water, he aimed and tightened his trigger finger, then heard a click and a multi-leveled *woosh* above him.

This time he wasn't trying to find a way to escape a Boston ambush, so he clearly saw what looked like tracer bullets seemingly making a multi-directional sculpture of an opening blossom in mid-air. He watched as the tendrils curved and shot into the bodies of two dozen helmeted, visored, uniformed guards all around the fountain.

He saw them react as if they had been punched or lanced, their helmets cracking and their bodies crumbling. Once again surprise was with Dan and Alex, but that only compensated slightly for the fact that it wasn't enough. There were at least two dozen other helmeted visors keeping guard on the gamblers, and maybe, by quick glance, even more.

Dan stopped caring about the numbers. His feet hit the fountain base, and he shot five of those two dozen one after another, running toward them as they fell. As his PPK clicked on the final round, he grabbed one of the falling needle guns and swung it around just in time to see Alex land. She had already dropped the H-gun, and her double Sig Sauers were in her fists.

That made thirty more rounds, and Dan couldn't help but be a little sorry for the survivors of the Morgans' initial drop. As he heard her automatics start roaring, he marched over to the sixth man, whom he had purposely shot to drop, not kill. Standing on no ceremony, he kicked off the man's helmet to find a young Asian face wracked with pain.

"More hired help?" Dan seethed, mostly for R-comm listeners' benefit.

"Has to be the elite hired help," he heard Bloch in his head. "No way they have unlimited human resources."

"Speak English?" Dan yelled at the man, drowning out the end of Bloch's statement.

The man answered frantically. "Yes, yes. I speak English."

"What are you doing here?" he demanded over the sound of Alex's guns.

"I don't know!' the man babbled. "I swear I don't know! We just guarding the gamblers. That's all we told to do! They move, we shoot! That all. I swear!"

Dan kicked him in the jaw and stood, amazed by the sight that met him. First, the elevator doors had opened and Lily Randall, Karen O'Neal, Lo Liu, and Valery Dobrynin had appeared, protecting Bloch, who was behind them. But neither they nor Alex had to shoot anymore, because all the gamblers were attacking the remaining guards with a ferocity that wouldn't have been out of place in the jungle.

"Hell hath no fury like a gambler stopped," Dan's daughter muttered as she placed her back against his.

"But why guard the gamblers?" Dan wondered. "What the hell..."

"Stop this!" The words were bellowed, and contained unmistakable strength and command. "Stop this at once!"

They all turned to see General Deng Tao Kung, in full military uniform, framed in the doorway of the Pai Gow Ultimate room, holding his QSZ-92 nine-millimeter automatic out in front of him.

Just inside the door was Amina, holding a Yugoslavian M84 Skorpion submachine gun on Feng San Wu with one hand, and an M75 Serbian hand grenade in the other hand. She leered at Dan from over the old man's shoulder.

And behind them, lying on the Pai Gow table, was something neither the Morgans had seen before. But the metal, half-casket-sized rectangular thing was something they both recognized. It was a bomb. A big bomb.

And beside it, leaning over it, was Paul Kirby.

Amazingly, everyone did stop at the general's command. But that didn't stop him.

"Are you insane?" Kung continued, berating the mob. "Do you know what this is? Do you know what will happen if you set this off?"

Dan heard one word in his head. It was Smith's voice.

"Azide."

He recognized it as a rumor about a catalyst that was more powerful than atomic and hydrogen power, combined.

And then the general saw Dan and the rest of the Zetas. His reaction surprised even them.

"You're all supposed to be dead!" he yelled at them. "Why aren't you dead?"

Dan answered him. "Your fault." He took a step toward Kung.

"Stay back!" the general warned, motioning at Amina and Kirby. "If this thing goes off..."

Dan knew how bombs worked, especially big bombs. A small explosion had to set off a fusion reaction, which set off a fission reaction, which set off the real bad boom.

"If this thing goes off," he replied, taking another step, "you're screwed. You didn't do all this just to set up an elaborate suicide."

The entire casino seemed to stop. For a second, only the smoke moved.

"No," the general admitted bitterly. "Curse you." He looked over Dan's head to Bloch, pointing his gun at her. "For a dozen years I planned this. A dozen years."

"Are you sure it wasn't thirteen?" Dan asked, seemingly quietly, but the general heard it.

"Yes," Kung said. "Yes, it was thirteen …when I first met with your Mr. Smith. Even then I was playing you." His gaze shifted back to Bloch. "I played you all, testing this thing on your homes, your headquarters. Then I knew it was powerful enough, but I had to get you out of my way long enough to get it here."

"It was powerful enough," Dan told him. "But you weren't."

"Not to kill you, no," Kung admitted. "Not then. But now?"

General Deng Tao Kung stuck the gun out in front of him, pointing it full in Dan's face. Perhaps he wanted to surprise the rest of them so much he might have managed to escape. Perhaps he simply wanted to exterminate the man who had been a thorn in his side for so long. Whatever the reason, it made no difference because just then, as before, a hook appeared—this time sinking deep into Kung's gun hand.

The man screamed, and all hell broke loose. The remaining helmeted Alpha ops grabbed their weapons and started shooting. Amina shoved her submachine gun over Feng's shoulder and started shooting. Bloch and Smith dove to the ground as the Zetas returned fire with precision and expertise.

Lulu reeled her catch in, dragging Kung toward her along the wall, but Kung was not a milk fish. He charged her, shouting savagely, and planted his boot in her chest. Wrenching the wire from her hand, unmindful of the hook in his own, he scrambled for his fallen automatic.

Alex tried to get a bead on Amina, but the Serb mercenary was dragging Feng in front of her, shooting and laughing all the while. Just as Amina got a perfect bead on Alex, Feng seemed to spasm in her grip, sending her stumbling back, her face a mass of surprise.

As the old man stepped away, still blocking Alex's aim, Amina pointed her Skorpion's barrel at the center of his back. But before she could pull the trigger, Dan smashed into her.

Deciding that he had to get a gun with more rounds, he grabbed Amina's arms, holding her M84 and grenade wide. His greater weight sent her back, but they both struggled to kick each other as hard as they could. Although his dark gray Zeta outfit had subtle padding and protection, he still had to adjust some of his kicks to shield his crotch.

He slammed her back into the Pai Gow table. Ignoring Paul Kirby's terrified face as it swept through his vision, they both went down onto the bomb, then rolled off it. Amina sprang back up, sweeping her chattering gun in an arc across the space, while Dan rolled and scrambled under the table in the opposite direction, hoping to come up behind the mercenary. Instead he slammed right into a retreating Kirby.

Kirby waved his hands and tried to say something, but Dan was interested in only one thing. Using all his might, he wrenched the man off his feet and hurled him into Amina. The submachine gun went wide and the grenade popped out of her hand. Only problem was that the pin stayed wrapped around her thumb.

Ignoring everything, Dan leaped, grabbed the grenade, rolled, and came up throwing at the deepest part of the fountain. It was a perfect shot. The M75 had been domestically designed in Serbia and didn't have the sophisticated destructive power of more solvent nations. Even so, its explosion sent metal, cement, and water shards everywhere, as well as knocking down everyone in the area closest to it.

That did not include Dan, already charging back toward Amina and Kirby, who were coiling about the floor like a cat trying to escape a clumsy dog. Just as Dan neared, Amina launched Kirby off her with a savage kick, practically sending the man back into Dan. But Dan blocked Kirby aside like he was a pesky running back in Dan's college football days.

Dan then all but bounced off Kirby back at Amina, but she, at the same time, was bringing her M84 around. He could see by the timing that it would be centered on his chest before he could reach her, and he was going too fast to stop. But just as it seemed he'd be perforated, Alex caught Amina's gun arm in hers while kicking the Serb savagely in the left knee.

Even after all the evil she had done around the world in general, and to the Morgan family specifically, Amina didn't have a chance. Caught between the father and daughter, she screamed as they systematically took the mercenary apart like a homicidal tag team. Alex worked the woman's body with kicks, breaking one joint after another, while Dan made a mess of her face, jaw, nose, and ears with a rain of punches.

Dan slammed Amina in the front of the throat, while Alex gave her a massive kick to the kidney. The Serbian mercenary crumpled down like a puppet with its strings cut. But before her body hit the floor, the Morgans heard Jenny's voice in both their heads.

"Diana."

They spun to see General Deng Tao Kung stalking Bloch with his still hooked hand straight out, his finger twitching on the double action trigger of the QSZ automatic, a Chinese-made armor-piercing round targeted for her head.

Alex brought up a Sig Sauer to stop it, but there were still too many gamblers in the way. Dan opened his mouth to shout at the other Zetas, but the noise was still too great in the devastated hall. Dan felt a pang in his heart that he was about to witness the unavoidable execution of his superior, when something moved in the corner of his eye.

Kung pulled the trigger, Paul Kirby leaped into view, the bullet splattering his chest. A moment after that, Lo Liu appeared behind the general, plunging a sword-shaped hunk of dried lava into his back.

The centuries-old petrified blade that had fallen from the peak just minutes before tore open Kung's kidney, pancreas, and colon, then drove under his ribs to rip his liver, gallbladder, and spleen apart. As the general fell, clawing and screeching, Lo Liu planted her knee between his shoulder blades, and put all her weight on the lava sword, driving it all the way through him.

As Dan got close, he heard Lulu whisper to Kung, "Don't worry. We'll make sure the authorities classify this as an accident."

Chapter 44

"The bomb would not have gone off," Diana Bloch told Dan. "No way. Paul saw to that. We had been feeding him fake azide for months. His last words to me were 'Don't worry.'"

Dan wanted to see her eyes through the dark, large, sunglasses, but even with the bright, late morning light, he could not.

They, like the others, were lounging ten miles from the nearest village, and, even so, that village only had a population of about three hundred. Framed with inspiring high cliffs on three sides, and faced by the glorious Purakaunui Bay in the South Pacific Ocean, peace and privacy were the words of this new day.

Dan, however, had a few more choice words for his nominal boss.

"W.T. F., Diana," he said in response to her contention about the bomb, as well as the late, somewhat lamented Paul Kirby.

She lowered her head, and then lowered her sunglasses, to look at her favorite blunt instrument. Then, without a word, she popped the sunglasses back over her eyes before leaning back in the beach lounge chair to watch the others enjoying themselves.

Linc and Karen were playing in the crystal clean blue water. Alex and Lulu were successfully trying to surf. Danhong and Conley were walking—among other things—in the expansive grasslands behind them. Lily and Scott were attempting sun tans. Jenny was sitting beside Dan, so she heard Bloch's next words as clearly as her husband.

"I play the long game, Cobra. You know that." Then, remembering the thirteen years Kung had been plotting, she added, "Apparently we all do."

Dan leaned down in his deck chair to put his elbows on his knees. "Not just long, Diana, deep. What was Kirby? A double agent? A quadruple?"

"He was *our* agent, Cobra," she stressed. "Alone. Undercover. Doing what he had to in order to be ready for the most important double-crosses."

Dan sat back, shaking his head. He had to begrudgingly admire the guy. He couldn't have gone undercover. He'd be chewing off faces and breaking balls the first hour.

"Really," he said, still not being able to get his head around it. "That devious, huh? I mean, did he act like a bureaucrat with a bug up his bum simply as cover?"

Diana made a dismissive sound. "No," she said. "That was actually him. But, his general sense of officious disapproval certainly made him an easy target for enemies trying to find possible traitors, so it served our purposes." She turned back to Dan and lowered her sunglasses again. "But make no mistake, he was as loyal as you."

Dan felt honest regret. "I did make a mistake about him, Diana," he admitted. "And, for what it's worth, I'm sorry."

Diana leaned back, slipped her sunglasses up, and let the sunshine bathe her as Jenny took her husband's arm, her expression one of appreciation and pride.

"For what it's worth, Cobra," Bloch responded, "Paul probably wouldn't have accepted your apology, so don't worry about it."

Just as everyone was getting back to their much-deserved, long-postponed down time, they felt a now instantly recognizable downdraft. They looked up to see what they now were calling Palecto II hovering above them. Conley and Renard had brought them here in Palecto One almost immediately after the general's grisly death. Almost immediately, because they had wanted to stay and help until Feng San Wu all but threatened them with physical expulsion if they didn't make themselves scarce.

"We can handle this," he had told them, "as we've handled every other Mainland incursion onto our freedom. But not if the authorities find a bunch of *gweilo*." Then, of course, he added a Confucius quote as he turned to direct the clean-up. "'If you are the smartest person in the room, then you are in the wrong room.'"

Zeta could take a hint, and Renard quickly decided on the destination while Smith made sure the azide, counterfeit or not, was stowed and the rest of the bomb was carefully disassembled. But still Zeta's exodus was further delayed when a still somewhat stunned Lulu had insisted on getting them all the proper beach wear and accessories. Turns out friends of the family had them available wholesale, since the supply at Happiness Place was now filled with needles, rips, and holes.

So now all the operatives started to make their way under the Flying Fox in perfectly fitting bathing suits, cover-ups, sandals, and towels. As they looked up like gawkers at a U.F.O., one hatch opened and Mr. Smith, in a tailored lightweight suit, slowly lowered to the sand in the center of their circle.

"Hmmm," he considered as he looked at all of them and their serene surroundings. "Everything in neighboring Australia is poisonous. Nothing here in New Zealand is."

"Outside of us, of course," Bloch reminded him as she stepped up.

"Outside of us," he agreed. "Could be worse though. At least General Kung isn't here."

"Where *is* the bad general?" Dan asked mildly as Lulu and Alex trotted up from the surf, carrying boogie-boards and wearing short-sleeved, short-panted, surfing wetsuits.

Smith raised his arm and made a fluttering motion with his fingers. "Dust in the wind," he said mildly before trying to give them his best serious look. "Wheels are in motion now to convincingly explain his absence from this mortal coil."

"What was his deal, anyway?" Alex asked as Conley and Guo arrived from the opposite direction. "What was he trying to do?"

Lulu sniffed. "Create an excuse to invade Taiwan, of course." She looked at the others. "They've been trying to do that for years." Her eyes reached Danhong. "No offense meant."

"None taken," the Chinese woman said. "She's right, you know."

Smith straightened, looking at the horizon. "Yes, looks that way, sadly. Our...discussion with the Alpha survivors leads us to believe that Kung wanted to have his mooncake and eat it too. If the bomb had had the effect he planned, it would have set off a tidal wave of earthquakes that could have torn the fragrant island apart."

"Then the Chinese would either be blamed," Danhong surmised, "or, if it was seen as a natural disaster, rush in with humanitarian aid..."

"*Humanitarian*," Lulu said with equal amounts of derision and disbelief.

"Either way," Smith interjected, "Kung was prepared to take the lead in occupying Taiwan, which would cement his reputation and power within his own country."

"Nonsense," Bloch countered. "What's in that for Alpha?"

"Ah," Smith smiled at her. "I think all this rest and relaxation is softening your brain, Diana." He turned to Dan as she pouted. "Because Cobra was right. Alpha essentially consisted of rich despots who had to rely on a network of hired help."

Dan stood straighter, giving Conley and Alex an I-told-you-so look.

"But they knew that would never work in the long run," Smith continued. "So they needed an ever-growing source of dissatisfied youth to solidify its Alpha Army."

Both Danhong and Lulu's expressions displayed growing awareness.

"Ooh," Guo marveled. "The Party would not have liked that." She looked around the circle. "They want the one-point-four billion Chinese to serve China, not Alpha."

"Which is why I'm sure the bad general wasn't planning on telling them," Smith said. "Just bask in his power while finding Alpha recruits in private, and maintain his pragmatic, fiercely patriotic face in public." Smith lowered his gaze to the sea. "Now," he said, motioning slightly toward Lulu, "if you'll excuse us…"

The others watched as the two walked off along the water's edge.

"Oh, to be a fly on the sand for that conversation," Linc mused, getting yet another arm swat from O'Neal.

"With your luck," Karen told him, "You'd get stepped on."

"It's okay," Alex assured them. "Lulu and I had a long talk during the flight here. Seems Smith had an unrelated meeting in Taiwan with four different South Asian movers and shakers thirteen years ago. Hoping not to be seen with any of them in public, he reserved a room at a hot spring spa that he thought was far away. But Kung being Kung, he had Smith shadowed, and for whatever reason, decided the spa's landlords were a security risk." Alex shrugged. "Or maybe he was just a demented, sadistic, power-mad bastard."

"He certainly acted like one in the casino," Jenny said to her daughter. "Did Lulu guess the truth?"

Alex looked after the pair, who had stopped about a hundred yards down the beach. "Nah. When Smith called to arrange the Alpha ambush at her place, he led with that."

As the others watched the two return, Renard checked in with Chilly, who was on board Palecto II, while Dan checked in with Valery, who was back at the classic car dealership in Massachusetts.

"You're welcome to come here," they had both basically told their employees.

"Not much of a beach guy," the others basically replied. "Besides, somebody's got to hold down the fort, don't they?"

"Especially now that the hacker who must not be named is up on more charges than I care to count," Chilly had added.

"Especially with Yuri wanting to kill me half the time," Dobrynin had added. "But don't worry. They don't call me Tarakan because I'm an insect. They call me that because I'm hard to kill."

By the time Scott and Dan signed off, Smith and Lulu had returned to the group, looking like they completely understood each other. Then the Taiwanese girl and Alex ran back to the surf. Conley and Guo returned to their "hike." Linc and Karen retraced Smith's steps along the beach. Scott and Lily started preparing a picnic. And Dan and Jenny returned to their beach chairs beside Diana's lounge.

Smith stood over them, casting the trio in shadow.

"So, Diana," he said. "You never answered my question."

She looked up as she took her sunglasses completely off. "What question, Jonathan?"

Dan's eyebrows raised at her first-time use of what may, or may not, have been Smith's first name.

"What are you going to do now?" he repeated.

"Whatever do you mean?" she replied with a bit of pseudo-innocence. Jenny assumed it was payback for the crack he'd made about her softening brain.

"Well," he smiled. "You have no headquarters, you have no homes of your own. You are down to your very few, very best agents. You can go anywhere, do anything."

He looked off toward the grasslands, then to the mountains, and finally to the sea—before settling his beneficent smile back on her as Palecto II's embarking handle lowered toward him.

"So what is it going to be, Diana?" he asked. "Same-old same-old, or something new, lean, and mean?"

She did not reply. In fact, she all but ignored him, stretching out like a satisfied feline in the sun.

"Well, let me know what you decide," he told her, "and I'll start arranging the financing for it."

And with that, he seemed to float up toward the stealth craft. It shot into the clouds, then off in the general direction of America.

Dan just tried to relax and enjoy the company of loved ones and trusted friends. But all too soon, he found himself thinking about what Feng had told him while hustling them out of the devastated casino. First the old man had revealed that he'd used his tai chi to push Amina off him, then he'd given Dan a glimpse of the future.

"Do not worry, *Yanjingshe*," he had said, using the classic Chinese for Cobra, "all evidence of this gambling will soon be gone, so we can start to repair the unfortunate natural gas explosion." The old man may not have winked, but he might as well have. "If ever you return to our fragrant isle, I hope you will visit our new, improved farm. You shall be most welcome."

Then, of course, he left Dan with a quote as the elevator door closed. "'Think of tomorrow,'" Confucius and Feng San Wu had said. "'The past cannot be mended.'"

Dan turned and got in Diana Bloch's face.

"So," he said to her point blank. "Whatcha gonna do?"

Sneak Peek

Don't miss the next exciting Dan Morgan thriller by Leo J. Maloney

DEEP COVER

Coming soon from Lyrical Underground, an imprint of Kensington Publishing Corp.

Keep reading to enjoy a sample excerpt...

Chapter 1

As soon as he stepped off the elevator, Dan Morgan knew that something was different in the hallway. His hand found the butt of his Walther PPK as his brain registered what it was: perfume.

He could smell a few distinctly different brands lingering in the air. That meant the women they had booked had arrived.

The models were necessary for their cover. American arms dealers operating in their particular corner of the business would have a parade of attractive women coming in and out of their suite.

Peter Conley had been making those arrangements with local modeling agencies. He had a knack for it, though the task was tougher in Turkey now than it had been in years past. It was a sign of the ways things were going in that country.

First they came for the swimsuit models, Morgan thought.

The smile died as it reached his lips when he heard the cries from inside the room. His Walther was in his hand and he was running down the hallway before the sound had fully registered.

As he got closer, he heard more cries and shouting. Though the sound was muffled by the door, he could definitely hear female voices. Something was going on in the suite.

Morgan's key card was in his free hand by the time he reached the door. There was no time for a stealthy entrance. As soon as the light on the lock turned green, he pushed the door open and threw himself inside.

What he saw stopped him cold. He'd run a dozen scenarios in his head as he raced to the room and he wasn't even close.

This is new, he thought.

Peter Conley was sitting at the small dining table that had been moved to the center of the living area of the suite. Four very attractive young women in cocktail dresses were sitting around him, laughing loudly.

There was a small pile of cash in the middle of the table and everyone there was holding playing cards.

All sound had ceased in the room and five pairs of eyes were now on him. Morgan holstered his gun and said, "Sorry, I heard some noise outside and thought there might be a problem in here."

"There is, these women are robbing me blind," Conley said.

The girls laughed as Morgan looked on, still baffled by what he was seeing. Peter Conley was in a room full of professional models and was playing cards...

"Sorry ladies, that is all of my money that you will get for today," Conley said. There were disappointed sighs from the women. "I'm afraid my partner and I have got to get to work. It will be time to go in a few minutes anyway; our clients will be arriving soon."

The women got up and headed to the other room to get themselves ready to leave.

As Morgan and Conley moved the table and chairs back against the wall, Morgan said, "Who are you and what have you done with my partner?"

"Run of bad luck. And one of those women is a graduate student in math. She was unstoppable. But give me another hour and I could have won it all back."

"Right," Morgan said.

Morgan hadn't been referring to the card game and Conley knew it. Something had been different about Conley since he'd met a former Chinese agent named Danhong Guo—or Dani—who was now part of Zeta. They'd had some sort of vacation romance and now there was something complicated going on between them.

And whatever it was had stopped Conley from calling the three women he knew and occasionally saw in Istanbul. That was not only interesting, it was unprecedented.

If they'd had more time, Morgan would have ribbed his friend a bit more. But Conley was right, they did have a meeting.

They neatened the room, making sure that it wasn't too neat. After all, the penthouse "Sultan" suite, the beautiful women, and the expensive suits they were wearing were all designed to paint a picture—a picture that would attract the right kind of attention.

They had also spent money like rich idiots for the last two weeks in Istanbul. Their cover had been good enough to get them their first client meeting, which was now minutes away.

Right on time there was a call from Nadim, the concierge, telling them that their guests had arrived. Nadim added that the men looked like good businessmen. That was a code that meant they didn't look dangerous.

That was as close to security as Morgan and Conley would get on this mission. No guards, no pat downs. The lax atmosphere would fit their cover as dilettante arms dealers.

The men arrived at the door and Morgan let them in. He recognized them from their photographs and ushered them into the suite.

The two Kurds wore Western suits. The senior partner was middle-aged and bald with a greying beard. He introduced himself as Barnas. He was with a thin, nervous-looking young man named Hilmi.

"We spoke on the phone, I'm Dan and this is my partner Peter," Morgan said as they all exchanged handshakes.

"Can I offer you a drink?" Conley asked pleasantly.

Just then, the four women came bursting out of the other room. The two Kurds nearly jumped out of their skin and then looked in shock at the women.

"Excuse me," Conley said. "Ladies, thank you for coming. I regret that we have to do some business now."

Conley led them to the door and the women made a show of kissing him good-bye. Morgan saw two of them press slips of paper into Conley's hand.

That would be their private phone numbers, Morgan thought, shaking his head.

Whatever was going on with Dani, Conley had not lost his touch. Maintaining a cover was as much stagecraft as it was spycraft.

And Peter Conley excelled at both.

He returned to the men and said, "Where were we? Can I get you a drink?"

The two men didn't respond, watching as the last of the women left the room.

"A drink?" Conley repeated.

"No thank you," Barnas said. "We would like to begin."

"Business first, that's fine." Conley said. "If you can come to the computer we'll show you—"

"With all due respect, we'd like to see the actual merchandise," Hilmi said.

"We can take you to our warehouse now. Will that be soon enough?" Morgan said.

"That would be ideal," Barnas said apologetically. "We have pressing concerns. We are from Diyarbakir, which is close to both Syria and Iraq.

The new leadership in Ankara insists on intervening in Syria. We have no doubt this is a pretext for the new president to—"

"Let me stop you right there," Conley said. "We're sure your cause is just but please understand that this is just a business for us. And if you have cash, we can do business."

"So you would just as soon sell weapons to our enemies?" Barnas asked.

"The only thing you need to concern yourself with is that we are willing to sell you the weapons you need to defend yourselves, or fight for your cause, whatever it is." Morgan said.

Ten minutes later, the four men were in the hotel limousine. Morgan was not sorry to leave the hotel. It was expensive and depressing. When he had a choice, he always stayed in the Old City, much of which dated back to the Roman Empire.

Their hotel was in the aptly named New City section, and when you went outside it could have been any modern city in the world. Why anyone would come to this ancient place and stay there was beyond him.

They headed south for the town of Zeytinburnu, where they had rented a warehouse near the waterfront industrial section of the city. They were only a few blocks away from the hotel when Morgan saw that they were being followed. The tail car was a nondescript sedan. Though the vehicle was unmarked, Morgan recognized it as Turkish police issue.

Like most drivers in Istanbul, the hotel limo driver seemed to think the gas pedal had two options: off and to the floor. What made the driver good at his job was that he was even more aggressive than the drivers around him who all seemed to view traffic rules as mere suggestions.

Remarkably, the police car managed to stay on their tail. After a few minutes Morgan turned to his partner.

"Do you see it?" Morgan asked.

"Yes, I admire their professionalism."

That was the problem with establishing yourselves as high-profile arms dealers. To attract customers you had to attract attention.

And not all of that attention was commercial.

Well, that was the job, Morgan thought. Looking behind them, he could now see that the driver and the passenger of the police car were wearing the distinctive blue uniforms and caps of the Turkish police.

"What is it?" Barnas asked.

"The good news is that we are making good time, the bad news is that we're being followed by the police," Morgan said evenly.

"What?" Hilmi said, nearly jumping out of his seat.

"Don't worry, I suspect they are primarily interested in us. And since we haven't done business yet, I don't think they will pay much attention to you, at least not immediately. My partner and I will be getting off in a minute. Stay with the car. I will instruct the driver to take you back to the hotel. Then I recommend you leave Istanbul."

As instructed, the driver let them off at the next light.

They were six blocks from the warehouse and the two agents walked casually on the sidewalk. Morgan could smell the salt water from the strait of Bosporus that separated the two halves of the city—and the two continents of Europe and Asia. Up ahead he could see the Roman walls that had protected the Old City for a thousand years, before it had fallen to the Ottomans in the fifteenth century.

Morgan regretted that he wouldn't see the inside of the walls on this trip—not with the police car pacing them. They were getting braver and coming closer, and Morgan wondered if he and Conley would make it to their warehouse before being approached.

The agents passed an olive oil factory and were in front of the electronics warehouse next door to their building when they heard the unmarked car pull over behind them. Two doors slammed.

"*Pardon, bakarmısınız?*" Morgan heard behind them. Though he knew almost no Turkish, he knew that was the equivalent of *excuse me* in English.

Morgan and Conley ignored them and kept walking.

Now they were in front of their own building. Morgan would rather have been inside. They were far too exposed on the street.

"*Dur!*" he heard one of the police shout behind them.

Before they could take another step, Morgan felt a hand grab his arm from behind.

Well, it looked like they would have to do this outside, he thought as he turned around.

When they were facing the two stern-looking police officers, he glanced over at Conley. His partner was smiling broadly.

"Is there a problem, officers?" Conley asked, his tone friendly.

The policeman closest to him fired off a series of instructions in Turkish.

"I'm sorry, I didn't get that. Do you speak English?" Conley said, though Morgan had no doubt that his friend had understood every word.

"I'll handle this," Morgan said and then he said one of the few phrases he knew in Turkish. It was a phrase he had made a point of learning in a number of languages. "*Hoverkraftımıniçiyılanbalığıdolu,*" he said as pleasantly as he could. Or, in English, *my hovercraft is full of eels.*

He heard Conley chuckle as the phrase had the usual effect and the two policemen looked at him dumbfounded.

Before they could say anything in response, Morgan and Conley sprang into action. Morgan punched the policeman in front of him as hard as he could, square in the nose. Disoriented, the policeman raised his hands to his face. His vision would be compromised and blood was already flowing from his nose.

Morgan relieved the man of his handgun and then clocked him two more times until he fell to the ground, unconscious. Conley's policeman collapsed next to his partner.

Looking around, Morgan saw that though the street wasn't exactly crowded, they had attracted the attention of several people nearby.

"Let's get inside," Morgan said. As soon as he'd finished speaking, they heard the first siren.

And then the second.

By the time Morgan had the key card in the lock to their building's front door Morgan had lost count of the sirens.

Stepping inside Morgan said, "I'm not impressed by your plan so far."

As Morgan slammed the door shut, he could see three marked police cars screech to a stop and heard even more nearby.

"What do you mean?" Conley said. "It's working perfectly. They are taking us *very* seriously."

Acknowledgments

I would first like to thank the following people for their friendship and encouragement over the years since I began writing in 2009. My closest and dearest friend Nancy K. Schneider; Dr. Rodney Jones; Alicia Schmitt; Bill Ross; Mayur Gudka; John Gilstrap; my niece, Lianne Webster Limoli; Michaela Hamilton, my editor at Kensington; Marian Lanouette, a fellow author at Kensington; Caio Camargo, Steve Hartov, Ric Meyers, and Kevin Ryan—all members of my extraordinary writing team—and Linda M. Maloney, who encouraged me to write my Dan Morgan novels.

I have been blessed to have every one of the people in my life, with each one contributing something special. Last, I want to recognize my friend, brother, and partner John, who has been gone twenty-one years already. I miss and love you and think about you many times every day. I know you are up there and still have my back.

About the Author

Leo J. Maloney is the author of the acclaimed Dan Morgan thriller series, which includes *Termination Orders, Silent Assassin, Black Skies, Twelve Hours, Arch Enemy, For Duty and Honor, Rogue Commander, Dark Territory, Threat Level Alpha,* and *War of Shadows.* He was born in Massachusetts, where he spent his childhood, and graduated from Northeastern University. He spent over thirty years in black ops, accepting highly secretive missions that would put him in the most dangerous hot spots in the world. Since leaving that career, he has had the opportunity to try his hand at acting in independent films and television commercials. He has seven movies to his credit, both as an actor and behind the camera as a producer, technical advisor, and assistant director. He is also an avid collector of classic and muscle cars. He lives in Venice, Florida.

Visit him at www.leojmaloney.com or on Facebook or Twitter.

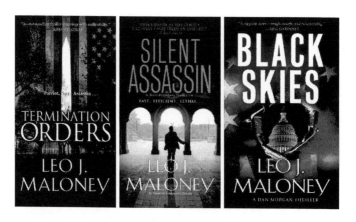

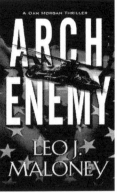

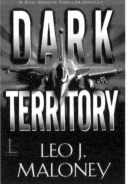

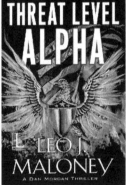

Made in the USA
Middletown, DE
22 June 2023

33245146R00161